BASED ON WRAITH: THE OBLIVION™

RICHARD LEE BYERS

WHITE WOLF
PUBLISHING

THE WORLD OF
DARKNESS

Caravan of Shadows
A White Wolf, Inc. Publication

Disclaimer: The characters and events described in this book are fictional. Any resemblance between the characters and any person, living or dead, is purely coincidental.

The mention of or reference to any companies or products in these pages is not a challenge to the trademarks or copyrights concerned.

Because of the mature themes presented within, reader discretion is advised.

Cover Illustration by George Pratt
Cover design by Michelle Prahler

Printed in Canada

Dedication

For Mark and Terri

-ONE-

San Francisco, November.

Long ago, before a fire swept through it, the derelict building had been a tavern, a casino, and, Joey Castelo suspected, a whorehouse. A charred wheel of fortune stood in one shadowy corner, and the wreckage of a fallen crystal chandelier lay in the middle of the floor. Tonight, however, the place was a market. Vendors displayed a meager but eclectic selection of goods on the dusty tables. Customers fingered them, quietly haggled over them, and paid in trade or with ancient-looking coins. A black man in a Giants cap sat on the bar, playing mournful blues guitar for a circle of listeners. Guards in green domino masks stood at the foot of the staircase and on the balcony that circled the room.

Joey was a tall, muscular man with a square jaw and coarse black hair. As he strode toward the stairs, surveying the scene before him, he thought, These people are all dead. And the reason he could see them was that he was dead, too.

For a second, he felt like he was trapped in a bad dream. Then the hard, cold weight of the shackles on his wrists and the clinking chain between them reminded him that his situation was all too real.

George Montaigne, the ghost who'd enslaved him,

scurried on ahead of him, his grimy brown trench coat flapping behind him. He was short, scrawny, and, like the sentries and some of the other spooks, wore a mask, a clumsily sewn gray leather hood. "Hurry up!" he said. "Tonight the artful Mr. Montaigne begins his rise to fame and fortune."

Specifically, he meant to "rise" through the efforts of his new slave, a heavyweight boxer, by pitting him against other fighters in the ring. Joey, who hated being a slave, wanted to deck the little weasel, but he couldn't. The manacles George had snapped on his wrists were magical. If he tried to hurt or disobey his master, they sucked all the strength out of his muscles.

George led him to the foot of the stairs. Somehow, the crowd sensed that something was up. Perhaps most people who visited the market tried to avoid attracting the guards' attention. At any rate, people turned to look at Joey and George.

Two masked guards, standing at the base of the steps, sneered at the approaching pair. Each sentry had a club in his hand, and a big bowie knife hanging from his belt. Joey felt glad that George had let him hang on to his own weapon, a collapsible steel baton. He'd carried the thing around with him all the time before he died, and somehow, like his favorite T-shirt, jeans, and sneakers, it had accompanied him into the afterlife.

"Kindly tell the Regent that Mr. Montaigne is calling," said George to the guards. From his tone, a person might have thought he was a king talking to a peasant.

The smaller of the guards was a squat, barrel-chested black man with the word CRIPS branded on his left forearm. "Run," he said. "We'll give you three steps."

"Don't be obtuse. A shrewd fellow like Mr. Montaigne wouldn't have returned if he weren't prepared to work things out," George replied. Joey wondered what the hell he was talking about.

The guard shrugged. "It's your neck." He turned, ready to climb the steps, then hesitated.

Joey looked up. At the top of the staircase stood a man in dress fatigues. A saber hung at his hip, and a brass cat-mask covered his entire face except for his mouth and chin. Joey noticed with a twinge of surprise that the mask displayed no eyeholes. "It's all right, Clarence," said the man at the top of the steps to the stocky guard. "I already know he's here. I heard his snotty little voice."

George peeled off his hood, revealing a beak of a nose and a weak, stubbly chin. "Vincent. How nice to see you."

Vincent started down the stairs. "I can't say the same. You look even sleazier than I remember."

"Now that wasn't very gracious," George replied. "I could make personal observations too, if I weren't so impeccably well-bred. I could point out that the troops are not wearing proper Ninth Legion masks, or any kind of uniform at all. I could ask why you're still stationed here, managing a grubby little swap meet, miles from the Presidio and the pulse beat of Hierarchy affairs. I could speculate that a once-promising officer has fallen out of favor with his superiors."

Though a newcomer to the world of the dead, Joey had already learned that it had a sort of government, known as the Hierarchy. In San Francisco, the reigning Hierarchs were based in the Presidio. The members of the Hierarchy, soldiers and bureaucrats alike, belonged to a system of Legions, whose uniforms nearly always included masks.

"You'd be wrong," the Regent growled. "Supplies aren't coming in from Stygia the way they used to. The Spectres are cutting the roads and sea lanes." Stygia was the Hierarchy capital. Apparently it was located someplace other than on earth, though Joey hadn't yet grasped how that could be. Spectres were supposedly crazy, evil ghosts, the enemies of all the other dead. "And whether a fool like you can see it or not, this Citadel has strategic importance.

It pretty much controls this half of the city."

As Joey surveyed the scene from his chained position, he noticed a red and brown glow outlining Vincent's body. Startled, he blinked. Then he remembered that George had mentioned that people had auras, halos; and ghosts, or wraiths as they called themselves, could see them. Evidently Joey had begun to see them, too.

George shrugged. "If you say so. At least, I'm sure that's what your commander told you. I suppose that if he's concerned with morale, he has to tell you something."

Vincent continued his descent. It occurred to Joey that by rights, the fire-blackened risers ought to groan or even crumble under the regent's gleaming boots, but they didn't. That was because wraiths were stuck in something called the Underworld, their own ugly level of reality. Except in special circumstances, they couldn't affect the world of the living.

"What the hell are you doing here?" Vincent asked. "Don't you even know that you were outlawed?"

"Yes," George said, "without a trial." He turned to the crowd of silent spectators. "I ask you, friends: Was that the justice of Charon?"

"I wouldn't appeal to them for sympathy," Vincent said, reaching the foot of the stairs. "They're the people you cheated and stole from, remember? And you could have had a hearing. You ran and hid instead."

"That's a gross distortion of the facts," said George. His voice was still as smooth as glass, but he started wringing the hood in his hands. "But let's not rehash old, petty misunderstandings. Let's talk about something interesting. You are still interested in pugilism, aren't you?"

Vincent said, "You know I am."

"Well, this" — George gestured — "is Joey Castelo. A newly deceased heavyweight boxer. A seasoned professional. And since our Mr. Montaigne is a sportsman through and through, he's come to match the lad against one of your fighters."

The gleaming brass cat-mask swiveled toward Joey. Despite its lack of eyeholes, he could feel the weight of Vincent's stare. "It might be interesting," the Regent said at last. "But there's no reason why it should have anything to do with you. I'm going to chain you, claim the slave for myself, and then he can fight whenever and whoever I want him to. Legionnaires, arrest the fugitive!"

The two guards stepped forward. George squawked and recoiled. Retreating beside him, Joey uncertainly lifted his baton. The onlookers muttered. Someone booed.

"Do you hear that?" George cried, backpedaling just beyond the soldiers' reach. "Your clients, the people who lend this miserable outpost what little importance it possesses, don't like what you're doing! They understand that since I returned of my own free will, I deserve a chance! And if you don't give me one, you're no sportsman at all, just a heartless bully!"

"Hold up, men," said the Regent grimly. The guards stopped advancing. "What are you babbling about?"

"We'll wager on the fight," said George, "and here's the bet: If Joey wins, you pardon me for all past transgressions, and pay me, oh, a hundred oboli. If your fighter wins, you own Joey, and you can do whatever you want with me."

"In other words," said Vincent, "I win what's already mine for the taking. What a deal."

George sneered. "Take it, then. If you're too greedy to pass up a sure thing, even when it means denying these fine people a flash of drama to brighten their tedious lives." He turned to the crowd again. "How about it, noble hearts? Wouldn't you like to watch two savage gladiators battle, with the fate of the desperate Mr. Montaigne hanging in the balance?"

A woman with a purple Mohawk yelled, "Torch the little creep and his Thrall, too! That's my kind of drama!"

But the guitar player shouted, "Take the bet!" And most of the crowd agreed with him.

Vincent stood, head bowed, fingering the hilt of his saber, obviously considering. Finally he said, "All right, it's a bet." The audience cheered. "You always were a smartass, George, but this time you've outsmarted yourself. I have a fighter who's never lost." He looked at Clarence. "Take them to the ring and keep them there."

The guards escorted Joey and George toward a doorway. The crowd followed. Joey said, "Jesus. Why did you bring me here? Wasn't there anyplace else to pick up a fight?"

"Of course," George replied. "But I *need* this pardon. No matter how much money we win, I can't live openly, in the proper style, without it."

"What did you do?" Joey asked. "Con games? Shoplifting?"

"More or less. That is to say, those were the official charges." The little man lowered his voice. "Actually, Vincent was upset with me for another reason, one he couldn't publicize. A while back, discerning young George's innate sagacity, the good Regent employed him in a confidential, intelligence-gathering capacity. Unfortunately, when Vincent and his forces tried to act on the information he provided, the results were less than satisfactory. An unexpectedly well-prepared band of Renegades crushed them on the battlefield, destroying Vincent's career prospects in the process, I imagine. Whereupon—"

"He decided that you'd sold him out," Joey interrupted.

George smirked. "Can you imagine? As if a high-minded spirit like Mr. Montaigne would even contemplate such a thing."

They stepped through the doorway, while many of the wraiths around them simply oozed through the wall. Supposedly, any spook could do that, too, though Joey had yet to master the trick.

In the center of the next room stood an elevated boxing ring with rows of chairs around it. The moon floated outside the top of a tall, broken window. It provided more than enough light to see by.

"You're really a piece of work," Joey said. "I ought to take a dive and let Vincent have you."

"And then go through eternity without the strength to lift a finger? I do order you to do your best."

"It might be worth it," Joey said. But he didn't mean it.

"Don't be silly," said George, squeezing Joey's shoulder. "I *like* you. When I get rich, I'll share it with you. You're going to live like a prince."

"If you like me, then set me free," Joey said. "Let's be partners, not master and slave."

George shook his head. "I told you before: No. You represent poor, persecuted George's one chance to reverse his dismal fortunes. He's not about to risk losing you. Now, let me tell you what to expect. There won't be a referee, any rules, or any rounds. You'll fight until your opponent can't continue. Don't worry about getting winded. You can't — that's for the living, though you can be hurt. I'll hold on to your baton."

Joey had grown attached to the weapon when he was alive, and he was even more so now. Maybe that was because it was a familiar object in the midst of a strange new world. Still, he reluctantly handed it over. His manacles clinked. "Am I supposed to fight chained up? If I am, you might as well throw in the towel right now."

George sneered. "You'd like me to take the shackles off, wouldn't you? But Mr. Montaigne is more clever than that." He pointed his finger, and the chain disappeared. Only the bracelets remained.

Joey gingerly spread his arms, half expecting an invisible bond to arrest the motion, but nothing did. Tired of feeling like a rube, gaping at every new marvel, he tried to hide his surprise. "Okay. Do you have gloves for me?"

George shook his head. "It's bare-knuckle fighting, like in the nineteenth century. You don't use a mouthpiece, either. And look, you *have* to win. For your sake as well as mine. Whatever you think of Mr. Montaigne, you'd like serving Vincent considerably less."

Joey smiled crookedly. "You know, for some reason, I believe you. Vincent must be an *incredible* prick."

"He is. Go on and get in the ring. Limber up, if that's what you do. Vincent and his man will be here momentarily."

Joey peeled off his T-shirt. The dank air chilled his skin. He climbed onto the canvas-covered platform, and to his surprise, the scratchy ropes flexed under his hands. The ring wasn't part of the Skinlands, the living world. It had been constructed by and for the dead. Evidently even a Hierarchy official in disgrace could afford certain luxuries.

Below the ring, wraiths took their seats. Despite the buzz of conversation, the room seemed unnaturally quiet. The metal folding chairs didn't shift, rattle, or clank together.

Feeling self-conscious with hundreds of strangers looking at him, Joey stretched, then threw some punches. It was weird. He was nervous. Angry over being enslaved, to say nothing of being dead. But at the same time, he felt exhilarated.

Or maybe it wasn't so weird. Prior to his death a couple of days ago, he'd spent years in a coma. Whatever was wrong now, at least he could think and move. Hell, he could fight, even if it wasn't exactly the kind of fighting he was used to. Who knew, maybe he'd finally win the victories that had eluded him in life.

Someone laughed. Startled, he jerked around, then realized that the noise was inside his head.

Don't kid yourself, sneered a voice from a dark corner of his mind. He'd been hearing it off and on ever since he'd awakened into death. Invariably it mocked and taunted him.

He'd gradually come to the conclusion that it was a self-hating part of his own personality, somehow evolved into a kind of independent life. *You were a loser when you were alive, and you still are.*

Screw you, Joey thought. I didn't always lose.

You always lost the important fights, the voice replied. *Always choked, or maybe you just weren't good enough. And you're going to lose again, unless you let me help you.*

Can it, Joey thought. Go away. The voice sounded so malevolent, and seemed to loathe him so intensely, that he couldn't believe it meant to do him anything but harm. Besides, he wanted to win on his own, in a fair fight.

The crowd babbled. Some people clapped, or cheered. Joey turned.

Vincent was crossing the hall, and a shirtless man was strutting along behind him. The latter wore trunks the same shade of green as his domino mask, and for some reason his ears were pointed like a devil's. And he was *huge*. Despite himself, Joey felt a pang of apprehension.

I warned you, gloated the voice. *This guy's a champion. Champion, hell, he's a monster. And he's going to take you apart.*

I've beaten big guys before, Joey answered.

Listen to me, said the voice. Suddenly the scornful tone was gone. *I want what's best for you. How could I not, when I'm a part of you? Every spook has a friend like me inside him, and every spook who survives and prospers learns to trust it. Let me—*

Go away!

It's your funeral, said the voice.

Vincent sat down in a chair the audience had left vacant for him at ringside. The masked fighter climbed into the opposite corner from Joey, looked down at the Regent, and bowed. Joey gathered that he was supposed to do the same, so he did.

"Begin," Vincent said.

CARAVAN OF SHADOWS

The masked man raised his fists and shuffled toward the center of the ring. Joey went to meet him.

For a moment, the two fighters circled, sizing each other up. Then Joey threw a combination, a jab to the face followed by a punch to the belly.

The huge Legionnaire blocked both blows, then swung at Joey's head. Joey ducked, but then the masked fighter's foot shot up at his groin.

The kick caught Joey by surprise. Even though George had warned him that there were no rules, he'd still expected his opponent to fight like a boxer. He frantically twisted aside.

The masked man's foot slammed into his hip and sent him staggering. The Legionnaire lunged after him, kicking again. Somehow he slapped his opponent's leg out of line, then punched wildly. He didn't connect, but his effort broke the flow of the masked fighter's attack.

The two men circled once more. Joey's hip ached. He hoped that the masked man couldn't tell.

Just remember, it's a street fight, not a boxing match, he told himself. He knew how to brawl. He'd had a rough life, he'd done a lot of it. He faked a punch at the big man's jaw, then snapped a kick at his knee.

The masked man sidestepped, and the kick missed. Before Joey could set his foot down and recover his balance, the Legionnaire hooked a blow into his kidney.

The punch sent him reeling drunkenly. The masked fighter stayed on top of him, battering him mercilessly. He covered up as best he could. Finally he struck out blindly and landed a lucky punch to the other man's stomach, driving him back.

Now much of Joey's body throbbed. He imagined that he'd be dripping blood, except that ghostly bodies didn't bleed. They didn't need air, either, but something, fear or a kind of reflex, was making him pant anyway.

I told you, said the voice. *He's an expert kickboxer. You haven't got a chance, not in this kind of fight, not unless you let me help you.*

Shut up! Joey thought. He sprang at the Legionnaire, hoping to throw him down. The big man sidestepped, punching him in the ribs as he blundered by.

Over the course of the next few minutes, Joey fought as well as he ever had in his life, and used every move he'd ever learned in the gym or on the street, but it wasn't enough. Occasionally he landed a punch, but he could tell he wasn't doing any serious damage, and meanwhile, the masked man, with his superior strength and longer reach, was beating him into paste.

Joey's vision blurred. The crowd screamed for the Legionnaire to finish him off. Once, from the corner of his eye, he glimpsed George's white, anguished face.

The masked man hooked his foot behind Joey's ankle, then jerked his leg out from under him. Joey fell against the ropes. A fist slammed into his chin, snapping his head back. More blows pounded his chest and stomach. He tried to cover up, but suddenly he couldn't lift his arms.

For a few seconds, the punches hurt, and then he couldn't feel them anymore. Everything seemed dim and far away. His legs turned to rubber and dumped him on the canvas and the man with the pointed ears raised his foot to stomp him.

Joey didn't beg for the voice's help. Not consciously. Not with words. At that moment, dazed with pain, he didn't even remember that it was an option. But a cold despair engulfed him, and as soon as it did, the presence at the back of his mind said, It's all right. *Here I come.*

Heat sizzled through his muscles, burning the weakness away. When the Legionnaire's foot stamped down at him, he caught it and shoved.

The man in the green mask stumbled backward into the center of the ring. Joey got up and stalked after him.

Snarling, the Legionnaire punched and kicked. More agile then he'd been before, Joey blocked or dodged every blow. He felt as strong as ten men. At first he only counterattacked with a fraction of his newfound power. He didn't want to put the masked man down too fast. He wanted to humiliate the Legionnaire, just as he'd been humiliated himself.

But gradually, as the crowd started chanting, "Jo-ey, Jo-ey, Jo-ey," and fear seeped into the huge man's eyes, he grew impatient with the game. Rage was building inside him. The pressure would blast him apart if he didn't release it.

He roared and lunged in for the kill.

After the second punch, the Legionnaire started to fall. Joey saw that his opponent was unconscious. That he'd won by a knockout.

It wasn't enough. He hadn't vented all the anger yet. He caught the masked man and carried his adversary to the nearest corner. Laughing, he started to slam the Legionnaire's head against the top of the post. Bone, or what passed for bone in a spook body, crunched.

The next thing he knew, hands grabbed him. Tried to pull him off his victim. For a moment, he thrashed. Then his fury and unnatural strength disappeared. Half sickened by his own cruelty and half elated by his triumph, he lolled in the arms of a pair of Vincent's guards.

The crowd was still yelling. George climbed onto the platform and held up his hands. Gradually the other wraiths fell silent.

"I want you to give me my winnings now," said the little man. "Formally, in front of all these witnesses."

"I keep my word," Vincent gritted, rising. "By the authority vested in me, and in the name of the Onyx Tower, I pardon George Montaigne for all past crimes."

The spectators cheered. George leered down at the Regent. "Thank you. You were right, you know, I really did betray you." He turned. "Heroic work, Joey! We're friends forever." He pointed. The chain reappeared between the gray metal wrist bands.

-TWO-

February.

Joey stepped through the door. His muscles tensed. Some slow-witted part of him was still convinced that he was going to bang his face against the panel. But of course he didn't. He slipped effortlessly through the barrier and into the apartment beyond.

The place was as filthy as usual. A dead Christmas tree stood in one corner. Fallen needles littered the floor beneath it. Empty beer bottles, plastic cups, and dirty ashtrays covered the tabletops, and a spider web, glinting in the morning sunlight, spanned the dirty window. The air smelled of tobacco, marijuana, and rotting garbage.

Sarah wasn't in sight. Scowling away a reflexive urge to call her name, Joey walked to the back of the apartment.

A soft snore buzzed. Joey smiled. Thank God, his daughter was home. George didn't allow him to visit her very often. If he'd missed her today, he might have gone weeks without seeing her. He went into her bedroom.

Sarah was a pretty, black-haired woman who was just beginning to get pudgy. Except for the flab around her middle, and a certain hardness in her face, she looked like Emily, her mother, had when she was in her twenties. Still fully dressed in high-heeled boots, tight jeans, a halter top, and a rust-colored suede jacket, still wearing smeared makeup, she lay sprawled across the unmade waterbed. A half-empty bottle of apricot brandy, a dirty glass, and a wooden jewelry box full of joints, capsules, and pills sat on the floor beneath her dangling, red-nailed hand.

Seeing her in this condition always made Joey's heart ache. As he moved to her bedside, he noticed that a river delta of sparkling, somehow ominous-looking cracks had spread up the far wall. During the months he'd spent in the Shadowlands, the country of the dead, he'd learned that such fissures and holes were called Nihils. Supposedly they opened on the Tempest, a kind of storm eternally raging under the surface of existence. George said that while some were permanent, most opened and closed unpredictably, anytime, anywhere. But it seemed to Joey that he saw them most often in lonely places. Places that smelled of misery and sorrow.

Concentrating, he stared at Sarah. Gradually a halo of colored light appeared around her body. Now that he could see people's life energies, he was learning the significance of the colors and patterns. In his daughter's case, the dull gray indicated sadness, the red and green sparks her addictions to sex, alcohol, and drugs, and a series of churning vortices the sickness stemming from last night's overindulgence.

He caressed her cheek. It felt warm and soft, the way it was supposed to. But he knew that if he applied any pressure, it would become as hard as stone. Because he wasn't really touching her at all. He was only touching the Shroud, the barrier that separated the living and the dead.

"I'm back," he said. "Daddy's here, baby." She didn't stir.

He sat down beside her. The waterbed didn't give or slosh under his weight. He stroked her silky hair. "You have to straighten up," he said. "Otherwise, you're going to ruin your life. You might even wind up dead. It almost happened once already." Last Halloween, just after his arrival in the Shadowlands, a couple of punks had tried to hurt her. Fortunately, George had had the power to send him into the Skinlands for long enough to rescue her. The price for this assistance had been Joey's freedom. "Trust me, you wouldn't like death, not if you wound up where I am." Apparently, many souls didn't wind up in the Shadowlands. Some wraiths believed that a number of the dead went straight to some Heaven or Hell. Nearly everyone agreed that many plummeted straight into the Void, the hungry nothingness at the heart of the Tempest.

Sarah snorted. Then the phone on the nightstand rang.

For the first two rings, it looked like she wasn't going to wake up. Finally, though, she groaned, blinked, and squirmed. Her dangling arm knocked over the brandy bottle, and the fragrant contents glugged onto the rug. She groped for the receiver. Her hand would have to pass through Joey to grab it. He jumped off the mattress an instant before her fingers could penetrate his body. It wouldn't have hurt him to let her reach through his torso, but it would have made him feel even more wretchedly nonexistent than he did already.

Sarah picked up the phone. "Yeah," she said groggily.

"Hello, sweetheart." It was Emily's voice. With his wraith ears, Joey could hear it clearly. As always, the sound of it wrung a pang of longing out of him.

Sarah grimaced. "Jesus. What time is it?"

"After ten. Mark and I just got in from the airport." Joey's jaw tightened. Mark was her new husband. He seemed like a decent guy, but Joey couldn't help disliking him anyway. "We, uh, got the message you left on the machine."

Sarah said, "What are you talking about? I didn't call you." Joey assumed that Sarah had called, but couldn't remember doing so now. She sometimes had blackouts when she'd been drinking.

Emily hesitated. "But you did. And you were crying. You said you didn't want to go on living."

For a moment, the younger woman looked scared. Ashamed. Then her mouth twisted. "That's stupid. Somebody must have pretended to be me, to yank your chain."

Emily hesitated again. Joey figured that she was choosing her words with care, trying to avoid another quarrel. Her conversations with Sarah frequently ended with her daughter blowing up at her. "All right. If you say so. Would you like to come and stay with me for a while?"

"No," Sarah said. "You know that never works out."

"Well," said Emily, speaking even more gingerly, "have you thought any more about trying some kind of counseling? I'd pay—"

"No!" Sarah barked. "I'm not crazy! Just because I like to party doesn't mean there's anything wrong with me! Get off my case!"

"I'm sorry," Emily said. She sounded like she was struggling to hold back tears. "I just want you to have a good life. I don't mean to pressure you into anything."

Joey's muscles tightened in frustration. But you've *got* to force her, he thought. You've got to drag her out of this dump and into rehab.

Sarah said, "Just leave me alone, okay? That's the only help I need." She hung up the phone, then reached for the items on the floor.

"No!" Joey said. "You're still wasted from what you had last night." He grabbed her wrist. Her dainty hand dragged his massive fist along as if he had no strength at all.

She fumbled up a few capsules and stuck them in her mouth. A swallow of apricot brandy remained in the fifth, and she used it to wash them down. Then she lurched out of bed and stumbled into the bathroom. Joey stayed where he was, out of respect for her privacy. After a minute, he heard the toilet flush, and then the shower hissing.

When she returned, her makeup was gone, her hair was wrapped in a towel, and she was wearing a shimmering blue silk kimono. She looked younger, vulnerable, more like the sweet little girl he remembered. He smiled at her. At that instant, her knees buckled, and she clutched at the door jamb for support.

Frightened, he looked at her aura. The whirlpools in the cloud of light were bigger now, and spinning faster. The whole field was wavering, fading in and out. It looked as if it might gutter out altogether.

She staggered across the floor, kicking the jewelry box, spilling her stash, and then collapsed back onto the bed. Eventually, her eyes glazed, she started to giggle, an ugly, brittle sound like the whine of a jigsaw.

Joey watched her until her halo stopped flickering. As he'd learned from observing other ailing mortals, this meant her sickness was abating. She wasn't going to stop breathing, or have a heart attack. For a moment, he felt relieved. Then rage engulfed him.

How could the little fool endanger herself this way? What the hell was the matter with her? What was wrong with Emily, that she didn't intervene? Was she too busy humping Mark to take care of her only child? For an instant, trembling, he hated them all for their perversity. For making him worried and sad. Then he wheeled and strode away.

-THREE-

George had taken up residence in a suite of rooms on the top floor of a ruinous Victorian mansion in Pacific Heights. His new possessions looked out of place in such desolate surroundings. Bracketed by filthy sheets of cobweb, an ormolu clock ticked on the mantel. Books, CDs, a stereo, and various bric-a-brac lined sagging shelves, atop a layer of dust their presence couldn't disturb. A pachinko machine stood in one shadowy corner, beside a rat hole in the baseboard. It all constituted a modest collection of belongings by Skinlander standards, but in the Shadowlands, where nearly all goods were imported from Stygia, the Hierarchy's island capital in the center of the Tempest, it was a display of affluence.

When Joey strode in, George was reading a sheaf of papers on the moldy couch. Looking startled, he hastily folded them up and tucked them inside his red velvet smoking jacket. "Back so soon?" he asked. "Couldn't you find your widow or your daughter?"

"I found Sarah. And I almost watched her die."

George's beady eyes blinked. "What, again?"

"Yeah. She drank too much, and took too many pills. For a minute, I thought it was going to kill her."

"But I take it she's all right."

"No. I mean, yeah, she'll recover from the overdose. But I found out she told her mother that she doesn't want to live. She said it when she was high, and claims she doesn't remember now, but still, if those feelings are inside her, she could commit suicide. I have to make contact with her, so I can help her get better."

George shook his head. "It can't be done. Samhain is a special occasion. The Shroud is weaker then than at any other time."

"I believe you that you can't carry me across the way you did before. But I've been talking to people about the powers that some spooks have. And everybody says that if you could carry a passenger into the Skinlands on Halloween, then you can go yourself, whenever. I want you to teach me to do it."

George rose and put his hand on Joey's shoulder. "I'm sorry about Sarah. But she has to live her own life, even if she makes a botch of it. Suppose you could appear to her. What could you accomplish, other than scaring the willies out of her?"

"I don't know, but I'm going to find out."

George frowned. "Not if Mr. Montaigne has anything to say about it. And you may rest assured, he does."

"You owe me, George."

"You're forgetting, you were paid in advance."

"Not enough. I win every fight." He did, too. When the voice fed him fury and strength, he was unbeatable. He sometimes wondered why his opponents' Shadows didn't give them the same edge. All he could figure was that every wraith's dark half manifested itself in a unique way.

Curiously, the stranger in his head rarely spoke to him anymore. Maybe it was because he was already giving it what it wanted, namely, a chance to do some damage.

"I'm making you rich," Joey retorted.

"And realizing your lifelong dream in the process."

"You're right, I like being a champion, even if I'm a slave, too. But—"

"Then relax and bask in the glory! Stop worrying about problems you can't do anything about." George smirked. "Why don't you get acquainted with some of the beauties who come to cheer you on at every match? They'll keep your mind here in the Shadowlands where it belongs."

Joey sneered. "I don't believe you. Do you honestly think I can forget about my family? Didn't you ever love anybody?"

George turned away, toward the grimy window. Outside, sunlight gleamed on the gargoyles, battlements, Moorish domes, flying cupolas, and dormers of the neighboring houses, and, beyond them, on the blue waters of the bay. After a moment, he said, "No. Young George was capable of great love, but he never found a heart that could reciprocate. Just petty souls, consumed by jealousy and spite."

"Well, I'm sorry about that. I could've been your friend, if not for this." He shook his arms and made the shackles rattle. "I still will, if you'll help me."

Scowling, George turned back. "I can't. I'm too busy to teach you."

"Busy doing what? You just book fights and make bets. I do all the work."

The smaller man smiled slyly. "There's affluence, and then there's influence. Authority. A man of Mr. Montaigne's talents would be wasting himself if he didn't strive to rise as high as possible."

Joey felt a vague pang of apprehension. "What does that mean?"

"You'll find out when the time is right. As my stalwart myrmidon, you'll have a part to play."

Joey could see that George wasn't going to tell him any more. Trying to stifle his irritation, he said, "Fine. Whatever you say. But I'm sure you can free up enough time to teach me one lousy trick."

"Very well," said George. "Someday. When you've helped Mr. Montaigne achieve all his ambitions, then he'll assist you with yours."

"'Someday' won't cut it. My kid is falling apart right now. Why do you have a problem with this?" Suddenly he thought he knew the answer. "It's the manacles, isn't it? You don't know if their magic will work in the Skinlands. After all, the Skinlands are a different world, with different laws of nature. You're afraid that if I jump over there, I'll find a way to get them off."

"Aha!" cried George. "So you *have* thought of it!"

"No! Not until this second. And I swear that if you get me through the Shroud, I won't mess with the chain. You must know that I mean it. If Sarah didn't mean even more to me than freedom, I wouldn't be wearing shackles in the first place."

George shook his head. "No. I want you to be happy, but this is out of the question. I forbid you to ask me about it again, or to seek the same knowledge elsewhere."

A wave of anger swept through Joey's mind. He flicked his wrist. The baton shot out to its full length, and he swung it over his head.

George recoiled, his mouth falling open.

A lightning strike of freezing cold blasted down Joey's arms. The dark room tilted, and he collapsed among the scattered rat droppings on the grimy mosaic floor. The baton tumbled from his fingers and rolled clattering away.

Too weak to stand, he lay curled in a ball, shuddering. Nausea cramped his stomach. George stood looking down at him for what seemed like a long time. Finally he waved his hand and said, "Enough." Joey's pain eased. Warmth trickled back into his muscles.

To his surprise, George helped him get up and limp to the sofa. "That was foolish," the little man said. He sounded like a father scolding a child. "You knew that would happen."

It was true, Joey *had* known. But when the rage had seized him, he hadn't been able to control himself.

-FOUR-

March.

Dank fog veiled the back streets and alleys of Chinatown, diffusing the few visible lights into blobs of phosphorescence. The buildings, with their turned-up tile roofs, reared above the mass of pearly vapor like cliffs rising from the sea.

Joey hated the hindrance to his vision. He irritably tugged at the mask George had insisted he wear, as if the position of the eyeholes were to blame.

A soft footstep scuffed somewhere behind them. Joey pivoted, only to see nothing but shadows and coils of mist, and the crescent moon grinning overhead.

He frowned. Even this late at night, there was nothing inherently sinister about the idea that someone else, Quick or dead, was walking through the darkness. But it did seem suspicious that the person had stopped moving when he did.

George turned. He had on his old leather hood and dirty raincoat, garments he hadn't worn since he'd purchased better. Joey gathered that they were both supposed to be in disguise. "What is it?"

"I heard a noise. I think somebody might be tailing us," Joey whispered.

"I'm sure everything is fine."

"If I'm supposed to be your bodyguard" — his muscles tightened at the thought — "you ought to listen to me. And you ought to tell me where we're going and why."

"It's not that I don't trust you," said George condescendingly, "but one never knows who might be eavesdropping. I assure you, the wily Mr. Montaigne has matters well in hand. Protect me, but don't try to think too much. Don't do *anything* until I tell you to, unless it's clear that someone's about to assault me."

"Fine," Joey growled. I hope something happens, he thought, and that I can't protect you. I hope your lousy ego gets you killed.

They skulked on, into a small open area. For a moment, the cold fog thinned, revealing more of their surroundings. Cracks snaked up sooty walls and across the pavement. The kites in a kite shop window hung in tatters. The shapely model on a faded billboard had an eyeless, noseless skull face.

Such vistas still gave Joey the creeps, even though he understood that he wasn't seeing them the way one of the Quick would. George had explained to him that spooks inhabited a semi-hallucinatory world laced with illusions of ruin and decline. A living woman's new dress could look stained and threadbare. Cheerful songs often sounded as gloomy as dirges. Fresh food sometimes smelled rotten. Supposedly the phenomenon was a manifestation of the Oblivion eating away at the fabric of the universe, though he wasn't sure he completely understood what that explanation meant.

He and George slipped into another cramped, lightless passage. Behind them, something clicked. His manacles rattling, Joey turned. He still didn't see anyone. Scowling, he decided there was no point in mentioning the sound again.

They walked a few more paces. Then a figure stirred inside the darkness at the bottom of a recessed doorway. It looked like a living tramp, huddled there for warmth.

But evidently George knew it wasn't. Turning toward it, he murmured, "The mask is lost."

"The scythe is drowned," the wraith in the shadows replied. Joey realized that they'd exchanged sign and countersign, like spies in a movie.

George beckoned, urging Joey on. They walked past three dented, overturned garbage cans vomiting a pungent spill of spoiled dim sum. Then George led the boxer through the substance of a door. On the other side was a narrow flight of stairs.

It brought them to a Buddhist temple. Candlelight gleamed on black, gold, and red lacquered wood. Sticks of sandalwood incense smoldered, filling the air with perfume. Three wraiths were loitering in the room, and, despite the lateness of the hour, a wizened, wispy-bearded old Quick man and a demure-looking young mortal woman knelt in prayer or meditation, oblivious to any ghostly presence.

The nearest wraith was a rangy guy in a black overcoat. The top of a small red book peeked out of his pocket. Tangled, dirty-blond hair tumbled over his shoulders, and a rack of antlers rose above his shiny cobalt mask, a body modification which, in Joey's view, made his attempt at disguise absurd.

Joey had gotten used to people with horns, pointed ears, extra breasts, and similar deformities. A few of the Restless had the power to sculpt ghostly flesh, and other wraiths availed themselves of the sculptors' talents much as the Quick used cosmetic surgeons and tattoo artists. Most spooks did so to become more conventionally attractive, but a few wanted to appear uniquely inhuman or grotesque.

A pale, petite female wraith with short auburn hair was at the far end of the room, possibly checking out the decorations. She wasn't masked, but with her huge black sunglasses, she might as well have been. A silver owl hung around her throat.

A plump Asian ghost in a conservative brown suit stood with his back against the wall. His flinty eyes and the naked Chinese sword in his meaty hand belied his peaceful, prosperous-businessman appearance. "I thought we were all supposed to come alone," he said coldly.

"We agreed to come unarmed, too," the horned guy said.

The woman snorted. "Right." She ambled closer. "Like you don't have a weapon inside that coat."

George raised his hand. "Please. Obviously, I did bring a protector, in violation of the letter of our arrangement. I suspect that each of us made some provision for his or her security. After all, we're freedom fighters. We have to be wary to survive. The important thing is that I got you here. The three greatest Renegade leaders in California are forging an alliance!"

Joey had barely picked up the basics of Underworld politics. But he did know that seven spooks called the Deathlords headed up the Hierarchy that ruled the Shadowlands. As near as he could make out, their government was as worldly and ruthless as any police state in the Skinlands. And like many such regimes, it had its rebels, a grab bag of conspiracies collectively known as the Renegades.

"Keep it in your pants," said the horned man. "We're meeting to talk about an alliance, that's all."

"For once, you got something right," the woman said. "We have to see if we can establish some common ground. And some things aren't negotiable." She gave George a challenging stare. "For instance: In the new world order, there won't be any Thralls."

"Ridiculous," said the man with the sword. "Every society has masters and servants, even if it calls them something else, and this one needs the latter more than most. Captive souls are its only resource. Perhaps we could establish automatic manumission after a proscribed period of indenture."

"I don't have a problem with that," said the horned man. "Let's be realistic. Revolutions always produce a shitload of prisoners. It happened in China, Cambodia, Vietnam, and anywhere else you can think of. Unless you want to melt all the Hierarchs down into cuff links, we're going to have to ride herd on them until we reeducate them. They might as well earn their keep while we're doing it."

"No," the woman said. "Once we've overthrown the governors, we have to set the rank-and-file POWs free. We can't build a culture of peace and love by perpetuating cruelty." Joey wondered if she'd been a hippie when she was breathing.

"Please remember," the Asian said, "that you and your kind will not decide anything about the social order in Chinatown, Japantown, or any similar community. The tongs are fighting to restore the rule of the Jade Emperor."

"In your dreams," the horned man said, sneering. "My underground is going to liberate the proletariat, not replace one gang of tyrants with another."

"Then there's nothing to discuss," the Asian said. "I'll thank you to leave without delay."

"You got it," said the horned man.

"Wait!" George cried. "This is why the Hierarchy is still oppressing us. We Renegades can't stop fighting one another."

"You might be right," the pale woman said sourly. "But when the rest of you are such assholes, what am I supposed to do?"

"Stay put," George said. "Deliberate, as you agreed. Give it one hour. Don't you see that we have a unique opportunity here? The resistance is stronger in San Francisco than anywhere else. If we can forget our differences, we can drive the Legions out. Establish a free state and a fortress. It would be the first real victory we've ever had, and the first milestone on the road to the overthrow of the Onyx Tower."

The three leaders hesitated. Finally the auburn-haired woman said, "You know, he's got a point. Maybe we should concentrate on beating the Hierarchy now, and worry about what to replace it with later." Behind her, the elderly worshipper started a soft, monotonous chant.

The horned man shrugged. "I guess that makes sense. I have to admit, my people are nowhere near strong enough to storm the Presidio by themselves. To tell you the truth, the Legions have been giving us a lot of grief."

"Our efforts haven't been going well either," said the man with the sword. "How many warriors do you each of you have?"

They began to talk about troops, weapons, and strongholds. The more involved in the discussion the other three became, the less George contributed.

And that bothered Joey. George might be ignorant concerning the theory and practice of terrorism, but ignorance had never stopped him from pontificating on any other subject. He ought to be yacking nonstop, particularly since he was the mastermind who'd brought the leaders together. Instead, Joey had the feeling that the little weasel was nervously waiting for something.

Suddenly, in midsentence, the woman cried out, swayed, and clutched at her head.

"What is it?" asked the horned man.

"Danger," she moaned. Evidently, like some other wraiths that Joey had met, she was psychic. "Enemies are coming."

Tearing open his coat, the horned man rounded on the Asian. "You back-stabbing bastard. I knew it was a mistake to meet on your turf." He whipped out a billy club. "But guess what. I'm taking your fat ass hostage."

"If anyone is attacking, it's not my people. Stay away from me." Dropping into a kung fu stance, the Asian lifted his sword above his head. George backpedaled, putting space between himself and the combatants.

Joey was pretty sure that if anyone had betrayed the others, it was his master. He wanted to say so, but fear of the magic of the shackles made him hesitate.

Footsteps pounded up the stairs. Legionnaires with crossbows burst into the room. The points of the quarrels were glinting black darksteel. Supposedly the Stygian metal, charged with the essence of Oblivion, was one of the few things that could destroy a wraith forever.

George gasped and cringed at the soldiers' entrance.

Maybe Joey had done his master an injustice. Maybe George hadn't ratted out the Renegades. Or maybe the little man was alarmed because the intruders were wearing the green domino masks of Vincent's troops.

-FIVE-

"Everybody, freeze!" yelled one of the Legionnaires, a bald, square-faced guy with sergeant's stripes sewn to his denim shirt. "Drop your weapons!"

The horned man's club and the Asian's sword clattered on the floor. Joey was glad that his baton was in his pocket, though considering the pair of crossbows leveled at his chest, he doubted that it was going to do him any good.

"You people ought to run while you have the chance," said the tong leader. "My men are all around you."

"Afraid not," said the sergeant. "We neutralized your sentries on the way in. We're the ones who have guys all over Chinatown tonight."

Moving slowly, George peeled off his mask. "I believe I'll go downstairs," he said, a subtle quaver in his voice.

The sergeant snorted. "Yeah, right."

"You don't understand. I'm George Montaigne. I led you people here."

"You bastard!" the red-haired woman said.

"I set it up with Marcia O'Hara, Overlord of the Skeletal Legion," George continued. "Ask her, and she'll vouch for me."

Vincent walked into the room. "I'm afraid the Skeletal Legion didn't make it," he said, the firelight gleaming on the brazen contours of his cat mask. "Marcia owed me a favor, so she let me handle the operation."

George was still trying to appear nonchalant, but his face turned gray. "Well. That's splendid. This is quite a coup for both of us. It must be a sign that fate intends us to be friends."

"Think so?" Vincent asked. "I'll tell you what I think: Nobody makes a fool out of me and gets away with it. Not even once, and definitely not twice. Tonight an anonymous source supplied intelligence leading to the arrest of *four* notorious Renegades. Each of you will be punished as severely as the law allows."

"No!" George said. "You can't do that!"

"You're wrong," said Vincent, smirking. "Your presence here gives me license to do whatever I want. Subversives *usually* vanish into the guts of the system without a public trial. Considering your criminal history, no one will bat an eye. You're going to spend a long, long time in my torture chamber. And if I ever get tired of listening to you scream, I'll ship you to the furnaces. The artificers can smelt you into jockstraps."

Two more Legionnaires carried rattling sets of manacles into the room. Joey's own bracelets began to grow cold. It was a warning that he had to protect George, as he'd been commanded.

That was all right. He would have made a move in any case. He had plenty of reason to dislike his master, and, except for the pale woman, he wasn't much taken with the Renegades, but he had no doubt that any punishment that befell George would befall his slave as well.

Acutely conscious of the black-pointed arrows aimed at his torso, Joey unmasked and took a step forward. "Marshal!"

Vincent turned. "Of course, the boxer." The soldiers with the chains moved warily toward the horned man and the tong leader.

"Yeah. Look, I'm a Thrall. I wasn't any part of this, not

of my own free will." He took another step. "This chain is magic. It sucks out my strength if I don't do what George says."

Vincent peered. "Really. I've heard of artifacts like that. Supposedly Nhudri himself made them. But I've never seen one."

Joey lifted his hands and moved forward again, as if to give the Marshal a better look. "Please, get it off me, and let me join your Legion. I'll fight for you, the way you wanted me to in the first place."

"If the stories are true, only the man who locked the irons on can remove them," Vincent said, head still bent to inspect the shackles. "But I'll bet that after a day or two on the rack, George will be glad—"

The ecstatic fury of the voice surged through Joey's mind. Suddenly he wasn't even a little afraid anymore. He lunged and grabbed Vincent by the throat. The chain between his cuffs disappeared. George must have willed it away. Joey tried to swing the Marshal around in front of him for use as a human shield. But the man in the cat mask resisted frantically. Despite Joey's unnatural strength, he couldn't manhandle his opponent into position. So instead, he shoved him at the crossbowmen who were preparing to shoot him. Vincent reeled into the soldiers and knocked them backward. One of their crossbows discharged its bolt, which bounced off the ceiling. Becoming insubstantial, as he would if he were stepping through a wall, one of the marksmen fell into the space the old man occupied. Clearly sensing nothing amiss, the wizened Buddhist continued his droning chant.

Joey pivoted, to discover that another Legionnaire had drawn a bead on him. He didn't see any way to spoil this one's shot.

The pale woman shouted, and her fist shot into the air. The Legionnaire's arms jerked, and his shot flew wild. Joey pounced on him and clubbed him to the floor.

Other soldiers turned in Joey's direction. Taking advantage of their distraction, the Asian dove for his sword, rolled to one knee, and buried the weapon in a crossbowman's groin. The blond man lowered his head, rammed his antlers into a green mask and the eyes behind it, then snatched up his club.

Snapping his baton to its full length, Joey took a stride toward another enemy. A hand grabbed his forearm. Snarling, he whirled to meet George's wide, frightened eyes.

"We've got to get out of here!" George wailed. "Others will come! You can't win!"

Joey was so frenzied with rage that for a moment, the words didn't penetrate. Then he heard new voices shouting and babbling. The shrill shriek of police whistles. Footsteps drumming up the stairs.

"Run!" Joey bellowed to the Renegades. He couldn't afford to wait and see if they'd heard, or if they'd heed him. He and George dashed at the wall.

A crossbow bolt whizzed by an inch in front of Joey's nose. Then he plunged into the wall and out the other side.

He and George plummeted through coiling strands of fog toward the broken pavement twelve feet below. Joey landed heavily, pain jolting through his joints, sprawling forward onto the asphalt. He scrambled up.

The sergeant had been telling the truth. The Legion was out in force. One soldier stood gaping beside a red pagoda-roofed phone booth a few yards to the left, and two more pounded toward the fugitives from the right.

George was still crouched on his hands and knees. Joey grabbed his arm and yanked him up.

George hissed. "My ankle!"

"Shut up! Run!" Joey shoved him, and the little man staggered forward. They sprinted at the crumbling brownstone wall and black window on the far side of the street.

Beyond the grimy glass was a tiny bakery. Ovens lined the righthand wall, racks of fortune cookies in plastic bags stood by the door, and a conveyor belt ran half the length of the room.

Joey grabbed George, spun him ninety degrees, and pushed him through the ovens and the wall behind them. Now they found themselves in an apothecary shop, beside a display of ginseng and powdered antler. The spices in the air tickled Joey's nose. He led his companion through one more store, then into the fog again.

For the next few minutes they played hide-and-seek with Vincent's men, dodging on and off the street, in and out of shops stocked with jade, teak, dried lotus, silk, and lychee wine. If they'd been alive, they wouldn't have stood a chance. But being able to pass through barriers afforded them constant opportunities to give their pursuers the slip.

Finally they darted down another alley and through a boarded-up screen door. Behind it was a room so dark that even a wraith could barely see. Rows of battered workbenches with corroded manual sewing machines bolted on top lined the walls. Perhaps the place had once been one of Chinatown's infamous sweatshops. At any rate, a feeling of misery hung in the musty air. Joey sensed it at once. It was like the echo of a scream, too faint to hear, yet poisoning the silence forever.

Paradoxically, he liked the way the vibration jangled his nerves. Any ghost would. Places with tragic histories nourished wraiths somehow, made them feel stronger and more real. When it was feasible, wraiths took these places for their homes. Peering about, he didn't see any signs that this one was occupied.

"Wait," gasped George. "I have to stop, at least for a second."

Joey listened. The night still echoed with cries and whistles, but, as near as he could make out, none arose in the immediate vicinity. "All right," he whispered. George slumped down on the floor. A minute passed. "Maybe we should just hide here for a day or so. They can't search every room in Chinatown, can they?"

"They wouldn't have to," George replied. "Some of them have the ability to track us. Our only hope is to get far, far away." Somewhere in the night, something howled. Joey still had a trace of the voice's fury seething inside him, pumping him up, yet nevertheless, he felt a twinge of fear. His companion flinched. "Barghests!"

"Bar who?"

"Creatures that can sniff us out." He lurched to his feet. "We have to go."

"Is your leg okay now?"

"It will have to be. Come on."

They slipped back out into the fog. Hoping to sneak out of the district, they tried to work their way south, but kept doubling back to avoid the search. Their progress was as circuitous and frustrating as running a maze.

The barghests bayed on. By the sound of it, the creatures were all around them. The ghastly wailing gnawed at Joey's nerves. He felt as if the black ranks of the buildings were closing in around him. It became hard to remember what direction he wanted to travel, or that he needed to move cautiously. He realized that his fear was partly artificial, that the howling was casting a kind of spell, yet he couldn't shake it off.

Then two naked figures loped out of the dark. Joey gasped and lurched backward. George screamed.

The barghests were as gaunt as greyhounds and moved on all fours. Foam dripped from wolfish muzzles lined with jagged fangs. Their pointed ears were set on top of their heads, and they had crisscrossing strips of gray Stygian iron embedded in their faces.

Joey knew that they must be wraiths, transformed by a flesh sculptor. The Shadowlands didn't have any animals.

But no trace of human intelligence remained in their crimson eyes.

The creatures threw back their heads and howled. Terror ripped through Joey's mind. He whirled and ran. George sprinted after him.

Strangely, running away seemed to make the baying louder, the dread even more overwhelming. When a third barghest howled, somewhere up ahead, the sound hit Joey like a hammer. His legs tangling, he fell. George dropped to his knees. Sobbing, the little man began to pound his fists against his temples, as if the monsters were a nightmare he could hammer out of his head.

Joey had to fight the urge to squinch his eyes shut. Through slitted lids, he watched the barghests alternately slink forward, one howling while the other advanced. A Legionnaire with a whistle and a whip, no doubt the handler, emerged from the billowing fog behind them.

Whimpering, Joey tried to stand up. His twitching muscles wouldn't oblige. Please, he thought, help me.

Of *course*, replied the voice smugly.

Anger flared in Joey's breast, like a coal fanned fiery hot by the draft from a bellows. He dragged himself to his feet, then started toward his tormentors.

The terror wasn't gone, just counterbalanced. Every lurching step was an act of will. As he neared the barghests, pain lanced through his body. Bloodless slashes opened on his face and arms. The monsters' cries were actually shredding his substance.

But the pain steadied him. It fed his anger and his strength. Screaming, clenching the baton in his flayed, cramped fist, he managed to break into a run.

The barghests reared onto their hind legs and lunged to meet him, striking with fangs and barbed yellow talons.

He smashed in the top of one creature's skull. As it started to fall, its partner plowed into him and knocked him down.

Straddling him, snarling, it dug its claws into Joey's chest. It tried to bite him, and he pummeled it frantically. The barghest's grip loosened, and its attacks faltered. Joey tumbled it off his body, then scrambled on top of it. He pounded its head against the pavement. Something crunched, and the creature went limp.

New pain blazed across Joey's back. Spinning, he caught the whip before the Legionnaire could pull it back, then yanked it.

The soldier stumbled forward. Joey sprang to his feet and dropped the guy with one whizzing sweep of the baton.

He looked around. He didn't see any more hunters, not yet, but he could hear them converging on him from all sides. His fury started to fade, the fear to trickle back. His wounds ached.

He ran back to George, who was still on his knees. The howling had cut him, too. "God," he whispered. "God."

Joey jerked him to his feet. "Move!"

"Don't you hear them?" said George. "There's nowhere to go!"

"They're going to put you in a torture chamber, remember? You can't just quit!" He gave George a push. Moaning, the little man ran.

They dashed through a souvenir shop full of T-shirts, chopsticks, fans, and leering plaster Buddhas, then into another crooked alley where a chunky Asian teenager in a nylon windbreaker was locking the door of a battered, primer-spotted Cutlass. The boy looked edgy, as if he sensed the howling echoing through the district even though he couldn't really hear it. "Jump into the Skinlands!" said Joey. "Get his keys and drive us out of here."

George gaped at him. "What?"

"You heard me. Try!"

George closed his eyes and muttered under his breath.

A whistle shrilled. It sounded like it was just around the corner. The teenager started to walk away.

George kept muttering.

He isn't going to make it, Joey thought. The Shroud is too thick here. Or fear and pain are messing up his concentration. He opened his mouth to tell George to give up and keep running, and then the little man grunted, and his legs folded.

Joey grabbed him and tried to hold him up. It was like trying to support a man made of lead.

George recovered his balance. "You!" he called. "Hey, you!"

The kid jumped, spun around, and squawked, alarmed by the way George had appeared out of nowhere. To say nothing of the gashes on his face, which were now beginning to bleed.

Edging forward, George held out his hand. "I need your keys."

The teenager backpedaled. "Keep away!" His voice broke, as if it hadn't finished changing.

"Please," said George. "I don't want to hurt—"

The kid wheeled and ran.

George pounced clumsily onto his shoulders. The impact tumbled the boy to the ground. They started to wrestle.

It was obvious to Joey, hovering impotently over the struggle, that his scrawny companion was no match for such a beefy opponent. He was horribly sure that the kid would pin George, or beat the crap out of him.

But the boy was blubbering with terror. He didn't want to fight, just get away. And when he tore himself free, leaped up, and fled, he left his key chain on the asphalt.

George grabbed it and dashed back to the Cutlass. His bloody hands shaking, he tried one key after another. "It's the gold one!" Joey said. George didn't respond. Evidently the little man couldn't hear him. Finally George got the door open.

Suddenly realizing that, if he was invisible, he was in

danger of being left behind, Joey scrambled into the passenger seat.

George climbed in, then gawked blankly at the controls. When Joey figured out the problem, he didn't know whether to laugh or cry. George had never learned to drive.

At last the little man put the key in the ignition and turned it. He jumped when the warm engine roared to life. Looking down, he gingerly positioned his foot above the accelerator. Then he clutched the wheel in one hand and moved the shifter with the other. Joey thanked God that the Cutlass had an automatic transmission. The car rolled forward and clipped a garbage can. George stamped on the brake, and the vehicle jerked to a halt. The motor missed a beat. For a second Joey was afraid it was going to stall.

Still not giving the car any gas, George let it creep forward again. His oversteering sent it weaving from one side of the passage to the other.

Three Legionnaires and four barghests appeared in the fog ahead.

If the car kept inching along, the hunters would be able to reach through its substance and grab Joey. They could jump aboard, wait until George popped back into the Shadowlands, and nail him. The fugitives' only chance was to race through them. And George evidently couldn't even see that they were there.

Joey screamed in his ear: "Floor it!"

George didn't react. The hunters spread out.

"George!" Joey shouted.

"Joey? I can hardly hear you. The Shroud—"

"Roadblock! Go fast!"

George cringed. "I'm still trying to get the hang of this. I can't—"

The Legionnaires and the slavering barghests were just a few feet ahead. "Fast!" Joey shrieked. "Fast! Now!" His hands opened and closed with the futile desire to drive the car himself.

George closed his eyes and stamped on the accelerator.

The Cutlass hurtled forward. One Legionnaire, evidently still possessing a live man's instincts, sprang out of the way, but the other hunters stood their ground. For an instant, hands shot at Joey, clutching and clawing, and he lashed at them with the baton.

Then the Cutlass was in the clear, and it hadn't picked up any unwanted passengers. But it was speeding straight at a rust-spotted trash bin.

"Look out!" Joey yelled.

George's eyes snapped open. He froze for a moment, then jerked the wheel.

The Cutlass veered just enough to sideswipe the trash bin instead of ramming it head-on. Tortured metal screamed. Then the car bounced away from the bin and rocketed on through the night.

-SIX-

Nevada.

George felt the truck decelerate, make a series of turns, and come to a complete stop. Perhaps the driver needed fuel, food, or rest.

George had managed to take the Cutlass four nerve-wracking blocks out of Chinatown before being drawn back into the Underworld. With no one in control, the car had crashed into a lamppost. Fortunately it was all but impossible for such a Skinlands event to harm a spirit on his proper side of the Shroud. He and Joey fled the wreck, ultimately stowing away on an eighteen-wheeler headed east.

Once they had left the threat of Vincent and his minions behind, George sank into a kind of bitter lethargy, which had yet to relinquish its grip. Still, he supposed that he might as well find out where he was. Even if it wasn't anywhere that he cared to get off, it would do him good to stretch his legs. And to escape from the truck's cargo of fish. To him, it seemed to be reeking with decay.

He gingerly stepped through the side of the trailer, down onto cracked, oil-stained tarmac. The sudden shift from refrigerated darkness to hot glare was almost more than his ghostly senses could tolerate. Squinting, he peered about.

His unwitting chauffeur had conveyed him to a desert truck stop, a shabby asphalt and aluminum oasis in a vast expanse of sand. Looking as enticing and unreachable as paradise, the Rocky Mountains rose on the western horizon. Off to the north, on the other side of the empty highway, vultures floated in the raw, white sky.

Joey hopped through the side of the truck. His wounds had healed, but his T-shirt could not. It was in tatters. Recalling that the lad had prized the garment, that it was one of the items he'd carried from life into death, George felt vaguely guilty. He quashed the sensation with practiced ease.

Blinking, Joey shielded his eyes. His shackles clinked. "What's up?" he growled. He was surly, the way he always seemed to be these days.

"Nothing," said George. "I merely wanted a respite from the stink. Let's get out of the sun." They followed the trucker, a hatchet-faced man wearing a Jack Daniels cap and an NRA tank top, toward the diner entrance.

Inside, a ceiling fan turned sluggishly, without seeming to stir the stuffy air. Strips of flypaper dangled.

A ruddy-faced waitress scowled from behind the greasy Formica counter, her underarms sodden with pungent sweat. A derelict slot machine, with the front panel removed and its mangled works exposed, stood in the corner, beside a ragged-edged Nihil two feet across. A faint bubbling sound rose from its inky depths.

As was his cautious habit, George stood and studied the hole for a moment. As far as he could tell, nothing peered back, so he sat down in a chair behind the driver. The man jerked around, frowned, shrugged, and resumed reading the menu scrawled on the blackboard. His lips moved silently.

Joey perched on a tabletop. "You had it made," he said. George shrugged.

"You were rolling in money," Joey continued. "Buying whatever you wanted. Screwing high-priced hookers.

Partying with the fight fans. Being a big shot. It could have gone on forever, if you'd only had the brains to leave well enough alone."

George didn't appreciate being needled. He was tempted to *order* Joey to be quiet, but he didn't like to exert his mastery needlessly. Despite the boxer's chronic hostility, he hadn't abandoned hope that they could be friends. "You still don't comprehend. The gifted Mr. Montaigne has a high destiny awaiting him. Something grander than mere prosperity. Besides, my scheme worked. It's just that Vincent and the Overlord turned it against me. Miserable, treacherous—"

Joey startled him by laughing. "Yeah, those 'treacherous' guys are a real pain."

Though wraiths didn't have blood, and thus couldn't blush, George imagined that he felt his face grow warm. "The Legionnaires are no saints, but at least they keep order. If the Renegades overthrew them, the Spectres would rise out of the Tempest to slaughter us all."

Still ensconced behind the counter, the waitress asked if the driver knew what he wanted. He ordered a chili dog, fries, and a Coke.

"Give me a break," Joey said. "Last time around, you sold the Hierarchs out to the resistance. You don't give a rat's ass about what's good for anybody but yourself."

"That isn't so! And even if it were, who could blame me? All young George's life, he was a visionary. He should have achieved miraculous things. All he needed was a helping hand. But no one ever offered one. Instead, he was rebuffed at every turn."

"If you were as slimy then as you are now, then everybody was smart to hate you."

George grimaced. "We've both been through an ordeal, so the long-suffering Mr. Montaigne will pretend he didn't hear that. The point he was making is this: He died in the gutter. Then, awakening in the Shadowlands, he realized he had one last chance to realize his potential. You may be certain that he doesn't intend to waste it."

Joey sneered. "I'll bet he doesn't. So what's your next move, Napoleon? Actually I have an idea. If we find a body shaper, we can get new faces, head right back to Frisco, and pick up where we left off."

George sighed. "If only it were that easy. But if you resumed your career, someone would surely realize who we were. Even if we eschewed our former activities and associates, the Hierarchs have agents capable of discerning our true identities."

"So we'll have to sneak back, and lie low. Maybe use fake names."

George hesitated. "Naturally, false names are a good idea. I've already thought of a couple. You can be Peter Wilson, and I'll be Martin Pryor. But I'm afraid they wouldn't provide protection enough, not in San Francisco. We simply can't go back at all."

Joey stared at him. "What?"

"If I know Vincent, he'll hunt me relentlessly. I don't dare return to his sphere of influence, or linger in any one place too long. We'll have to be rovers—"

"Free me," Joey said. "I'll go back alone."

"Don't be ridiculous. At this point, the good Marshal has a rack awaiting you, too."

"I'll take my chances."

"Perhaps you would, but it's not an option."

"God damn it!" Joey cried. "I have to be where I can see Em and Sarah."

"Why? It only depresses you."

"It's the only thing that makes this whole bleak world of slavery and death bearable."

George felt another twinge of remorse. He extinguished it as effortlessly as the first. "I know that isn't true. I've seen how you come alive in the ring. And you'll still fight. We'll find the action in a town, pick up a match or two, and move on. Oh, it won't be as glorious—"

Joey shook his square-jawed head. A lock of his coarse black hair tumbled down his brow. "It's not enough."

Any compassion that George had felt for Joey began to give way to annoyance. Hadn't he helped him save his sluttish daughter's life? Hadn't he rescued the man himself, extracting him from the Hierarchs' clutches just a few hours ago? Didn't he deserve better than this whining ingratitude? "Isn't it? Then what would you like me to do with you, rent you out as a bodyguard? Do you think you could get it right this time?"

Joey's brown eyes blazed. His aura flickered into visibility, churning with the ebony light of hate. Even though George knew that the power of the manacles kept him safe from attack, he couldn't help feeling a jolt of apprehension.

"I'll get you," said Joey thickly. "So help me." He stood up and strode through the wall.

-SEVEN-

Las Vegas, May.

Joey spotted Emily and Sarah across the casino, at a roulette table. They seemed to be winning with every clattering spin of the wheel. The croupier, a smiling young man dressed in a milk-white tuxedo, a candy-apple-colored cummerbund, and a matching bow tie, kept shoving chips at them. Grinning, Emily stacked the tokens into multicolored towers. Enthroned on her mother's lap, tiny Sarah squealed with excitement.

Smiling, Joey ambled toward them. Strangers kept greeting him. As champ, he'd had to learn to deal with such attention. He acknowledged the well-wishers without giving them a chance to bog him down in conversation.

He reached the table and leaned over his family. Emily smelled of perfume, Sarah of chocolate ice cream. "How's it going?" he asked. "Has mommy wiped out our life savings yet?"

"No!" Sarah said. Her eyes sparkled. "We're winning a bunch!"

"We sure are," said Emily. "I've just about got enough to buy a new husband. What do you think, a movie star or a handsome Italian count?"

Joey stiffened. He didn't know why, since she was obviously joking, but something about the comment bothered him. Trying to stifle a sudden sense of foreboding, he said, "I think I'd better get you high rollers away from the game. Especially if you still want to see Bill Cosby."

"Why not?" said Emily. "We can finish breaking the bank tomorrow." Sarah slid off her lap. Emily tipped the croupier a five-hundred-dollar chip and stood up. She gazed at Joey for a moment, then threw herself into his arms. Onlookers murmured in sentimental approval.

Joey gave her a passionate kiss. Her lips were soft and sweet, and as they moved against his, the color faded from the roulette table behind her. The rainbow of chips, the red spaces on the wheel, and the green felt all turned gray.

It was odd. It might even have been disturbing, if Joey had let himself notice it, but he didn't. Closing his eyes, he gave his wife another kiss.

But he couldn't blind himself forever. And when he looked up, color was draining from the whole casino, leeching the scarlet from the croupier's tie and cummerbund, the blue from a cocktail waitress's sparkling sequin dress, and the pink of every face in the room. Only Sarah and Emily retained their natural hues.

Joey couldn't ignore it any longer. For all he knew, he was sick, or going crazy. "Do you see that?" he asked.

"Don't think about it," Emily said. "Don't think about anything but Sarah and me." She pressed her mouth and body against his. Her tongue slipped between his lips.

Most of the lights flickered out, plunging the hall into gloom. A craps table split down the middle and collapsed. Chiming, whirring slot machines fell silent. The smell of mildew rose from the carpet.

People changed, too. Locks of hair turned white, then fell out. Teeth tumbled from bloody gums. Fingers shriveled into twisted claws. An eyeball slid from its socket and plopped in a glass of whiskey.

Though the crowd hadn't seemed to notice the loss of color, they understood that they were withering into corpses. Croaking with tongues too desiccated for coherent speech, they tottered toward Joey and pawed him feebly, leaving trails of stinking slime on his clothes.

Suddenly he realized, without questioning how he knew, that the kissing was *making* them rot. Horrified, he pulled back.

Emily clung to him. "No!" she said. "Love me, love me!"

"I do," he said, "but—"

"If you won't love us, we'll have to go away." The darkness behind her seemed to stir, to open, like jaws gaping to swallow her up.

Sarah threw her arms around his waist. "I'm scared, Daddy! I'm scared!"

He looked down into her tear-streaked face and started to cry himself. "It's all right, baby." He shoved one of the walking cadavers away. "Get off me! I don't owe you bastards anything! You were already dead when I walked in here!"

He kissed Emily. The dead men wailed and gobbled. Then the bodies of the remaining gamblers, waitresses, and tourists thudded to the floor.

When Joey looked around, the corpses had crumbled into piles of dust. Watches, buttons, rings, eyeglasses, and splinters of bone stuck out of the powder littering the room. The casino had continued its transformation as well. The rest of the lights had gone out. Mice scurried through the shadows, and bats hung from the chandeliers as though they had slept there for years.

"You did it!" Sarah cried. "The bad things are all gone!" Her jubilation made Joey feel like a hero.

Laughing and trading silly jokes, he and his family explored the ruin. Sarah and Emily glowed like sunlit stained glass in the monochromatic gloom. But when he passed a fly-specked mirror, he saw that his own body had turned dark and misty. His face was just a blur.

CARAVAN OF SHADOWS

For a moment, the change upset him, but he decided that if it didn't bother Emily and Sarah, it couldn't be any big deal.

A hand tapped his shoulder.

Thinking it was Emily's touch, he turned. No one was within reach of him.

He wondered if he was imagining things. Then the invisible fingers prodded him again, more insistently. His wife, his daughter, and the derelict casino itself shattered into a million tiny pieces, flecks of glitter tumbling through an ebony void.

He screamed and bolted up on the king-sized bed. Wrapped in his filthy, now bloodstained raincoat, George was bending over him. Outside, beyond a panoramic expanse of window, the neon displays of Vegas's great casinos, the Excalibur, Bally's, the Wheel of Fortune, the Luxor, the Inferno, the Circus Circus, Caesar's, and the Valhalla among them, blazed against the blue-black desert sky.

"I can scarcely believe you were sleeping *again*," said George.

Joey grunted.

For the first few months of his afterlife, Joey had found himself without the need for sleep. But not long after George had told him that they weren't going back to San Francisco, some instinct had prompted him to take a nap. He'd only been looking for a break from awareness, from grief and frustration, but he'd found something better. Vivid dreams of Emily, as loving as she'd been on their honeymoon, and Sarah, restored to innocent childhood. Visions of a family that could see and hear him.

Sometimes morbid elements in the dreams, like the images of death and decay in the one he'd just experienced, worried him. So did the fact that he was sleeping most of the time, wallowing in an experience he knew to be unreal. But it didn't bother him enough to make him stop. Except for the satisfaction Joey found in beating an opponent in the ring, waking existence didn't hold a single pleasure that compared to the satisfaction he found in his dreams.

"Get up," George said.

"Why?" Joey asked as he swung his bare feet onto the floor. Somehow the pile carpet felt soft, even though the fibers didn't give under Joey's weight. "Do we have a match?"

"Not yet," said George. "But Mr. Montaigne is about to introduce himself to some new people. With his steadfast retainer at his side, he's bound to make a suitably posh impression."

"Yeah," said Joey sardonically, pulling on one of his sneakers. "And his new buddies won't be as likely to try to mug him for his clothes, or peddle his ass to slavers." Neither possibility was particularly farfetched. Joey had lived a rough life, but he was still amazed at what ruthless predators many of his fellow spooks could be. Maybe the neverending shortage of material goods was to blame. Or maybe, now that they were dead and seemingly condemned to an eternity in the dreary limbo of the Shadowlands, they figured they had nothing to lose by giving their evil side free rein.

"I doubt that we'll be in any such peril tonight," said George, "although I'll grant you, one can't be too careful." He shifted his weight like a kid who needed to take a leak. "Will you hurry? You're going to want to see these people, too."

"Oh, yeah? Why?"

George smirked. "The sooner we get there, the sooner you'll find out."

Joey stood up and grabbed his baton off the nightstand. Then he and George stepped out of the hotel room and into the corridor, slipping through the door and the wall respectively.

On their way to the service stairs, they encountered an elderly female wraith carrying a Bible bound in white leather. She gave them a sad smile, but didn't speak.

Joey had already noticed that a number of other spooks were inhabiting the building. Ordinarily, ghosts wouldn't have found the ambience of a resort hotel especially compelling. But this one was also a casino, and to a wraith, casinos buzzed with an undercurrent of greed, desperation, and despair, a vibe that made Joey think of flat-broke gamblers blowing their brains out. The atmosphere was as invigorating as the climate in a cancer ward.

The joint had been designed in such a way that no matter where a guest was headed, he had to cross the casino proper. Despite the hour, gamblers mobbed the slots and tables. Perhaps, with no clocks or windows in view, dazed by the drone and the free drinks, they had no idea how late it was. Still squeamish about walking right through living bodies, Joey had to weave and dodge to avoid them.

George led him into a darkened lounge. On stage, a high-prowed boat like a Venetian gondola sailed down a stage-set river. It was the most amazingly realistic theatrical set that Joey had ever seen. The black water rippled. On the bank, rushes swayed, while black clouds churned in the overcast sky above.

A bare-chested actor poling the gondola, a guy with the physique of a champion body-builder, shoulder-length golden hair, and an ornate black mask, boomed his way through a soliloquy. Cigar in hand, a skinny guy in a straw hat and striped blazer lounged in the front of the boat. Mugging, he conveyed that he found his companion's oration excruciatingly dull. When the speech thundered to a close, he offered a quip that convulsed the audience with laughter.

Meanwhile, a man in the back of the room wiped down tables, just as if the stage were empty. Obviously because for him, it was. The actors were wraiths, presenting a play for their own kind. Judging from the scythe gleaming in the gondola, it must be a spoof of one of the legends of Charon, founder of Stygia and the Deathlords' predecessor. The king of the dead was invariably depicted carrying such a weapon.

The scene ended, and the stage went black. An instant later, when the light returned, a shadowy throne room, illuminated by a brazier of dim blue fire, had taken the gondola's place. Dark figures peeked from behind massive columns. Though the two actors were gawking about, they evidently didn't see the shadowy lurkers.

"What's with these sets?" Joey whispered, intrigued despite himself. "How can they look so good, and change so fast?"

"Remarkable, isn't it?" George murmured back. "Didn't I tell you that you'd want to see it? The sets aren't real. Neither is the lighting, nor, I suspect, the Spectres hiding behind the pillars. That girl is creating it all with her mind." He pointed at a figure sitting beside the stage.

When Joey looked at her, he felt as if he'd taken a hard punch in the stomach. The woman was Emily!

Then she turned slightly, and he saw that it wasn't so. In fact, the resemblance was superficial. This woman looked like she was in her twenties, and the real, living Emily was middle-aged. The illusionist's dark hair was longer and straighter, her face thinner, with finer bones, and her complexion paler. His sudden, stupid burst of excitement curdled into self-disgust.

"I'm told that her name is Elaine Forrester," said George, oblivious to Joey's distress, "and that she's the impresario. Ergo, the one we want to talk to."

"Why?"

"These are *touring* performers. I'd like to tour with them. As you yourself observed earlier, we dwell in a hazardous world, and traveling with a group is safer. Moreover, merging our exhibition with theirs might garner us bigger crowds, and bigger purses. And, in all candor, the sociable Mr. Montaigne would enjoy some fresh companionship. You've been dismal company of late."

On stage, the blond actor playing Charon reeled about, swinging his scythe at the nimbly dodging Spectres. The man with the cigar provided rapid-fire commentary in the style of a sports announcer. The audience howled.

"Wow," said Joey, "what a lucky break for them. I mean, who could pass up the chance to team up with a swell guy like you?"

George grimaced. "Don't be snide. A Renaissance man like Mr. Montaigne is an asset to any endeavor. And you, of course, will refrain from saying anything to put them off. Don't mention that we've ever run afoul of the San Francisco authorities, or that I ever did anything that could be construed, albeit unjustly, as a betrayal of any of my former associates."

"Don't worry," said Joey. "I know that if you get busted, I get busted." Besides, now that George had given him an order, he had the power of the manacles constraining him. Leaning back against the wall, he watched the performance unfold.

And despite his sour mood, he found himself smiling. After a while he got used to the utter realism of the phantasmal sets, but each had a somber beauty at odds with the farcical nature of the performance. And the pattern of the guy with the cigar, a dizzying mix of insults, cynical observations, bawdy innuendo, puns, and fractured logic, was hilarious. As the comedy built to a climax, the Skinlander janitor began stacking the chairs on the tables, to the annoyance of the wraiths sitting on them and everyone who was trying to see the stage. But the comic recaptured their attention with a malicious series of speculations about the live man's sex life, and the play drove on to a riotous conclusion.

Afterward, the cast, eight actors in all, lined up at the foot of the stage to take their bows. Charon removed his mask, exposing a face as striking as his build. His features were so perfect that they seemed stylized, like the image of a hero in a comic book. He gestured grandly at Elaine, who acknowledged the applause by nodding coldly.

The actors jumped down and began to circulate among the audience, passing the hat. Some of the crowd reached into their pockets, while the cheapskates beat a hasty retreat. Elaine went and stood in the far corner, beside a little girl with freckles and curly chestnut hair. George scurried over to them, and Joey followed a pace behind.

George clapped. "Bravo! The comedy was delightful, and the vistas you created were magnificent."

"Thank you," the woman said. Her expression was guarded and her tone cool. Seeing her so aloof, Joey wondered how he could ever have mistaken her for the vivacious Emily.

George smiled at the little girl. "And you sang like an angel." His voice was softer and less smarmy than usual. Surprised, Joey thought that he sounded almost human.

The child wraith smiled shyly. Elaine said, "I'm tired. Excuse me." She began to turn away.

"Wait!" George said. Her lips tightening, she turned back. "Allow me to introduce myself. My name is Martin Pryor, and my associate is Peter Wilson, a champion pugilist ready to face all comers. As I watched your show tonight, it occurred to me that it would be mutually beneficial to *combine* our—"

"No," said Elaine.

George blinked. "Please, hear me out."

"There's no point. I already know you wouldn't fit in."

The comic walked over to join the conversation. His hat was half full of money, a few whole iron coins and a number of pie-shaped bits. "Oh, come on," he said. "This is vaudeville, my kumquat, not the Royal Shakespeare Company. We've got jugglers and a stripper. We'd be guessing people's weights if we could get the scale. Which reminds me, why am *I* still getting scale? So what's a boxer more or less? If I'm any judge of beefsteak, this kid's the closest thing to an animal act we're ever going to find. And from the smell, I'd say he was standing *mighty* close." He leered at Joey.

The illusionist scowled. "Drop it, Artie. I told you, I don't want to add anybody to the troupe right now."

"Well, of course," said Artie. "We wouldn't want to *grow*. Imagine if we got successful. Imagine if success spoiled us. Never again to cavort through the heather like innocent little lambs! Why, just between you and me, I *came* to Vegas for quickie cavorts." Abruptly he smiled, not the smart-ass smirk he'd worn till now, but a more natural expression. It made him look tired. "I'm sorry, fellas. But when Her Majesty here makes up her mind like this, nothing can change it. Maybe next season, okay?"

"I hope so," George sighed. "A pleasant night to one and all." He and Joey turned away.

Just as the pair reached the door in the back wall, it opened, and three men walked in. The one in the lead was a rangy guy in a white silk jacket and an open-collared turquoise shirt. Gold chains gleamed around his neck, and his steel-gray hair was combed straight back. His lean face gave the impression of youth despite the lines around the eyes. In their black suits, white shirts, and black ties, the heavyset men behind him looked alike enough to be brothers.

Startled by the interruption, the custodian, who was plugging in a vacuum cleaner, jerked around. The gray-haired man asked him if he'd mind taking a break, and handed him a folded bill. Looking simultaneously greedy, scared, and puzzled, the cleaner grabbed the money and scurried out.

The goons took up positions flanking the door.

Beaming, the gray-haired man made a beeline for Elaine and her companions.

The janitor could see this guy, Joey thought, so the gray-haired man must be on the other side of the Shroud. Yet he can see us wraiths. How can that be? He looked at the stranger's aura.

It was a haze of colors, mainly blue but constantly shifting, that defied simple interpretation. George's halo often looked like that, especially when he was trying to manipulate or deceive someone. But the newcomer's aura was pale, paler than any that Joey had ever seen.

"I think that's Lorenzo Orsini," George whispered excitedly. "He owns the Inferno, one of the biggest hotels and casinos in Las Vegas. A place that caters to the living and the dead."

"Did I miss the show?" asked the gray-haired man, addressing all members of the cast with a sweeping gesture of his hands. "Damn! Business held me up, but I'll make sure to catch it next time. I'm Lorenzo Orsini, Larry to friends. No need to introduce yourselves. I know your names, and I've heard how talented you are. Which is why I want you working at my place."

"Thank you, but we're comfortable here," said Elaine.

"Oh, come on! What have you got in this toilet? A stage that's only available for a couple hours a night."

Drawn by the enthusiastic sound of his voice, other members of the troupe began to wander over.

"Mortals drifting in to screw up the performance. Small houses, because nobody knows you're here." He sneered at Artie's hat. "No wonder you're making peanuts.

"Now at the Inferno, you'll have your own theater, with stagehands, wardrobe, musicians, and anything else you want. I'll put your names on the marquee, print handbills, and pull in every wraith in Nevada. And since my place isn't a church, you won't have to take up a collection. We'll sell tickets."

Elaine shook her head. "We really aren't interested."

"It's because of my predecessor's reputation, isn't it? I know that he wasn't always a friend to the Restless. But that's why the family replaced him. These days, the Inferno is a *haven* for ghosts. Ask anybody."

"I've heard that, but the answer is still no."

Orsini smiled crookedly. "Is it racism? You hate me for the kind of critter I am?"

"No. I suppose that in our own way, we feed on the living, too. I simply think we're better off here. And now I'll say good night."

"For the love of Mike!" Artie exploded. "All right, you're the boss, it's your call. But why are we even *in* show business, if we're going to blow off a gig like this?"

Some of the other performers muttered in agreement. Elaine grimaced. Joey could tell that she felt guilty for disappointing them, yet also wanted to tell them to go to hell.

"I'd like to sing with a big band," the little girl said timidly.

Elaine heaved a sigh. "I know you would, button." She looked back at Orsini. "All right. You can book us for three weeks."

People cheered. Orsini grinned and said, "You won't be sorry. I'm going to head straight back to the Inferno and make arrangements. You get your belongings together and move in ASAP." He strode toward the door.

"What's the deal with that guy?" Joey asked. "What did Elaine mean by 'feed on the living'? How come he can see us?"

"Because he's a vampire," George replied, scrambling forward. "Mr. Orsini! Mr. Orsini! There's *another* attraction you should book! My associate—"

-EIGHT-

June.

Orsini found Elaine where he often found her, on the roof, at the opposite end from the huge, red-neon devil. She was staring east, away from the other casinos, in the direction of the old Mormon fort and the natural history museum.

Once again he was struck by how sad and lonely she looked. How like a phantom, even here in the Inferno, where his flunkies had done everything possible to help wraiths forget that they were dead. He wondered if she was gazing at the stars, or at nothing at all.

He only had a second to study her unnoticed. His heart didn't beat, nor, except for when he needed to speak, did breath whisper in and out of his lungs. But, sensing him anyway, she turned. She put on a wan little smile. "Hi."

Smiling in return, he ambled toward her. Traffic grumbled on Fremont Street below. The cool breeze carried the tantalizing scent of rain, falling in the mountains to the west. "You're on in twenty minutes," he said.

"I know. I'll be there. I just wanted to get away for a while." She turned back toward the edge of the roof and rested her hands on the railing.

"That's you. Always pulling back. It's a bad habit. It robs you of things that are worth having." He put his own hands on the rail.

She grimaced. "I see where this is going."

Orsini shrugged. "Okay, you got me. People have always told me that I'm about as subtle as a train wreck. So, *have* you decided whether to extend your stay?"

She shook her head.

"Some very successful entertainers spend pretty much their whole careers in Vegas. Look at Wayne Newton. Buddy Hackett. Siegfried and Roy. No reason a wraith can't do the same."

"Why does it even matter to you?" she asked fretfully. "I understand why you've got a section reserved for your own kind. But what's the point of building a playground for dead people? You can't spend our money, and you can't use our goods."

"True enough. But in a world full of violence and double-dealing, we can use *you*. Some of you have talents that can reach across the veil of death, abilities as powerful as ours. Entertaining you helps us recruit you."

"With your magic, you could just force us to do what you want."

Orsini sighed. "Sure, like in the old days. Like some of my clan brothers, in other parts of the world, do even now. But most of us have gotten smart enough to understand that making friends is better than catching slaves." A meteor flamed across the sky. He pointed. "Look."

Her dark eyes widened. Her face looked softer, younger, than it had before. "Wow." The shooting star burned out. After another moment, he said, "You asked why I'm interested in your kind. But I think what you really want to know is, why am I interested in you?" He could virtually feel her defenses snapping into place.

"Because you think *I'd* make a good soldier for the

Giovanni cause?" she responded, still gazing at the blackened clouds above.

"No. Aside from the fact that your illusions really are amazing, and I take pride in the quality of the entertainment here, I like you. I think we're two of a kind."

"Yeah, right."

"The elders, the ancient undead, of my family chose me to become a vampire. I didn't want it. Believe me, I know that I'm a monster. I understand that in some respects, my little kingdom here is an ugly place, and that sometimes I do ugly things to survive.

"Believe it or not, most vampires relish their power and eternal youth, but not me. If I could turn into a mortal and walk away from it all, I would. And I think that if you could throw *your* karma away and start fresh, you'd do the same."

"Maybe," Elaine said, her hand inching toward his, stopping a hair's breadth away and creating the illusion that the two were touching.

Orsini was glad that he was a good actor. Otherwise, he might have laughed. She was as intangible as air, and, like all Kindred, he had no real sex drive. It had vanished, never to return, the first time he felt the Hunger for blood, a lust fiercer than any mortal craving. And yet she was drawn to him, as he intended.

Perhaps recognizing the absurdity of her emotions, she pulled her hand away. "It's nice that you want to be friends. Still, I run a traveling show, and before long, it needs to travel on."

"I don't see why. Aren't your friends happy here? If you need something I haven't provided, just say the word."

She smiled wryly. "You've got to be kidding. This place is a palace. Who ever heard of a wraith swimming pool?"

She ought to be impressed, Orsini reflected. He'd accomplished the seemingly impossible feat of getting water into the Shadowlands by running a pipe through a Nihil,

into one of the rivers inside the Tempest. It had turned out
to be a hellishly dangerous job — for the ghosts who did it.

"Of course everybody's happy, for the time being. But—
" she stammered.

"Then why rush off?" He looked into her face. "Elaine,
are you in some kind of trouble?"

Her eyes narrowed. "What makes you think that?"

"Intuition. Sharpened by how closemouthed you always
are. You never talk about yourself, or your past."

"There's nothing to tell."

"All right, if you say so. But I hope you understand that
this place is a fortress. As long as you stay, nothing can hurt
you."

"I really don't need protection." Her hand inched toward
his. "But I guess we could stick around two more weeks."

He smiled. Despite herself, she was becoming dependent.
Someday soon she'd spill her secret, if, in fact, she had one.
Even if she didn't, she truly was talented. The time and effort
he'd devoted to her and her troupe would still have been
well spent.

-NINE-

July.

Resplendent in his new, canary-yellow suit, George sauntered around the hotel. He knew he was being vain, but he couldn't resist putting himself on display.

Completing a circuit of the ghosts' wing, he strolled into the living section of the resort. No doubt there were some wraiths hanging around there, too.

Someone sobbed softly. Startled, George glanced around. He didn't see anyone. The crying must be coming from inside one of the guest rooms lining the hallway.

If pressed, George would have admitted that, on occasion, he enjoyed spying on the living. Voyeurism was a sordid pastime, but in the barren limbo of the Shadowlands, sometimes the only one available. And now he was curious. Listening, he stalked up and down until he found the proper room, then stepped through the door.

The mortal section of the resort resembled, in a playful sort of way, the mansion of a debauched Satanist. In this suite, the wallpaper was a lush crimson, the furniture a gleaming lacquered black. Beside the wet bar hung a Hindu painting of a tusked demon copulating with a human woman. Dainty silver shackles hung from the posts of the canopy bed, and an elephant-foot umbrella stand full of switches, birch rods, and whips squatted in the corner.

George peered about. He still didn't see anyone. Then came another sob, from behind the closet door. He stuck his head through the panel.

Kimberly, the wraith troupe's child singer, crouched on the floor, beneath studded leather harnesses, a French maid's outfit, an SS uniform, and other costumes. Her eyes were red and swollen. Her aura shone with the silver and gray of misery.

George's morbid curiosity gave way to dismay. As far as he was concerned, most adults, living, dead, or vampire, were no better than riffraff, but he had a soft spot for child ghosts. Like him, they'd been expelled from mortal existence without ever having a chance to fulfill their potential. And during the weeks he'd spent socializing with the performers, fleecing Artie and Chris, the actor who played Charon, at poker and gin, he and the little girl had struck up an acquaintance.

"What's wrong?" he asked.

She looked up. Sniffed and wiped her nose, even though it wasn't really running. "Mr. Pryor. I'm sorry. I didn't mean to bother anybody."

"You didn't. But you are worrying me. Come out of there and tell me what's the matter." He lifted her to her feet, then drew her gently through the door.

"It's all right," she said, her eyes downcast. "Really."

He started to lead her to a chair, then thought better of it. She shouldn't stay in a suite full of sex toys. He escorted her into the corridor instead. "Balderdash. If it were all right, you wouldn't be hiding in the dark caterwauling, now would you?" He stooped and took her chin between his thumb and forefinger, lifting her head until he could look her in the eye. "Please tell me. I promise to fix it if I can. And there's very little the resourceful Mr. M — Pryor *can't* fix when he sets his mind to it."

Kim stared at him for a moment, then said, "You have

to promise not to think that Elaine is bad. Because she isn't."

"I won't." Haughty to the point of flagrant bitchiness, he thought sardonically, but not bad.

"Then okay." She frowned, evidently pondering how best to begin. "When she found me, I'd been dead a year. I was hanging around my mom and dad. And that's *all* I was doing. All I *wanted* to do."

George nodded.

"Elaine told me I should join the show, so I could be with friends who could talk to me and play with me and take care of me. At first, I didn't want to, but she kept after me until she talked me into it. You see how nice she is?"

"Absolutely," said George. He suspected that if Kim didn't sing like a nightingale, Elaine wouldn't have given a tinker's dam about her.

The little girl swallowed. "But here's the thing. She promised that every few months, I could visit mom and dad. Everybody in the show gets to see the people they care about. That's how we decide what towns to play, and it's my turn! We were supposed to go to Boulder a month ago! But Elaine won't!"

"Have you asked her about it?"

Kim nodded. "A bunch. She said I was nagging. She *yelled* at me."

George grimaced. "She's quite the little tyrant, isn't she? But the wise Mr. Pryor has noticed that if the rest of you present a united front, she sometimes agrees to your wishes. If I were you, I'd talk to Artie, Chris—"

"I did. And they don't care if we never go, either!"

"Well, we are living in the lap of luxury. You like having toys, and new clothes, and a bed where you can crawl under the covers, don't you? And we're making money hand over fist."

"They still should want to go! There's something wrong with them!"

George wondered how to explain that, to mature souls,

ambition and pleasure meant more than nostalgia. And then, abruptly, it occurred to him that it had been weeks since *he'd* thought about moving on.

The Hierarchy wasn't the unified force it had been in Charon's day. People whispered that the Deathlords, the fallen monarch's former deputies, were too busy scheming against one another to govern effectively. Spectres, those mad spirits pledged to universal destruction, assailed the regime from the outside, and rebels undermined it from within. As conditions worsened, the sundry Governors of the Americas, and George assumed, the rest of the Shadowlands as well, grew isolated and virtually independent, like provincial governors in the decaying Roman Empire.

Thus, once George had escaped from San Francisco, the risk of his recapture had diminished considerably. Still, it was possible that Vincent had dispatched agents to retrieve him. Or that the governor of San Francisco had prevailed upon the Hierarchs of other cities to hunt, arrest, and extradite him.

Such being the case, it was regretfully time to abandon the comfortable berth Larry Orsini had given him and seek out greener pastures. Yet if he hadn't spoken to Kim, who knew how long it would have taken for the notion to cross his mind?

"What's the matter?" she asked. He realized that he must have a troubled expression on his face.

"Nothing." He glanced at another of his new possessions, a Stygian copy of a gold Rolex. Thank god, hours of daylight left. Hours before the vampires would awaken. "Young Mr. Pryor is going to straighten everything out. You can help by returning to the troupe and staying with them."

Kim frowned. "Why? What are you going to do?"

"I'll explain later. For now, please trust me."

"Okay." She stepped through the wall, making a beeline for the theater. He headed for Joey's room.

- TEN -

The cool blue water caressed Joey's body. The yellow sunlight warmed his shoulders. A few yards toward the beach, the waves hissed and shredded into foam. To the north, the towering span of the Golden Gate swept across the bay. A hang glider, black and scalloped like a bat's wing, floated in the southern sky.

Drop-dead sexy in her red bikini, Emily tossed the beach ball, and Sarah caught it. The little girl yelled, "Here it comes, daddy!"

She threw the ball wild, to the left. Throwing up a sparkling wave of spray, Joey jumped to make the catch.

The ball flew past his fingertips, a bare inch out of reach. He splashed down into the waves. When he lifted his head, his hair plastered down, stinging salt water trickled into his eyes. As he cleared his vision, he saw Emily and Sarah twenty feet farther away than they should have been. Their eyes were wide with shock.

He started to wade toward them. Something tumbled him backward, dunking him. He choked on a mouthful of stinging water.

He tried to stand, but now he couldn't touch bottom. Treading water, coughing and sputtering, he looked around.

His family was half a football field away. Sarah was

keening wordlessly. Emily screamed, "Riptide! Riptide! Help! Help!"

Joey realized that he was being dragged out to sea.

Suddenly frantic, he tried to swim.

It didn't help. Though he kicked and stroked with all his might, every time he raised his head, Emily and Sarah, and the shore behind them, were farther away.

In a minute, he couldn't see or hear his family at all. Then, without warning, the current yanked him down. The sunlit water turned black. His lungs ached, and he fought the urge to gasp for air. Finally, he couldn't resist it any longer.

For an instant, seawater poured down his throat, strangling him. Then he was thrashing on his bed. As usual, George was standing over him.

At that moment, George *was* the riptide. Joey threw himself at his tormentor. The shackles blasted a wave of cold and sickness through his body.

At first, even that wasn't enough to calm him down. He writhed like an animal in a trap, tumbling off the mattress onto the floor. Finally the craziness loosened its grip. "Sorry," he croaked. "Sorry."

Clearly alarmed, George gawked down at him. "My god! What was that?"

"I had a nightmare. I thought you were part of it. I'm all right now."

George waved his hand. Joey's flesh started to warm up. "Good. Because we may be in trouble."

Grunting, Joey stood up. His chain clinked. "How so?"

"Larry Orsini belongs to a vampire clan called the Giovanni. Do you know anything about them?"

"They're the vampires who can see us." During his weeks at the Inferno, he'd discovered that many of the undead couldn't.

"They're more than that. According to legend, they're descended from Venetian necromancers, sorcerers who could conjure the dead. At any rate, the Giovanni have made a specialty of working with ghosts like us. The older ones have the power to hurt or control us, by magic spells."

Joey gaped at him. "And knowing that, you came here? Don't you have *any* sense?"

George glared back. "Everybody says that Larry doesn't use those abilities. His spirit employees claim they're here of their own free will."

"Then what's the problem?"

"I just talked to Kimberly. She was upset because no one in her troupe wants to move on, even though staying means that they can't visit their living relations. I realized that despite our need to keep ahead of Vincent's agents, I haven't been contemplating leaving, either. In the stories people tell, a Giovanni's magic snaps shut on a wraith all at once. The spirit knows he's being forced into service, and naturally he doesn't like it. But suppose Larry has found a way to influence us insidiously. A slow process, working in concert with his vampiric charisma and the seductions of life in the hotel. We wouldn't resist or rebel if we didn't even realize we'd been enslaved."

"I can see how this is a hot issue for you, but in case it's slipped your mind, I'm already enslaved. Is there any reason I should give a damn?"

George grimaced. "Your relationship with me doesn't twist your thoughts and emotions. And currently you only have one master, not two."

Joey sighed. "All right, I get your point. What are we going to do?"

"The wise thing would be to slip away this instant. But I promised Kimberly I'd free her associates from the spell, and Mr. Montaigne is a man of his word."

Joey stifled an incredulous laugh. "If you tell them what you think, maybe they'll come to their senses like you did."

George shook his head. "I doubt it. Kim has already remonstrated with them, to no avail. Evidently she and I have stronger wills than they do. And if one of Larry's minions overheard me exposing his master's machinations, the result could be most unpleasant."

"So what is the plan?"

George scowled. "How should I know? I'm not a Giovanni. I don't understand how their powers operate. Perhaps in this case Larry is using tools and props, like in ritual magic. Perhaps there's a room somewhere, with effigies of everyone he's trying to bewitch. If we could find it — but the search would be dangerous, too!" His fists opened and closed. "Damn it anyway! I truly am fond of Kimberly. But whatever I may have said in a moment of weakness, I'm not her guardian. Neither she nor her companions are my responsibility."

"In other words, why should you hang around and put your ass on the line to help them?"

"Crudely put, but yes."

Joey realized that if Elaine's troupe was really in trouble, he wanted to help them. Maybe it was because he didn't like the idea of anyone else being enslaved. Or because Kim was a cute little girl like the Sarah in his dreams. In any case, he decided to see if he could convince George to act like a stand-up guy for once. "You want to know what I think?"

"Please."

"First off, you're kind of panicking. You don't *know* that Larry is brainwashing people."

"I know the strength of the bond that links many wraiths to their living loved ones."

Joey's mouth twisted. "Tell me about it. Still, you're just guessing. It would be better to find out for sure than just assume the worst and run away. The guy's a big shot. If he isn't trying to hypnotize you, don't you want to keep him as a friend?"

George shrugged. "I suppose."

"And let's say that he *does* have a voodoo doll with your face stashed away somewhere. You've shaken off its mojo for the time being. But once he notices you've split, he might be able to run some extra juice through it and reel you back in. It would be safer to destroy the thing, or steal it."

"All right. Perhaps you're talking sense. Go look for the workroom. Report back when you find it, or at five o'clock, whichever comes first." He pulled off his watch.

"Screw that," said Joey. The bracelets grew colder. "If I'm going, you're going with me."

"I'm *ordering* you—"

"Then I'll disobey." His stomach churned. "Leave me shaking on the floor, I don't care. You know things I don't, and you can do tricks I can't. We need to tackle a job like this together." His knees went rubbery.

George waved his hand. Joey's weakness abated. "All *right*! If you're afraid of a simple little errand, I'll come along to hold your hand!"

-ELEVEN-

For the most part, the vampire wing of the resort lacked the mock diabolical trappings of the mortal area. Some of the decorations, like a painting of a gaunt, undead woman gazing down at a sleeping child, or a statue of what seemed to be a maimed, dying werewolf, were decidedly macabre, but there was nothing comical about them. They had such an eerie beauty that Joey wondered if somebody famous, a Rembrandt or a da Vinci, had created them.

He suspected that the whole high-ceilinged, dimly lit complex would look similarly lovely, or at least elegant and luxurious, if he could see it as the vampires did. But to his wraith eyes, the paper was peeling off the walls, refuse choked the crumbling fireplaces, and a web of jagged Nihils carved fissures in the floor. The air smelled of blood and decay.

As George had promised, there were no vampires wandering around in the middle of the afternoon.

Abruptly, a ghost with an eyepatch stepped through the wall. "Can I help you?" he asked.

"We're just giving ourselves the nickel tour," said Joey. "Checking things out."

The one-eyed man said, "No problem. You ought to come back tonight and catch the show. The new headliner sings like Sinatra." He crossed the room and disappeared through the wall on the other side.

George frowned. "That was easy enough. I don't know whether to be relieved or disappointed. Either he assumes we mean no harm, or he doesn't believe we can do any harm."

"Well, he doesn't know you can hop across the Shroud. Let's keep looking."

George nodded. "It occurs to me that the resident Giovanni may well live apart from the guests. Look for an area closed to the public."

They prowled on. George kept checking his watch, until Joey wanted to tear it off his wrist, throw it on the floor, and stamp on it.

They skirted a softly crackling Nihil big enough to fall in. A hint of sickly color, like the lights Joey saw when he closed his eyes and pressed on the lids, squirmed in its depths.

At last, turning a corner, they found themselves in a library. Dilapidated armchairs and crumbling books exuded the smell of rotting leather. Along the back wall, two rusty suits of plate armor leaned drunkenly on their halberds. Between them stood a black door with a tarnished silver plate. The engraving read, *NO ADMITTANCE*.

"Bingo," said Joey. He raised his arms, displaying the manacles. "Can we lose the chain now? If we get caught in a restricted area, I wouldn't count on being able to talk our way out."

George stared at the links. They disappeared. "Lead on. Stealthily."

" 'Stealthily.' Right. No wonder you're the boss. I would never have thought of that," smirked Joey.

"How sad to think that that sally represents the acme of your wit. Now get on with it."

Joey stuck his face through the door. On the other side

was a staircase. He beckoned to George, and they glided down the steps.

At the bottom, running at right angles to the stairs, was a corridor, even more dimly lit than the rooms above. The stench of blood and rot was stronger. Joey peeked around the corner.

Three feet away slouched a slack-featured man with a gash in the side of his neck. His gaudy Hawaiian shirt was filthy with dried blood, but the wound had long since stopped bleeding. An ant crawled on his blistered, greenish cheek, and he cradled an automatic rifle in his swollen hands. As Joey recoiled, he glimpsed an equally gruesome guard standing on the other side of the opening.

"What is it?" asked George. He looked ready to bolt back up the steps.

Joey knew just how he felt. He struggled to get past his instinctive terror. After all, it was pretty stupid for one dead guy to be scared of another. "Guards. I guess you'd call them zombies. But I don't think they can see us. I stuck my head out right in front of them, and they aren't doing anything."

George swallowed. "Then let's proceed."

Gripping his baton, half expecting the zombies to shoot, or lunge at him, Joey made himself step back into the corridor. The animated corpses didn't stir. Adjusting his vision, he saw that they scarcely had auras at all, just faint wisps of phosphorescence crawling on their soft, discolored skin.

George stepped gingerly out behind him. The little man screwed up his face at the sight of the guards, then pointed at a door. "Let's look in there."

Beyond the door was an apartment. Joey didn't doubt that it was lavishly furnished, though to him, everything looked worm-eaten and threadbare. "I suppose they're wise to live in a bunker," murmured George. "Even if some calamity razed the hotel, a rival clan bombing it or something like that, the sunlight wouldn't reach them here."

"Hitler thought it was a good idea, too."

They skulked on. In the bedroom, on a waterbed covered with tiger and leopard skins, slept a nude female vampire. Her fangs were extended, indenting her full and blood-smeared lower lip. Last night's rumpled garments lay discarded on the Persian carpet. So did what was left of last night's supper, the naked corpse of a towheaded teenage boy.

Joey felt sick. Larry had told him that, unlike movie vampires, real-life undead only drank from willing mortals, and were careful not to do them any harm.

He turned to George. "You know, maybe you could kill every one of these bastards. Jump across the Shroud, waste one, jump back, and sneak on to the next."

George looked disgusted, too. But he said, "Remember, we came down here partly because we've considered Larry a friend. We're hoping that we won't find any evidence to indicate otherwise. At the end of our search, hopefully we'll feel comfortable with the conclusion that he truly *is* a friend."

Joey scowled. "You've seen this, and those monsters in the hall. But you're still willing to go on kissing his ass, just as long as he isn't messing with you."

"That's a simpleminded way of looking at a complex situation. Besides, even sleeping vampires are notoriously difficult to kill. I don't have the proper tools, and there may well be alarms and defenses we don't perceive. We'll be doing well to make our search and get out safely, without trying to conduct a pogrom while we're at it."

Joey supposed that George was right, but he hated to admit it. Anger seethed inside him, just as if he were about to climb into the ring. It made him want to see the vampires die. "Okay. If we can't croak the bitch, then let's get out of here."

They stalked on. Found five more sleeping vampires, and two more zombie sentries. Then Joey tried to step through another door. A jolt like an electric shock threw him backward.

"What the hell was that?" he asked.

George cautiously sank the tip of his index finger into the panel, then jerked it back. "Ouch! I think it's a ward."

"What's that?"

"A protection that keeps wraiths out of an area. I dare say that Larry's personal quarters are behind here. Try to slip through the wall."

"Give me a break," Joey growled. "Do you think he doesn't know that we can go through a wall as easily as a door?" The bracelets chilled his wrists.

George grimaced. "All right, forget that." The cuffs grew warm. "Damn it! If there's anything to be found, it's here, but there's no way to get at it. We'll simply have to do the prudent thing and run away, as I proposed in the first place. Hope that we aren't needlessly alienating a benefactor, and pray that he doesn't have the means to draw me back."

Suddenly Joey got an idea. "Maybe not. Here's the plan. We're going to jump into the air, and when we come down, we'll let ourselves fall through the floor. See if we can go under the ward and come up on the other side."

George eyed him dubiously. "Do you think that will work?"

"Who am I, Merlin the magician? How should I know? It's worth a try, isn't it, now that we've come this far?"

"I suppose. On three, then. One, two, three!"

Joey jumped. He half expected George to stay put and let him try the experiment solo. But after a split-second's hesitation, the little man leaped too. For a moment, Joey watched him sink into the linoleum. Then his own eyes slipped beneath the floor.

The world went black and silent. Nothing remained but the sensation of falling. Suddenly he was sure that he wouldn't be able to stop. That he'd plummet to the center of the earth.

Terrified, he flailed, fighting gravity the way he'd fought the riptide in his dream. The emptiness around him clotted into semisolidity. He felt a mushiness beneath his clawing hands and kicking feet.

He struggled to move forward and up. At times, he felt like he was swimming. At others, it was like trying to flounder up a mound of slime. He tried to stifle the stupid, mortal instinct that insisted he was going to suffocate.

He wondered if the impression that he'd stopped his fall, that he was moving under his own steam, was an illusion. Or if he'd gotten turned around and was crawling in the wrong direction, parallel to the floor above or deeper into the earth. Then a pain like jabbing needles stung his fingers.

It was the ward. It protected the floor of the space beyond the wall, too. But it hadn't flung Joey back. It didn't exert as much force in this direction.

Joey clambered upward. The needles stabbed down his arms. Ripped his face and torso. Then his upper body flailed out onto a tile floor. Clutching at it, shuddering, he hauled his legs out of the torture zone like a man dragging himself out of a hole in the ice of a frozen river.

In a moment, the agony faded. He looked around. He was sprawled in a spacious living room with Southwestern decor. Displays of Indian artifacts, war bonnets, lances, pipes, turquoise and silver jewelry, pottery, and buffalo robes, occupied display cases or hung along the faux adobe walls. An oil painting of a pueblo adorned the space above the mantel. Cacti bristled in clay pots. An ornately carved cabinet full of delicate glassware, which to Joey's eyes looked chipped and cracked, was the only thing that clashed with the overall tone.

George was nowhere in sight.

Joey stuck his arm back into the floor. Instantly, it began to feel as if it were on fire. Doing his best to ignore the pain, he groped.

At first, he found nothing. Finally his fingers grazed what

felt like cloth. Fumbling, he got a weak grip on what he thought was a shoulder. Two hands clutched his forearm. He stuck his other arm into the floor, got a strong hold with both hands, and heaved, yanking George into the light.

"Thank you," George whimpered. "The pain. Hammering at me. I couldn't…"

For a moment, Joey felt sorry for the little guy, and glad that he'd gotten him clear. Then he remembered that this was the man who'd enslaved him, and pity withered into self-contempt. He stood up. "We'll see if we can find a different way to leave."

"That would certainly suit me." George clambered to his feet and looked at his watch. "Let's hurry. It's already four o'clock."

The suite in which they found themselves was a lot bigger than the other Giovanni apartments. From that fact, and the magic that protected it, Joey surmised that it really was Larry's private quarters. Sneaking on, the two ghosts found an office. An armory filled with swords, bows, and modern firearms. A hot tub. A huge aquarium, filled with a rainbow of tropical fish. And finally the chamber where the vampire slept.

The lean, gray-haired undead lay on a red marble bier in the middle of the floor. Several tables stood along the walls. On top of them sat abstract sculptures, twists of copper wire and scraps of garnet. Entangled in some of these, like animals locked in cages, or crucified men hanging from trees, were charcoal sketches of George, Elaine, Artie, Chris, and other members of the troupe. A crimson fire axe leaned in the corner.

Joey didn't see any pentagrams, zodiac wheels, satanic idols, wavy-bladed daggers, or any of the other customary trappings of ritual sorcery, at least as it was practiced in the movies. But he didn't doubt that the sculptures were magical. The interior of the room wavered as if he were seeing it through a curtain of heat, and something in the air was making his skin itch.

He noted sardonically that Larry hadn't bothered to sketch him, or Kimberly. Evidently he'd assumed that the Thrall and the child would stay if their keepers stayed.

He turned to George. "I've got to hand it to you. You guessed there might be a workroom, with something like voodoo dolls, and by God, here they are."

"I've always told you, young George is a most insightful fellow. Odd that there are no representations of the ghosts on the resort staff."

"Maybe they really do work here of their own free will. Or maybe, once a spook is totally enslaved, Larry doesn't need the gadget anymore. Anyway, who cares? Jump across the Shroud and trash the drawings."

George swallowed. "I wonder if that would be prudent."

"He can't wake up, can he, not in the middle of the day?"

"People say not, but I don't *know*!"

"Just do it *stealthily*. And if anything happens, step back here and we'll run. Do it for Kim. Do it to protect your own back. Show some guts."

George grimaced. "Very well." He closed his eyes, clenched his fits, and muttered. Then, giving the sleeping Larry as wide a berth as possible, he tiptoed into the magic room. Joey followed.

George removed his own picture from its wire cage and began to tear it. The hiss of ripping paper seemed horribly loud. The little man cringed. Joey did too. But Larry didn't stir.

Even so, George didn't keep tearing. Instead, he moved to Kim's portrait. Joey guessed that he meant to collect them all, carry them into another room, and destroy them there.

Behind George, the red axe floated into the air.

Joey screamed, "Look out!" George didn't react. The little man couldn't hear him.

Joey looked frantically around the room, trying to spot whatever was moving the weapon. The air seemed to shimmer and ripple even more violently than before, hampering his vision.

The axe drifted toward George. Tilted upward, poising itself.

At that moment, Joey saw a shadow crouching against the back wall. The distortion in the air had concealed it up to now. He charged it, and it swam into clearer view.

The figure was a hulking, naked man, evidently one of those wraiths who could move Skinland objects with his mind. Joey had no doubt that Larry had used his powers to enslave this ghost. With his blazing eyes and bestial snarl, the man looked almost as bereft of humanity as a mad dog.

The naked man sprang to meet him, hands outstretched. Full of rage and loathing, Joey dodged, then clubbed the sentinel as he blundered past. The baton rang, and the guard crashed to the floor.

And so did the floating axe. George screamed and whirled around. Larry groaned and shifted restlessly on the bier.

His face a mask of terror, George squinched his eyes shut. Larry mumbled, then visibly relaxed, seemingly sinking into deeper slumber.

George cracked his eyes open, and then, sweat streaking his face, he gathered the remainder of the drawings. The papers rattled in his shaking hands.

When he had them all, he scurried into the living room with Joey striding along behind him. The little man tore the sketches to shreds, fumbled open the four locks on the door, swung it open, and then slipped back into the Shadowlands. "Let's make ourselves scarce," he said.

-TWELVE-

When Joey and George reached the wraith theater, a rehearsal was in progress. Larry's ghost orchestra played fast, brassy, circus-style music. While on stage, the jugglers tossed gleaming daggers back and forth.

One juggler fumbled a catch, knocking a knife pinwheeling sideways. It clanked down and skidded off the stage, into the orchestra pit. The conductor lowered his baton, and the music staggered to a halt.

"No, no, no!" Artie's voice called from the darkened balcony. "I told you, aim for the trombone player. He's over there!" The musician in question grinned and flipped him the bird.

Joey spotted Chris, the handsome blond actor who played Charon, sitting in the aisle seat in the fifth row. He strode over to him. George scurried along a pace behind.

Chris twisted in his seat. "Hi, guys, come to watch? If you like screw-ups, you picked a good day. We're all making mistakes, and I feel weird. If we were Skinlanders, I'd think we had the flu."

"Larry sort of hypnotized you," said Joey. "George and I broke the spell. That's probably why you feel peculiar."

Chris blinked. "Excuse me? What the heck are you talking about?"

George said, "You have family in Dallas. The show has to travel if you're ever going to see them. But when was the last time you thought about moving on? When did you last hear anyone but Kimberly discuss the possibility?"

The actor shook his head. "I — I don't know. Now that you mention it, that's not like us, not even a little bit. And people say the Giovanni have the power to mess with our heads. But my god, why would they? What makes us important?"

The band resumed playing. Above them, flashing blades arced through the air. Joey looked at Artie's watch. It was nearly five o'clock.

"Aside from the fact that you're talented entertainers," said George, "I can't imagine. Perhaps that sufficed. In any case, what's important is that he did do it. My associate and I have seen the proof. And unless you and your compatriots want him to do it again, unless you want to stay here forever like trained, happy house pets, you have to leave now."

Chris set his jaw. "Okay." He stood up and bellowed, "Hold it!" The music died. "We need a meeting. Elaine's people only. Back of the theater."

The musicians watched curiously as their fellow performers clustered. Joey noticed that Elaine herself was absent. Probably moping around alone as usual.

"This better be important," Artie said.

Chris looked at George and Joey. "Tell these guys what you told me. This time, with the details."

George laid it out for them. At first they babbled in shock and disbelief, but after a few minutes, he had them convinced. Joey gathered that they'd all heard horror stories about the cunning and unearthly talents of the Giovanni, and that helped to undermine whatever skepticism they might otherwise have felt.

A juggler hefted one of his knifes. "We ought to tear this dump apart."

"Rest assured, Mr. Pryor shares your righteous outrage,"

said George. "However, sagacious as he is valiant, he advocates flight, not reprisal. Who knows what other tricks the fiends might be holding in reserve?"

"Spoken like the yellow-bellied worm you are," said Artie. "And as one wriggler to another, I approve. The problem is that not everybody is here to hear this little news flash. Let's split up, collect the others, and meet in front of the building. And don't anybody take the time to gather up all your new belongings. Grab the things you really need, and vamoose."

The performers murmured in agreement, then started to disperse.

"What's going on?" the trombone player shouted.

"We're blowing this pop stand," Artie answered. "Do you want to come?"

"No!" said the musician, obviously astonished. "Why would we? What's wrong?"

"For you, maybe nothing. Anywho, there's no time to explain. Shalom, you tin-eared mugwump! Do the music world a favor — get a hammer and put that overgrown ocarina out of its misery!" Artie said as he stepped through the wall. Joey and George were right behind him.

The two wraiths began to range through the resort. At first, Joey yelled, "Elaine's people! Elaine's people!" Then he heard the performers shouting, "Hey, rube!" Remembering that it was the traditional carnival distress call, he switched to that instead.

Rounding a corner, he and George came face to face with Elaine. Her lower lip quivered, and her pupils were dilated. She stared at them with no sign of recognition.

Joey guessed that either she was more susceptible to Larry's power than the rest of the troupe, or he'd given her a stronger dose of it. Either way, the termination of the spell had evidently plunged her into a daze. "Elaine?" he said. "Do you know us?"

She peered at him. "Reverend Saul?"

Joey glanced at George. "This is helpful," he said sarcastically.

"At least she seems docile," the little man said. "I imagine she'll recover by and by. Just take her where she needs to be. I'll meet you there as soon as I fetch my trench coat."

"That filthy thing? Leave it."

"I brought it with me when I passed from life into death. I'm not going to lose it now." He trotted down the hall.

Joey cursed him, and took Elaine's arm. For a moment, he was acutely aware of the soft, smooth feel of her skin. He realized that he'd not touched a female wraith in the nine months since his death. Scowling, he led the illusionist back down the corridor. She came along cooperatively enough, though not as quickly as he would have liked.

The shouting began to die down. He guessed that most of the troupe was already outside. In another minute, he and Elaine would be there too. He urged her on, into the mortal lobby, a mock infernal cavern. Stalactites dripped from the ceiling, colored fountains gushed, and a towering statue of a bat-winged Satan with an Elvis haircut and jumpsuit leered from a marble pedestal in the center of the floor.

Four of Larry's wraith security guards were standing at the effigy's disco-booted feet, talking excitedly. One was waving his gray iron billy club around.

Joey tried to haul Elaine back out of sight, but he was too slow. A guard spotted them, pointed them out to his buddies, and they all strode forward.

Still guiding Elaine, Joey sauntered to meet them. He hoped it would keep him from looking suspicious. Besides, every step took him and the illusionist closer to the rendezvous point.

"What's going on?" asked the guard in the lead. He was a beefy guy with a chipped front tooth and a sprinkle of white in his black mustache.

It was obvious that the troupe was leaving, so Joey didn't

try to deny it. "We're moving on to another gig. See you next time."

"That's nuts," said a second guard, a willowy black woman with several gold rings in her left ear. "You people are booked for another month."

Joey shrugged. "I don't make the decisions. I just do what they tell me." He tried to edge around the guards.

The wraith with the chipped tooth sidestepped, blocking his path. "Yeah, but the lady here does decide. Is there a problem, Miss Forrester? Whatever it is, I'm sure that you and Mr. Orsini can work it out."

Elaine stared at him blankly. Then her legs went rubbery. For a second, Joey had to hold her up.

"Something's wrong with her," said Chipped Tooth.

"Maybe, but that's none of your business," said Joey.

"It's not yours, either," said the black woman. "You don't work for her. You're that boxer."

"That's true," said Joey. "But come on outside with us and you can talk to Chris or Artie."

Chipped Tooth shook his head. "I don't think so. I don't understand this at all. But I know that Mr. Orsini expects people to honor their contracts, and I know that he likes this girl. I don't want to have to tell him that I let you skip out without even finding out why you were leaving. Or that I let you drag Miss Forrester away when she was too punchy to know what was going on."

"What if I told you that Orsini is a bad guy, just like the nastiest Giovanni anybody ever heard of," Joey said. "That he's the one who made her sick."

A lanky guard with acne-pitted cheeks sneered. "We'd say you were full of—"

Releasing Elaine's arm, Joey whipped his baton at Chipped Tooth's face.

The blow cracked home, and Chipped Tooth stumbled backward. Joey pivoted and struck at the black woman.

Meanwhile, oblivious Skinlander tourists strolled by not more than a yard away.

The black woman lifted her club in time to block the attack. Metal rang on metal. She swung at Joey. He twisted out of the way and kicked her in the stomach. She doubled over.

Something crashed down on his head, and the world went dark. When the light came back, he found that he was swaying on his knees.

The lanky guard hit him again, smashing him to the floor. Then the fourth goon, a bald guy with stubby gilded horns, took a swing. They alternated attacks like a pair of section hands driving a spike into the ground.

Pain ripped through Joey's body. His vision was getting hazy. He tried to strike back at his tormentors, tried to tap the power of the voice, but this time, it wasn't enough.

Shuddering, Elaine backpedaled to the edge of a crimson fountain. She looked terrified of the violence, but still too confused to take any kind of action.

Then suddenly, someone sang, a sustained note so high and piercing that, despite the agony already wracking Joey's body, his ears began to ring. The horned man screamed. The flesh on his head ran like melting ice cream.

Joey whirled around in the direction of the noise. Chris and Kim stood several yards away. The little girl was doing the singing. Joey had never realized that her voice could be so destructive.

The three remaining guards rushed her. It broke her nerve, and she recoiled. Chris jumped between her and her would-be assailants. His skin thickened into silvery hide, and his hands swelled into misshapen appendages segmented like an insect's body, with long claws and spiked knuckles. Evidently he was a flesh shaper, one skillful enough to grow natural armor and weapons.

The black woman tried to club him. He blocked the swing, then punched her in the face, virtually obliterating her features. She reeled.

But she'd held Chris's attention long enough for the lanky man to circle behind him and hit him over the head. Evidently the glinting hide wasn't thick enough to cushion the impact, because Chris pitched forward onto his hands and knees. Chipped Tooth pounced on Kim. The little girl squealed till he grabbed her by the throat.

A surge of rage blunted Joey's pain. He tried to scramble up. Finally his unnatural strength kicked in. He ran at the lanky man and dove over Chris to take the thug down. The guard's club streaked at him, glancing off his shoulder, but he barely felt it. He slammed into the guy and knocked him down. Dropping onto the guard's chest, Joey beat him until he lost consciousness.

Joey leaped up while Chris clambered to his feet. Still clinging to Kim, Chipped Tooth backed away. "Take it easy," he stammered. "We can still work this out."

"Take this easy," Joey growled, charging forward.

Chipped Tooth dropped Kim and turned to run. Joey bashed him from behind. Then he dropped to one knee and started to batter him to pulp.

A huge hand, hard as iron, gripped his shoulder. Talons pricked his skin. He jerked around, ready to swing.

Chris peered down at him, his big blue eyes out of place in his now inhuman face. "Come on," he said. "We haven't got time for this. We have to get Elaine and Kim away."

Joey knew Chris was right, but he was so angry, so eager to punish the guard, that it was hard to care. He forced himself to stand up.

Chris scooped up the weeping Kim in his body-builder's arms. "It's all right," he told her. "They can't hurt us now."

Elaine was still cowering beside the fountain, and when Joey started toward her, she shrank back, stumbling off the rim and into the foaming scarlet water.

With the voice's fury still boiling inside him, it wasn't easy to make his tone gentle, but he did his best. "Please.

It's okay. We're your friends — you know Chris and Kim — and we're going to take you to a safe place."

Trembling, Elaine hesitantly held out her hand. He led her across the lobby and through the exterior wall.

Outside, the desert sun was dazzling, and the dry heat seared his face. The stink of exhaust hung in the air. The chattering troupe had clustered around a red and white Coca-Cola truck. Triangles of cloth stuck out of their hastily packed bundles and valises.

Joey looked around for George. It was pleasant to imagine the little snake getting left behind. But Joey had standing orders to appear before his master every day. It was one of several directives intended to make it absolutely impossible for him to escape. Thus, not only was he unable to flee of his own volition, he couldn't allow happenstance to separate them unless he wanted to spend eternity crippled by the power of the shackles. After a moment, he spotted George at the edge of the crowd, surreptitiously transferring iron coins from his pockets to a money belt.

Artie hurried forward. "You people are the last. What kept you?" His head bobbed forward. Evidently he'd just noticed how beaten-up the four latecomers were. "My god, is everybody all right?"

"We will be if we get out of here fast," Joey said. "We had to mix it up with some thugs to get out of the building."

"I think the Coke guy has taken in his whole delivery," Artie replied. "We should be able to hitch a ride any second."

"If not," said Chris, "we'll have to jump into whatever cars are passing. Hook up down the road."

Artie scowled. "It isn't safe to split up."

"This time, it's safer than hanging around."

"All right." The comic raised his voice: "Everybody climb aboard this luxury liner! But if things get ugly, and we're still sitting here, run for it! We'll meet up at the next stop on the card."

The wraiths began to pile onto the truck. Joey escorted Elaine on board, then stuck his head through the side to watch the hotel.

Armed ghosts, some clad in brown fatigues and bronze lion masks that marked them as Legionnaires, began to gather under the porte cochere. Evidently the Inferno wraiths had sent for reinforcements. When a sufficient number arrived, they'd rush the truck.

What was keeping the delivery guy? As the minutes crawled by, Joey grew convinced that the driver wasn't coming. He was about to say as much to Artie when the mortal, a fat man with a gingery Abe Lincoln beard, finally wheeled his hand truck out the front door.

Joey quivered with impatience while the guy ambled across the tarmac, stowed the dolly, put a stick of gum in his mouth, and riffled through the papers on his clipboard.

Then, chewing noisily and open-mouthed, he took a leisurely look around. One of the troupe yelled, "Get going, moron!"

At last the mortal climbed into the cab. The engine rumbled to life, and the truck rolled toward Fremont Avenue. The performers cheered. Artie thumbed his nose at the goons in front of the casino. "So long, suckers!"

Swaying with the motion of the truck, Elaine blinked. "My key," she moaned. "My things." She stepped through a row of clinking, lead-colored soda canisters and the side of the vehicle.

Whirling around, Joey grabbed her arm and yanked her back to safety. "No!" he said. "Stay put!"

She squirmed, struggling to break free. "My things, my things!"

Artie held up a green carpetbag. "Calm down! They're here. I picked them up for you."

She stared at the bag for a moment, then crumpled to the floor and started to cry.

-THIRTEEN-

Pioche.

A round, yellow moon floated over Boot Hill, illuminating the weathered crosses and crumbling tombstones so brightly that even a mortal could have made out the inscriptions. The one closest to Joey and George read, *FANNY PETERSON, JULY 12, 1872. THEY LOVED TIL DEATH DID THEM PART. HE KILLED HER.*

Kim's clear soprano voice throbbed through the cool night air, singing a lullaby. She seemed fully recovered from her ordeal, as did the rest of the troupe. Even Elaine was as cold and reserved as usual.

No doubt the atmosphere of the historic graveyard was partly responsible. Even more than most cemeteries, the place buzzed with an undercurrent of suffering and fear. One of the wraiths who made his home here, an old guy with white mutton-chop whiskers and a derby, claimed that in the 1870s, Pioche had been the roughest mining camp in Nevada. Supposedly, the first seventy-five people buried here had all died violent deaths.

Switching vehicles several times, the troupe had spent the day putting miles between themselves and Vegas, a journey that carried them into the mountains. When darkness had fallen, they'd looked for a good spot to rest, and stumbled on this place. Fortunately the resident spirits had been willing to share their turf in exchange for a show.

Joey wished that he could join in the general mood of celebration, but he felt edgy and blue. All he wanted was to be by himself. To sleep. He was just about to slip away from the crowd when George said, "You're frowning ferociously. Why so glum? We saved ourselves and everyone else, just as we wanted."

Joey shrugged. "What difference does it make? We had trouble in San Francisco. Then again in Vegas. Someday we won't run fast enough, and some terrible thing will happen to us. Maybe it would have been better to get it over with."

George lifted an eyebrow. "Well. Aren't you the optimist. I concede, in the past few months, we've gotten into one or two scrapes. But we escaped unscathed — well, relatively — and our luck is bound to improve."

"Luck has nothing to do with it. People will never stop trying to hurt us, because we're in Hell. Everybody wants to rob or enslave everyone else."

"Don't tell me you're afraid. Mr. Montaigne knows his steadfast champion better than that."

"I'm not," Joey said. "I just wish that everything wasn't so ugly. So useless. I'm sick of it."

"It isn't all unpleasant, not by a long shot." George opened his grubby trench coat, exposing the garish yellow suit he'd bought at the Inferno. "One can lay one's hands on a great many luxuries, provided one has the means to purchase them. And thanks to your pugilistic prowess, and my managerial skills, we do."

"Holy Mike," cried Artie's voice, "that suit is a putrid spectacle! It's enough to make a man embrace nudism, or at least a nudist of the feminine persuasion. Don't stare directly at it, it'll burn your eyes out."

Joey turned. Artie and Mike were standing a few feet away, beside a gray tumbleweed twitching in the breeze. The blond actor had returned to his usual handsome appearance.

George sniffed. "I suppose one can't expect a clown to

appreciate high fashion."

"I'll let you know next time I see some," Artie said. "Now, how's about a little five-card stud?"

"That sounds good," George said. He looked at Joey. "If you're all right."

"I'm fine," Joey said. "At least, I'm not in such rotten shape that I want to talk to *you* about it." He hated it when he caught himself confiding in George. After all, the little man wasn't a friend. He was the guy keeping Joey away from his family.

George grimaced. "Fine. Sulk or doze as usual, just as you please." He followed Chris into the shadows.

To Joey's surprise, Artie stayed behind. "I'll catch up with you lunkheads in a minute," he said.

"Do you want something with me?" Joey asked. In the mountains to the north, a coyote yipped.

"As a matter of fact," Artie said. "I thought we could have a chat, without the ferret that walks like a man kibitzing. You know, I overheard some of what you were saying, and I agree with you. The Underworld is Hell, or at least Purgatory, just like some of the Heretics say it is." The Heretics were wraiths who, in defiance of the sordid facts of existence in the Shadowlands, clung to their old religions, or embraced new faiths unique to the dead. Since they believed in an authority greater than the Deathlords, the Hierarchy regarded them as subversives, and persecuted them as relentlessly as it did the Renegades. "I figured that out the day I woke up deceased and found this in my pocket." He pulled a plastic tube out of his blazer, then unscrewed the end and slid out a cigar. "I guess my kids buried it with me.

"You've seen that I use a stogie in my act. I was also addicted to them. Sucked them down nonstop. And now I'm carrying this last one. But I can't smoke it, or I won't have it to wave around anymore. Sometimes I think I hear it calling my name." He drew the cigar under his nose. His face contorted into a comical mask of mingled pleasure and pain.

"That's rough."

Artie grinned. "Thanks for the sympathy. I can tell you're on the verge of tears, you heartless swine. But on the other hand, being a wraith isn't *completely* bad. It's better than not existing at all. Maybe we can't smoke, knock back hootch, or eat, but we can still screw."

Joey grimaced. "Yeah. We're lucky guys. Is this why you came over here? To give me a pep talk?"

"Not me, *paesan*. If you weren't surly and brooding, you wouldn't have any personality at all. Actually, Goldilocks and I have been talking about you and your boss."

Joey felt a pang of apprehension. He wondered if the performers had figured out that he and George were fugitives. "What have you been saying?"

"My, my," said Artie. "You look mighty furtive all of a sudden. Relax. Half the people you meet in the Shadowlands are keeping secrets. Nobody here cares about yours. Chris and I were just remembering that your esteemed master asked to join the troupe. I think that if we push for it now, we can convince the Ice Queen over there." He nodded at Elaine, standing alone by the graveyard's low stone wall. A scatter of Nihils the size of dimes glittered in the bare, rocky soil at her feet. "You couldn't tell it by looking at her, but she must feel grateful for what you did, freeing us from the Giovanni trance. We'll twist her arm if you want us to."

Joey sighed. "Talk to Martin. It's not up to me."

"It is if we decide it is," Artie replied. "I like Martin, god knows why, and I guess we have reason to be thankful to you and him equally. But nobody in the troupe approves of slavery. That's probably why Her Nibs turned him down in the first place. Obviously, we aren't Lincoln and the Union army, we can't go around emancipating people. But we can make sure that one particular Thrall, namely you, doesn't have to stick around this two-bit gilly unless he wants to. So what do you say?"

Joey hesitated. He was starting to like Artie and his companions. It might be fun to travel with them. Yet at the same time, a part of him suspected that any relationship with a fellow wraith would turn out to be hollow and worthless, a mere distraction from the few real satisfactions his existence provided.

But he supposed he could sleep and box whether he and George were traveling by themselves or in a group. He opened his mouth to say yes, and then his shackles started getting cold.

Abruptly he remembered that, on the night they'd met the troupe, George had ordered him to say nothing that could keep them from being allowed to join. That meant that he couldn't say no to Artie now. Not unless he wanted a humiliating wave of weakness to dump him on the ground.

Grimly, any pleasant anticipation of new friendships smothered by the bitterness of being coerced, he said, "Sure. Go ahead, talk to her."

-FOURTEEN-

Colorado Springs, August.

Joey raised his eyes. The redwoods towered over him, so tall that they seemed to be holding up the sky. The branches whispered in the cool breeze, patches of clear blue showing between them.

He smiled, and let out a long breath. A visit to Muir Woods always made him feel happy. Peaceful. Emily squeezed his hand, and he sensed that she felt the same.

"Daddy! Take my picture!" Sarah cried. When he looked at her, she was standing at the base of one of the trees. She'd tilted her head, half closed her eyes, and stretched out her left arm. He suspected that she was imitating a model she'd seen in an ad.

"Okay," he said. His Kodak was hanging around his neck. He peered through the viewfinder, then frowned. Something was wrong. He didn't know why, but his daughter didn't look right.

Emily murmured, "She's really growing up, isn't she?"

And he realized that was the problem. Sarah was getting taller by the second. Breasts swelled on her chest, and her baggy Snoopy sweatshirt shrank into a tight red halter. Rouge and lipstick encrusted her face like a rash.

"She's sick," he said, starting toward her. "It's all right, sweetheart, daddy will help you."

"Stay away from me!" she said. Her breath smelled of gin and marijuana. Her voice was a drunken rasp.

"This is for your own good," he said, "so please, be a brave girl." He grabbed her, catching her hair with one hand and her belt with the other.

She struggled to break away, but her strength was no match for his. Straining, he squashed her body smaller, forcing the bones to telescope like his baton. In a few seconds, she was a little girl again.

"Now isn't that better?" he asked.

She nodded. "I'm sorry I was naughty." She opened her arms to hug him, then froze as motionless as a mannequin.

This time, he didn't know what to do. He spun around to ask Emily, and got another shock. There was still a slender, dark-haired woman standing behind him, but it was no longer his wife. Emily had turned into Elaine. And when he saw the illusionist, he realized he was dreaming. That he was actually dead and lying asleep in a derelict movie theater in Colorado.

He grimaced. He always felt cheated when a dream went wrong. And for some reason, it particularly bothered him that Emily had changed into the show boss. He wondered if he could wake himself up.

Elaine blinked. "Your real name is Joey Castelo. And Martin is really George Montaigne. I hope you don't mind me knowing that. Sometimes, when I'm walking in somebody's dreams, flashes of information come to me. I promise not to tell anyone."

Joey peered at her. He couldn't put his finger on the reason, but she seemed different from Emily, Sarah, or anyone else he'd seen in the last few hours. More substantial. "Are you telling me" — he groped for words — "that you aren't just something my brain made up? That you're *really* Elaine?"

"Uh-huh. You've seen my illusions. Well, I can put myself in people's dreams, also. They're two different uses of the same skill."

Of course, a figment of his imagination could conceivably make the same claim, but Joey found that he believed her. Going into somebody else's sleeping fantasies wasn't *that* much weirder than reshaping your body, walking through walls, or a lot of other stunts he'd seen the Restless do. In fact, he felt a spark of amazement, but considerably more resentment. "Where do you get off, screwing around with what's inside my head?"

"When I'm ready to leave, I can put everything back the way it was. When you wake up, you won't even remember I was here."

"Isn't that swell. You still don't have any right to stick your nose in here in the first place. You're like a peeping Tom."

"You have a point, and I apologize. But I wanted to thank you. You and George saved everyone, but me especially. It was insane, but Larry was making me" — she hesitated — "have special feelings for him. Intimate feelings. They're gone now, but it still makes me sick to think about."

She was such a private person that it must have been hard for her to reveal such a thing. But recognizing that fact didn't relieve Joey's irritation. "You're welcome. Now get lost."

"I didn't just want to *say* thank you," said Elaine. "I want to help you in return. I can see you have problems. People in the troupe try to be your friends, but you turn away. All you want to do is fight and sleep. If I hadn't followed you here, I don't know when you would have given me a chance to really talk to you."

Never, he thought reflexively. "Yeah, well, not everybody's a social butterfly like you."

She grinned. It was the first indication he'd seen that

she actually had a sense of humor. "I guess I have my own problems. But we're talking about you."

"You're talking about me. I'm just asking you to leave me alone."

She sighed. "You aren't making this easy. I suppose that under the circumstances, that's to be expected. But I'm intruding here because I truly am worried about you. Do you know why I didn't want to let you and Mart — George join the show?"

Joey shrugged. "Artie said he thought it was because you don't like slavery."

"That was part of it. So was the fact that Spectres ambushed us a few months back, when we were traveling from Helena to Missoula. We lost four people. Maybe it wouldn't have happened if I'd been a better leader. In any case, I didn't feel like taking responsibility for anybody new. But the main reason was your Shadow. Do you know what I mean by that?"

"I guess so. I've heard the term. Everybody has a bad side, and that's what the Restless call it."

"That's correct as far as it goes, but there's more to it. Everyone does have a dark side, but for most of the living, it isn't too hard to control. But if a soul becomes a wraith, the evil inside him gets stronger. Sometimes he can sense it splitting off, becoming what amounts to a separate creature with its own thoughts and powers, a parasite inside his head. Sometimes he can't, sometimes it keeps itself hidden. But either way, it works to hurt him and often the people around him. To kill whatever goodness is inside him."

Joey thought of the voice, always goading and taunting until he'd cut a deal with it. He thought of George, clever, yet so insatiable for *more* money, *more* status, that he always wound up sabotaging himself. He held in a shiver. "What happens if your Shadow does wipe out your nice side?"

"You turn into a Spectre. That's where they come from. Or Oblivion grips you and burns you away to nothing."

Joey grimaced. "Great. Every time I think I've gotten used to being dead, I find out it's even worse than I realized." The sky darkened as if an eclipse were in progress. Pine needles fell, and denuded branches twisted. Bark flaked, the smell of rotting vegetation rose, and Nihils pocked and cracked the ground. Now that he was thinking about being a wraith, the dream forest looked as if he were viewing it through the Shroud. "But how come you're more worried about my Shadow than anybody else's?"

"Because I can see it growing inside you. Only vaguely, I just have a touch of that talent, but enough to alarm me. And I've watched you fight. Something terrible comes over you. I understand that a boxer has to be aggressive, but you're like a rabid dog."

He felt scared. Ashamed. Angry at her for confronting him with this stuff. "Okay, let's say you're right. What can I do about it?"

"There are people called pardoners. They know how to break a Shadow's power. We should find one and let him treat you."

For a moment, it sounded like a good idea. Then he realized the implications. If this whole thing wasn't just crackpot mumbo jumbo — and unfortunately, he had the feeling that Elaine knew what she was talking about — then it seemed likely that his Shadow and the voice were one and the same. And it was the voice that had made him a champion. If something drained its vitality, he'd turn back into a loser, and then his existence really would be unbearable.

"No," he said. "Thanks for the advice, but like I told you, I don't want anyone messing with what's inside my head. Besides, I think I know how to manage my Shadow. I let it out when I box, it gets to do some damage, and that satisfies it."

Elaine shook her head. "It doesn't work that way. You can't draw strength from it without increasing its hold on you. Someday, when you've given it enough power, it will seize control. You can't imagine how horrible that will be."

On the mountainside to the right, something cracked and crunched. Then came a thud that shook the ground. Apparently one of the now-dead sequoias had fallen.

Joey said, "Are you one-hundred-percent sure that it's going to happen?"

The illusionist hesitated. "Well, no. It's as if you were obese, with high cholesterol. You *might* escape a heart attack, but you'd be at far greater risk than the average person."

"If it's just a risk, I'll take my chances."

"That doesn't make sense."

"Maybe not to you, but it's how I feel."

She grimaced. "All right. You're being incredibly foolish, but I don't know what else to say to convince you. I suppose I should go."

To his surprise, he felt a twinge of guilt for rebuffing her. "I do appreciate that you even care about me. You don't have to leave if you don't want to. It's nice here, or it used to be. Maybe if we hike a little ways, we'll find a part that still is."

She smiled wanly. "Okay."

They set off down the trail. It bothered him a little to leave Sarah behind, but now that she'd frozen into a statue, she didn't seem like her real self anymore.

After a while, Elaine said, "Perhaps there's another way."

"What do you mean?"

"What we're worried about is the balance between your bad side and your good side. If we can't weaken the one, maybe we can strengthen the other."

He frowned. This was starting to sound like religion. He'd never been interested in that when he was breathing, and he wasn't now. He'd been raised Catholic, but he'd dumped what passed for his beliefs without a second thought as soon as he awoke into death and found that the Blessed Virgin and Baby Jesus weren't waiting to greet him. "What do you want me to do? Go to church? Read the Bible?"

She scowled. He guessed that for some reason, what he'd said had struck a nerve. "No. Contented people usually find it easier to be virtuous, so I want you to get whatever would make you happy. Above and beyond winning fights."

He sighed. "There's zero chance of that."

"You need the people you left behind, don't you? The ones you conjure up in dreams like this one. The little girl, and the woman who looks like me."

He frowned. "She doesn't look like you."

Elaine waved her hand. "Whatever. The point is, you can still spend time with them. We can add your hometown to the route."

Hard rings formed around Joey's wrists. His arms jerked with the sudden added weight. Glancing down, he saw that his manacles had appeared. "No. George won't let me go back there."

She cocked her head. "Why not? He's hardly the most unselfish person I ever met, but he doesn't seem especially cruel, either."

"I'm not supposed to talk about it, and it doesn't matter anyway. Even if I could get back, just seeing them wouldn't be enough."

"Why not?"

He didn't want to tell her. It was too personal, too painful, and she was virtually a stranger. A bitchy one, most of the time. But for some reason, he found that he couldn't hold it in. "When I was alive, and my boxing career was going nowhere, I moonlighted as a bodyguard. I screwed up a job, and somebody shot both me and my client.

"I spent years in a coma before I finally croaked. In the real world, Sarah, my kid, is grown up. She's also a drunk, a drug user, and god knows what else."

Elaine lifted her hand as if she wanted to touch him, then lowered it again. "Do you think it's your fault? That she has problems because you weren't there to raise her?"

Joey shrugged. "In my shoes, wouldn't anybody think it?

In the end, it was obvious that I was never going to make it as a fighter. I couldn't handle being a failure, and I took it out on my wife. The last thing Sarah ever saw me do was slap her mom across the room."

This time, Elaine did touch him, a contact so light and brief he barely felt it. "I'm sorry."

"Yeah, me too. All this crap happened a long time ago, so I guess that if I were smart, I could get over it. But I keep thinking that if I could talk to Sarah *now*, maybe I could help her straighten out."

"It can be done."

He laughed bitterly. "I know. Some spooks can jump across the Shroud. George can. But he told me that I'm not allowed to learn."

"You don't strike me as a particularly submissive person. You must have thought of learning on the sly."

"Sure." He hesitated, then decided that if he was blabbing his embarrassing secrets, he might as well go all out. "But this chain is magic. It makes it pretty impossible for me to disobey him. It's also the reason he doesn't want me to step over. He's afraid that it won't have any power in the Skinlands, and I'll get it off."

"All right, I understand. But there are other ways to reach the living."

He remembered Larry's slave, lifting the axe by sheer force of will. "I know. I've seen a little of that, too. But I don't think it would help to make my photo float around in front of Sarah, or make a pencil write her a note. That would scare her, but it wouldn't *influence* her, not enough, not over the long haul. We need to *meet*, face to face. Have real conversations."

Elaine smiled. "And if you knew my art, you could. You could slip Sarah's soul out of her sleeping body and into the Shadowlands, then talk to her here. Or shape her dreams, insert a facsimile of yourself into them the way I've incorporated myself into this one. Would you like me to teach you how? Since your true, shackled form would never leave the Underworld, I don't see why George would object."

Joey hesitated. He'd never doubted that, given a chance, he could learn to jump the Shroud, or levitate objects in the Skinlands, for that matter. To him, they seemed to be essentially *physical* acts, like skipping rope and working a speed bag. In contrast, the idea of molding dreams and extracting souls from bodies was mysterious. Arcane. It was hard even to imagine how anybody might go about it. "I don't know if I could learn."

"You could try."

"I guess." God knew how many hours it would take, time he might otherwise spend enjoying his dreams. "But even if it worked out, what would be the point, when George won't let me go home?"

"If we work on him, perhaps we can change his mind. Anyway, we'll figure out something when you're ready."

"I need to be ready now. By the time I learned your tricks, and made it home to Frisco, it would probably be too late. Sarah nearly died twice, just in the few months I was watching her. I wouldn't be surprised if she's dead already." The thought made his throat feel clogged.

Elaine took hold of his arm and made him stand still. She stepped in front of him and gazed up into his eyes. "Are you sure you want to say no? Is this the *real* Joey, speaking from the heart?"

Annoyed, he opened his mouth to tell her that of course it was. Then, suddenly, everything looked different, as if someone had thrown a switch inside his head.

Elaine was offering him a chance to talk to Sarah, to hug her, to save her. Who cared if it was a long shot? How could he even consider turning it down?

He suspected that something had been prompting him to do so. Abruptly the idea of an enemy inside his head, trying to hurt and corrupt him, seemed a lot more real. He wondered how many other thoughts his Shadow had planted in his mind, and if from now on, he needed to weigh every feeling, every urge, to determine if it was truly his own. The notion made his skin crawl.

"You're right," he said. "That's not how I really feel. Please, teach me."

He felt the voice sneer.

-FIFTEEN-

Las Vegas.

Holliday ambled down the Strip, his boot heels clicking on the sidewalk. Most of the Skinlander tourists stepped out of his way. They couldn't see him, but unconsciously they sensed that *something* was moving among them, something that it was prudent to avoid.

Though Holliday had business to attend to, he kept his pace deliberate, even leisurely. A gentleman didn't scurry around like a rabbit. It was apt to give people the wrong impression.

Thus, he was able to take in the sights: the Mirage, with its gardens, waterfall, and volcano blasting flame into the night sky; the Excalibur's banners, ramparts, drawbridge, and spires of scarlet, gold, and blue. Everything was impressive, if only in a gaudy, childish way, even though he was viewing it through the patina of decay imposed by the Shroud.

He shook his head. He remembered this peculiar town as it had been in its infancy, a tiny, adobe village dwarfed by a neighboring stand of cottonwoods. For a moment, he felt a twinge of melancholy.

Scowling, he strangled the emotion. He was damned if he'd get nostalgic over life on the frontier. It had been a hellhole, full of clods and ruffians, discomfort and disgrace.

Precious little that was good had ever happened to him there, not until he'd crossed over into death.

The facade of the Inferno appeared ahead, caked with grime and riddled with Nihils. Humming and crackling, one marquee flickered, while the other shone clean, bright, and steady. Evidently the latter existed in the Shadowlands, confirming the reports that the hotel catered to vampires, mortals, and wraiths alike. Holliday had to wonder what kind of ghost would accept the hospitality of the Giovanni, but then again, most people were idiots. Even the majority of the dead had short memories for everything but their personal obsessions.

He walked into what appeared to be the wraith section of the hotel. Finding himself in a dimly lit lobby, he absently pushed his blue-tinted spectacles back to the top of his nose. He'd started wearing them in 1876, when quacks proclaimed that doing so would cure any sickness, including consumption, and he'd never lost the habit. He unbuttoned his black duster and Prince Albert coat, then approached the desk.

The clerk was a stooped man with a weak chin and wispy, mouse-colored hair. He goggled at the Colt revolver tucked in Holliday's vest, and his aura flickered orange with anxiety. Clubs, knives, and similar weapons were common in the Underworld. Guns, however, which had to be imbued with the mystical substance known as soulfire, were a rarity.

Holliday took an instant dislike to the clerk. The fool is rude, he thought, cowardly, and a Giovanni flunky. "It's not polite to stare," the gunman said.

The clerk twitched. "I'm sorry, sir. I was just" — he swallowed — "admiring it. May I help you?"

Holliday nodded. "I'm looking for Lorenzo Orsini. I understand he's the head bloodsucker hereabouts."

The clerk looked shocked. But, evidently deciding to withhold comment on Holliday's disrespectful language, he reached for a phone. "Yes, sir. His secretary should be able to give you an appointment."

Holliday covered the phone with his hand. The clerk flinched. People often did, when the shooter showed them just how fast he could move. "Let's not do it that way. I'm in a hurry. Just tell me where to find him. Better still, you can show me."

"I'm afraid he's not available—"

Holliday grabbed for the clerk's head. The stooped man tried to jump back, but he was too slow. Holliday gripped his ear, twisted it, and yanked him through the substance of the desk. "Just take me to him, and I'll worry about the rest." He turned the flunky loose.

As he did, he heard a foot scuff on the carpet. He turned. Two wraiths, a black woman and a white man with pockmarks, were advancing on him with iron clubs in hand.

Holliday rested his fingers on the grip of the weapon he'd put on display. He had a second Colt hidden in a shoulder holster, a two-shot derringer in his hip pocket, and a knife in his boot as well. "There's still time to be sensible," he told the clerk. "Or I can shoot you, then them, then find the dago on my own."

If the clerk had had any sand to him, he might have defied Holliday. After all, he couldn't tell whether the stranger's bullets were made of darksteel, or something similarly lethal, and the odds were actually against it. But, looking at his associates, he stammered, "Hold it! Let's not turn this into a public brawl. We've had too much of that kind of thing around here already. This man just wants to see the boss, so let's oblige him." No doubt exerting every ounce of courage he possessed, he managed a sneer. "Larry, that is to say Mr. Orsini, knows how to deal with people like him."

Holliday smiled. "If he does, he'll be the first." He waved his hand, signaling the clerk to lead on.

His reluctant guide conducted him into what was evidently the vampire wing of the resort. To his senses, the place looked and smelled like a palace falling into ruin. It reminded Holliday of plantation houses looted and defaced by Sherman's vandals. Glaring, the two guards trailed along a few paces behind him.

Ahead, voices murmured. Light spilled through a doorway, and the tang of tobacco smoke tinged the air. "That's the casino," said the clerk. "Mr. Orsini is in there."

"I'd appreciate it if you'd introduce me." He told the man his name.

When they entered the room, Holliday got a surprise. In many respects, the place resembled a boom-camp gambling hall, the kind of place he'd frequented in Deadwood, Leadville, and Tombstone. The floor looked like hard-packed earth. Confederate battle flags and portraits of Jackson and Lee decorated the lucky numbers on the wheel of fortune. Dice rattled in a spinning chuck-a-luck cage. At one table, people were playing Spanish monte, and over in what was presumably the quietest corner, someone was operating a faro bank. On the stage, behind a row of faux kerosene footlights, a fresh-faced youth with a banjo sang one of the comical "Mulligan" songs of Harrigan and Hart.

But the casino was by no means an accurate re-creation. Gamblers with a taste for modern games could shoot craps or even play slots. The room was air-conditioned, and the chairs were padded. It was all soft, prettified, distorted, and despite Holliday's disdain for the squalid original article, he found himself sneering.

The clerk led him past the undead patrons. Some wore elegant evening wear, some tattered, faded denim and black, studded leather. Most were pallid, lean, and, judging from their lack of reaction, no more able to see wraiths than the mortal croupiers.

In a moment, Holliday realized that he and his escort

were heading for a table in the rear, where three vampires sat playing draw poker. One was a handsome man dressed in a white sports coat and an open-collared purple shirt. He gave the impression of youth despite steel-gray hair and wrinkles around the eyes.

To his left slouched a freakishly ugly undead, his features marred by an exaggerated widow's peak, large, pointed ears, a broad snout of a nose, and fangs that he evidently couldn't retract. His flesh emitted a musky stench like an animal's.

Beside him was a woman with striking emerald eyes, an elaborate powdered wig, and a black, heart-shaped beauty mark affixed to her cheek. Her ruffled crimson gown left her creamy shoulders bare. She'd dabbed perfume behind her ears and between her breasts.

Sizing them up, Holliday decided that each of the trio had an air of authority. He suspected that he was interrupting a convocation of princes. Not that he cared.

The gray-haired man glanced up at his approach. Evidently, he *could* see the Restless. "Hello, Wally," he said, giving the desk clerk a pleasant smile. "I hope you understood, I'd rather not be disturbed unless it's important."

The woman in the wig said, "Are you talking to one of your phantoms?" The gray-haired vampire raised a manicured hand, requesting her silence.

The clerk, Wally, squirmed. He *looked* like he was sweating, even though a spirit couldn't really do so. "This man, uh, *insisted* on seeing you. He says he's Dr. John Henry Holliday."

"Really," said the Giovanni chieftain. "*The* Doc Holliday?" Holliday sensed that he was intrigued, but skeptical. In a way, the shooter didn't blame him. The Shadowlands were crawling with impostors claiming to be the ghost of someone famous. Still, like any sort of challenge or disrespect, it galled him. His mouth tightened.

"The only one I've heard about," Holliday said.

"I'll be damned." Orsini glanced at his table mates. "There's a wraith here who claims to be — well, you heard. He looks like the descriptions, too. Thin and pale as one of us, with a droopy, ash-blond mustache." He turned back to Holliday. "You wouldn't believe how eager I am to talk to you. But unfortunately, despite the cards and chips, this is a business meeting. Why don't you let Wally show you to the wraith theater, or the wraith casino, and I'll join you as soon as I can."

"I'm afraid that's not convenient. I'm here on business myself." Holliday sensed movement at his back. No doubt it was more wraith guards and other Giovanni, slinking into the room to protect their master. "These days, my line is bounty-hunting, and I mean to collect someone from the premises. A few weeks ago, you brought a pretty, black-haired wraith here. Some kind of entertainer, I believe."

Orsini frowned. "Who told you that?"

Holliday dismissed the question with a wave of his hand. "This sorry world is full of snoops and gossips. Even your corner of it. As I was saying, I believe that a smart fellow like you must have known that agents of the Laughing Lady were willing to pay a substantial reward for the girl." The Laughing Lady was one of the seven Deathlords. "Yet you didn't turn her in."

"I wasn't obliged to. I'm not a vassal of the Deathlords."

Holliday shrugged. "The point is, if you weren't willing to give her up then, you probably aren't eager to do so now. So I'm not going to let you out of my sight till you produce her."

Orsini sneered, his veneer of affability crumbling to expose the natural arrogance of a vampire elder. "I hope you're not threatening me."

Holliday said, "Yes, I am. I'll spell it out if you like. Give me the woman or I'll kill you."

"You can't be serious. You're in my stronghold,

surrounded by my minions and my brood." Holliday sensed the stooges in question edging closer. "We're Giovanni, masters of the living *and* the dead." He smirked. "Maybe you expected your reputation to awe me. Sorry. But as you may have gathered, I'm something of a Western buff. I know that, even if you are who you say you are, the real Doc Holliday was scarcely the deadly creature he made himself out to be. He was a drunk who couldn't even shoot straight."

Rage flared in Holliday's breast, all the more fiercely because Orsini's gibe was true. "I've been practicing my aim." He snatched the Colt out of his vest and shot the ugly vampire in the forehead.

The man screamed, leaped up, and clapped his hairy, yellow-clawed hands to his face. Waves of black, crackling light swept down his body. He collapsed, but vanished before he could hit the floor.

For a moment, the onlookers goggled, and why not? Those who could perceive what had actually happened had every right to be impressed by a bullet that existed on both sides of the Shroud, a projectile charged with the power of Oblivion. Hell, they ought to have marveled at Holliday's shooting, too. "Now let's have the girl," he said.

"Get him!" Orsini shouted, trying to duck under the poker table.

He was quicker than a mortal, but so was Holliday. He shot Orsini in the shoulder, then, by force of will, dampened the dark flame surging from the slug. He didn't want this man disappearing.

Holliday pivoted. Onrushing wraiths brandished clubs at him. He felt the coercive powers of the Giovanni, prying at his mind. From past experience, he knew that he could resist the mesmerism for at least a few moments. With luck, that would be long enough.

He shot the nearest ghosts before they could bludgeon him. Since wraiths existed on the lip of Oblivion anyway, they vanished in a heartbeat. Now his first revolver was empty. He tossed it into his left hand and drew the other.

But he didn't want to gun down everybody, because he knew that if he ran out of bullets prematurely, the enemy wouldn't give him a chance to reload. Concentrating, he floated the craps table into the air, then slammed it down on two Giovanni. The impact wouldn't kill them, he knew, but it did stun them sufficiently to keep them down. The non-Giovanni bloodsuckers squealed and scurried for the exit, panicking like a bunch of mortals.

For the next few seconds, Holliday threw furniture with abandon and fired when necessary. He thinned out the enemy considerably. Then a wraith darted into striking range and swung a saber at his head. He barely managed to duck. As he shot the swordsman, he felt a Giovanni's magic boring into his mind. His legs went rubbery, and his vision blurred. Peering desperately about, he finally spotted his assailant's eye gleaming between the curtains at the back of the stage. He put a bullet in the eye.

He whirled back around to confront the next attacker. He didn't see one, and, though his ears were ringing from the roar of his Colts, he could tell that except for groans and whimpers, the casino had fallen silent.

He inhaled, savoring the pungent odor of gun smoke. Then he walked to Orsini, over cards, chips, and scraps of wood, none of which shifted or clinked beneath his feet. The vampire was shuddering uncontrollably. A pistol lay by his twitching hand. Evidently he'd pulled it from a pocket or holster, but lacked the strength to hold on to it. His white flesh had a dusky tinge from the malignant energy roiling inside it, and his shoulder was wet with fragrant blood.

"Now let's talk," Holliday said.

"If I help you as much as I can, will you take the bullet out?" Orsini's voice was a feeble rasp.

"All right." Holliday sat down in a chair, pulled a handful of cartridges out of his duster, and began to reload the Colts.

"Okay, then. Remember, you gave your word. To tell you the truth" — Orsini paused to gasp in a ragged breath — "she isn't here anymore."

Holliday smiled. "Sure she isn't. You just let her wander away." He almost admired Orsini's grit. Not many men, breathing, Restless, or undead, would try to bamboozle him with the flames of the Void licking at their vitals.

"I swear it's true. I did have her, but she escaped."

The dago actually sounded sincere. Holliday lifted an eyebrow. "You might have saved yourself some trouble if you'd tried to convince me of that before." He understood why Orsini hadn't, though. The vampire couldn't bear to look as if he were truckling. In that respect, they were two of a kind. "Maybe you should tell me the whole story."

"All right. Back in May, I glanced in on a traveling revue that had just hit town. I like to check out the competition. The illusionist looked familiar somehow, even though I was sure I'd never met her."

Orsini grunted. His body shook through another spasm. When it passed, he said, "Several days later, I remembered that I'd seen her, or someone who resembled her, on Hierarchy wanted posters a few years back. I keep documents like that, so I checked to be sure, and it turned out I was right."

And you left the poster lying around, Holliday thought, for a spy the Hierarchs had planted in your organization to discover. The spy told his bosses you were harboring a fugitive, and they sent me to fetch her.

"As I recalled," Orsini continued, "the Laughing Lady's soldiers were chasing the girl hot and heavy for a while."

Holliday glanced around, checking for a second wave of enemies, but didn't see any signs of one. "You recalled right," the bounty hunter said. "But the fugitive, Margaret Elaine Rochelle, vanished without a trace, so eventually they packed it in."

"The performer called herself Elaine Forrester. I decided

to bring her under my influence. Find out if she truly was the outlaw, and, if so, what made her so important. Once I knew that, I could decide whether to sell her to the Laughing Lady, dispose of her elsewhere, or keep her for myself. It seemed like a no-lose proposition, because even if she turned out to be just a lookalike, she is one of the best illusionists I've ever seen."

Orsini's mouth twisted. "It should have gone off without a hitch. The way the magic operated, Elaine didn't even know she was being subjugated, so she didn't fight it. I put a lot of her friends under the same kind of whammy, so they didn't suspect anything, either. But *somebody* smelled a rat, because one day, while I was sleeping, he trashed the foci that sustained the spell, and then the whole troupe ran away. My people tried to stop them, but they blew it."

Holliday asked, "Do you know where the players went?"

"No. If I did, I would have gone after them."

"Well, don't fret about it. After I died, I learned how to track. I'll find them quickly enough, now that I know I'm on the right trail."

Orsini's face contorted, and his back arched. "That's all I can tell you. Now please, keep your part of the bargain."

"Fair enough," said Holliday. He shifted himself into the Skinlands, then drew his knife. "Do you want to bite on something?"

"Your throat," Orsini wheezed. "No. Just do it."

Holliday knelt beside him and began to probe the wound. After a minute, he levered the black, deformed slug from a nest of splintered bone. He wiped it off, then dropped it in his pocket. Even ordinary darksteel was too valuable to waste, and his ammunition had been forged with far more potent enchantments.

Orsini tried to crawl, to put some space between them, but he was still too weak. "Now get out," he said. "I have more spirit soldiers, and other progeny. They'll be here any second."

"You could be right," Holliday said. "But as a 'Western buff,' you know I was always a gambling man, and I'll bet I have time to cut your head off. With a sharp knife it doesn't take that long."

Orsini gaped at him.

"I promised to take out the bullet," Holliday said. "I never said I'd let you live, and I don't need you coming after *me*. Look at it this way. Maybe you'll continue on as a wraith. Maybe some kind Giovanni will give you a job." He grabbed the vampire and started to slice his neck.

-SIXTEEN-

Salt Lake City, September.

Every house on the block was dark. It seemed to Joey that by midnight, the entire city had shut down. The living part of it, anyway. The troupe had drawn a decent crowd. He'd had to defeat three challengers, and his fists were still a little tender.

"Pick a house," said Elaine. She sounded slightly impatient, and he didn't blame her. Presumably every home had someone asleep inside it, so one ought to be as good as another.

But so far, he'd barely scratched the surface of her art. He was afraid that he'd never learn enough to talk to Sarah, and that made him superstitious about his lessons. He wanted to train in a place that felt right.

He studied the double row of houses. Perhaps they were actually pleasant, well-maintained tract homes, but to his eyes, the lawns looked scorched and dead. Some of the windows were cracked, and paint was peeling from the doors. One house had a porch with a sagging roof and torn screens, a chimney with a broken top, and Nihils the size of rat holes deepening the shadows under the eaves.

Joey pointed at it. "That one." Maybe it was just his imagination, but it seemed to him that the dwelling was giving off a vibe of grief and fear. That it was the kind of place where the Shroud was weak, and the Restless felt powerful.

He and Elaine headed toward it. For a moment, a gust of breeze brought them the briny smell of the Great Salt Lake. They slipped through the substance of the twin-paneled door, then up a flight of stairs with broken newel posts and loose, worn carpeting.

As Joey reached the second-floor landing, he heard the complex susurrus of several mortals breathing, then caught the sour smell of sickness. The odor was seeping from the first room on the right. Curious, he stuck his head through the door. Elaine did the same.

On the other side, a wizened old woman slept in a four-poster bed. The sound of her lungs was a labored wheeze, her heartbeat so faint and irregular that it made Joey wince. A chunky female ghost in a hot-pink jogging suit sat on the chair in the corner. A set of leg irons and a tomahawk with a darksteel head lay at her feet.

With a snarl, she grabbed the hatchet and leaped up. Joey, who now occasionally glimpsed people's halos even when he wasn't trying, saw hers flash the rippling red of fury. "Get out!" she cried. "This one belongs to me."

He understood what she meant. She was a Reaper, someone who, by accosting a newly dead wraith, awakened him to existence in the Shadowlands. Some Reapers were kindly benefactors, but many, including, by all appearances, this one, were slavers intent on capturing helpless, disoriented victims.

Perhaps because George had tried to do the same thing to him, and had succeeded in enslaving him in the end, Joey felt an answering burst of rage. He snapped his baton to its full length. The chain between his bracelets rattled.

Elaine gripped his arm. "We didn't come here for this," she said. "Suppose you chase her away. She'll just come back later."

"Not if I stick that axe in her head," he replied. But he knew Elaine was right. He couldn't free even a tiny fraction of the slaves in the Shadowlands. Hell, he couldn't even free himself. So why borrow this particular piece of trouble? He let his companion drag him back into the hall. Inside his mind, the voice, cheated of a chance to hurt someone, squirmed, as restless as a tiger pacing in a cage.

Joey watched for a moment, making sure the Reaper didn't come after them. Then he and Elaine slipped into another room.

The sleeper here was wrapped in twisted blankets, but Joey didn't have to see him to know he was a little boy. A T-shirt and jeans of the proper size lay discarded on the floor. An aluminum baseball bat leaned in one corner, and a scatter of video-game cartridges and *X-Men* comics littered the desk. *National Geographic* maps and posters of fighter planes and spacecraft adorned the walls.

"Is this boy all right?" asked Elaine.

"I guess."

"Then you might as well get started. Don't worry about our friend with the hatchet. I can help you and keep an eye out for her at the same time."

He closed his eyes and tried to relax completely. Elaine called it making himself receptive. He had a hunch that he was entering a trance, although, since he'd never been hypnotized, he wasn't really sure.

At any rate, by now this first step at least was easy. In a few moments, his senses became even sharper. He heard a cat clawing a piece of furniture a block away. The whisper of tires on Interstate 80. Yet paradoxically, the world seemed quieter, as if all the sounds were merely tiny flaws in a greater stillness.

He narrowed his heightened awareness, focusing it into something like a searchlight. Then he projected it at the form in the blanket cocoon.

Instantly he knew the kid was dreaming. In fact, though he still felt his body standing in the bedroom, he also began to exist in the dream. Even after weeks of training, this still creeped him out. It was the strangest sensation he'd ever felt, something no mortal could ever experience. He truly was in two places at the same time.

It was night in the dream, too. The boy had a tiny white scar under his left eye, freckles, and straw-colored hair that shone in the gloom. He and a group of adults were walking silently through a field. No one reacted to Joey's sudden arrival. So far, he was as much of a ghost here as he was in the waking world.

Elaine shimmered into existence beside him. "Okay," she said, "you made contact. What now?"

Joey shrugged. "The usual. Try to influence the dream. Make myself a real part of it."

She sighed. "I keep telling you, it's easier to draw the soul into the Underworld."

He was sure she knew what she was talking about, but despite her assurances to the contrary, he had a morbid fear that he might yank a spirit out of its body, then find that he couldn't put it back. Besides, the thought of hauling Sarah, this child, or any other living person into the ugly world of the Restless was inherently repulsive. "I'd rather try it the other way first. What the hell, it's not like I've had any luck at either one."

Elaine said, "Suit yourself." She and Joey fell into step with the procession.

Joey imagined his body growing thicker and heavier. He imagined the sound the grass would make, swishing around his sneakers. But it wouldn't swish. Finally he whistled, then snapped his fingers. The boy didn't react.

The group trudged on through the darkness. Then Joey caught a vague echo of what the dreamer was feeling. The kid was nervous because he didn't know where the grown-ups were taking him. Periodically he tried to ask, but his mom, a tired-looking woman in a charcoal suit and a lacy white blouse, always shushed him. Joey scowled. "I'm not getting anywhere."

I told you this was a waste of time, jeered the voice.

Elaine said, "Try changing insignificant details. Sometimes that's the way to get a grip."

The parade started up a slope. Joey decided that when they'd gone a few more paces, a scatter of round white pebbles would appear on the ground ahead. It didn't happen. He imagined a yellow meteor arcing down the sky. The twinkling stars refused to fall.

At last he shifted the greater part of his awareness back into the Joey in the bedroom. He willed the boy's soul to slip out of his body. Maybe that was easier, if you knew what you were doing, but he couldn't manage it, either.

In the dream, the walkers reached the top of the hill. There they found an open-sided tent, fluttering in the wind. Inside it were a marble headstone, a selection of wreaths and bouquets, and a freshly dug grave. Her eyes closed, the elderly woman from the four-poster bed floated unsupported above the hole, occupying the same position the coffin would at a conventional burial.

When the boy saw her, he froze. His mother gripped his shoulder and forced him on.

Halting at the foot of the grave, she said, "Hello, mom. We came to show you how much we love you. And to say good-bye."

The floating woman didn't stir. Her wrinkled mouth didn't so much as twitch. But a quavering, disembodied voice said, "I'm not ready to go yet."

"Please," said the boy's mother, "don't be difficult. Everyone went to a lot of trouble to be here. We got you lovely flowers, and a nice marker. And you're right next to dad, just like you wanted."

"It doesn't matter. It isn't my time."

The younger woman's mouth twisted. "But it is. Please, I'm begging you. We can't stand to see you suffer anymore. It's tearing the family apart. Just *die*, and we'll give you anything you want."

"Anything?" the old woman asked slyly.

"Yes."

"Then give me Brigham, to keep me company. He was always my favorite."

"All right," the younger woman said.

The boy screamed and tried to tear himself away from her. She grabbed him with both hands.

Joey transferred his will back into the dream. Turning to Elaine, he said, "Help him. Change this."

"It's just a little nightmare," she replied. "He'll wake up in a second and be fine."

Thrashing madly, Brigham finally broke away from his mother. But with the grave behind him and a crowd in front, he had nowhere to go. Two men in black suits pounced on him, lifted him into the air, and carried him toward the pit.

His grandmother sat up and stretched out her spindly arms, and the men put Brigham in her twisted, spotted hands. Smiling, seeming not to notice the boy's shrieks and writhing, she clutched him to her chest as they started to drift down into the grave.

A surge of fury sent Joey lunging forward. Shoving people aside, he muscled his way to the front of the crowd. He wrenched Brigham out of his grandmother's embrace.

She tried to snatch the boy back. Joey reflexively clung to him with one arm and knocked her away with a backhand sweep of the other, realizing as he did so that his shackles had disappeared. He leaped back from the grave and set Brigham on the grass behind him. Pivoting, he raised the baton.

The crowd lurched one pace forward, then melted away to nothing. Brigham's grandmother and all the appurtenances of her burial vanished too. Abruptly Joey, the boy, and Elaine were alone on a quiet, starlit hilltop.

Joey looked down at Brigham. Trembling, the kid goggled back at him.

Joey squatted beside him. "It's okay now. You're safe. You're in your house asleep. This is just a dream, and the scary part's over." A thrill of excitement sang along his nerves. Yeah, by god, it was a dream, and he'd taken control of it. Somehow, wanting desperately to help Brigham had finally turned the power on.

Brigham kept shaking.

Joey decided there'd be time enough to celebrate the breakthrough after he got the boy over the worst of his funk. Putting his hand on Brigham's shoulder, he said, "I promise I'm telling the truth. Just think about it. This isn't a cemetery, so nobody would really be buried here. Real people don't float in the air, either."

Brigham swallowed. "Okay," he said. "I guess." But he continued to shiver.

Maybe if Elaine appeared to the kid, she could calm him down. Joey turned in her direction. "Don't look at me," she said. "You're the one who's been a parent. If you don't know what to do, I certainly wouldn't."

He scowled at her. She spent a lot of time with Kimberly, so as far as he was concerned, her statement was a cop-out. Evidently she just didn't want to be bothered. He turned back to Brigham. "I know what just happened was awful. But you have to remember, dreams are crazy. People do things they'd never do in real life. Actually, your grandma wants you to have a long, happy life. And your mom loves you too much to ever give you away to anybody, for anything."

"I know," Brigham muttered.

"Then maybe you can start to feel a little better."

Brigham shrugged, and then his face twisted. He made a

choking sound. Joey realized that the kid was struggling not to cry.

Joey put his arms around him. "Talk to me," he said. "Tell me what you're thinking, so I can help you fix whatever's wrong."

"I don't want grandpa and grandma to be dead! I don't want to be dead either!"

"But you aren't. You won't be for a long time."

"But I will someday. And I know what it's like." Joey caught a stray wisp of the dreamer's memory: Brigham and three other kids were watching a video called *Visions of Death, Volume Six* that had footage of shooting victims, autopsies, and exhumed corpses. "You *rot*, and worms eat you."

"But that's only the body. The spirit is somewhere else."

Brigham grimaced. "That's what everybody says. But nobody really knows."

Joey hesitated. He didn't want to risk scaring the kid all over again. But on the other hand, he didn't want him to go around worrying about death all the time, and he had the feeling that that was exactly what was happening. "I know, because *I'm* dead."

Brigham peered at him. "Really?" He didn't seem frightened, or particularly skeptical either. Perhaps in a dream, nothing seemed unlikely.

"Really. I left my body behind, and I don't look all slimy and maggoty, do I?"

Brigham stepped back and looked him up and down. "No, you look okay. Do you live in Heaven?"

Joey was tempted to say yes, to deliver the maximum amount of reassurance. But it would have felt contemptible to lie to the boy so blatantly. "No. Maybe some dead people go to some kind of Heaven, but I didn't."

Brigham's eyes widened. "Did you go to Hell?"

I'm still trying to make up my mind, Joey thought sardonically, but of course he couldn't say that. "No, that didn't happen either. People like me stay on earth, except not exactly."

"What do you mean? What's it like?"

Joey opened his mouth to reply, then realized that he didn't know what to say.

Seemingly dismayed by his hesitation, Brigham quivered. "It's bad like Hell, isn't it?"

"No! It's—" Joey hesitated again. How could he describe something as strange as existence in the Shadowlands? How could he make a living child understand, and make the knowledge comforting at that?

Maybe he could *show* him what it was like.

He'd changed the dream once, in the heat of anger. On some level, he was still influencing it, or Brigham wouldn't be able to see him. Maybe, now that he'd finally done the trick, he could work some other transformations.

"Do you want to see what's it like?" he asked. "You wouldn't die yourself. It would be fake, like a movie."

Now it was Brigham's turn to hesitate, but after a moment, he said, "Okay."

Joey closed his eyes and concentrated. For a few moments, nothing happened. He started to fear that nothing would, that the skill had deserted him as suddenly as it came. Scowling, he pushed his doubt aside and focused his will again.

He felt the power kick in. Brigham gasped.

Joey knew why. In effect, he'd given the kid the hyperkeen senses of a wraith. Overhead, the stars blazed with a new brilliance. There were more of them, and not all of them were white. Some burned red, blue, or gold. In the woods at the base of the hill, an owl hooted, too faintly for any ordinary mortal to hear. The scents of pine and oak filled the air.

"Do you like it?" Joey asked.

"Everything's" — Brigham faltered — "cool!" Joey held in a smile.

"Uh-huh. And having sharper eyes and ears isn't the only cool thing. You can do this." He stuck his hand into the earth. Brigham gaped at him. "Go on, try it."

The boy gingerly slid one fingertip into the ground, then grinned and rammed his arm in up to the elbow.

"I think everybody's wished they could walk through walls," Joey said. "Well, when you're dead, you can. You can stroll right into Fort Knox, the White House, or anyplace else. You can walk through fire or across the bottom of the ocean, or let a car run into you, and it doesn't hurt."

Wide-eyed, Brigham said, "Have you seen the bottom of the ocean?"

Joey smiled. "No, but I may get around to it. I've got time. I can stay strong and healthy forever. Here are some of the spirits that I've seen."

He marched a parade of gorgeous, exotic figures out of the darkness: a lithe woman with leopard-spotted fur and amber eyes; a man with silver feathers for hair, and skin that shone like molten ruby; a pudgy, grinning elf of a guy flapping the black and orange wings of a monarch butterfly. They passed in front of Brigham like models crossing a stage, then faded into nothingness again.

Clearly awestruck, Brigham stared at the procession. "Are they angels?"

"No, just people. You can pick up a lot of different powers, provided you have the talent. Some people learn to reshape bodies, so everybody can look like whatever they want. Some guys learn to fly. I'm learning to go inside people's dreams, so I can talk to my family. That's why I'm visiting you tonight. I'm practicing."

Abruptly a kind of weakness swept through him. It wasn't physical. His muscles stayed as strong as ever. But it still jolted him. Overhead, the stars dimmed, and the scents wilted out of the air.

Brigham gaped. "What's happening? For a second, I couldn't see you."

"You've worn yourself out," said Elaine. "You only have a moment of power left."

"Everything's all right," said Joey, "but I have to go. You might not remember all of this after you wake up." Elaine had said that it often worked that way. "But try to hang on to the idea that you shouldn't be afraid of death. It isn't the end, you just move to a new place, where you'll have friends and fun the same as always. Will you do that?"

"All right," said Brigham. He reached out, to hug Joey, shake his hand, or simply touch him.

He didn't make it. Without warning, something hurled Joey away, not up or down or over the ground, but in some indescribable direction that didn't exist in the waking world. For an instant, he saw the boy's hair, glowing like a lone star in limitless darkness, and then he only had a single set of perceptions and a single body, the one standing in the bedroom.

He half expected Brigham to sit up, but it didn't happen. The boy slept on. Joey wondered if the kid was still on the hill, or if that dream had ended.

To his surprise, Elaine threw her arms around him. "I knew you could do it!" she cried, then, looking flustered, let him go.

-SEVENTEEN-

The first things Holliday saw were the flames, strands of blue and gold light writhing against the blackness. When he advanced a few steps farther, he made out the shapes of the torches themselves. They were Thralls, whose bodies a flesh shaper had stretched into spindly, towering monstrosities. The slaves' legs had been fused into a single shaft, and their arms bonded to their sides. Their mouths had been erased.

At last the form of the Citadel itself began to emerge from the murk. Inside the perimeter ring of torches was a parking lot, and at the center of that rose a black, silent structure originally built as a trolley barn.

Holliday, who made at least a token effort to keep up with the news of Skinlands America, recalled that until recently, this place had been Trolley Square, a shopping mall and tourist attraction. One evening, most of the people inside had gone mad. They'd started looting and vandalizing the stores, and attacking any sane person who blundered into view. Holliday had never heard an explanation of why it had happened. Perhaps nobody knew.

In the aftermath, mortals had closed the establishment down. But, savoring the newly generated atmosphere of chaos and terror, a colony of wraiths had obviously taken up residence, just as he'd been advised.

Holliday walked between two of the torches. The flames radiated cold, not heat, but as he'd discovered on one unpleasant occasion, the burns they could inflict were no less painful for that. The fires hissed and crackled, and the stench of charring flesh suffused the air.

Nihils cracked and pitted the asphalt. He skulked forward until he was close enough for a good look at the trolley barn, then began to work his way around it.

NO TRESPASSING and THIS PROPERTY PROTECTED BY ARGUS SECURITY signs hung on the walls. Most of the doors and windows were boarded up. Bits of shattered stained glass littered the ground beneath them. Another torch stood beside a service entrance that wasn't boarded, merely chained and padlocked. On the stool next to it slumped a wraith, probably a doorman collecting tolls and doling out passes to visitors. His aura was gray with melancholy or boredom. Someone had sculpted lines of yellow, tear-shaped knobs onto his cheeks.

Holliday frowned. The time had come to make a decision. Should he enter the Citadel openly? Ask the permission of the Anacreons, the Legion officers who ran the place, to conduct his business? Or would it be better to do it on the sly?

In a properly ordered world, any Hierarchy official would assist in the apprehension of a fugitive. But the Shadowlands hadn't been truly orderly even in Charon's day, and the very pretense of such a thing was failing now. It was conceivable that no one in the Citadel cared about the will of his nominal masters in Stygia. Or that some opportunist would decide to cheat Holliday by seizing the prize for himself.

In Las Vegas, the shooter's pride had demanded that he march into the Giovanni fortress with all flags flying, but he was in a more pragmatic mood tonight. He'd just as soon avoid any complications. Therefore, he'd sneak in. And if anybody noticed and objected, well, he had yet to meet a Legionnaire as formidable as he was.

He stole away from the doorman and around the corner of the trolley barn. He peered at the sealed windows and doors, and at the roof, trying to spot the flicker of aura that would reveal the presence of a sentry. He didn't see any glow. Either the guards were well hidden, or security was lax. Maybe the local Renegades and Spectres had been quiet of late.

He dashed up to the base of the building. No one shouted, or took a shot at him. He stuck his face through the wall.

The space inside wasn't entirely dark. Dim shafts of moonlight fell through grimy skylights. The beams illuminated overturned planters, antique lampposts with broken bulbs, fluttering strips of yellow police tape, and chalk body outlines. Shops and restaurants occupied refurbished trolley cars, or had facades like Victorian mansions. Most of them were scarred by bullet holes, obscene graffiti, and splashes of gore. The air smelled of blood and gun smoke.

Holliday could see other wraiths wandering around, but none seemed to notice him, nor were any of them nearby. He transferred the Colt from his vest to the pocket of his duster, concealing it, stepped through the wall, and began to stalk through the shadows.

Despite his caution, he soon turned a corner and came face to face with a teenage ghost who was gliding along as silently as he was. She would have been pretty had she not allowed a flesh sculptor to mold her mouth into a fixed and exaggerated grin, a common sign of allegiance to the Smiling Lord.

Holliday was jumpier than he'd realized. He almost drew his gun. But the girl only looked startled, not hostile or alarmed. He touched the brim of his hat.

The girl looked him up and down. Her aura shone red with desire or greed. She said, "Do you want a date? If you don't have any money, we could do a trade. Maybe those sunglasses—"

"Another time," Holliday said.

He walked on, past a candy shop rustling with roaches, evidently still thriving on whatever spoiled sweets and confectioner's supplies remained within. Then by a women's clothing store, with swastikas, crossed hammers and sickles, and pairs of eyes sloppily painted on the walls.

Four Legionnaires appeared in the gloom ahead. Their outfits were an incongruous combination of white, leering, red-lipped clown masks and blue and gold uniforms like those of the U.S. Cavalry. Each soldier wore a saber. One, a burly man with sergeant's stripes, had a pistol as well.

Holliday ducked into the narrow gap between two trolley cars. A Nihil seethed in the floor at the back of the space.

The Legionnaires tramped by without glancing in his direction. He gave them a little time to get farther away, then skulked on, over some of the trolley tracks that crisscrossed the floor.

Rounding a kiosk, he spied a pale rectangle floating in the darkness. When he stalked two paces closer, he could see that it was a marquee, with a ticket booth like a crystal sarcophagus centered underneath. A theater. Surely the place where his quarry had set up shop. Smiling, he edged forward. Then a little girl with chestnut hair and a small man wearing a filthy raincoat over a garish yellow suit stepped through the broken plate-glass facade.

"I would too understand," said the child. "Why does Joey have to be a Thrall?"

"He agreed to it of his own free will. Don't you fret, the magnanimous Mr. Pryor will free him by and by."

"Chris says Joey's already made you a fortune." They moved apart. Holliday noticed a softball in the little girl's hand. Evidently she and her companion were going to play catch.

The man in the trench coat scowled. "'Chris says.' 'Artie says.' Does everybody in the troupe regard me as some sort of Simon Legree?"

"No," said the child. She threw the ball. Accurately, though her companion nearly fumbled the catch anyway. "But Elaine says you need your consciousness raised."

Holliday grinned at the mention of his quarry's name. He glanced around. No one else was in sight. Still avoiding the pools of moonlight, he crept toward the little girl.

The man in the raincoat threw the ball. It flew too high, and the child had to jump for it. "Well," said the man, "in all candor, our haughty impresario should mind her own business, too. These ingrates seem to be forgetting who, at great personal risk, liberated you all from durance vile."

The girl tossed the ball. This time her companion caught it a bit more deftly. "What does 'consciousness-raising' mean?" she asked.

The man in the trench coat sneered. "It doesn't mean anything. It's an example of what the more intelligent Skinlanders call psychobabble." He threw the ball so wildly that the girl couldn't catch it. It hit the floor and rolled to Holliday's feet. He picked it up.

The little girl whirled and scampered after it. She said, "What does psychobabble—" Her eyes widened, and her words caught in her throat.

Smiling, Holliday proffered the ball. "Hello, little one. I'm looking for Miss Elaine Forrester. Do you know where she is?"

He was trying to be pleasant. But either he looked menacing anyway, or the girl and her companion had good instincts. She recoiled, and the man said, "Kimberly! Come away!"

Inwardly, Holliday sighed. So much for the genteel approach. Fast as a striking snake, he tossed the baseball into his left hand, whipped the revolver out of his pocket, gave the kid and her caretaker a moment to discern what it was, then put it away as rapidly as he'd drawn it. "Calm down," he said.

-EIGHTEEN-

Joey and Elaine turned down East Street. Most of the buildings were ruinous, just as the illuminated copper dome of the state capitol, seemingly floating in the night sky, was green with corrosion. Nihils hissed, and a faint stink of decay hung in the air.

Joey said, "You were pretty smart, making me help Brigham by myself."

She shrugged. "I had a hunch all along that you were looking over your own shoulder too much. That if something got you stirred up enough to just *act*, spontaneously, the power would respond. Mind you, I'm pretty sure that you still can't do everything that I can. Most people *never* get good enough to make other wraiths fall asleep, or spin illusions."

"It doesn't matter. Thanks to you, I got what I needed." He felt an urge to take her hand. He didn't. He was sure she'd pull away, and besides, the impulse made him feel guilty. Disloyal to Emily. "If the magic hadn't kicked in, would you have helped the kid?"

"I doubt it. He was just having a bad dream, and I try to avoid getting involved in other people's lives. I don't think I'm very good at it."

"You're helping me."

"I owe you."

"You lead the troupe."

"I didn't ask for the job. I had it dumped on me. And that's running a business, not dealing with people's personal problems."

"You help take care of Kim."

"She's a child. Somebody has to." Elaine grimaced. "I'm not consistent. Sue me. What do you care anyway?"

"I don't." His mouth tightened. "That didn't come out right. I mean, I'm just trying to get to know you."

"Well, stop."

They walked on. Their footsteps clicked on the sidewalk, and the sound echoed. Off to the east, two dogs growled, evidently at one another.

After a while, Emily said, "I'm sorry if I snapped at you. It's just that I don't like personal questions."

"No kidding."

She frowned. "You don't have to be sarcastic. Your past isn't exactly an open book, either."

He lifted his arms, drawing her attention to his shackles. "That wasn't my choice, remember?"

"I know. Sorry again." They walked a few more paces. Then, her tone wistful, she said, "In the dream, you made death seem wonderful. Is that what you really think?"

Joey snorted. "Of course not. I wanted to make Brigham feel better, so I left out the parts that bother the hell out of me." Three of the Citadel's torches appeared in the murk ahead. "Like slavery. And the fact that most of the time, our sharp eyes just let us see all this crud" — he waved his hand at the derelict buildings — "more clearly. And hey, let's not forget the way watching the Quick enjoy their world makes you feel. Like a starving man with his nose pressed against a restaurant window."

Elaine sighed. "It certainly does. I remember the moment when I realized just what a terrible place the Underworld really is. I was watching someone break an obolus into bits. When the chisel split the iron, the coin *screamed*. Up until then, I hadn't understood that except for the few odds and ends we carry over from life, every trinket we have is forged from the essence of our own kind. It gave me the dry heaves.

"Sometimes I wonder why we don't all just dive into the Void and put ourselves out of our misery. Who cares if it would make Oblivion stronger, maybe strong enough to destroy the universe? What's the universe done for us lately?" She scowled. "I don't mean that. The Skinlanders deserve their chance to live."

He thought of Emily and Sarah. "Yeah."

"You know, I think the Shadows are the worst part of the whole rotten deal. You can never trust anybody, especially yourself."

Joey felt an urge to say that she could trust him, but it would probably sound glib and phony. Hell, how could he expect her to believe it when he wasn't sure of it himself? When he felt the voice sneering inside him?

But she suddenly seemed so depressed that he wanted to say *something* to cheer her up. Himself, too, for that matter. The jubilation of finally learning dream control was slipping away, and he wanted to snatch it back. "On the other hand, death isn't *all* bad."

She raised an eyebrow. "You could have fooled me."

"Come on. Sometimes there *is* beauty. Like the images you make."

"They're just illusions. They don't last." Quickening their pace, they walked between two torches. Joey tried to keep his eyes pointed straight ahead, so he wouldn't see the burning Thralls clearly. The whispering fires chilled him.

"While we're watching them, they're as real as they need to be. And they live on in our memories."

She smiled. "You should leave the flowery talk to George."

They veered to the left, avoiding one of the larger Nihils in the parking lot. For an instant, a sickly green light flickered out of the hole. Joey gripped his baton, but nothing else happened. "I'm just saying that sometimes we have fun. I like Kim's songs and Artie's jokes, don't you? And I do trust some people, even knowing they've got Shadows inside them. Heck, sometimes I even kind of like George. He did save Sarah's life, and I did sell myself to him, so maybe I don't have a right to hate him. And once in a while you can see that there's a halfway-decent guy trapped inside him."

They neared what was now the official Citadel entrance. Joey still thought it was weird that the strongholds had such things, considering that wraiths could slip into or out of the building at any point. But it was a way of keeping tabs on the flow of traffic, and everyone was expected to honor the convention.

His experiences over the last few months had convinced him that he and George were in little danger of arrest outside of San Francisco. Even so, he tensed when the doorman, a Legionnaire with tear-shaped bumps on his cheeks, looked up at him and Elaine. But the soldier merely glanced at their passes, disks of gray Stygian iron stamped with the emblems of the Beggar Lord, the Smiling Lord, and the Ashen Lady, the three Deathlords with representatives in the stronghold, and waved them on.

Joey stepped into the high-ceilinged trolley barn. The stale air smelled of rotting food and mildew. Wan shafts of light oozed through the skylights.

Elaine glided through the door. "If you like everybody so much, why do you still spend so much time asleep?" she asked.

He shrugged. "I just need to."

"In other words, despite your little pep talk, a dream of life is better than the reality of being a ghost."

They started across the trolley barn's cavernous interior. Occasionally they spotted other wraiths in the distance. Some of these were sitting or walking alone, and radiated a tangible feeling of sadness. Somewhere, someone sobbed.

"Maybe it is," Joey admitted. "For now. But I have hope that my spook existence can get better."

They strolled past what had been a children's play area. Bullet holes riddled the miniature trolley cars and the grinning statues of cartoon characters, and rusty stains spattered the floor. Like a huge white fish, the theater marquee swam out of the gloom ahead.

Nearly home, or as close to home as their motley caravan ever got. Joey felt a little sorry that the excursion was about to end.

Elaine sighed. "Maybe your existence can get better. Perhaps if you get your freedom, and help Sarah, you'll be happy. I hope so."

"Thanks. I think I've got a shot." They stepped through the theater's plate-glass facade. "You have to understand. All my life, I wanted to be a winning fighter. Now I am, and I love it." Sometimes, when the rage drained out of him, and he looked down at some knocked-out opponent that he'd played with like a cat tormenting a mouse, he was ashamed of just how much he loved it. "Now that I've got it, though, I'm starting to wonder, is this it? Will I still be fighting in a hundred years? Will it still be a thrill? Don't get me wrong, I like the idea of existing forever, but it can be scary, too."

They stepped into the lobby. Chandeliers shrouded in filthy cobwebs hung from the ceiling. A plaster copy of a Greek or Roman statue lay in pieces on the ratty carpet, and someone had hacked the phrases *GENERATION LAST* and *NO MORE CHILDREN* into the wall. The room smelled of mold and rat droppings.

"At least, for now, you're living your dream," said Elaine, turning toward a staircase. "Some people…" She faltered.

"What's the matter?" Joey asked.

She shook her head. "For a second, I felt, I don't know, apprehensive."

He peered at the shadows at the top of the steps. "I don't see anything."

"I'm sure there isn't anything to see. It's not like I'm psychic. I guess I'm just tired. We did two shows, then walked around in Brigham's head." She started up the stairs, and Joey followed.

"I'm sorry. I didn't mean to wear you out."

"Don't be silly. All I need is a rest." She hesitated. "I enjoy teaching you."

The office in which she'd taken up residence was right at the top of the stairs, opposite one of the entrances to the balcony.

Elaine and Joey stopped outside her brown, matchboarded door. "Good night," he said, feeling awkward. "Thanks again."

"See you tomorrow." She stepped out of sight.

Or at least she started to. Then she froze, leaving the back half of her body in the hall. Joey started to ask her what was wrong, but then she finished disappearing.

Puzzled, he stared at the door. The halting way she'd moved had looked peculiar, but if something was truly the matter, surely she would have spoken, or hopped back out into the corridor. Trying to squelch a pang of anxiety, he turned away. He could use some rest, and the dreams that came with it.

After three paces, he stopped. He wasn't psychic, either, at least no more than any other wraith, but he couldn't shake the feeling that something was wrong. He tiptoed back to the office and pushed his face through the wall.

Despite his attempt at stealth, he found himself looking down the barrel of a revolver. The gunman was sitting on top of the dust-covered desk. He was pale, thin, just under six feet tall, and dressed like a character in a western movie, in a long, caped overcoat and slouch hat. Round, blue-tinted glasses perched in front of his light-colored, piercing eyes.

George and Kim were huddled on the green leather couch by the righthand wall. Elaine was standing just inside the door. All three looked scared.

"I'm hard to sneak up on," said the cowboy. "Come in and join the party."

Joey wondered if he could jump back and dive to one side before the gunman pulled the trigger. It didn't seem likely. He stepped through the wall. "Who are you?" he asked, trying to sound unafraid. "What's this all about?"

The cowboy smiled. "My name is John Holliday. Doc to my friends."

Joey blinked. "You're kidding."

Holliday's lean jaw tightened. "It's not polite to question a man's word. I am Holliday. As for my business, I'm here to escort Miss Forrester to an interview. The Hierarchy's wanted to chat with her for years. That doesn't have to be your trouble, unless you decide to deal yourself in. I'd recommend against it."

"There must be some mistake," said Elaine. She sounded completely unconvincing. "What's supposed to be the charge?"

"Heresy."

"That's crazy," said Joey. "She's just an entertainer, running a show."

Holliday shrugged. "It doesn't matter. I collect the bounty whether she's guilty or not. Now, here's what we're going—"

"If you want to turn me over to the authorities," said Elaine, "do it here. We're in a Citadel. You don't need to 'escort' me anywhere."

"That could be true," Holliday said. "But I've never met the Anacreons here. They might like you. They might be corrupt. I'd rather turn you over to somebody I know is honest, and loyal to the Laughing Lady." It seemed to Joey that Elaine flinched at the Deathlord's name. He had to help her, but how? It would probably be suicide to rush Holliday's gun. And yet, once the bounty hunter and his prisoner vanished into the night, Joey might never find them again.

He could only think of one thing to do. Persuade Holliday to take him along, and hope that he got a chance to jump the gunman later. He tried to say, "Look, if you'll let her go, you can take me instead. I'm wanted too, in California."

He got the first four words out. Then his manacles burned freezing cold, and nausea churned his stomach. His legs folded, and, chain clanking, he toppled to the floor.

He tried again to force the proposition out. His face went into spasms. He couldn't even mouth the words.

Though pain was blurring his vision, he could see that everyone, including Holliday, was staring at him. Probably hoping to slip silently through the couch and the wall behind it, George started to stand up. Instantly the bounty hunter's revolver pivoted to cover him. The little man slumped back down.

"What's the matter with him?" Holliday asked.

"He's epileptic," George lied. Occasionally spirits had the bad luck to carry their illnesses or deformities from life into death.

"Or maybe he's shamming to distract me, and give one of you the chance to try something foolish. Either way, it doesn't matter. Here's what's going to happen. I'm taking Miss Forrester and Kimberly out of here. If I hear an alarm, or notice I'm being followed, I'll kill the child. If I see that I'm really in trouble, I'll kill Miss Forrester, too. I'd rather have something tangible to peddle, but if I swear that I shot her, the Laughing Lady's people might pay me the reward anyway. They know I'm an honorable man.

"If nobody interferes with me, I'll let Kimberly go at the

edge of town. Everybody understand?" His prisoners stared at him. "Excellent. Ladies, if you'll be so kind as to precede me into the hall."

As Holliday passed, Joey tried to grab his ankle and yank him off his feet. His cramped, trembling fingers brushed the gunman's boot, but he couldn't make them grip. Holliday made a contemptuous spitting noise and stepped through the door.

-NINETEEN-

Shuddering, Joey peered up at George. The little man looked not only shaken but overwhelmed, as if he were trying to grapple with too many unpleasant thoughts at once.

"George!" Joey croaked. "Snap out of it! We have to do something."

Perhaps fixing on his slave as a safe target for his outrage, George glared down at him. "You were going to tell him that *we're* fugitives, weren't you? Offer us in Elaine's place. That's why the chain paralyzed you."

"I was going to turn myself in. I wasn't going to say anything about you."

"You belong to me! How could you accuse yourself without implicating me as well? How many times have I ordered you to keep my secrets? How many times have I told you to protect me?"

"I get the point," Joey growled. A cramp ripped through his belly, and he grunted. "Now that your precious ass is out from under the gun, will you shut the shackles off, so we can help our friends?"

George raked his fingers through his hair. "Holliday has darksteel bullets. He told me so. And he said that if anyone tried to stop him, he'd kill Kim."

"Do you really believe that if we don't try, he'll let her go? In the old West, Doc Holliday was a psycho." Joey wasn't really sure that was true, but it was no time to let a little thing like facts get in his way. Certainly the man he'd just met seemed ruthless enough to murder anyone. "And even if the son of a bitch was telling the truth, don't you care about Elaine?"

George swallowed. "We don't truly know what she's accused of doing—"

"We know you don't have to do anything terrible to piss off the Hierarchy. They're a bunch of Nazis. And we know Elaine's our friend. Come on, be brave! We did okay in Vegas, didn't we? Hell, I'll do the dangerous stuff."

"If you imperil yourself, you imperil Mr. Montaigne's pocketbook." The little man grimaced. "But all right." He waved his hand. The chain between the iron cuffs disappeared, and Joey's strength began to trickle back.

When he was able, he hauled himself to his feet. "If I don't get after them right away, we'll lose them. Send help."

"I'll find the patrol—"

"No! Think! If we bring Legionnaires into this, they could wind up arresting Elaine themselves. Get some of our people, ones who know how to handle themselves."

George gave a jerky nod. "All right."

Joey flicked his baton to its full length, strode to the top of the stairs, and peered down. The lobby was empty. He listened. The theater was silent.

Which way would Holliday go? Out into the mall, where he stood a fair chance of running into Citadel soldiers? Probably not. It was more likely that he'd taken the shortest route to the parking lot, which meant cutting through the theater proper. Joey hurried down the steps, then through the nearest entrance to the auditorium. Above his head, beams sighed and creaked. Specks of grit drifted down from the underside of the balcony.

As he trotted down the aisle, he couldn't help wondering

if Holliday had paused in the shadows at the back of the stage, just to make sure that nobody did pursue him. He couldn't help imagining that he felt the bounty hunter's six-shooter staring at his chest. His skin crawled.

But no shot came. Joey scrambled onto the platform, across it, and out the back. Groped his way through a cramped space choked with props and painted flats. He warily stuck his face through the rear wall.

As far as he could tell, the Nihil-pitted parking lot was empty. At the edge, the ring of Thrall torches popped and hissed. The cool night air smelled of roasting flesh.

Evidently Holliday was hustling his captives along at a good clip, and had already reached the street. Torn between the need to catch up and the need to move quietly, still half expecting a gun to blaze, Joey loped across the tarmac.

Reaching the highway, he peered up and down. All he saw was decrepit storefronts and inky pools of shadow.

They didn't come this way, said the voice. *You guessed wrong.*

Shut up! Joey thought. I'm not listening to you.

Or maybe they're moving through buildings instead of open spaces, the voice continued, *like you and George did that night in Chinatown. In that case, you'll never spot them. Maybe they already hitched a ride. There's some traffic, even at this hour.*

Stop! Joey commanded. He closed his eyes and tried to think. After a moment, it occurred to him that if Holliday *did* mean to catch a ride out of town, he might well make for the nearest major highway. Joey headed in that direction.

He squinted at the murk ahead. As far as he could tell, nothing was moving. At every intersection, he stared up and down the cross street. Nothing there, either.

Over the next few minutes, he grew more and more afraid that the voice was right. Holliday and the prisoners were gone for good. Finally, he snarled in frustration. Swung the baton back to slam it against a battered white Corolla sitting at the curb. Then a faint noise murmured through the night. It sounded like a child whimpering.

It was so soft that Joey assumed he was right on top of the source. Otherwise, he wouldn't be able to hear it. He looked around, but couldn't find it.

Straining his ears, he started to follow the sound. After a few moments, during which he didn't seem to get appreciably closer, he wondered if it was actually coming from far away. He had a hunch as to how that could be.

Kim could do uncanny tricks with her voice. Maybe she could project it over a long distance, to attract would-be rescuers, yet simultaneously make it seem so nearly inaudible that Holliday wouldn't tumble to what she was doing.

But the risk! If the gunman did suspect what she was up to, he'd probably kill her at once. Joey quickened his pace.

The weeping led him north. The sound stopped twice, filling him with apprehension, but each time it started up again a minute later. Finally, looking cautiously around a corner, he saw Holliday, Elaine, and Kim about a hundred feet away. Thank god, they weren't moving along inside buildings after all. Evidently Holliday felt confident enough that no one would chase him, or that he could handle anyone who did, to have decided against what could be an awkward, disorienting, and tiresome mode of travel. In fact, he was so self-assured that he'd put his revolver away.

Holliday started to glance over his shoulder. Joey jerked himself back out of sight.

His mouth felt dry. He almost imagined he could feel a heart, hammering in his chest. Okay, he thought, I found them. Now what?

He remembered Holliday's threat. At the first sign of trouble, Kim would die. And if the gunman decided he was in any real danger, Elaine would die too. Still, Joey guessed that all he could do was try to sneak close enough to jump the guy. He reflexively took a deep breath, and then something tapped him on the shoulder.

Raising the baton, he whirled. Now masked in his gray hood, George cringed. Joey was surprised that the little weasel had dared to venture out himself.

But he had, and he'd brought Chris with him. "Take it easy," the handsome actor said.

"Keep your voices down," whispered Joey. "They're around the corner." He peeked out to see if Holliday had heard Chris, but the thin man and his captives were simply walking on up the street.

"We followed Kim's voice," breathed Chris. "What do we do next?"

George said, "Now that we've found them, I can go for reinforcements."

"No time," said Joey. "There's a main drag up ahead. He's going to herd them on a truck and disappear if we don't stop him fast." At least they now had Holliday substantially outnumbered. But Joey still didn't think much of their chances, not against a gun. What they needed was a long-distance weapon of their own, and a marksman to snipe with it.

"Do you have a plan?" asked Chris.

"Yeah," Joey said. "You two sneak through these rows of buildings and get ahead of him. Then distract him while I come up behind him."

"He'll shoot Kim," said George.

"Maybe not," said Joey, "if you get him rattled, and I get on top of him fast enough. Do you have a better idea?"

He expected George to argue some more, out of anxiety for Kim, or reluctance to put himself in the line of fire. But after a moment's hesitation, the little man said, "No. Let's do it." He melted through a grimy brick wall. Chris stuck his head around the corner, then darted across the street and disappeared into the building on the other side.

Joey was almost sure that he could hear his companions scurrying through the storefronts. And if he could, maybe Holliday would, too. He prayed that the sound was just his imagination. He started gliding forward himself, passing through one wall after another. He crept through a deli, a hardware store, a religious supply house full of crumbling leather-bound copies of *The Book of Mormon*. Peering out windows, he watched for the right time to make his move.

Suddenly, glass or porcelain shattered in one of the shops ahead. He guessed that George had shifted himself into the Skinlands, so he could throw things around and make a lot of noise. And in the hope that by doing so, he'd take himself out of Holliday's reach.

Holliday pivoted toward the noise. But it had already stopped, and presumably he had no way of knowing whether it had actually had anything to do with him. After a moment, he said, "Little one, this makes the third time I've asked you to please stop whining."

"She can't help it," said Elaine. "She's frightened. She's a little girl."

"Perhaps so," said Holliday. "Still, I warned you what would happen if anyone got up to any foolishness." Suddenly he had a revolver in his hand. He'd drawn it so quickly that Joey hadn't seen him move.

Something stirred behind one of the windows on the far side of the street. Holliday turned, but Chris had already ducked out of sight.

Holliday glanced at the prisoners. "I'm afraid your friends don't value your safety very highly, Kimberly. I sincerely regret that."

"This isn't the troupe!" cried Elaine. "We don't know who it is."

Joey skulked closer.

Another shadow, squat and horned, bobbed in a second window. Holliday whirled toward it, a split-second too late to shoot. Almost immediately, a tall silhouette with some sort of growth wriggling on its shoulders appeared in yet another store. Joey realized that, by dashing back and forth and changing shape, Chris was doing his best to make it look like several spooks were lurking in the stores across the street.

As the actor ducked, Holliday fired. To Joey's astonishment, the window shattered. The falling pieces crackled with black fire, and vanished before they hit the ground. Evidently the gunman's bullets were charged with some kind of magical energy, and could destroy targets on either side of the Shroud. From Joey's vantage point, it was impossible to tell whether Chris had been hit.

Smiling, Holliday turned back toward the captives. Elaine stepped in front of Kim. "I'm telling you, it's not our friends!" the illusionist said.

Joey was all but certain he was out of time. If he didn't make his move right now, Kim was going to die. He wished that he were closer to Holliday, but at least the bounty hunter had his back to him, and was trying to watch both the prisoners and the street ahead. Baton upraised, Joey charged through a smeared window with flaking gilt lettering and out into the street.

His sneakers didn't squeak on the pavement nor did Elaine react to his sudden appearance and give him away. But Holliday turned at once. "I told you I'm hard to surprise," the gunman said. I'm going to die, Joey thought. All the way, this time. Holliday pulled the trigger.

But as he did, Kim screamed, a screech like a thousand train whistles going off at once. Holliday staggered, and his arm jerked. The bullet whizzed past Joey's forehead.

The cry had rocked him, too, but somehow he kept driving forward. He managed to close with Holliday an instant before the gunman could swing his weapon back into line. He lashed the baton against Holliday's wrist. The impact cracked, and the six-shooter flew from the thin man's hand.

Holliday tried to reach inside his coat. Joey clubbed him across the face, shattering the blue-lensed glasses and flattening the nose on which they sat. The bounty hunter reeled backward.

Joey pursued him. His ears still ringing from Kim's shriek, he almost didn't hear Elaine shouting, "Behind you!" And then, furious, as eager to deal out pain and injury as he'd ever been in the ring, he nearly ignored her. But she sounded so scared, so insistent, that after a moment he had to glance around.

The revolver was floating in the air. The barrel swiveled in his direction.

He dove behind a rusty green Jeep Eagle parked by a newspaper box. The revolver barked. The vehicle lurched, then sizzled as one fender burned to nothingness.

Holliday gave his head a shake, as if to clear it. The gun flew into his hand, and he started toward the car.

It was obvious to Joey that he couldn't hide behind the Eagle for long. Not when Holliday could blast it out of existence, or flow right through its substance. Joey decided to lunge through the vehicle himself, using its mass for cover, and try to close with the bounty hunter again. It almost certainly wouldn't work, but the only other option seemed to be jumping up, running, and getting shot in the back.

He flexed his legs to spring. Then another Joey shimmered into view beside him, leaped up, and dashed into the open. Holliday turned and fired. The figure kept running.

For a moment, the real Joey was too astonished to take advantage of his enemy's distraction. Then he realized that Elaine, despite her exhaustion, had managed to cast an illusion. From the corner of his eye, he glimpsed her pulling Kim through a graffiti-covered wall. He jumped up and charged through the bulk of the car.

Holliday turned and fired. The first shot would have hit Joey in the chest if the Eagle's hood hadn't blocked it. As it was, his proximity to the seething, disintegrating metal brought a wave of pain and dizziness. He fell to his hands and knees. Holliday aimed at his head.

Then Chris hurtled into view. Now armored in gleaming gray hide, his fists huge masses of spikes and claws, he jumped Holliday from behind. He ripped and battered the gunman's head and shoulders.

Yes! Joey thought. He was sure that Chris was about to finish the fight. But somehow, his head mashed out of shape, his eyes torn out, Holliday twisted out of the actor's embrace, sprang back, and pointed the revolver at him.

Chris dove sideways, through a wall. Holliday fired. Joey doubted that the bounty hunter had missed by more than an inch.

But now Joey's dizziness had passed. He scrambled up, determined once again to take Holliday from behind, by surprise.

Holliday spun. Tossed the six-gun from his right hand into his left and whipped a second one out from under his coat. Joey hurled himself through the same wall that Chris had fled into.

He landed on the linoleum floor of a shadowy music store. The trumpets and saxophones looked dented and corroded. The guitars had missing strings, and the drums broken heads. The racks of sheet music smelled musty.

Chris was crouching by the display window, peering out. Scraps of Holliday's flesh hung from his knuckle spikes. He shot Joey a glance that said, What does it take to stop this guy?

Joey shook his head to say he didn't know. He guessed they were going to get another chance to find out, because Holliday was stalking toward them.

Then laughter pulsed through the night, louder and louder. Joey realized that George, still on the other side of the Shroud, had found a store full of televisions, and was quickly turning them on. An instant later, Kim started wailing, a ghastly, wavering howl that scraped the nerves. Her voice skipped and cracked with fear or fatigue. But it seemed to come from everywhere at once, and it raised the ambient noise level by several hundred percent.

Holliday stopped advancing. Blind, he'd been willing to keep fighting. Blind and deafened, he evidently wasn't. He began to back into the middle of the street.

Joey quivered with rage. He yearned to dart into the open air and attack. But he hadn't managed to surprise the bastard yet, and despite the bounty hunter's seeming handicaps, his instincts warned him that this time wouldn't be any different. When Chris beckoned, he reluctantly followed him out the back of the store.

-TWENTY-

Joey crept down the hall toward the entrance to the theater balcony. He wondered if he was being foolish. It had only been a couple hours ago that he, Elaine, George, Kim, and Chris had sneaked away from the blinded Holliday, and, figuring there was safety in numbers, had returned to the Citadel to rejoin the rest of the troupe. It was hard to believe that another problem could arise so soon. And yet he had a hunch that that was exactly what was likely to happen.

He slipped into the gallery and began to sit down in an aisle seat, and then, from the corner of his eye, glimpsed a shimmer of aura by the tarnished railing in front of the bottom row of seats. His shackle chain clinking, he jerked around.

It was Artie's aura. The comedian was sitting on the floor in the lotus position. "I see you had the same idea I did," he said. "Amazing, considering your customary stupor. Come farther away from the doorway, and don't make a lot of noise. If we catch her dead to rights, we can cut through a lot of crap."

Joey tiptoed on down the aisle stairs and sat down beside Artie. The comic stared into space and breathed slowly. His halo began to turn the light blue of tranquillity.

After a while, Joey's curiosity got the better of him.

"What are you doing?" he whispered.

"Meditating, you fathead," Artie murmured back. "I'll grant you, the breathing part seems kind of silly under the circumstances, but it's part of the program."

"Does this mean you're a Heretic?" Joey asked.

"Yeah," Artie said, grinning, "just another wacky Transcendentalist, busting my chakras to achieve satori and vanish from the Underworld into a higher state of being."

"Wouldn't that be nice," said Joey wistfully. "Unless Transcendence is just another name for the Void. That's what some ghosts say."

Artie shrugged. "In my case," he said, sounding more serious, "I don't figure it matters. I'm mean, you don't think a schmuck like me has what it takes to achieve spiritual perfection, do you? I'll be satisfied if the effort just makes me a better person. I'm not very proud of some of the things I did when I was alive. Hey, did you hear that?" Whatever he was referring to, Joey hadn't. "Be quiet!"

A moment later Elaine crept past the doorway with her carpetbag in hand. Artie smirked at Joey, pressed his fingers to his lips, and tiptoed after the illusionist, hoisting his knees absurdly high. The boxer crept after him.

Joey soon formed the impression that if left to his own devices, Artie would have followed Elaine all the way out of the theater, mugging and improvising bits of silent comedic business every step of the way. But the fighter was far too worried to wait that long to confront her. When she reached the landing midway down the staircase, the spot with the fanged mouth painted in stinking dried blood on the wall, he said, "Where are you going?"

Elaine jerked around. "Just, just walking," she stammered.

"You said you wanted to rest," Joey replied. In fact, she'd claimed that after her ordeal, she needed a rest so badly that she couldn't possibly explain why Holliday had abducted her until she got one. That hadn't sat particularly well with any of the people who'd been desperately searching for her, but in the end they'd had no choice but to accept it.

"I'm edgy," she said. "If I stroll around a little, maybe it will calm me down. Don't worry, I won't go outside the building, even though I can't imagine Holliday coming after me again tonight. He can't have grown new eyes already."

Artie shook his head. "It won't wash, my prevaricating little pork chop. Judging by the smell, neither will the palooka here, but let's not digress into that sordid topic. You left Kim alone up there, even though, when she came in, she was even more frazzled than you. And you look like you could frazzle Haystack Calhoun. You've got your satchel of sundries and unmentionables. You're taking a powder. The least you could have done is lifted the receipts, in the time-hallowed vaudeville tradition."

Elaine said, "I'm sorry. I wanted to say good-bye. But I knew that if I did, you'd give me a hard time about leaving."

"You bet we would," said Joey. "Everybody here is your friend. You can trust us. We were all willing to risk our necks to get you back, weren't we?"

She grimaced. "That's the problem. I don't want anybody getting hurt on my behalf."

"And nobody did," said Artie. "Look, we've all been through a lot together. If you're going to cut out, don't you think you at least owe us an explanation?"

"I think that the less you know, the safer you'll be."

"Put yourself in our place, and try not to step on my feet. Wouldn't you want to understand, no matter what?"

Elaine sighed. "I guess."

Turning to Joey, Artie said, "Round up the cattle and heard 'em into the theater, buckaroo. I'll stay with this little heifer, and make sure she doesn't cave in to another urge to vamoose."

-TWENTY-ONE-

Elaine sat on the edge of the stage, feet dangling, her carpetbag beside her. Clustered in the first three rows of the orchestra, their faces pale smudges in the gloom, the troupe gazed up at her. Chris, Artie, Kim, Joey, and George had claimed the nearest seats.

Elaine had butterflies in her stomach. She was no good at talking to people unless it was as the boss, and that wasn't appropriate now. What made the situation even more awkward was that her story was complicated, strange, and, in her mind, shameful.

She supposed that the best way to tell it was to start at the beginning. She swallowed, then asked, "Has anybody here ever heard of the Church of the Holy Covenant?"

A couple people raised their hands.

"It's not one of the world's hugest religions," Elaine continued, "but it's been around for centuries, and it has hundreds of thousands of parishioners around the world. It's a Christian sect, but with some odd features." She frowned. Even now, it felt wrong to talk about the faith in such a detached and therefore disrespectful manner.

"Odd how?" asked Artie quietly.

"The bishops choose leaders called Saints to rule over

the church. They examine the babies born to the congregation, and pick out the ones that God supposedly wants to have the job. There are never more than a handful in any generation." She hesitated. "I was one of them."

Expecting her audience to laugh, or scoff, she tensed. But nothing happened. Even Artie held back whatever wisecrack had sprung to mind.

After a moment, she said, "And so I grew up believing I was special. I think that in my place, anybody would have. Everyone kept telling me how wise and pure I was. I thought I felt the Holy Spirit guiding my every step. Sometimes I could heal the sick, or at least it seemed like it.

"When I got leukemia, and found out I was going to die young, I was only a little scared, because I was sure I was going to Heaven." She grimaced. "In fact, since the church taught that Saints led the faithful in the afterlife, too, I guess I expected eternity to be business as usual. Instead, I wound up in the Shadowlands.

"Not that it seemed so bad for the first few minutes. At least I still had this." She took a glass sphere the size of baseball out of the carpetbag and lifted it for everyone to see. Her touch made it pulse and ripple with a blue and scarlet sheen.

Joey said, "That's the 'key' you were worried about in Vegas, isn't it?"

She nodded. "My symbol of office. Of Sainthood. I'd carried it into death, and in the Shadowlands it began to glow with beautiful light, like everyone imagines a sacred relic should."

She put it back in the satchel. "When my Reapers turned up, that was comforting, too. They said they were members of the church, and had come to escort me to my rightful place.

"At the time, I was still too dazed from dying to ask many questions. Now I understand what the Reapers meant, or at least I think I do. A version of the faith exists as a Heretical sect in the Underworld. It has its version of Heaven in one of the Far Shores lands, and that's where we were headed.

"But we never got there. We hadn't gone a block from the crematorium when a force of Legionnaires attacked us. They made it clear that it was me they really wanted." Chris raised her hand, as if she were a teacher and he a student. "Yes?" she said.

"I don't know much about how the Hierarchy goes about persecuting Heretics," the blond actor said. "But they don't ordinarily arrest every priest or rabbi who dies, even if the guy was a big deal in the Skinlands. Normally you have to set up shop as a religious honcho on this side of the Shroud to get their attention. So what was the deal with you?"

Elaine shook her head. "I didn't know then," she said, "and I still don't. It's not like there's anybody I can ask. Anyway, to continue my story, my escorts were outnumbered, but they were tough, and they fought hard. They all died, or I think they did, but their sacrifice, and a lucky break, gave me the chance to run away.

"The next few months weren't easy. I'd never had to take care of myself anywhere, and now I was trying to survive as a fugitive in the Shadowlands. Looking back, I can't imagine how I made it."

For a moment, she smiled. "But as you can see, I did. And as I learned my way around, I found out that it was the Laughing Lady's servants who were after me."

Artie said, "That's another peculiar aspect of your situation. People say the Deathlords are all plotting against each other to seize Charon's throne. But generally speaking, they still work together to put down Heretics and Renegades. That being the case, why is it specifically the Laughing Lady who craved, and apparently still hankers for, the pleasure of your company?"

Elaine sighed. "I don't know that, either. Maybe other members of the church could tell me, but I've never run into any. I guess they aren't that numerous in the Shadowlands, either, and of course, over here, they'd have to keep their heads down. Anyway, much as I hated to leave my mortal home behind, I figured clearing out of Chicago was the only way to keep from getting arrested. So I came west, but I was still afraid. Of the whole world, because anyone could be a Hierarchy spy. I stayed away from people until I met Ben Strickland, the illusionist who ran the troupe before me. I guess he saw how lonely I was, because he bent over backwards to win my trust, then convinced me to join the show."

Kim cried, "Like you and me!"

Elaine smiled at her. "Sort of. He made me his apprentice. I found that I loved his art, and, though I guess I didn't show it much, I came to care about him, too. He was like a father to me, in a way my real dad wasn't. Not that my parents didn't love me, but I think it was hard for them to treat me like their daughter when I was supposedly a mouthpiece for the voice of God.

"Anyway, after a few years, Ben seemed to get tired, old on the inside, the way some wraiths do. The last of his Quick friends and relatives died, and didn't turn up in the Shadowlands, and I think all the ugliness here just wore him down. I tried to cheer him up, but it didn't help. Finally, one night, Oblivion took him — ate him away to nothing in just a few seconds. He never even changed his expression. I can still see his sad little smile."

Her eyes ached as if they could shed tears. She wondered why she was babbling about Ben's destruction. She didn't need to relieve that particular pain to relate the gist of her story. "Afterwards, those of you who were already members of the troupe asked me to take over as manager. I felt that if you wanted me, I owed it to Ben to accept. I was reluctant, because it was a high-profile job. But since I'd run away from Illinois years ago, no one had bothered me, so I thought that if the show stayed here in the west, everything would be all right.

"And for a while, it was, but now someone's found me. I'm sorry I brought trouble down on your heads. At least if I leave now, it shouldn't happen again."

"Hang on," said Chris. "You're panicking. We handled Holliday. I admit it wasn't easy, but we weren't expecting him, either. If he comes back, we'll be ready."

"Thank you," said Elaine. "But don't you see, it isn't just him. I hoped that Larry Orsini just wanted to enslave us because we're good entertainers, but now I'm sure that he recognized me, too. The secret is out. The hunters will keep coming. My only chance is to drop out of sight again."

Artie peered at her thoughtfully. "In all the time you spent hiding, weren't you ever tempted to go looking for your church's Paradise? If you found it, you could be queen or Popette or something, right? And it may be the only way to get the Madwoman's agents off your back."

Joey glowered at him. "Give her a break. I fell into the Tempest for a few minutes right after I died. I was damn lucky to get out again. Elaine would have to be an idiot to travel into it if she didn't know exactly where she was going."

Elaine sighed. "Thanks for sticking up for me. But the truth is, of course I thought of looking for Heaven. I was just too cowardly."

Now Joey glared at her. "That isn't cowardly, it's smart. People say there are a billion twisting, forking paths in the Tempest. Supposedly, a few people know how to find their way, but you aren't one of them, are you?"

She shook her head. "But I have a guide." She felt the key throb inside the carpetbag. "The crystal ball I showed you. In the Skinlands, it was just a lump of glass. In our world, it's become something more, the way a wraith's most cherished possessions occasionally do. It's alive, or at least it talks. I can hear its voice in my mind, and it says it can lead me to Heaven." She sighed. "You can't imagine how tired I am of listening to it nag!"

Artie leered. "Obviously, you never met my first wife. But I notice you never smashed the doodad, or threw it away."

"No. I couldn't. And now" — she hesitated — "now I think that, if people are still hunting me after all these years, hundreds of miles from my mortal home, maybe the stupid thing has been right all along. I should go. Otherwise, I'll be afraid forever."

"Now that's showing some moxie," Artie said. "We ought to hit the trail pronto, before our saddle pal Doc sprouts new peepers, or puts together a posse."

"I can be ready in five minutes," said Chris.

"What are you talking about?" said Elaine. "I didn't ask anyone to come with me."

Artie snarled, "What's the matter, we're not good enough for you? I'll have you know that my ancestors were tarred and feathered by some of the best people on three continents!" He smiled. "You don't have to ask, *bubele*. We're volunteering. Some of us, anyway. Hard as you work to keep us at arm's length, we like you anyway, just to spite you."

"I, I like you, too. That's why I forbid you to risk your lives for me."

"It's not up to you," said Chris. "we won't let you go without us."

Kim said, "I'm coming!"

"No!" said Elaine. "*You* definitely aren't." As the words left her mouth, she realized that she'd tacitly conceded that others were. "I love you, and I hate to part with you, but I can't take a little girl into danger."

Chris put his hand on Kim's shoulder. "I'm sorry, sweetheart, but she's right."

Kim knocked his arm away. His mouth fell open. "No, she isn't!" the child wraith shrilled. "I know I look like a little kid. Unless I let a flesh shaper change me, I always will. And I know that in most ways, my brain still works like a kid's. It's like it's stuck that way. But I'm *sixteen*! I have a right to try to be a grown-up. And you need me! I helped in the Inferno, and tonight, too."

Artie frowned. "I'm sorry if we've made you feel bad. That's the last thing we'd ever want to do."

"You didn't," she replied. "You're nice to me. But now I just *have* to come, and that's all there is to it."

"Or you won't feel like a real person," murmured Chris. "I understand." He looked at Artie. "And now that I do, I'd say she does have a right to go."

Artie shrugged. "Maybe. At any rate, I'm pretty sure we'd have to do her bodily harm to keep her from following us. Look at that mulish glint in her beady eyes." He grinned up at Elaine. "I wonder where she gets it." He turned toward the rest of the troupe. "Okay, suckers, who else wants to go on a romp through the great beyond?"

One hand went up. Then another. People muttered back and forth.

"I'll tell you what," Artie said. "It's a big decision. Take a few minutes to talk it over privately with your loved ones, your agents, or whoever. If you decide you're in, the boat leaves in half an hour."

Most of the troupe began moving toward the exits. Elaine looked down at Artie in mingled dismay and admiration. She said, "You should have been the leader all along."

"And give up insulting people, and making light of everything that happens? Not a chance! Besides, anything I know about being the boss, I picked up from watching you. No, my little ptarmigan, this ragtag and bobtail band is yours to command. Just not to ditch."

-TWENTY-TWO-

To Joey's annoyance, George led him all the way upstairs and into the conference room they'd taken for their quarters. Artie had suggested that people talk privately, and the Restless had keen hearing. Still, Joey thought that any quiet corner would have done, because he couldn't imagine that anyone would bother to eavesdrop. What would be the point? But George evidently felt differently. Or perhaps it was just his natural sneakiness, coming to the fore.

The little man sat down on the long, dusty table. "You know," he said, "now that I've had the leisure to mull it over, it really was unfair."

Joey blinked. "What was?"

"Becoming our traveling companion, without ever warning us she had enemies and thus her presence constituted a danger."

Joey stared at him. "Where do you get off, complaining about that? We did exactly the same thing to her."

George rolled his eyes. "I know that. It was a joke. Did you think that young Mr. Montaigne is bereft of any sense of irony?"

"Let's just say that this is the first I've seen of it."

George's mouth tightened. "Tommyrot. You're simply too

obtuse to appreciate the subtleties of your witty comrade's discourse. But never mind. Do you think we ought to lend our support to this endeavor?"

Joey's fist tightened on the baton. "I don't know. I care about Elaine—"

"Quite a lot, I think."

Joey irritably waved his hand, flicking the idea away. His manacles clinked. "Don't be stupid. I don't have those kinds of feelings for anyone but my wife. But Elaine's a friend. If she's in trouble, I owe it to her to stand beside her.

"But she's going into the Tempest! That's like" — he paused, groping for words — "a whole different universe. I know people say you can come back from the other side, but have you ever *met* anyone who did?"

"I assume you mean besides Spectres and Stygians. Actually, yes, a few. Once I even saw a Ferryman, one of old Charon's special pathfinders. It's said that *they* wander the Tempest with impunity. But for most of us, it's a hellishly dangerous place. Imagine a maze the size of a planet, or a galaxy, for all I know, crawling with monsters and Hierarchy patrols."

Scowling, Joey paced along a row of rotting, musty-smelling drapes. "How can we let Elaine go into trouble like that without us? But on the other hand, how can I vanish off the face of the earth? Isn't my first duty to Sarah? And now I have a way to get to her! To straighten her out! I finally learned how to talk to people in their dreams!" He shook his head. "I can't believe it was just a few hours ago. So much has happened, I feel like it's been weeks."

"That's nice," said George absently. "You're right, of course. There's something to be said for either course of action. If we stay, we'll be safer, and continue to prosper on the proceeds of your prizefights."

Suddenly, a feverish light glittered in the little man's eyes. Joey's stomach sank. "Ah," said George, "but if we *go*!

If Elaine reaches her Far Shores haven, she'll be an empress, or at least a great lady. And then, surely she'll elevate her faithful paladin Montaigne to a station befitting his merit."

"You can't be serious."

George smirked. "Au contraire. Why so dismayed? Aren't you the one who always exhorts me to be valiant?"

"Free me. I want to stay here."

"Don't be ridiculous. I need your assistance now more than ever before. Anyway, a moment ago, you more or less wanted to go."

"I thought I did. But when you made up your mind, when I realized that I might actually *have* to go, I understood what was really important to me."

"That's just human nature. In retrospect, the option a fellow declines always looks more attractive than the one he chose. You'll get over it soon enough."

"The hell I will."

George stood up. The tail of his raincoat swished across the tabletop without disturbing the dust. "You're forgetting that we wouldn't return to San Francisco even if we remained in the Shadowlands."

"That's what you think. I'd get there somehow."

George spread his hands. "There's no point even discussing this if you're going to be irrational. Suppose I promise to free you when the prize is won."

"Like I trust you to keep your word. Even if you mean it, and we don't get killed on the way, who knows how long the trip is going to take, or if I could make it back through the Tempest without Elaine and her magic eight ball. Damn it, Sarah needs me *now*! Why did you even ask my opinion, if you don't care what I think?"

"Because I was hoping for an intelligent appraisal of the situation, untainted by your morbid sentimentality. Why can't you accept that your *life* is *over*? You have to let go of your mortal attachments and invest yourself in the present."

Joey sneered. "That's easy for you to say. You never loved anybody, and nobody was ever stupid enough to love you."

George trembled. "That... that was uncalled for. You heard Artie. The expedition is departing soon. You'll depart with it, and that's that."

Joey pivoted and began to melt through the wall. Then an idea struck him. One so disturbing that, though the last thing he wanted was to continue the conversation, he had no choice. He turned back. "George."

The little man had just picked up his suitcase, a brown leather valise with golden hinges, snaps, and buckles. He set it on the table. "What?"

"You've betrayed people before. Twice that I know about. No matter what happens, you'd better not try to sell out Elaine. Or somehow, I'll make you pay."

George looked shocked, but Joey knew him too well to assume it was an honest display. "What do you take me for? The performers are our friends!"

"They sure are. But if your life was on the line, or the Hierarchs offered to make you a big shot, I wonder if you'd let a little thing like that stop you from switching sides."

George scowled. "One day, you'll appreciate just how grievously you've wronged the steadfast Mr. Montaigne. Meanwhile, keep your suspicions to yourself. I won't have you poisoning anyone's mind against me."

-TWENTY-THREE-

Holliday caught the astringent smell of the hospital morgue as soon as he slipped through the double doors. He felt the bleakness that fouled the atmosphere as well. As he'd expected, the Shroud was weak here, making it a propitious place for a divination.

He reached to adjust his blue glasses, then remembered that the ghost with the club had broken them. Scowling, he strode past a wall of square drawers, and shelves full of bottled hearts and kidneys, and into an autopsy room beyond.

The white, naked body of a chubby, middle-aged man lay on one of the nearest tables. A female pathologist in green surgical garb spoke into a hanging microphone, then made a Y-shaped incision in the corpse's chest. Two young men, medical students, Holliday supposed, looked on. Since they were masked, too, it was hard to be sure, but he thought the tall one with the sharp nose looked queasy.

A ghost with a gray crew cut and a conservative navy-blue suit sat in a chair in the far corner, reading a book. Looking up, he said, "Yes?"

"I need to borrow this room," said Holliday. "I'm afraid I need privacy, too. Please, take a stroll."

The doctor sheared through the corpse's ribs with a buzzing electrical saw.

The wraith in the corner stood up. His aura flickered orange and red with mingled fear and anger. "This is my home," he said. "You can't just order me out."

After last night's fiasco, Holliday was in such a bad mood that he was tempted to kill the fool. But he realized it would only waste a bullet. Or, if he used his knife, a smidgen of effort. It wouldn't even cheer him up. Only capturing Elaine Forrester would do that. He opened his duster to display the Colt in his vest. "Go or die. It doesn't matter to me."

Evidently trying to decide if Holliday was serious, the other spirit peered into his eyes. The rosy tinge bled out of his aura, and the orange flared brighter. He swallowed and scuttled through the wall.

Holliday moved to a table at the back of the room, then took a deck of cards out of his coat. They were big and square-cornered, the kind he'd learned to play with while growing up in Griffin and Valdosta. Though modern cards had come into use before his death, he retained a fondness for these. They had no figures or pips in the corners, and the court cards weren't double-headed. A poker player had to *know* the pack, had to be able to tell the shoes of the King of Diamonds from those of the Jack of Clubs, and the skirt of the Queen of Hearts from those of her royal sisters. Otherwise he'd have to turn his cards right side up, and give away his hand.

As Holliday removed one Joker from the deck, he pictured the big, black-haired wraith with the bludgeon again, and felt his jaw clench. He made an effort to put his anger aside. The cards spoke more clearly when he was calm.

The doctor droned into her microphone. One of the students asked her a question. When Holliday felt ready, he cut the deck into three stacks, shuffled each from his left hand into his right, and put them back together. Then he dealt out fifteen cards, face up.

The one in the middle of the layout represented himself. It was the Ten of Spades, a card of opposition and frustration. To the left lay the Queen of Spades, and on the right the Jack — Elaine Forrester and the man with the baton. Despite the involvement of Kimberly and the transformed wraith, these other two bore primary responsibility for Holliday's humiliation, and would prove the greatest impediments to avenging it.

The pathologist lifted a lump of tissue out of the cadaver's chest and set it on the scale. The tall student made a choking sound and bolted out the door. Holliday wondered if his presence had contributed to the mortal's distress.

In the upper righthand corner of the spread were the Seven of Diamonds and the Three and Seven of Clubs — tokens of failure and a loss of reputation. The divination was warning that if Holliday proceeded as planned, Miss Forrester had a fair chance of escaping him.

Glaring, the shooter consulted the pasteboards in the upper left corner. Here lay the Deuce of Clubs, and the Ace and Seven of Spades.

Holliday's grimace turned to a thoughtful frown. Ordinarily, confident of his ability to face down any opponent, he preferred to hunt alone. But the cards were suggesting that this time around, he'd better recruit some high-powered help if he wanted to win.

In the lower left were the Ten of Diamonds and the Three and Five of Hearts. Cards of ill omen that supposedly revealed the cornerstones of the Querent's character. As was his habit, he barely spared them a glance. He read the future to spy out how to trap fugitives, not to study his own nature. He hoped that after a century and a half of existence, he already understood himself as well as a man needed to.

The cards in the lower right wing hinted at forces operating outside his sphere of influence. They were the Jack of Hearts and the Five and Six of Spades. Love, separation, and fear. The preoccupations of Elaine and her companions, he supposed.

Holliday stroked his mustache. He'd absorbed the surface meaning of the layout, without learning everything he needed to know. Fortunately, a skilled cartomancer like himself could delve beneath the surface. He held his hands an inch above the cards, fingers spread and palms down. He closed his eyes and emptied his mind.

The voices of the doctor and student whispered on. The cadaver hissed, popped, squelched, and cracked as its demolition proceeded. Eventually, Holliday's hands began to tingle. An image wavered into existence behind his eyelids.

At first, it was just a tantalizing blur, but gradually it sharpened into focus. Though he seemed to be looking down on it from high above, somehow he could see every detail. Beaches. Green waves slapping against a seawall. Iron-fronted Victorian buildings, and streets lined with white and crimson oleanders.

Holliday smiled. He'd been a little worried that the cards would show him a vision he couldn't interpret. It happened that way sometimes. But this message was a cinch. He'd visited this island town last year. He opened his eyes, gathered up the deck, and went in search of a phone he could use in private.

He found it in a lounge adjacent to the Emergency Room. In the far end of the room stood two sagging cots with stained, sour-smelling linen. Holliday inferred that weary physicians napped here during slack times, but no one was present now. He shifted himself into the Skinlands, picked up the receiver, and dialed the governor of Little Rock.

Someone who was probably a mortal servant answered. Holliday told her his name, and Clement Purvis himself came on the line. "Doc!" he boomed. "How's it hangin'?"

The governor was one of those wraiths who'd mastered the art of possessing the Quick. He kept a number of lobotomized, broken-willed hosts in his Citadel, slipping in and out of them as casually as if they were bathrobes. His current body's voice was a fruity bass. It made him sound as jovial as Santa Claus.

Holliday wondered just how long Purvis's geniality would last. Each of the Deathlords supposedly reigned over the Restless who'd died of a particular cause. The Smiling Lord, for example, ruled the victims of violence. Generally speaking, this traditional division of the spoils didn't mean much anymore. Unrestrained by Charon, a lord of Stygia would claim any soul he could get his hands on. But the Laughing Lady theoretically held sway over those wraiths who had, in some sense, succumbed to madness, and in Holliday's opinion, many of her minions did indeed act crazy. In Purvis's case, the aberration took the form of abrupt mood swings, frequently for no discernible reason.

"I'm in Utah," Holliday said. "I found her. Lorenzo Orsini was right. It's the same woman."

"Well, I'll be damned!" Purvis boomed. "Who would have thought she'd turn up after all this time? Bring her in, and expect a bonus."

"It isn't quite that simple. She's on the move again. I just verified that she and her troupe hit the road last night, while I was... indisposed."

"'Indisposed!'" the Governor snarled. "What the devil does that mean?"

Holliday sighed. "It means that my first attempt to catch her didn't pan out. I had bad luck, and frankly, I didn't expect her associates to be anywhere near as tough as they turned out to be. Don't worry, it's only a temporary setback."

"The hell you say!" Purvis's anger was rapidly crumbling into anxiety. "Now that she knows you're after her, she could get her face changed."

"She can't change her deathmarks." Deathmarks were patterns of scars, ridges, or discolorations found on the face of virtually every wraith. Visible only to ghosts like Holliday, who'd mastered the trick of seeing them, they were as individual as fingerprints, and no flesh sculptor could alter or erase them. "And I know where she's headed. Galveston."

"What does she want there?"

"That, I don't know. Strange as it seems, she didn't confide in me."

"I don't appreciate your sarcasm! This matter is important. The woman is a threat."

"From what you've told me, I doubt it. I don't think she has the information she'd need to cause any mischief. Where would she get it?"

"From her Heretical acolytes."

"If the Hierarchy couldn't locate her until now, what makes you think her people did any better? Looks to me like all she's been doing is lying low."

"Biding her time! Scheming! Waiting for the proper moment to strike!"

Holliday's fist tightened on the receiver. "Calm down. You sound like you're foaming at the mouth. It doesn't matter what she means to do. I'll catch the next plane to Galveston and nail her there."

"Excellent!" said Purvis, jolly again. "I knew I could count on you. Doc Holliday always gets his man, hey? Or in this case, woman." He laughed heartily.

"That's right." Holliday hesitated. Despite what he'd gleaned from the cards, it galled him to admit there was any job he couldn't handle alone. "And just to make sure, I plan to bring in some help."

"Legionnaires?" Now Purvis sounded dismayed. "We don't have many people in Texas. That's Smiling Lord and Emerald Lord country. And I'm not sure the Anacreons we do have are really loyal. I suppose I could send some of my personal forces—"

"Don't bother. I have somebody else in mind, someone who owes me a favor." The person he was thinking of was a lot more useful than the average Legionnaire. Besides, accepting support from Purvis would be tantamount to inviting him to reduce the amount of the reward.

"Oh," said the governor slowly. "I guess that's good, then. If they're competent. They are, aren't they?"

Holliday decided he'd had enough. He was beginning to feel the strain of holding himself in the Skinlands. And more to the point, nobody was paying him to soothe the governor's nerves. He broke the connection and dialed again.

-TWENTY-FOUR-

Galveston, October.

The llama delicately nibbled the last feed pellet out of Sarah's hand. The animal allowed her to stroke its neck a second longer, then turned and trotted toward another little girl, who still had food to give away.

"Should we move on?" Joey asked. He hoped that the answer would be yes, but his daughter always found it hard to tear herself away from the petting zoo. "There's still a lot we haven't done."

"Okay," Sarah said reluctantly. Grabbing onto Joey's hand, she led him and Emily. She, Joey, and Emily wove through a tangle of children, parents, lambs, and goats. Finally the trio escaped out the gate. Smiling, Joey took another look around.

The Golden Gate Park children's playground was particularly pleasant today. A balmy breeze blew from the east. Maybe it was just his imagination, but the wind seemed to carry the scent of flowers. Sunlight gleamed on the Troll Bridge and the Mouse Tower. At the top of the hill, the antique carousel, with its tub, rocker, and chariots, shone invitingly.

"How about the merry-go-round?" he asked. "We haven't ridden that yet."

Sarah tensed. "No. I don't want to."

Puzzled, he peered down at her. "Why not? I thought you liked it."

She hesitated, then said, "You'll ride away."

He grinned. "Are you teasing me? The horses just go in a circle."

Sarah scowled. "No. You'll go off and never come back."

"That's silly, sweetheart. Daddy would never do that."

Emily laid her hand on his arm. "I'd rather we didn't ride, myself," she said.

He stared at her. "If we act like the kid is right, it will spook her even more. I want to show her there's nothing to be afraid of."

Emily's dark eyes gazed into his. "I'm frightened, too. Please, don't leave us again."

An unpleasant memory tugged at him, demanding recognition. He brushed it away as if it were a gnat. "What do you mean, 'again'? Have you both gone nuts?"

"You did go!" Sarah shrilled. "You were gone for years and years. I cried all the time."

"That isn't true!" Joey said. "Both of you, just shut up!"

And they did. At first, their lips kept moving, but no sound came out. When they realized they couldn't speak, the agitation bled out of them, and they started smiling again. Evidently, by willing away their voices, he'd also removed the crazy fears they'd been jabbering about.

"So," he said, "are we going to ride the carousel or what?" Sarah started to scamper toward the slope.

But after three strides, she lurched to a stop. Her mouth melted away, leaving a blank expanse of skin beneath her nose. Her legs went stiff, and she pressed her arms to her sides.

Emily cried out and lunged toward Sarah. Then she froze, too.

The entire park began to change. The sky darkened. The grass withered, and dry leaves fell from the trees. Cracks split the ground, and the Mouse Tower collapsed. Everyone but Joey, Emily, and Sarah vanished. A buzzing of flies and the stench of death arose from the petting zoo.

The bodies of Joey's wife and daughter began to stretch. When they were twice as tall as he was, their hair burst into crackling yellow flame. They writhed, though their limbs were so rigid that the motion was almost imperceptible.

Joey tried to tip Sarah over, so he could reach her head and beat the fire out, but her feet had sunk in the earth. He struggled to uproot her until, behind him, something whinnied.

He spun around. A black wooden horse, with blank white eyes and a crimson bridle and saddle, tossed its head impatiently. It still had holes in its belly and spine where the brass pole had impaled it. He wondered vaguely how it had gotten loose.

He knew he mustn't get on it. He had to save Emily and Sarah. But an invisible force lifted him into the air and set him in the saddle. Once there, he found that he couldn't get off.

The unliving horse hurtled forward, across the blighted field. Joey twisted to peer wretchedly back at his family. After a moment, all he could see were two sparks gleaming in the murk. Then his mount plunged into a hollow full of petrified pines, and even the wavering points of light were gone.

Joey awoke screaming and thrashing, with George and Elaine crouched over him, and the other members of the expedition, eleven souls in all, looking on. "It's all right!" said George. "You were having a nightmare."

Joey took a deep breath. Sometimes the gesture steadied him. "Yeah. I'm okay." He noticed that the metal floor beneath him had stopped vibrating. Evidently their transportation, a semi loaded with microwave ovens, had stopped. "Are we getting off?"

"Yes," said Elaine. "I think we might be close."

"Terrific," he said sardonically. In the days since they'd fled Salt Lake City, he'd decided that Elaine's crystal key wasn't exactly the last word in navigation. If Artie's theory was right, it was guiding them to a Nihil, which would open on a Byway through the Tempest, taking them to the place Elaine called Heaven. But the globe couldn't tell her where the opening was. It just enabled her to sense, vaguely and intermittently, in which direction it lay.

That had made catching rides cross-country a time-consuming, frustrating business. The travelers kept having to jump from moving vehicles when Elaine abruptly declared they were heading the wrong way.

The travelers began to rise, gather their belongings, and step through the side of the trailer. In a moment, Joey and Elaine were the only ones left. He got up, shackles clinking, made sure that the collapsed baton was still in his pocket, picked up the suitcase that George had left for him to carry, and started to follow the others.

"Wait," said Elaine.

He turned back around.

She hesitated, as if hoping he'd speak, then said, "I saw the end of your dream. I didn't mean to. Sometimes you can't help seeing."

Joey grimaced. "I know. Don't worry about it."

"It's obvious what it meant. I'm sorry that George is making you come along. I mean, I want you here. But I'd rather take my chances without you, and feel that we're still on good terms, then drag you along and know that you resent me."

He didn't know what to say. He didn't resent her. Not at all. But every time he looked at her, he remembered he was abandoning Sarah, and something inside him twisted.

"I'll tell you what," she continued. "I'll tell George that he can't come unless he frees you. How about that?"

Now it was Joey's turn to hesitate. Finally, he said, "No. He wouldn't go into the Tempest without me along as his bodyguard. And then he'd make damn sure I never got to Frisco, just for spite."

"Are you sure?" she asked.

"Yeah." Actually, he wasn't. At that moment, he wasn't certain what he thought, or exactly why he'd said what he had. He just knew he didn't want to talk about it anymore. "Come on. Everybody's waiting." He jumped through the side of the truck.

He landed on tarmac. Carpetbag in hand, Elaine hopped down beside him. Joey looked around.

They'd boarded the truck in the afternoon, but now the sky was dark. Their unwitting chauffeur, who'd already wandered off somewhere, had backed the vehicle up to the crumbling concrete loading dock of what appeared to be a warehouse. A lone yellow bulb shone dimly above the door. Black, square-edged masses, probably other commercial buildings, rose on either side.

The travelers had spread out and were rubbernecking. "Anybody have a clue where we are?" asked Rick, twirling one of his juggling knives in his fingers.

Nadia, one of the actresses, said, "Somewhere on the gulf." As soon as she mentioned it, Joey smelled saltwater, and heard the murmur of surf.

Artie straightened his candy-striped blazer. "I think we're on an island. When I peeked out of the truck a few minutes ago, we were going over a bridge."

If this was an island, and the crystal ball actually knew where it was going, then Elaine was right. Unless the Nihil was underwater, in which case it might be miles offshore, they really must be close. Joey couldn't help feeling excited at the prospect of finding their objective, even though he didn't want to go through the thing. He looked at the illusionist. "Which way?"

"I'll try to find out." She took the globe out of the carpetbag, cradled it in her hands, and stared into it. Waves of gold and purple pulsed through the crystal, painting her face with ripples of colored light. Eventually, she led her companions toward the battered chain-link fence at the back of the lot.

-TWENTY-FIVE-

Holliday watched Ambrose Shelley studying his cards. The strange eyes behind the mercenary leader's feathery black mask, one silvery and faceted like an insect's, the other yellow, with an oblong pupil, narrowed.

Holliday wondered idly if Shelley imagined that his false face gave him an advantage. It didn't. Holliday had already spotted his tell, just as he had the tells of the four other hired toughs seated at the table. Shelley's head invariably craned forward a fraction of an inch when he drew a good hand.

Holliday and his associates, wraith and mortal, had set up shop in a penthouse suite with cafe au lait-colored furniture and reddish-brown carpet and drapes. Snoring sounded from two of the bedrooms. Roger Weiss, a handsome, rawboned man who looked a little like Wyatt Earp, sat babbling into a cordless phone about "focus groups" and "market share." His hair, pomaded and dyed raven black, gleamed as if shellacked. He was wearing a gold shirt, a pastel-yellow, double-breasted suit, and a matching tie. An ashtray full of half-smoked butts and a tumbler of bourbon sat on the table beside him. The smell of the liquor made Holliday crave a drink, just a little, even after all these years.

Withdrawn as usual, bald and blubbery as an enormous infant, Milo Waxman sat slumped by the window, staring out at the night. Even with his fat ass in a chair, he wheezed. Occasionally, he glanced surreptitiously in the wraiths' direction. Since he was Weiss's staff psychic, he could see and hear them as clearly as he could his Quick employer, but for some reason he preferred to pretend otherwise.

Suddenly Milo let out a squeal.

Weiss gave a start. "What's wrong?"

"She's in the city," said the psychic.

Holliday stood up.

Weiss hung up the phone, rose, and peered about. "Dr. Holliday? Are you here?"

The shooter shifted himself across the Shroud. Weiss lurched backward. "Of course," said Holliday. "I told you I'd hang around."

"I wish you wouldn't do that," said Weiss.

Holliday pushed his new blue spectacles up his nose. He'd bought them, and another duster, at a market during his layover in Dallas. Fortunately, since many inhabitants of the Shadowlands had lived during the nineteenth century, and many younger ones considered tinted glasses an indispensable accouterment of style, neither item had been hard to find. "What did you want me to do, go out in the hall, materialize, and knock? What would be the point of that?"

"None, I suppose." The sudden pallor in Weiss's face dissolved into pink blotches. He took the gold handkerchief out of his breast pocket and dabbed at his hairline. Holliday wouldn't have been surprised to see drops of dye-stained sweat ooze down his forehead.

Weiss was a preacher, mainly on cable TV, where he sold divine blessings like a medicine-show drummer hawking patent elixir. In Holliday's judgment, the mortal was about as covetous and lustful a sinner as had ever come down the pike. But Weiss never questioned the validity of his beliefs, including the notion that he was God's particular pet, and somehow this irrational faith lent him certain powers. He used them to wage war against the Restless, whom he considered demons. Frequently he performed with cameras rolling, and for a substantial donation.

Holliday had run into him in St. Louis, where the clergyman had been striving to exorcise a derelict apartment house, so it could be razed without the interference of the spirits who dwelled inside. Unfortunately for Weiss, a couple of the occupants wielded powers as formidable as his own. He was losing the battle, with a pack of tabloid journalists looking on.

At first, Holliday had watched the struggle out of curiosity. But eventually, his preference for working alone notwithstanding, he'd realized that someday it might prove useful to have a bona fide mortal exorcist beholden to him, particularly one with millions of dollars and an extensive organization at his disposal. He'd appeared to Weiss and offered an alliance.

His back to the wall, the minister had accepted the offer. Working together, the two new partners had cleaned out the building in short order. The bounty hunter had helped Weiss on three occasions since, but he still made his mortal partner as nervous as a cat. That was because, despite Holliday's assurances to the contrary, Weiss took the shooter's presence as a guilt-provoking reminder that he had forged a pact with a minion of the devil.

Holliday turned to Milo. The psychic quivered in his chair. "Are you sure you're picking up Elaine Forrester?" the bounty hunter asked.

Milo nodded. His jowls wobbled.

"Good. Then get over to the map and show us where she is."

Milo struggled out of his seat and waddled to the worktable. His plump, rosy mouth going slack, he stared at the chart for half a minute. Finally he jabbed a stubby sausage of a finger at it. "There, more or less. Moving east."

"Thank you," said Holliday. He glanced at Weiss, making sure the mortal was paying attention, then pointed at the map himself. "I'm here, you're here, Hall's here, and Frink's here. We do it just the way we planned." He started to slip back into the Shadowlands, then realized that Weiss was staring at him uncertainly. "Is there a problem?"

Weiss shook his head. "I just never thought it would come to this. Somehow I never really believed I'd wind up doing something because *you* told me to."

"You never thought I'd call in the debt? Come on, you're smarter than that. Hell, I'm just asking you to chase a spook. You live for that anyway."

"But how do I know what the consequences will be? Solomon forced unclean spirits to build the Temple of Jerusalem, and God smiled. But if he'd permitted the demons to command him, that would have been an abomination."

"We don't have time for this." Holliday stared the preacher in the eye. "Keep your word like a man, and you can count on my help in the future, just like always. Balk, and you can fight me, here and now. And I believe you know who'll win."

After a moment, Weiss lowered his gaze. "All right. But not because I'm afraid of you. Because our association helps me do the Lord's work."

"Sure," said Holliday. "Wake up your people." Turning, he stepped back across the Shroud.

Shelley was adjusting his khaki combat belt. Clipped among the pouches was a soulfire-powered radio. His men had them, too. Aside from their reputation for cold-blooded efficiency, that was the principal reason Holliday had engaged them. Since they were going to split up into teams, they'd need radios to coordinate their operations.

"For a second, I thought he was going to wimp out on

you," the mercenary leader said.

Holiday snorted. "Not likely. You know the plan, too. Weiss, his two assistant Biblethumpers, and Milo all get protection from Elaine's people. Except for Milo, the mortals won't even know your people are there, so don't expect them to work with you. It won't be pleasant duty, but if your boys stay behind them, they'll be out of the worst of the fireworks."

"Got it," said Shelley. He loosened his darksteel shortsword in its scabbard, then picked up his crossbow and quiver, which were on the wet bar.

"I don't know how many performers came with Miss Forrester. Surely not all, but quite possibly enough to outnumber any one team of your men."

"The more the merrier," Shelley said. "I hear there's a Thrall shortage in Houston. Talk about your golden opportunities." Holliday had told the mercenary that he only wanted Elaine. Shelly and his men could keep anyone else they could catch, to sell into bondage.

The bounty hunter frowned. "Don't underestimate these people. They're tough."

"Maybe," said Shelley, sighting down the crossbow, "but we're professionals. As long as your tame Holy Rollers hold up their end, little Miss Forrester doesn't stand a chance."

-TWENTY-SIX-

For a few blocks, Joey enjoyed the walk. He liked the soft glow of the gaslights, the horse-drawn carriage that clip-clopped by, the salty, slightly fishy smell of the cool sea breeze, and the old-fashioned stores and restaurants, even though Artie sneered and called them tourist traps. For once, nothing looked dirty or broken.

Soon, however, Elaine stopped, glanced around, and took the key out of her carpetbag. She stared into it, and it turned a deep green that reminded Joey of pine trees. "This way," the illusionist said, and led her companions down a side street.

The old shops gave way to old houses, but these were dilapidated to the point of collapse. Trash littered the street, and the yards were overgrown. Jagged Nihil cracks cut through everything, and a rotten stink hung in the air....

Tugging on the straps of his backpack, Chris peered up and down the street. "This place looks like it's been stepped on," he said.

"A hurricane pretty much flattened all of Galveston back in 1900," Artie answered. "Maybe there are areas that nobody ever cleaned up."

A flicker of aura appeared in one of the broken windows

on the left. A stooped old man in an undershirt, pants, and suspenders peeked out at them. Kim waved, and the stranger ducked out of sight.

"Look, Artie," said Chris, lowering his voice, "there's something I've been meaning to ask you."

Artie nodded. "I've been expecting it. When a husband and wife decide they want a baby—"

"Be serious for a minute. You're a Transcendentalist—"

"Say it louder. There might be a couple Hierarchs up in the panhandle who didn't hear you."

"—so how do you really feel about taking Elaine to her church's Far Shore? When she gets there, they'll declare her a Saint, won't they?"

The gleam in Artie's eyes indicated that he'd thought of another smart answer, but then he sighed and let it go unspoken. He glanced at the head of the procession, where Elaine stood gazing into the key, seemingly oblivious to her surroundings. "The way I see it," the comic said, "just because I think Elaine's religion is bunk doesn't mean it isn't useful. If it teaches people to love, be brave, and forgive, maybe it prepares them for Transcendence."

Gasping, Elaine fell to her knees, the key tumbling to the sidewalk.

Everyone clustered around her. "What's wrong?" Joey asked. The boxer's manacles rattled as he knelt beside her.

"I don't know," whimpered George. "I feel sick. Afraid."

"Maybe we should turn around," said George. "Perhaps we're heading into something toxic."

"Let's go back a ways and see what happens," said Joey, taking Elaine in his arms and standing up.

After several steps, Joey's stomach began to churn and ache. He started to feel afraid, not just for Elaine, but for himself. Looking around, he saw that his companions all felt the same way, though no one else had been hit as hard as their leader.

"You were wrong," said Joey to George. "It isn't ahead. It's behind us."

"But what is it?" said Chris. "Spectres?"

"I don't know," said George. "I've never felt anything like it."

Seeing the growing panic in the faces of his companions, Joey realized that with Elaine incapacitated, someone needed to take command. "You guys can figure it out while we move," he said, turning again.

As they trotted along, the sickness and fear faded, but not completely. They nipped at the travelers' backs like a pack of wild dogs. The group quickened its pace, trying to escape the unpleasant sensations altogether, some even dropping their baggage in an effort to increase their speed.

Then George stopped dead in his tracks. "Oh, no!" he said.

"What?" said Joey.

George turned, the skirt of his grimy trench coat flapping around his skinny, yellow-clad legs. "It just occurred to me. We feel like we're being pursued, but what if we're being *herded?*"

"That," said Artie, "is a very sharp guess, especially for a weasel of your ilk. Let's see if we can move off at a right angle."

They turned and hurried toward a sagging, three-story house with dormer windows and a shingleless, triple-pitched roof. Now Joey felt the sickness and anxiety scratching and shoving at his right side.

At first, he couldn't feel any comparable pressure ahead. Then, as they trotted into the next street, a slender blond wraith in an emerald necklace and a fancy green dress stumbled through the clapboard wall of a dilapidated house on the other side. "What is it?" she wailed. "What's happening?"

"We don't know!" yelled Chris. The woman melted back through the warped and decaying wood.

CARAVAN OF SHADOWS

A second later, Joey felt the sickness and the fear jabbing him in the face. Kim sobbed.

Still cradled in Joey's arms, Elaine thrashed, then stopped moving altogether. Her arms and legs dangled as limply as a rag doll's. Her eyes were open, but showed only white. They'd rolled up. Then, to Joey's horror, her flesh began to steam, as if she were melting away.

Kim looked up at him. "Do something!" she cried.

"We will," Joey said. He looked at Artie. "We could try the other way."

"Let's not waste the time," the comedian said. "If it's true that we're being driven, and I think it is, there'll be a force shoving from that direction, too."

"So do we go where it wants, or try to break out of the box?"

"We escape," said Artie. The others muttered in agreement. "But which way?"

"Look at how we're drifting," said Joey. "The whole group has been edging to the left! It seems like the power pushing from the right is stronger than the one in front of us."

"An unwarranted assumption," said George. "It may well be that the source to the right is simply closer."

The fighter scowled. "Okay, Einstein, what direction do you want to go?"

George blinked. "I, ah, don't know."

"At least if we keep on this way, we won't be heading directly away from the entrance to the Tempest," Artie said.

"That makes sense," said Joey. "Let's go."

They hurried on, past ruined houses, twisted, leafless trees, and narrow, crooked lanes full of potholes, which in some cases were also glinting, hissing Nihils. The sickness and fear became worse and worse. People cried, retched, and staggered from side to side. Then, suddenly, a white light appeared ahead, to the left.

"Hold it," Joey said. Everyone stumbled to a halt. "I'm

going to find out what that glow is." He placed Elaine in Chris's arms. "And I want to lose the chain." George waved his hand, and the gray iron links between the fighter's bracelets disappeared.

Joey took his baton out of his pocket, pulled it to its full length, then, using the ruined houses for cover, crept toward the glow.

The fear and sickness grew worse and worse. His skin began to smoke. Finally he drew close enough to see that the glow was a car's headlights. A man in a suit, a mortal by the way he was sweating, stood beside the vehicle, waving a book around. He was yelling about Elaine, about "driving her forth," "commanding her by the power of Jesus Christ," and "sinking her in the lake of fire." Joey surmised that that was why she was sicker than her companions.

Joey turned and skulked back to his friends. "What did you see?" asked Artie.

Joey told them. "I got the feeling that the mortal's raving along with somebody else he hears coming over his radio headset," he concluded.

"The man's probably an exorcist," said Artie. "One of a team, apparently. They've raised the same force they use to chase ghosts out of their homes."

"Who are these clowns," asked Chris, "and why are they picking on Elaine? How do they even know she's here? We didn't know where we were until a few minutes ago."

"Let's ponder those questions later," said George. "It's conceivable that the force the exorcists have raised weakens with distance. If so, perhaps by giving the mortals themselves a wide berth, we can find a weak spot in the fence. A place where we can break through."

"Sounds like a plan to me," said Artie, "especially since I don't have any other ideas. Let's get ourselves out of this torture chamber."

Swinging well to the exorcist's left, the travelers drove

forward. Terror and sickness hammered them from two sides, growing stronger with every second. Their vision blurred, they kept tripping, and their skin steamed and itched. Elaine's body gave off a thick plume of vapor.

Finally, Joey croaked, "Stop. We aren't going to make it. Even the weakest part of the fence is too strong. And even if the rest of us get through, I'm scared it will destroy Elaine."

With shaking hands, George wiped his eyes, as if they were streaming tears. "We can't stay put, either. Eventually the power will drive us mad, or grind us away to nothing. We'll have to go into the snare."

"Maybe not," said Joey. "Everybody, fall back." The travelers began to blunder back the way they'd come, and the psychic pressure eased slightly. The boxer moved to Kim's side. "Sweetheart, I think you're our one chance."

"Me?" She gaped.

"You're the only one who can shut the exorcist up. No one else could get close enough. But you and I will go as near as we can stand, and then you'll zap the guy with your voice. Give him a taste of his own medicine. Okay?"

She swallowed. "I'll try."

He smiled. "Good girl."

"Are you sure this is a good idea?" George asked.

"Do you have a better one?" Joey replied.

George grimaced. "No."

"Then I'm as sure as I need to be," the boxer said. He and Kim started toward the light.

Joey instinctively led her from one patch of cover to the next, as if that could blunt the edge of the mortal's power. But it didn't. He shuddered, and his body smoked and charred.

Kim fell. She tried to stand, but at that moment, she was too weak. His face twitching, Joey picked her up and staggered on with her, deeper into the sickness and fear.

The white light grew impossibly big and bright. Joey

realized it couldn't be just the headlights anymore. Up close, the exorcist's power was visible. Squinting, Joey could just make out the shape of a huge cross, floating over the mortal's head in the heart of the glare.

Joey stopped behind a blighted tree a few yards from their tormentor. He set Kim down, swayed, and clutched at a gnarled branch for support. "This is as close as I can get," he croaked. "Let the jerk have it."

Kim took a ragged breath, then tried to wail.

Nothing came out but a wheeze.

She tried again. Still nothing.

"Come on," said Joey. "I know you can do it."

She tried again and again, but still, nothing happened. "I *can't* do it!" she moaned.

Joey slapped her.

Stunned, she stared at him, and he glared back. "You promised we could count on you," he snarled. "You said you could be an adult, not a helpless little baby. Don't you *dare* let everybody down!"

Kim struggled again to sing. This time, the music came. Her voice rose in a grating, quavering imitation of a barghest's howl.

For a while, Joey was afraid it wouldn't work, that Kim's nerve and last bit of strength would fail before anything happened. Or that the man's headphones would block out the sound of her voice. But finally, the exorcist's ranting faltered, and the glare dimmed.

"Yes!" said Joey. "You've got him! Put him away!"

Kim howled even louder, giving it everything she had. The glow in the air blinked out, leaving only the headlights. The psychic pressure in front of Joey disappeared. Dropping the book, the exorcist screamed, tore off his headset, clutched his ears, and fell to the sidewalk.

Kim's legs folded. Joey clumsily caught her and held her up. "That was great," he said. "I'm sorry I hit you." A crossbow bolt with a darksteel point streaked out of the darkness. He scooped her up and leaped sideways. The arrow whizzed through the space where'd they'd been standing.

Peering, Joey glimpsed several masked wraiths advancing with weapons raised. Still carrying Kim, he dove through a wall and into a dilapidated home. Much of the roof and upper story of the house had collapsed, filling the ground floor with debris. Stars burned in the opening overhead.

Joey fell down. "Run," he whispered. "I can't protect you. I'm still too weak from the exorcism."

Kim tried to clamber up, barely making it. "I don't think I can go fast enough to get away."

"Damn!" He crawled to the window, peeked out, and saw the armed ghosts stalking toward the house. Clutching his baton, he tried to invoke the power of the voice. "Come on!" he said. "Make me strong!" Nothing happened.

Then footsteps pounded the ground. The attacking wraiths pivoted. To get a better view of what was happening, Joey stuck his face through the wall.

The members of the caravan, except for Elaine, who was nowhere in sight, charged the crossbowmen. The strangers shot at them. Three of the performers dropped. Waves of black light pulsed through two of them, and then their bodies disappeared.

The travelers who were able raced on. The enemy wraiths coolly set aside their crossbows and drew their swords. Though slightly outnumbered, the strangers had better weapons, and obviously knew how to use them. Joey was terrified that his friends wouldn't be able to beat them.

Then the voice sent a surge of inhuman might through his muscles. He'd only needed a moment for the power to kick in, and his companions had bought it for him. He sprang to his feet, dashed through the wall and on across the Nihil-cracked ground, faster than any living athlete could run.

Two of the masked wraiths turned to face him. It didn't matter. He hurtled into them like a lightning bolt, laid out each with a single blow, and plunged deeper into the battle.

The rest of the fight only took a few seconds, as he smashed down one attacker after another. Then, abruptly, he and his companions were the only ones standing.

Kim stumbled out to join them. George ran to her. "Are you okay?" he asked.

"Yes," she said.

"I'll get Elaine," said Chris, his hands flowing back into their usual shape. He loped into the darkness.

"Can everybody walk?" asked Joey.

"Everyone who isn't dead," murmured one of the dancers sadly.

"Good," said Joey. "Let's gather up some weapons, and anything else that looks useful, as fast as we can."

By the time they had, Chris and Elaine were back. She'd awakened, though the flesh sculptor was still carrying her.

Artie buckled a sword belt around his narrow waist. It looked peculiar on top of his red and white-striped coat. "Okay, folks," he said. "Judging by the squirming in our guts and the pressure in our nonexistent bladders, there's at least one more exorcist still praying against us. My guess is, there's a minimum of two, and if the chump Kim just KO'd had spirit bodyguards, chances are, the others do, also. In other words, chewed up as we already are, we'd better get where we're going pronto, before somebody else bushwhacks us." The carpetbag was sitting on the ground beside him. He took out the key and gave it to Elaine. The globe shone blue and silver upon her touch. "That's where you come in, my little bundle of marzipan. You've got to plug your mind into this gimcrack like never before. Lead us straight to the right Nihil."

She stared at him. "What makes you think I can? I feel awful. What if the direction I pick takes us right where the enemy wanted us to go? Look, it's me they're after. The rest of you, leave me, and you'll be all right."

"I—" George began, then hesitated, like he didn't know what he really wanted to say.

"You're wasting precious time," said Artie. "Nobody's going to ditch you, so get to work."

She grimaced. "All right." She stared into the key. The blue and silver glow turned to whirling golden sparks.

-TWENTY-SEVEN-

Holliday and his team had hidden themselves in three derelict brownstone tenements at the end of a dead-end street. Since ghosts could pass through solid objects, the cul-de-sac wouldn't box in Elaine Forrester the way it might a living fugitive. But the horseshoe configuration of the buildings would allow the hunters to attack from three sides.

Not that Holliday was particularly worried about holding a tactical advantage. The illusionist and her friends might collapse before they even got there. And if not, surely they'd be too decrepit and demoralized from prolonged exposure to the exorcism to put up much of a fight.

Sitting with Shelley behind a fourth-story lancet window, Holliday surveyed the empty street. Abruptly, the mercenary leader's radio crackled. "This is Rodriguez," said the voice on the other end. "Our Bible banger's down. That singer kid Holliday told us about freaked him out with her voice."

Frowning, Holliday wondered how this incompetent had missed spotting Kimberly until it was too late. "Who else do you see?" Shelley said.

"Just the slave."

"Hm." Shelley fingered one of the feathers projecting from his asymmetrical mask. "I wonder if the group split up. I take it that the kid and the Thrall don't see you."

"It doesn't look like it."

"Well, I hate to throw good merchandise away, but maybe you'd better kill them before they do any more damage. They're supposed to be two of the dangerous ones. Call back when it's done."

Rodriguez said, "We're on it."

Holliday didn't have an exorcist in his squad. Since the whole idea was to drive the fugitives toward his position, he didn't need one. But he did have a Skinlands radio, to keep tabs on Weiss and his assistants. He shifted himself across the Shroud and grabbed the apparatus off the filthy wooden floor. "Milo!" he said.

After a moment, the psychic stammered, "Yes?"

"The enemy knocked out Frink."

"Oh, my Lord! I knew it! I felt it! Is he all right?"

"I don't know. Even if he's not, you'll have to sort him out later. Right now, his side of the barrier is gone. Can Weiss take up the slack?"

"I wouldn't think so, not from here. Perhaps not at—"

"Then put him in the car and move him. Radio the other exorcist and tell him to move closer, too."

"I don't know if they'll be able to continue the exorcism properly while they're riding."

"They'll have to do the best they can. You get me a current fix on Miss Forrester."

"I lost her a few minutes ago. I can't guarantee—"

"Stop arguing and do what I tell you!" Holliday snarled.

Milo swallowed audibly. "Okay." The bounty hunter allowed himself to sink back into the Shadowlands.

After three more minutes, Shelley lifted his own radio. "Rodriguez. Talk to me, Rodriguez." No one answered. "Damn it! Something's happened to them."

"Thank god for professionalism," said Holliday bitterly. He jumped back into the mortal world and picked up his radio again. "Milo! Forget the exorcism. By now, the rabbits are out of the trap. All that matters is finding Miss Forrester." He made his voice as cold and ominous as he could. "*Don't* let me down."

"I, I won't!" Milo stuttered. Five minutes of silence crawled by. Holliday wondered if he'd scared the fat man too severely. Maybe the mortal had decided to run away. He would have spoken again, to find out, except that, if the sensitive *was* on the job, he didn't want to break his concentration.

Finally, Milo babbled, "I've got her! She's already past you. She swung around to your left. She's going east on Campeachy, just past Cotton Street."

"Right," said Holliday. No longer able to sense Shelley across the Shroud, he looked at the section of floor where he'd last seen him. "You heard that. Get our men on the bus. Radio the other squad to give chase, also."

Holliday sprang to his feet and hurried downstairs. Groping his way through a narrow hall and out the door he'd forced earlier, he emerged into an oblong brick courtyard. Jagged rows of broken gargoyles leered from the roof line. The gray bus Weiss had rented for him sat beside a dry fountain.

By now Holliday had begun to ache from the effort of holding himself in the Skinlands. But since he couldn't carry the radio into the Shadowlands with him, he couldn't let himself slip back across the Shroud until he got the apparatus on the bus. He hurried on board, dropped into the seat nearest the front door, and flowed back into the spirit world.

Until that moment, the carriage, indeed, the entire courtyard, had seemed empty. Now he saw that three mercenaries had boarded the bus ahead of him, and the rest were trotting toward it.

He grimaced in contempt. Considering that he'd had to make his way here like a mortal, *all* the hired hands should have beaten him on board. This kind of lollygagging was part of the reason he preferred to work alone.

The remaining mercenaries scrambled into the carriage. All but Morris, a chunky wraith with dreadlocks who had the power to possess machines. He laid his hands on the nose of the bus, and his body dissolved into the metal. The engine rumbled to life a moment later.

Crossbow in hand, Shelley sat down across from Holliday. "Let's do it," the mercenary said.

"May I assume that you told our driver where we're going?"

Shelley scowled. "Hey, give me a little credit."

The bus rolled through the dark, twisting streets, bouncing over bumps and potholes. As it neared Campeachy Avenue, Holliday started scanning the blackness ahead, looking for a gleam of aural fire. All he saw was shadow.

After a while, his radio hissed. "They're not on Campeachy anymore!" Milo cried. "I see them more or less opposite you, on Ashton, going into a big house with satyrs, centaurs, and nymphs carved in the stonework around the door." He paused. "Dr. Holliday? Do you hear me?"

Holliday didn't have time to answer. The bus was rapidly approaching a cross street. He stood up and pounded the dashboard. "Turn left! And hurry!"

For a moment, he was certain that Morris wouldn't hear him, that this step of the hunt would go wrong like everything else. But then the steering wheel rotated, and the bus sped up.

"Thank you," Holliday said. "Left again at the next corner."

As soon as the vehicle rounded the turn, Holliday spotted the fugitives on the porch of a ruined Italianate house with the decoration Milo had described. The performers were slipping through the recessed door and grimy sandstone facade.

Holliday thrust his upper body through the windshield, pointed his Colt, and fired. One of the men on the porch reeled and vanished in a blaze of black fire. The bounty hunter felt a pang of satisfaction, but it turned to frustration as soon as he discerned that the rest of his potential targets had already made it inside.

"What do they want in the house?" Shelley asked.

"Catch them and you can ask," Holliday replied. He thumped the dashboard with the butt of his revolver. "Faster!"

Morris swerved onto the house's barren lawn, and the bus lurched to a halt in front of the porch. Holliday and the mercenaries leaped through the side of the vehicle and rushed the abandoned dwelling.

Gun at the ready, Holliday led the others through the door. On the other side was a spacious foyer, with flaking, nearly unrecognizable mythological scenes painted on the molded stucco ceiling. The psychic residue of suffering hung in the stagnant air. At the far end of the hall, an arch opened on a shadowy parlor full of drop cloth-shrouded furniture. A hissing sound issued from the right of the entrance.

Holliday lunged through the doorway and toward the noise, which came from a massive fireplace. From the dim blobs of light squirming in its depths, it was clear that the space under the cracked marble mantel was a Nihil.

As soon as he spied it, Holliday was certain that the fugitives had fled inside. Still, he listened, just in case he was wrong. He only heard his own men and the whisper of the Nihil.

He waved his gun at the hearth. "They went this way. Come on."

Behind the black mask, Shelley's mismatched eyes narrowed. "We didn't sign on for the Tempest." Some of his men muttered in agreement.

"You craven sons of bitches!" Holliday said. "They're

only a few seconds ahead of us! We'll catch them and be out again in no time!"

Shelley hesitated, then said, "All right."

Stooping to get under the mantelpiece, Holliday stepped through the portal.

He found himself on a narrow path paved with flags of rough gray stone. Cold gusts of wind swept back and forth, constantly changing direction. Bordering and arching over the trail like the walls and ceiling of a tunnel were expanses of thick, churning, charcoal-colored vapor. Blue and purple flashes, flickering in the depths of the mist like heat lightning, provided the only illumination.

Holliday loped down the passage. Shelley and the others crept along behind him. Rounding a sharp bend, the shooter discovered that the way split into three branches, each of which immediately twisted out of sight.

Hoping to catch the sound of the fugitives' retreat, he listened at the mouth of each tunnel. All he heard was the laughter of the wind. He supposed he could use his cards to divine which way the performers had gone, but it would take too long. Who knew how far ahead they'd be by then, or how many additional forks they'd pass, in the interim? Impossible as it seemed, he'd lost them again.

-TWENTY-EIGHT-

The Tempest.

Joey turned, surveying the island. At least he thought of it as an island, though it would have been just as descriptive to call it a hill inside a cave with walls and a ceiling made of storm clouds. On the island's highest point, a rocky outcropping, sat three weathered, blue-stone pyramids. Below them was a stand of oaks and elms, and a pool of clear water. Artie, who'd apparently heard a lot about the Tempest, said that most likely no one had built the pyramids, nor were the trees and lesser plants truly alive. They were just *here*, parts of the landscape no different than the soil.

Assuming their various timepieces were working properly, the caravan had been traveling the Byways for four days. Most of the time, Elaine's key guided them along cold, claustrophobic paths, with the black fog pressing close on either side. Sometimes, creatures hidden inside the mist screamed, giggled, or gibbered obscene endearments. Periodically the mist thinned enough to provide a glimpse of dilapidated towers, what appeared to be burial mounds, or, once, a colossal beast so hideous that, after they averted their gazes and fled down the trail, no one could remember what it looked like.

Occasionally, though, the way would widen into an oasis similar to the one in which they were currently camped, a kind of miniature, uninhabited Far Shore, where the scenery was more pleasant, and the freezing wind abated. Then, their nerves frazzled from watching out for Spectres and other threats, the travelers would stop to rest, though they always posted guards.

At such times, despite Joey's troubles, he couldn't help feeling a kind of elation. Because here, beyond the Shadowlands, he was *real*. When he walked, the grass gave under his feet. If he pulled on a branch, it bent. Since dirt would stick to him, he had to wash. After a year of being intangible in relation to nearly everything around him, even a coating of grime was a delight. He could see why some spooks were willing to brave the dangers of the Tempest to live in a place like this. Smiling, he picked up a white pebble, savored the cool, smooth hardness of it, then threw it. It cracked against a tree trunk. He ambled on through the perpetual gloom, down the slope toward the pond.

Nearing the water, he heard crying coming from behind an oak. The sound was soft, and kept hiccuping, as if the sufferer was trying to stop, or at least muffle the noise as much as possible, so none of the travelers scattered about the island would hear it.

Holding his shackle chain to keep it from rattling, Joey tiptoed forward and peeked around the tree. Her face in her hands, her halo orange and gray with worry and sadness, Elaine sat hunched on the mossy ground. Her carpetbag, one of the few pieces of luggage to make it out of Galveston, lay beside her.

He squatted and hesitantly touched her shoulder. "Hey," he said, "what's wrong?"

"Nothing," she said. "Go away."

"No way. You wouldn't go away that night you came into my dream, and now it's my turn to bug you. What's the matter? Are you thinking about the people we lost?"

She finally lowered her hands and glared at him. "Of course I am! Four people are *gone*, because of me!"

"I miss them, too," said Joey. "But they knew they were going into danger. They wanted to come anyway, because they cared about you."

"Do you think that makes it better? This stupid trip isn't worth anybody's life."

He struggled for a response. "I don't think you can know that until you get to the end."

"I know because the whole thing is based on my religion."

"It's based on the need to get you to a place of safety."

She waved her hand impatiently. "I know. But the enemy is only hunting me in the first place because I used to be a Saint. We understand that much, even if we don't know what it all means. The refuge we're trying to reach is my church's Far Shore. And that makes me think it's not worth reaching, because my religion's turned out to be a crock. It doesn't teach about the Tempest or the Deathlords, so what good is it?"

"Just because it doesn't tell the *whole* truth, in a way you can understand, doesn't mean there's no truth *to* it."

She sighed. "Maybe. But even if I could regain some faith in the Holy Covenant, I wouldn't have any in myself. I told you that Spectres attacked the troupe before you joined us. What I didn't say was that one of the people they mauled clung to existence for a couple minutes. I tried to heal him. Nothing happened."

"Even when you were breathing, it didn't work all the time, did it? Heck, maybe nobody can heal a dead man."

"And maybe I never really healed anybody, ever."

Joey didn't know what to say.

"And if that's true," she continued, "what will happen if I do make it to Heaven? Everybody there will expect me to play the part of a Saint again, and I can't! Not without belief!"

"Maybe not," Joey said, "but you're one of the smartest,

kindest people I've ever known. God knows what would have become of Kim, or me for that matter, if you hadn't decided to help us. I'm sure your people will make you welcome, even if you're not quite what they expect."

"'God.' I wonder a lot about Him." Her lips quirked upward. "I guess somebody like me would, wouldn't she? Some ghosts believe the whole Underworld is Hell, and we're all here because He's damned us."

Joey brushed a stray strand of hair away from his eye. "Frankly, I don't have a clue about how this place works, or why some souls land here and others don't. But I can't believe that people like you or Kim did anything God would want to punish you for."

"A week ago, I didn't believe it, either. At least, not usually. But the exorcists hurt me with *prayer* and *Bibles*. How could they do that if God hasn't forsaken me?"

"People say that belief, no matter what kind, has power even in the Skinlands. Maybe they were able to blast you just because they thought they could."

Elaine grimaced. "Whereas I don't know what to think about anything."

"Whatever you believe, or can't believe, the rest of us believe in you. We're going to get you through this mess, no matter who gets in our way, or what it all turns out to be about."

She gave him a wan little smile. "Thank you. You're good friends. I don't deserve you."

"You ought to stop talking like that. Someday you might convince somebody. Not me, but someone."

She put her hand on his.

For a moment, a thrill sang up his arm. Then he pictured Emily's face. "Well," he said, "you wanted some time alone." He started to clamber to his feet.

Her fingers took hold of his. Her grip was gentle, tentative, but it locked him in place. "I don't anymore." She hesitated. "I mean, unless you do."

He felt something give way inside him. With mingled joy and guilt, awkwardly, because of the chain, he put his arms around her.

-TWENTY-NINE-

Galveston.

Holliday stepped through the back wall of a shabby seafood restaurant and found himself in the kitchen. Pots bubbled, the griddle sizzled, and the stink of half-spoiled fish, laced with the metallic tang of the pollutants they'd ingested, hung in the muggy air. The linoleum was humped and stained, the counter tops scarred and grimy, and voices babbled out in the dining area.

He walked past the cook, a squat bulldog of a man, and on around a corner. There he discovered a phone, and although he wasn't looking forward to making this call, he supposed he owed Clement Purvis a report.

He slipped across the Shroud. For once, emerging into the living world didn't make his surroundings look any cleaner. He picked up the phone and started to dial, when he heard heavy footsteps, and smelled tobacco smoke. Frowning in annoyance, he turned.

The cook lumbered around the corner. His bloodshot eyes widening, he stopped abruptly. After looking Holliday up and down, he sneered. "Who are you supposed to be, Maverick?"

Holliday didn't understand the reference. He suspected

it was an insult, but perhaps that was because he was in a bad mood. Staring the mortal in the eye, he said, "I'm the man who's borrowing your phone."

"I can see that," the living man said. "The only trouble is—" His ruddy face turned a shade paler. He shivered almost imperceptibly, dislodging flakes of ash from the tip of his cigarette. "The hell with it." He disappeared back around the corner.

Holliday reflected wryly that it was too bad the mortal hadn't forced the issue. His demise at the shooter's hands could only improve the health of the city at large. He finished dialing.

Tonight Purvis had the high, clear voice of a little boy. But his tone was sullen, as if the child in question had been switched and sent to bed without supper. "About time you checked in," he said. "Are you in Little Rock? I guess you can bring the Heretic on in, although I don't know why I should have to be the one—"

"Be quiet and listen," Holliday said. "I don't have Miss Forrester. I found her again, but she and her friends escaped into the Tempest. Evidently I was wrong about her ignorance. She must at least know how to find her particular Far Shore, and is probably heading there now."

For a few seconds, Purvis was silent. Then he started chortling. Holliday's fist tightened on the receiver.

"I'm sorry," gasped the governor between giggles. "I'm sorry. It's just that I told the Laughing Lady you were about to catch the girl. I'm going to look so silly!" He laughed some more.

If Purvis had been in communication with the Laughing Lady, he must have some mystical telegraph or telephone link with Stygia. Holliday filed the fact away for future reference. He couldn't imagine what good it would ever do him, but he hadn't prospered as long as he had by ignoring any intelligence that came his way. "No, you won't. I am going to catch her. I guarantee it."

Purvis's tone shifted again. For once, he sounded rational and appropriate. "I trust you, Doc, you know that, but are you sure you can handle this one? You haven't gotten a break yet, and unless I'm mistaken, you don't have a lot of experience in the Byways."

"I'm telling you, I'll get her, no matter what it takes." He meant it, too. His pride demanded no less.

"Okay, then. The Lady told me that Danziger has decided that if we can take the illusionist alive, he wants her."

Holliday blinked. "I thought the whole point of the exercise was to keep her away from him."

"He doesn't want her showing up of her own free will, able to make trouble." Purvis's momentary calmness started to crumble. An antic quality crept into his voice. "I guess he thinks it would be a hoot to have her groveling in chains at the foot of his throne." He tittered. "The point is, if you catch her deep in the Tempest, you might as well take her on to him."

"He'll pay the bounty?"

"Yes!" the Hierarch snarled. "Do you think—"

Holliday hung up and slipped back into the Shadowlands. Adjusting his slouch hat and blue glasses, he ambled through the wall and turned left.

The seafood restaurant was just outside the ruined part of town. It didn't take him long to reach the house of the nymphs and satyrs. He melted through the door, strode on into the parlor, and took up a position in front of the seething fireplace. He transferred his derringer to his duster pocket, ensuring instant access to each of his weapons.

Holliday was indifferent to the ideological and political squabbles that divided the Underworld, and generally sold his services to the Hierarchs simply because they were on top. Working on their behalf was both more convenient and more profitable than hiring out to any of their rivals.

But despite his conviction that when push came to

shove, *all* spirits were venal and treacherous, he always hesitated before dealing with Spectres. But sometimes he didn't have a choice. Now that Miss Forrester had vanished into the Tempest, only its inhabitants were likely to be much help in tracking her down.

This being the case, Holliday spread his arms and began the incantation that would call on the Spectres. Though he wasn't speaking loudly, the grating words, jumbles of too many consonants and too few vowels, seemed to echo through the derelict home. He had no idea what they meant, only that they hurt his throat and ears.

The whole chant took five minutes, but he'd known Spectres to answer before it was finished. He watched the Nihil carefully. Nothing stirred inside it, nothing but the usual squirming flecks of phosphorescence.

Raising his voice, he bellowed and croaked through the final lines. Still, nothing happened.

The attempted magic left him weary, as if he'd been jumping back and forth across the Shroud, or flinging Skinlands objects around by force of will. His shoulders slumped, and he glared at the gate in frustration. He'd been trying for days now. "Why don't the Spectres respond?" Holliday muttered. "The spell always worked before."

A pleasant baritone voice said, "Perhaps we didn't want you to take us for granted."

The blackness inside the Nihil seemed to explode into fragments, which hurtled out of the fireplace onto the filthy parquet floor. Some of the figures swarming out were vague blurs of shadow, while others had forms as distinct as Holliday's own. Some looked like ordinary people, some had the rotten flesh and bare bones of corpses, and others sported horns, beaks, sharklike jaws, and other appendages that diminished their resemblance to *anything* human, living or dead. But they all possessed auras riddled with veins of black, the stigmata of their fealty to the Void.

Despite himself, Holliday took a step backward. His hand twitched toward the Colt in his vest.

"Doc," chided the voice he'd heard before. "Calm down. You're among friends." The speaker emerged from the Nihil. He was thin, well-groomed, and dressed in a handsome gray tuxedo. Surprisingly, given the overall elegance of his appearance, he reeked of a pungent odor similar to the scent of the whores Holliday had known on the frontier. Even in the gloom, his dark green eyes glittered. "Who was it who told you where and how you could buy those wonderful bullets in the first place?"

"You people," Holliday said.

The Spectre smiled. "Well then, there you are." He held out his hand, and the bounty hunter shook it. The newcomer's grip was dry and firm. "My name's Travanti. Are you ready to join us?"

"No."

Travanti shook his head. "Doc, Doc, Doc. Why do you think we always help you? It's because you're virtually one of us already. You chose to be like us when you decided that the wraith Holliday needed to live up to his Skinlands reputation. Well, you have, and everybody knows it. But now that you've proved yourself, isn't it time to move on to bigger and better things? The Shadowlands are a desert. Our realm is grander than you can imagine. Join us and we'll make you a prince."

"Maybe I don't want to be a prince."

"Of course you do. Everyone does. I can't imagine what's holding you back."

"I guess I've just never been much of a joiner."

Some of the other Spectres started to laugh. Travanti raised a manicured hand, and they fell silent instantly.

"All right," said the Spectre leader. "What the hell, there's no rush. We have until the end of time. When you decide to embrace your destiny, we'll be here for you.

Meanwhile, what can we do for you tonight?"

Holliday outlined his situation.

"It sounds straightforward enough," Travanti said. "What will you pay us?"

Holliday shrugged. The Spectres he'd dealt with before had generally wanted payment in the form of slaves, though once they'd asked him to assassinate a Heretical leader. "Souls?"

"Well, of course that's the standard trade, but my little band of wanderers tends to travel light. We had one petitioner who paid us in pain. We gave her her heart's desire, and she let us play with her from moonrise to moonset. After an hour or so, she decided she hadn't made a very good bargain, but still, how does that sound to you?" The other Spectres sniggered and fidgeted.

Holliday's jaw tightened. He reminded himself to mask his anger. "It sounds like a shabby way to treat a future prince."

"You'd be surprised," Travanti said. "When you join us, you'll find that your perspective on pleasure and agony will change. But I admit, I'm only joking. This time, we'll help you for free."

Holliday's eyes narrowed suspiciously. "Why?"

"Three reasons. First, we love you like a wayward brother. Second, Eric Danziger is one of us. I don't mean he's part of my particular tribe. But he *is* a lord of the Tempest, advancing our cause, and I'd be glad to do him a favor if I can."

The Spectre's sea-green eyes glittered. "And third, I know Joey Castelo."

"Who?"

"The black-haired prizefighter you mentioned. I invited him to join us right after his death. He couldn't just say no like a gentleman. He hit me with that rod of his. The scar still aches, even after all these months." He rubbed his cheek, and the skin stretched more than it should have. From the unnatural flexibility, Holliday realized that Travanti was wearing a mask, one so realistic that its maker must have flayed some other spirit's face for the raw materials. He wondered what lay hidden underneath. "And now, thanks to you, I have a chance to pay him back. Coincidence is a wonderful thing."

Holliday couldn't imagine how this particular Spectre had known to answer his call, but he was sure that "coincidence" had had nothing to do with it. "Do you think you can track Miss Forrester?" the bounty hunter asked.

"With the greatest of ease, if she hasn't lost her way. I know where her Far Shore is."

"Good. That only leaves the problem of her lead."

The Spectre smiled. "Which is no problem at all. You mustn't think of the Tempest as some boring piece of solid, three-dimensional earthly real estate. It's more like a four- or five-dimensional cloud in a constant state of flux, and at any given moment, I know all the shortcuts. Don't worry, we'll catch her." He gestured at the fireplace. "Shall we get started? Be careful not to bump your head on the way in."

-THIRTY-

The Tempest.

The fog thinned, giving Joey a murky view of the landscape. To the left of the Byway, backlit by green and violet flashes, rose what appeared to be the broken shells of bombed-out office buildings. To the right, the ground fell away sharply and became a swamp. Gnarled cypress trees, bearded with Spanish moss, leaned over channels of black water. The incongruously frigid wind carried the smell of rotting plants.

Joey found the scenery reasonably creepy. But in the week since he'd entered the Tempest, he'd seen worse. As long as nothing moved, or cried out, he refused to let this particular roadside attraction spook him.

He couldn't imagine taking the Tempest lightly. It was way too weird for that. But now that the caravan had traveled a long way without ever having to defend itself, he'd begun to suspect that the place wasn't *quite* as dangerous as people said. No doubt the Spectres were deadly, but maybe the odds of their actually attacking were slim. Perhaps the eternal storm was so vast that most sections of it were sparsely populated.

The way began to grow dimmer. Joey tried to stifle a pang

of anxiety, reminding himself that sometimes the flickering in the clouds abated, but it never stopped entirely.

Yet this time, suddenly, it did, plunging the caravan into total darkness. Kim squealed. He reached for her blindly, and then a wave of confusion crashed through his mind, wiping coherent thought away.

When the light came back, it was sunlight. Dressed in glasses and a corduroy sports coat with leather patches on the elbows, Joey stood on Castro Street, beside the entrance to a bathhouse. Something hard and heavy weighed down his jacket pocket.

Confused, he ran his fingers through his hair. Hadn't he been somewhere else just a moment ago? He couldn't remember, any more than he understood why he was dressed this way. He'd never owned a corduroy coat, and he had twenty-twenty vision.

As he gazed about in perplexity, a bar with smoked-glass windows caught his eye. Somehow, he sensed that he was supposed to go inside. He shuffled across the street and opened the door. The same vague intuition drew him to a corner table beneath a Tiffany lamp.

A moment later, Emily and Sarah walked in. Much to his surprise, his wife had chopped her hair into a crewcut and bleached it blond. His little girl had on a black Franklin's Gym T-shirt, and was glowering as if she wanted nothing more than to bust some heads.

Joey tried to greet his family with what he hoped would be a warm embrace, but he found himself too dazed and slow to rise from his chair.

As he struggled to move against the will of his body, Emily and Sarah appeared in the seats across from him. The waiter brought three beers and a platter of vegetables and dip.

"I want you to stop harassing me," Emily said, scowling.

Joey blinked at her in bewilderment. "What are you talking about?"

"You know very well," she replied. "The threats. The phone calls. The hate mail. Following me around. All of it."

"I *don't* know," he protested. "Has somebody been phoning the apartment?"

She glared at him. "Come off it, Stan!"

When she called him by someone else's name, a pang of alarm shot through him. He started to recall what was happening here, though the notion that he *could* recall was just as nonsensical as everything else.

This was the day he'd been... shot? Could that possibly be right? Yes, somehow he was reliving the day he'd been injured, only now different actors were playing the major roles. Sarah was himself. Emily was David, the gay surfer type who'd hired him to play bodyguard at a meeting with a jilted, angry ex-lover. And Joey was the guy David was afraid of, the man who wound up putting one bullet in his beloved's heart and two more in the would-be protector's forehead.

But it won't happen this time, Joey thought. I don't have to do it.

He opened his mouth to tell Sarah and Emily to get out of the bar, get out now, they were in danger. Instead he said, "I'm sorry, I'm sorry! It's just that I love you so much." He was helplessly babbling the same apologies and excuses that the killer had given that day.

His hand slipped into his pocket and fingered the gun.

Maybe Sarah could stop him. He stared at her, trying to make her sense that something was wrong. She obviously didn't notice. Slouched in her seat, she looked restless and distracted, the way he had been. Upset and preoccupied because he'd just come from slapping his wife.

Joey felt his hand grip the revolver, his muscles tense. He strained to stay in his chair, but that was just as useless as his previous efforts. He sprang up and pointed the gun at Emily.

She yelped and lurched backward in her chair. The legs squealed on the hardwood floor. Sarah struggled up from her seat — like her predecessor, she'd made the mistake of scooting it too close to the table to get up quickly — snapped a baton to its full length, leaned forward, and struck at his shooting arm.

Knowing that it wasn't meant to be, he still prayed that she'd hit him hard enough to spoil his aim. The club slapped him, and the stinging pain made his hand clench. The gun barked. A red dot appeared in the center of Emily's chest, and she toppled sideways out of her chair. Helplessly, he swung the revolver toward Sarah and shot her twice in the head. She collapsed, cracking her skull against the edge of the table on the way down.

Across the bar, people were shrieking and ducking for cover, but he was only dimly aware of it. Shaking with grief and self-hatred, he stared at the bodies of his family. This was all his fault. It had been his fault *twice*, and he couldn't bear it.

He put the snub-nose gun in his mouth. He wondered vaguely if he was still following the script, if the original killer had committed suicide, too. He'd never bothered to find out. He squeezed the trigger.

The revolver only clicked. Elaine appeared beside him and jerked his arm down. He gaped at her in astonishment.

"This isn't real!" she said. "It's like a dream!" She swung her arm and the bar shattered into nothingness, leaving the Byway standing in its wake.

The place looked different than it had before the lights went out. The rest of the caravan was gone, and thick vapor streamed across the path, from the swamp and into the shattered cityscape. A sickly blue light shone from several upright rectangles standing like doorways along the trail. Joey wondered if the rectangles were some kind of Nihil.

"Are you all right?" asked Elaine. "Is your head clear?"

Joey reflexively took a deep breath. "Yeah."

"I was stuck inside one of these lights, lost in a nightmare. So were you. I think everybody else is, too. We've got to end the dreams fast, before anybody hurts himself."

Inwardly, he winced. He'd only changed a person's dreams once, that last night in Salt Lake City. What if he wasn't up to this job? "I get it," he said.

She squeezed his arm. "Good. See you in a minute." She turned and stepped into one of the blue rectangles. For an instant, as she was passing through, he glimpsed the scene on the other side. Kimberly had shrunk into a frozen, doll-like figure less than a foot tall. She was standing on the edge of a table with her toes hanging over the drop. A fat, grinning man in a yellow windbreaker was about to pitch her over by poking a pencil point into her back.

Joey wanted to dash to her rescue, but he understood that that wasn't the plan. Elaine was going to save Kim, and he was supposed to help somebody else. Scowling, he stepped through a different light.

He found himself on a carnival midway. Roller coasters clattered, and the riders screamed. The amplified voices of the barkers chanted. The scents of fried food and animal waste floated in the air, and the red and yellow lights of a Ferris wheel shone against the night sky.

Curiously, one section of the illusion looked real, but the farther an object was from that area, the less convincing it appeared because of a lack of detail. On the outskirts of the show, the carnies and marks moved stiffly and had no faces, and the writing on the signs was a meaningless scrawl. Beyond the fence at the edge of the lot, the world shone blankly in a gray haze.

At the heart of the illusion was a trailer with the phrases FREAK SHOW, WORLD'S UGLIEST MAN, and SEE NATURE'S CRUELEST JOKE painted along the side. Interspersed with the lines of text were black ovals shaped like faces with red question marks snaking through the centers. Laughter rippled from the entrance and exit.

Joey dug a gray obolus bit out of his jeans pocket and approached the trailer. He wondered if the ticket seller, a bored-looking woman with sun-damaged, leathery skin and nicotine-stained fingers, would take it, but she didn't give it a second glance. Passing a notice warning that the attraction was not recommended for pregnant women, children, or people suffering from heart disease or nervous disorders, he climbed the rusty wrought-iron steps that led inside. The laughter grew louder.

The inside of the trailer was hot and stuffy, rank with the sweaty smell of the crowd. Joey had to shove and elbow his way through the mob to catch even a glimpse of what everyone else was gawking at.

Caged behind a chain-link fence, naked except for a harness of chains and leather that made it impossible for him to retreat to the rear of the enclosure or even turn his back, the freak cowered as best he could. He was both a dwarf and a hunchback. His right arm was too long, and had no fingers. The left was too short, and displayed eight. His genitals were huge, and covered with warts.

And his face was even uglier than his body. The flesh looked wet and raw, as if someone had scraped away the skin. His jaw was crooked, his mouth a puckered hole resembling an anus. His nose was off center, too far to the left, and had only one gaping nostril. Above it was a single eye with two pupils. A bulge of bone distended the right side of his forehead.

For a moment, Joey had no idea who he was looking at. Then he noticed the dwarf's golden hair, and realized that it had to be Chris.

Joey was sure that this dream, like his own, reflected real events. Before death, Chris had been deformed. No wonder he'd wanted to learn shape changing, and chosen to make his customary wraith form ridiculously handsome, Joey thought.

One of the marks yelled, "I bet the lady freaks love him! Look at that pecker! The warts are like French ticklers!" The crowd roared with renewed laughter, and Chris cringed.

Sickened and outraged, Joey tried to wipe the illusion away. Exerting his power, striving to shred the scene into nothingness, he used all the skills that Elaine had taught him.

It didn't work. It wasn't that Salt Lake City had been a fluke, or that he'd forgotten how to channel the magic. He felt the energy flow. But some other force, no doubt the same one that had dumped the travelers into these miniature hells in the first place, deflected it.

Maybe Chris can wake himself up and end his own nightmare, Joey thought. "Chris!" he shouted. At the same instant, the jeering and laughter blared louder. "It's J — Pete, do you know me? Remember, you're a ghost now, this isn't real! Try to snap yourself out of it!"

The freak didn't even turn his head to look at him, either not understanding or not hearing Joey's voice.

Abruptly Chris urinated. The stinking stream rattled on the metal floor. Some of the gawkers cried out in disgust. Many laughed so hard they had to clutch at their neighbors to keep from falling down. The mob lurched back and forth, bouncing Joey around. He almost thought he could feel the trailer rocking.

A darkness, the gathering power of Oblivion, washed through Chris's pasty, blemished skin. Joey understood that though his friend lacked a gun, or even the freedom to use his arms and legs, he too had a way of ending the torture, and he was about to do it.

The realization made him even angrier, intensifying what had been a merely human rage into the sublime fury of the voice. Someone bumped him, knocking him stumbling forward. Snarling, he pivoted, clubbed the offending party, a buxom woman in a Harley-Davidson T-shirt, then knocked down three more people, clearing himself some breathing room. That accomplished, he clenched his will and summoned his power.

The trailer exploded as if he'd set off a bomb. A split-second later, he and Chris were standing on the Byway. The actor had his clothing, gear, and gorgeous body back. Kim goggled at the two of them.

"Stay here," the boxer said. "Keep everybody together." He looked at Kim. "Which rectangle did Elaine go through?"

The little girl pointed. "That one."

"Then I'll take the one beside it." He turned and strode through the blue opening.

He found himself with George, in front of a window. The little man was sobbing, screaming, and hammering on the glass. On the other side was a portion of the Golden Gate Bridge. A crescent moon shone above it, and the vague mass of Alcatraz, dusted with a handful of lights, rose from the black expanse of the San Francisco Bay. Beside the guardrail stood a pale, pretty girl with curly brown hair. She was well-dressed in clothes that reminded Joey of black-and-white Bogart and Edward G. Robinson movies. Judging from the way her stomach bulged, she was pregnant. She was crying brokenly, and clutched a crumpled telegram in her hand.

George yelled, "Beverly, don't! I'm here!" The pregnant girl started to climb over the rail, and then Joey blasted the illusion apart.

He and George appeared back on the Byway. All the rectangles were gone, but two members of the caravan had failed to reappear. Evidently Elaine hadn't been able to rescue them. Without the blue glow, the path was dark, but fortunately, not completely so. Drawing on her powers of illusion, she'd created a floating bubble of silver light.

George looked wildly about, then glared at Joey. "Take me back!" the little man screamed. "There's still time to save her!"

"Don't be stupid," Joey said. A wave of fatigue, the price of using the dream magic, swept through him. He swayed. "She wasn't real. It was a nightmare. A trap."

"I said, *take me back!*"

Joey's manacles turned cold. "I can't!" he said. "That

place doesn't even exist anymore!" His stomach churned, and his knees buckled.

Chris grabbed George, spun him around, and slapped him. The blow cracked like a gunshot. Clearly stunned, the smaller man gaped at him.

"Pull yourself together!" said Chris. "Pete told you the truth. He saved your life. Stop hurting him."

George swallowed. "All right." He waved his hand. Joey's sickness, and some of his weakness, faded.

He clambered to his feet. "Let's move. Get out of this" — he waved the baton at the mist flowing across the path — "and away from the marsh."

"I'm tired," said Elaine. "I don't think I can make light and tap into the key at the same time."

"Don't worry about it," Artie said. "You can navigate us back on course later."

Shuddering, clinging to one another, the travelers scrambled forward. When they finally got clear of the fog, and the flickering in the clouds resumed, Kim started to cry.

-THIRTY-ONE-

Comfortable on a smooth stone shelf that formed a natural chair, his baton and a crossbow beside him, Joey scanned the slope below, watching for flickers of aura. Given the gloom and the profusion of outcroppings and boulders, he suspected that somebody could climb almost all the way to his vantage point before being spotted. Fortunately, he was well hidden within a shadowy notch in the hillside. He was fairly sure that no matter how close an intruder got, he'd at least see the stranger before the stranger noticed him.

Not that he was unduly worried about being attacked. Intuition told him that the thing lurking in the swamp wouldn't leave its lair to pursue escaping prey. And that was just as well. All the travelers desperately needed rest.

They'd kept up a brave front until they'd stumbled on their current refuge, a spot where the Byway widened out enough to contain an actual mountain. This side was barren, but they'd found water, grass, and trees on the other. There was also a huge chessboard with squares made of red and black moss occupying one level stretch of ground, and, scattered about the slope, the cyclopean marble chessmen to go with it. As soon as they decided to camp, people began to fall apart.

Joey guessed that he should have expected it. It was hell to relive painful experiences. When it came right down to it, he'd been hit as hard as anyone. But no matter how upset they all were, *somebody* had to take first watch. And it wasn't too bad. Being alone had helped Joey pull himself together.

He sat in his lofty guard position and drank in a panoramic view of the Tempest. Off to the right, high in the sky, a mass of vapor rotated like a whirlpool. Elsewhere, funnel clouds, darker than the surrounding fog, swayed back and forth. At the moment, most of the heat lightning was blue-green, like the fire in a giant opal.

A shoe scraping on a stone nearby broke Joey's trance. Startled, he jumped, then stuck his head out of the niche and looked up the trail. Expecting to see Artie, who was supposed to take the next watch, Joey was surprised to see George, clambering awkwardly down the path.

Joey's mouth twisted. "What is it?" the boxer asked. "Is everybody all right?"

George said, "I think they will be, given sufficient time. I, ah, just wanted to talk."

"Frankly, I'd rather be by myself. Your company's no big treat even when my nerves aren't shot."

"I want to apologize for hurting you. I was distraught."

"Forget it. The visions made us all nuts."

"And I want to thank you for saving me."

Joey snorted and held out his hands. "If you're really grateful, you know how to show it. Take the chain off."

"Soon," said George. "And when that day arrives, and you share in the bounty we've won, you'll rejoice that the generous Mr. Montaigne didn't dismiss you prematurely."

The wind howled, and chilled Joey's face. The skirt of George's grubby trench coat billowed. Copper-colored lightning flickered inside a cloud bank off to the left of the mountain. "Excuse me if I don't hold my breath."

"If only for the sake of your morale, it's a pity you can't

appreciate young George's acumen. How he honed an already brilliant mind through decades of intensive study. Of philosophy. History. Political science." Abruptly the little man grimaced, as if, for once, he'd grown tired of his own pretensions. "But since you won't, there's no use nattering on about it. He'll wait for events to vindicate his worth." He hesitated. "You learned something very private about me today. I've never told anyone about Beverly."

"I didn't want to poke my nose into your secrets. I just had to go into the nightmare to yank you out. I won't tell anybody what I saw."

"I know that," said George, sitting down on a round gray rock, "and I appreciate it. Now that you know as much as you do, I think I'd like to tell you everything. Perhaps confession will allay the grief the incident has awakened."

Joey frowned. He wasn't sure he wanted George confiding in him as if the two of them were buddies. The little man didn't have the right. But on the other hand, he was curious, and he couldn't help feeling a trace of pity for anyone else who'd been dragged kicking and screaming down memory lane the way he had. "I guess you can tell me if you want to."

"Thank you." George paused, evidently collecting his thoughts. Joey took another look down the mountainside. As far as he could tell, nothing was stirring.

"I believe I've alluded to the fact that I always had trouble fitting in," George continued. "I was born into grinding poverty, but I aspired to be cultured and affluent. Somehow, my efforts to improve myself alienated everyone, of whatever class. People thought I was... peculiar. A sham. A ridiculous upstart, giving myself airs."

"Boy, that's hard to imagine."

George grimaced. "Please, spare me your gibes, at least until the tale is told. This is difficult for me. Because no one liked me, my enterprises never bore fruit. To be candid,

I couldn't even hold a job. But finally, when I'd all but accepted that I was fated to live out my days destitute and alone, I found a position as a clerk in a dockside warehouse. And there I met the one person perceptive enough to discern my merits."

Joey nodded. "Beverly. The boss's daughter?"

George scowled. "It wasn't like that!" He sighed. "Well, to some extent, I suppose it was. Naturally I was delighted that her family had money. But I loved her too. She was beautiful. Gentle. Sensitive. Ethereal as I imagined an angel would be.

"At first, we were deliriously happy. At her urging, her father promoted me. My new salary and her cachet admitted me to the social milieu to which I'd always aspired, and it was every bit as glorious as I'd hoped.

"The problem was that she did come from a prominent family, and her father hadn't realized she was serious about me. Evidently he thought we were just friends, or that I was merely a passing fancy. When he learned that we intended to marry, he forbade her to go through with it. And when she defied him, he turned his powers of persuasion on me.

"He called me into his office and fired me. Then he said that if I continued to see Beverly, he'd cut off her allowance, disinherit her, and use every iota of his influence to ensure that no one else would ever give me a job. On the other hand, if I'd agree to throw her over and never contact her again, he'd pay me a substantial sum. Invested properly, it could grow into a fortune."

"And you took the money."

"Yes. It was the Depression. Even menial work was cruelly hard to come by. I couldn't face the prospect of reverting to the penniless wretch I'd been. But it wasn't only for myself. I was thinking of Bev, also. Sheltered and delicate as she was, I didn't think she could bear the kind of hardship I'd endured."

"You could have asked her. You could also have called her old man's bluff. Didn't it occur to you that when push came to shove, he might not have been able to stand the thought of cutting her off?"

George goggled at him. "No! My god! Is that what you think?"

Joey grimaced. "Hell, I don't know. I never even met the guy. Go on with the story."

"All right." George rubbed his eyes as if they were tearing up. "I sent Bev a telegram breaking things off. I thought that I wouldn't be able to go through with it in person. Then I forsook my apartment for a hotel, so she couldn't find me to talk me out of it.

"What neither her father nor, god forgive me, I realized was just how much she loved me, or that she was carrying my child. When she accepted that I truly was gone forever, she wrote a farewell note, drove out on the Golden Gate, and—" He faltered.

"Jumped," said Joey softly.

George nodded. "When I read about it in the *Chronicle*, I started drinking. Some time after that, I began to gamble. When, weeks later, I sobered up, my money was gone. I spent the rest of my life trying to make more, but nothing ever worked out. It was as if I'd been cursed."

For a moment, Joey felt himself hovering between pity and disgust. Then, as if something had given him a push, he came down squarely on the side of condemnation. "Now that part of the story is *really* sad. My heart bleeds for you."

George flinched. "I didn't mean to imply that that was what I regretted most. The way you miss your own wife and child, you must comprehend how I feel."

Joey's fists clenched. "Don't you dare compare yourself to me. I never wanted to leave Emily and Sarah. I'd give anything to be with them now. You *sold* your girl and kid like a couple of slaves. Hell, you *murdered* them."

"No! Don't you understand, I didn't know what would happen!"

Joey felt himself growing angrier by the second. He had to fight an impulse to get up and slap George around, even though he knew the manacles would cripple him as soon as he tried. "I understand that I was right about you. A guy who'd betray the only person who ever loved him would sell out anyone."

George shook his head. "That isn't so."

"The hell it isn't. In Galveston, when the exorcists were after us, you wanted to ditch Elaine, didn't you?"

"I admit that for a moment, I *considered* it, but only after she herself implored us to do precisely that. I thought it might be our only hope of saving anyone. In the end, I stayed with the rest of you. I didn't even *advocate* abandoning her."

"Only because nobody offered you a bribe."

George lurched to his feet. "That is not true! Mr. Montaigne is a man of honor. He keeps faith with his friends. And as for everyone else, the snobs and the bullies and the ingrates, why shouldn't he dupe them? They deserve it, and his wits are his only means of getting by. This conversation is over. I forbid you—"

"To tell anyone what you told me," said Joey, sneering. "I know the routine. Fortunately, I don't need to tell them. I'm sure they already sense what a bastard you are."

George shuddered, and his halo flared red with fury. He wheeled and disappeared down the trail.

-THIRTY-TWO-

Holliday noticed that the Byway was widening. The black hexagonal stones which had paved the last few miles gave way to the hard-packed earth and pebbles of a wilderness trail. "We're close," Travanti said.

Holliday nodded. He could feel it, too.

Travanti turned to the pack of horrors marching along behind them. "Everyone, move quietly. We've got the girl and her friends outnumbered, but I'd still rather take them by surprise."

The wraiths stalked on. The air grew a little warmer. When the hunters rounded a final bend, what had seemed a kind of tunnel opened into a huge dome with a solitary mountain in the center. Red and purple lightning flickered, glinting from the edges of a jumble of boulders. The trail proper switchbacked up the slope.

"Hold up," Holliday said. "I'm going to scout ahead a little ways."

"Be careful," Travanti replied.

The gunfighter began the ascent. Straining his senses, he glided from one pocket of shadow to the next. The wind howled. Off to the left, a mass of churning clouds took on the shape of a man's face. Until the image began to break up, it was as clear, detailed, and symmetrical as the creation of a master sculptor.

Abruptly Holliday heard a whimper, and something fluttering. He tiptoed on until he spotted Martin Pryor, the little rodent of a man he'd first seen playing catch with Kimberly. His face in his hands, Pryor sat slumped on a rock. His grimy coat flapped in the breeze, and his aura shone gray and brown with sorrow and bitterness.

Holliday wondered if Pryor was supposed to be a sentry, but was too upset to attend to his responsibilities, or if he'd simply wandered away from his companions to snivel in private. Either way, if he was as oblivious to his surroundings as he seemed, it was about to cost him.

Fortunately, this part of the mountain wasn't as steep as many of the stretches above. Holliday could leave the trail. Clambering above it, he slipped around behind Pryor. He clapped one hand over the little man's mouth and pressed a Colt against the side of his neck with the other.

Pryor gave a violent start. His aura blazed orange with fear. "Simmer down," Holliday said. "Don't make me shoot you. Will you behave?"

Pryor nodded. Holliday warily took his hand away from the captive's lips.

Pryor said, "Please—"

"Shut up. We'll talk at the bottom of the hill. Move."

The Spectres had done a good job of concealing themselves. Even Holliday couldn't spot them until he was nearly on top of them. When Pryor caught a glimpse of them, he recoiled. The shooter thought the prisoner might have soiled himself, were the Restless still capable of that particular humiliating reaction. It took two prods from the revolver barrel to make him continue forward.

Manifestly relishing the prisoner's terror, some of the more overtly monstrous Spectres crowded around him. Crooning threats and obscene endearments, they fondled him with tentacles and talons.

"Do you recognize him?" Travanti said.

"Yes," Holliday replied. He looked Pryor in the eye. "Were you on guard duty?"

For a moment, the man in the trench coat quailed, the way people usually did when Holliday gave them an intimidating stare, but then something surprising happened. Pryor drew himself up straight, and most of the orange bled out of his aura, replaced by the shifting, unreadable blend of colors that marked a successful lawyer, or an expert poker player. "If I should decide to assist you, what's in it for me?"

A female Spectre with long, platinum-blond hair and a leprous, noseless face put her arms around him from behind. "A quicker end, darling." Her gray, forked tongue slid into his ear.

Pryor ignored her. Still gazing at Holliday, he said, "If you like, I'll name a price."

"I like your nerve," said Travanti, "but I don't think you understand your situation. It would be nice to know what you can tell us, but we don't really need to know it."

Pryor looked at him. "Are you in charge here?"

The Spectre in the tuxedo hesitated. "Technically, I guess I'm second in command. My followers and I have placed ourselves at Doc's disposal for the duration of the hunt."

"Then with your indulgence, I'll negotiate directly with the commander-in-chief." Pryor's beady eyes shifted back to Holliday. His expression was calm and expectant.

The shooter felt a twinge of admiration. "Whatever you have to sell, don't you think we can torture it out of you?"

"I am a disciple of Zeno. A Stoic. I daresay that at the very least, you'd find it a time-consuming endeavor. And if you did manage to crack my composure, it might prove bothersome to keep my cries from resounding up the mountain."

"I think this is just a stall," said one of the Spectres, a blur of shadow with amber, faintly luminous eyes and the scratchy, querulous voice of a cranky old woman. "I don't believe he can tell us anything worth hearing."

"That's not true," said Pryor, still looking at Holliday. "You'll concede that Miss Forrester and her retinue are a resourceful lot. They have, after all, evaded you twice already."

Holliday shrugged. "I think the third time's going to be the charm."

"I can only applaud your optimism. However, permit me to point out that the terrain gives the caravan — Elaine's people — a considerable advantage. I, alas, was not the sentinel. He's well hidden higher up. Envision what might happen if he spies you before you detect him. He gives the alarm, and the remainder of your climb becomes arduous in the extreme. Shooting from cover, my erstwhile companions pepper you with crossbow bolts. The brawnier members of the opposition roll stones down on your heads. Kimberly assails you with her voice. And while this gallant rearguard fights a holding action, your prize flees down the other face of the mountain and vanishes into the storm."

"Even if she did," said Travanti, "we'd catch up with her again."

"Perhaps so," said Pryor, "but you'd suffer casualties first. And perhaps you wouldn't locate her. Even the wiliest hunter can be thwarted by bad luck. Now imagine how your raid might progress with my assistance. I point out the sentry's position. You silence the man without warning, preventing him from apprising his fellows of your presence. I guide you straight on to their campsite, and you catch them flatfooted, also. A far more satisfactory scenario."

"And afterwards," said Holliday, "we let you go."

The captive smiled. "Bravo. That's quite droll. No, I'm afraid that even an altruistic heart like mine requires a bit more compensation than that. I have a Thrall up there, an insolent, ungrateful brute sorely in need of correction." His aura pulsed red with anger. "I want him back. With my aid, you can take Elaine's companions alive, to sell into bondage. Entertainers ought to fetch a pretty penny, and I expect half. And finally, Doctor, I'd appreciate an introduction to whatever patron you're working for, so I can petition to enter his service also."

"I'm freelance," said Holliday, "but I take your meaning." He turned to Travanti. "What do you think?"

"That he talks a good game," the green-eyed Spectre said, "but if we actually start picking him apart, he'll sing like a nightingale."

"Maybe," said the bounty hunter, "but maybe not. He's already showing us he's got some sand to him. As far as I know, he's not one of the meddlers who came after me in Utah. I don't have a score to settle with him. If he truly can help us, I wouldn't mind making a deal."

Travanti stroked his chin. "And I suppose my people could get along without the fun of destroying him. But can we trust him? I can see his Shadow. It's strong. But that's not an ironclad guarantee that he's willing to sell out his friends."

"But they're not my friends," said Pryor. His aura burned reddish brown with resentment. "I have it on reliable authority that they hold me in contempt. Such being the case, I'd be delighted to switch sides."

"You'd better mean it," said Holliday. "Because if I even suspect you're playing us false, I'll kill you on the spot." He looked at the Spectres surrounding the prisoner.

"Let him go."

Muttering, the hideous ghosts stepped back. Pryor brushed ineffectually at the new stains on his already-filthy coat.

"Tell us about the Heretics," Travanti said.

"Everyone's on the other side of the mountain," said Pryor, "where there's water and vegetation. Everyone but one sentry. He's about three quarters of the way up, stationed in an alcove in the rock." He pointed. "Can you see it?"

Holliday squinted. "Not from here. Let's sneak up to where I can."

He and Pryor started back up the mountain. Travanti and four of his minions followed. Holliday wondered how, without speaking or gesturing, the Spectre chieftain had indicated who was to come along and who was to stay behind.

The party ascended as stealthily as Holliday could have wished. The cold wind rippled his cape and tried to steal his slouch hat. Finally he spotted a narrow gap in the face of the mountain, and the silhouetted figure inside. He never would have noticed it if Pryor hadn't told him where to look. Holliday raised his hand, signaling a halt.

"I see him," Travanti whispered. "Can you plug him from here?"

"Certainly, but his friends might hear it," Holliday said.

One of the Spectres, a gangly, shirtless, teenage boy with brass rings piercing his ears, septum, nipples, and navel, raised a small crossbow with a pistol grip. "Let me do it."

"No," said Pryor. "Our arrangement was that you'd make every effort to take them all alive. For sale."

"A few minutes ago, we were going to torture you to death," Travanti said. "Now you're on the payroll. Don't push it."

"A deal's a deal," Pryor said. He turned to Holliday. "Besides, I doubt that our youthful friend is as good a shot as you, or that he's using projectiles as lethal as your bullets. If the first one fails to dispatch the guard, he'll raise an alarm. Isn't there a more reliable way?"

A gaunt, stooped, hairless Spectre, whose intricately patterned scales reminded Holliday of a diamondback, said, "I can get him." He displayed the undersides of his hands. Suckers pulsed on his palms and elongated fingers.

Holliday nodded. "I'll cover you."

The Spectre dropped on his belly and crawled forward.

The fugitives had chosen their sentry position well. The notch opened in a sheer wall of granite. Except for the trail, there shouldn't have been any way to get near the guard inside. But, so suddenly that Holliday almost missed it, the scaly Spectre sprang to his feet and darted straight up the escarpment. He climbed higher than the guard, scuttled directly over his head, and pounced on him. The two wraiths plunged out of sight. For a moment, Holliday heard them grunting and thrashing around. Then the scaly Spectre rose from the shadows and gave his comrades the high sign.

Holliday looked at the kid with the crossbow. "Run back and fetch everyone else. Then we'll go collect our saint."

-THIRTY-THREE-

Holding hands, Joey and Elaine strolled toward one of the miniature groves of twisted trees along the ragged edge of the cliff. Once inside, they could enjoy some privacy while staying within earshot of their friends. A gleaming black bishop twelve feet long lay on its side next to the nearest trees. The giant chessmen were strewn around the mountainside as if a bad loser had dashed them off the board.

Before the two had even a moment to themselves, a scream erupted. Joey and Elaine spun around. Across the mountainside, lying by one of the pools on a pallet of moss, Kim thrashed.

"Damn," Joey sighed. "I thought she'd finally fallen asleep."

"Me too," said Elaine. "I have to go to her. I'll come back as soon as I can."

"Sure."

She squeezed his hand, then scurried away.

Joey tramped on past the fallen bishop. The trees had long, sickle-shaped leaves like eucalypti, but no discernible odor. Wondering if he'd been too rough on George, and annoyed with himself for even caring, he sat down with his back against one of the smooth white trunks and looked out at the Tempest.

At the moment, the lightning was predominantly orange, and brighter than usual. One patch of the churning vapor thinned, revealing a gigantic pit with battlements ringing the lip. Something with scalloped wings, maybe a bat or a dragon, dove into it and disappeared.

Seen from this perspective, the vast storm, always changing and always the same, was awe-inspiring. Hypnotic. And after watching it for a while, strangely restful. Joey's eyelids drooped. His chin bobbed toward his chest.

Maybe I should try to shake off the drowsiness, he thought. It would be tacky to let Elaine find me asleep, especially when she knows who I visit in my dreams.

Yeah, but she also knows how much my dreams mean to me, he reasoned. Sometimes they're all that keep me going. Surely she won't begrudge me a little nap, especially not now. After shooting Sarah and Emily, I truly need to see them safe and well.

Joey's eyes closed, and his body slumped. Floating in darkness, he realized he was dozing. He wasn't dreaming yet, but a dream was waiting. He felt himself sinking toward it like a pearl sliding through oil.

He couldn't remember passing through this in-between stage before. Up until now, he'd either been wide awake or with Sarah and Emily. Maybe he felt guilty, and that was slowing him down. He wondered wryly who he thought he'd betrayed, his wife or his new girlfriend. Knowing the way his mind worked, probably both.

Outside his head, in the waking world, someone shrieked.

Evidently Kim was still hysterical. Poor kid. But she was being taken care of, so he tried to shut her out. Below his dangling feet, or so it seemed, his own little girl's high, slightly off-key voice sang, "We all live in a yellow submarine, yellow submarine, yellow submarine!" He sensed that in another moment, the dream would swallow him until such time as someone shook him awake.

More cries, faint and tinny, sounded overhead. He

congratulated himself on how well he was blocking them out. Then, just as they faded away entirely, he realized that he wasn't only hearing Kim. A lot of people were yelling. Chris was bellowing his name.

He struggled to wake up. For a moment, it didn't seem that he'd be able to, any more than a drunk could sober up just by wishing his intoxication away. Then he felt himself floundering upward, the way he had under Larry Orsini's floor. His eyes popped open.

Dazed and dizzy, he scrambled around and peered out at the landscape. The heat lightning had become dim and sporadic. Even using the hyperkeen sight of a ghost, it was hard to make out what was going on. But evidently a gang of spirits, some human-looking, others gruesomely transformed, was attacking the caravan. A knot of people were fighting not far up the slope. Another member of the caravan, cut off from the others, stood with her back against a crimson pawn two feet taller than she was. Three Spectres charged her. She shot her crossbow, and one doubled over. But the other two grabbed her and tumbled her to the ground.

Joey ran to help her. A creature with the head of a woodpecker and a round iron shield lunged out of the gloom and swung a darksteel saber at him.

As he dodged, the power of the voice kicked in, spinning him out of the way with time to spare. Hampered only a little by the chain connecting his wrists, he lashed his baton over the shield and against the swordsman's beak. With a crunch, the appendage broke in two. His black-veined aura changing from scarlet to a haze of multicolored sparks, the injured wraith collapsed.

A crossbow trigger clicked. Pivoting, Joey batted the flying quarrel aside, knocking it over the edge of the cliff. The second attacker was a skinny, bare-chested kid with multiple piercings. Joey slammed the baton against his neck.

Something cracked, and the ghost fell down. Writhing, he screamed.

"Joey!" cried Elaine. "Where are you?"

He whirled, peering, trying to locate her. Agony blazed down his back from shoulder to hip.

Lurching around, he saw that he'd been facing three opponents, not two. The last one had long talons, gleaming and black like darksteel, but the rest of the attacker was translucent gray shadow, nearly invisible in the darkness, an attribute which had allowed it to sneak up and claw Joey savagely. Instead of pressing its advantage, it was standing back and watching him. Pumped full of the voice's fury, Joey was sure it was gloating.

He tried to lunge at it, but a spasm froze him in place. This second burst of pain showed him just how badly hurt he really was. It went on and on, waves of excruciating torment alternating with moments of faintness, of nothingness. His mind was flashing on and off like a strobe. Tides of darkness washed through his skin. The creature danced with obvious glee, hopping from one foot to the other.

It can't end like this, Joey thought. It would be stupid. This freak can't beat me, I'm a champion!

But he could tell it was ending exactly like this. He was dying for the second time.

Though his vision was blurring, he glimpsed a smear of brown. With immense effort, he managed to turn his head. Wrapped in his grubby raincoat, George was standing beside him.

"Help me," Joey croaked.

George smirked. "It's time for that reward I promised you. The equitable Mr. Pryor is about to give you exactly what you deserve." He grabbed Joey's arm, and, with a grunt, flung him stumbling backward.

Joey felt his left foot land on the very edge of the cliff. The back of his heel hung over the drop. He tried to windmill his arms for balance, but the manacles made it impossible. Momentum carried him on, into empty space.

A third of the way down the mountain, his skull smashed into an outcropping. He decided that it felt a lot like getting shot in the head, and then everything vanished in a flash of red.

-THIRTY-FOUR-

The Labyrinth.

Joey took a deep breath, let it out slowly, and felt the tension drain out of his body. For some reason, he'd been edgy, but now he was feeling better by the second. He guessed that a family outing was just what he needed. If Emily didn't insist on shopping for *too* many hours, it ought to be a great day.

Savoring the cool breeze, the golden sunlight, and the lush emerald grass, he looked around Union Square, a small park surrounded by towering, gargoyle-encrusted hotels and office buildings. Two hunched old men on a bench tossed popcorn to pigeons. Hissing, the bronze fountain in front of the Hyatt sprayed sparkling foam into the air. A cable car rumbled by, clanging its bell.

Sarah clutched Joey's hand. "Daddy! Daddy!"

She sounded frightened. Both startled and struck by a sense of déjà vu, he peered down at her. "What is it, sweetheart?"

"You've got to cut it down!"

He shook his head. "I don't understand."

Emily said, "She means that." She pointed.

Joey turned, then twitched in astonishment. Commodore

Dewey's memorial column was gone. In its place stood a leafy green stalk, thick as a telephone pole and taller than the skyscrapers, rising up and up until it vanished inside a mass of fleecy clouds. It looked just like the magical plant in *Jack and the Beanstalk*, Sarah's favorite fairy tale.

Joey said, "But I don't know what it's doing here. Why should I chop it down? What's wrong with it?"

"If you don't get rid of it, the giant will come," said Sarah. "He'll spoil things like before."

Now that she mentioned it, Joey dimly recalled some happy times that had turned scary and miserable. He sure didn't want any more of that. Still, none of this was truly making sense. "Maybe we should talk to the cops. Heck, it's not like I have an axe—"

Emily smiled smugly. "Sure you do." She opened her handbag and pulled out a red fire axe.

"Hurry!" said Sarah. "Please, daddy, before it's too late!" She tugged him forward.

He let her tow him across the square. Maybe she and Emily had the right idea. God knew, he didn't have a clue. He was utterly bewildered.

When they reached the foot of the beanstalk, he squinted up its length. At this point, he wouldn't have been too surprised to see a huge figure clambering down, but he didn't. "Nothing's happening," he said.

"It will," Emily said, strands of her dark hair stirring in the breeze. "It will unless you stop it."

Hesitantly he touched the smooth green surface of the plant. If something big were descending, he ought to feel a vibration. He didn't, not the slightest quiver. Abruptly, intuition told him what this was really all about.

Emily and Sarah were trying to trick him. They weren't worried about something coming down the beanstalk. They were afraid he'd climb it and never come back.

For a moment, the notion seemed silly, if not insulting.

Then murky memories flickered through his head. A snub-nose revolver. A hospital bed. An eighteen-wheeler. A fancy fireplace full of squirming darkness. He realized that somehow, he *had* abandoned his family, time after time.

If the beanstalk could make him do it again, then he should destroy it. He grabbed the axe and started chopping. Green and white chips flew.

From the corner of his eye, he glimpsed Sarah and Emily leering, as if he were falling victim to a particularly mean practical joke. Other visions flooded his mind. His daughter, surly, drunk, and grown to adulthood. His wife with lines in her face, holding another man's hand. A burial. A sad, lovely woman gazing into a glowing glass ball. He realized again how strange this all was, how lost he felt, and dropped the axe on the ground. "I'm sorry," he said, "but I can't do this. Not until I'm sure it's right."

Emily opened her mouth like she was going to argue, and then her eyes widened. She shrugged and stepped back. Sarah followed her lead.

Joey noticed that the sun had stopped shining on him. Glancing down, he saw that he and the beanstalk were standing at the center of a swelling blot of shadow. Looking up, he confirmed what he'd already guessed. Now a King Kong-sized figure *was* climbing down from the clouds.

At least it was Kong-sized at first. But as it hurtled earthward, as fast as if it were sliding down a fire pole, it shrank. By the time it reached the ground, it was Joey's size.

And the resemblance didn't end there. It had his swarthy skin and coarse black hair. His broad shoulders, massive arms, scarred knuckles, and square, homely face. As soon as he looked into its eyes, he remembered everything that had happened to him, from the shooting on Castro Street to his plummet off the cliff. Apparently he'd cheated annihilation again. Or maybe not. He had a hunch the jury was still out.

The double said, "You're a big disappointment to me,

brother. I've treated you fairly. This is all for the best. Why don't you get with the program?"

Joey realized what he was looking at. An instinctive fear quivered in his guts. "You're the voice, aren't you? The part of me Elaine called my Shadow."

The other Joey smiled. "You're getting smarter in your old age. What is it they say? Too little too late?"

"And I'm guessing this is no ordinary dream."

"Right again." The blue sky melted into the boiling black clouds of the Tempest, though the island of white at the top of the beanstalk remained. At the same instant, Emily and Sarah disappeared. Joey felt a reflexive pang of horror, even though he now understood they hadn't been real.

"You're in the Labyrinth," the voice continued. "The basement of the Tempest. The last stop before the Void." The ground shook, split, and rumbled as if wracked by an earthquake. Black light shone out of the cracks. The ring of high-rises crumbled. Joey staggered. For a second, the earth beneath his sneakers felt paper-thin, and yet another image popped into his mind. Artie, whose many interests included astronomy, had once bored him with a description of a black hole, a mysterious, unstoppable engine of destruction crushing and devouring anything that came too close, growing stronger and stronger as it fed on its prey. The concept didn't seem so dry and abstract when Joey pictured it happening a fraction of an inch beneath his feet.

The quake ground to a halt. Joey's Shadow, who'd kept his balance easily, said, "But at the same time, we *are* inside your dreams." He shrugged. "Go figure. I don't understand it myself."

"What am I doing here?" Joey asked, still trying to sound tough and unafraid.

The voice grinned crookedly. "Don't you know? It's time to pay your tab."

"What 'tab'?"

"For almost a year, you've been borrowing my strength. Elaine warned you there'd be a price. It's your identity. Your place in the outside world. From now on, *I'm* Joey Castelo."

"And that will make me evil," Joey said. He didn't think he'd ever used that word, at least not since he was a kid. Maybe it should have sounded corny, but it didn't. "A Spectre."

His twin nodded. "Evil is in the eye of the beholder, but you've got the general idea. Look, I know you don't like this, any more than you'd like a repo man towing away your car. But at least I'm willing to give you a break. You can live on here, inside me, with Emily and Sarah. After a while, you'll forget it isn't real. And isn't that your idea of Heaven?"

Joey hesitated. The dreams were pretty close to Heaven. For months now, he'd craved them like a junkie craves a fix. Would it be so bad to exist in them full-time?

He grimaced. Yeah, it would. Because up in the real world, there were real people who needed him. And he couldn't give his existence to a devil, or every terrible crime the creature committed would be his fault. Shoving aside temptation, he said, "Forget it."

The Shadow sighed. "Do you understand why you wound up here tonight?"

"Because I got hurt?"

"Yeah. Hurt to the point of death. Some spirits have the strength to climb back up to true existence, and some slide on into Oblivion. I know I could make it, and save us both. Can you say the same?"

"I don't see why not."

The voice smiled. "Really? Think about all the tight spots you've gotten into since you died. *Every time*, you used my muscle, my speed, and my determination to make it through."

Joey realized it was true. He struggled to squelch a twinge of uncertainty.

"Even if you could make it upstairs," the voice continued, "you wouldn't be able to tap into my power anymore. I'm cutting you off. You'd be the same loser you were when you were breathing. What good would you be to anybody then? With your talent for getting into trouble, how long do you think you'd even survive?"

Joey's throat felt dry. Swallowing, he picked up the axe, gripped it in both hands, and, straining, snapped it in two, so the voice couldn't use it to attack the beanstalk. "I guess I'll find out," he said, "because I'm going up."

"I don't think so," said the Shadow. His fist shot out at Joey's face.

Joey saw the punch coming, but he couldn't dodge it in time. The voice's knuckles slammed into his nose, breaking it, and he reeled backward. The pieces of the axe tumbled from his hands and disappeared.

Sneering, the double said, "Come on, come on, show me what you've got." His face throbbing, Joey raised his fists.

He hooked a punch at the voice's gut. The Shadow twisted out of the way, then hit him twice, once in the kidney and once in the side of the head. Joey staggered.

"Pitiful," said the voice, dancing and bobbing. "Just pitiful. I thought you were a champ."

Joey edged toward him. The Shadow lowered his hands, opening himself up, daring his opponent to take a shot. Joey jabbed at his face and snapped a kick at his knee.

The double brushed both attacks aside, then punched him in the Adam's apple. Pain blasted through his entire body. Feeling as if he were choking, black blobs swimming at the edges of his vision, he fell to his knees.

"Had enough?" asked the voice.

Screw you, Joey thought. He would have said it aloud if his throat hadn't hurt so much. He lurched to his feet and went after the voice again.

The next few minutes were some of the worst of his

existence. He never landed a solid blow. The Shadow flitted around him like a will-o'-the-wisp, taunting him, beating him with surgical precision. Bone cracked.

Even dazed with pain, Joey realized he should have known from the start that the fight was hopeless. He and the voice were the same person, with the same reach, the same moves, the same level of skill. It was inevitable that the inhumanly strong twin would humble the other.

He imagined he could hear an audience, cheering his enemy on, booing and jeering at him, the way they had on his most miserable nights in the ring. Maybe it was really the jangling in his ears. Or the rumble of another quake. The way he was staggering, he couldn't tell if the ground was shaking or not.

And then he was sprawled on his back. Joey couldn't remember the punch that had knocked him down.

The voice smiled down at him. "We can stop this any time."

For what seemed like quite a while now, Joey had yearned to do precisely that. Throw in the towel. What was the point of inviting any more pain? But something, pride, rage, or sheer irrational stubbornness, held him back. He struggled unsuccessfully to get up.

"Damn you!" said the Shadow. "What's *wrong* with you? Are you stupid?"

Despite the fog in Joey's head, he noticed a whiny note in the double's tone. The bastard actually sounded upset. He couldn't imagine why.

The voice dropped to his knees on Joey's chest and started hammering his face. Teeth shattered. "Just give up!" the Shadow growled.

Joey squirmed futilely, trying to buck his tormentor off. He fumbled feebly under the pounding arms, trying to hold them back. That didn't work, either. One tiny portion of his mind, disconnected from the pain and terror ripping through his body, wondered how a person could soak up this much punishment and not pass out.

Then something odd began to happen.

Joey's vision was so cloudy that at first, he didn't know if he was really seeing it. But when he squinted, he was sure. The voice had started to wither. The muscular body inside the T-shirt and jeans was shriveling to skin and bones.

Evidently the Shadow realized it, too. Snarling like a rabid animal, he pounded Joey even more savagely than before.

The withering didn't soften the punches, but it lightened the crushing pressure of the knees on Joey's chest. Then with a final spasm of strength, Joey flailed his arms, wrenched his body sideways, and dumped his attacker on the ground.

His face as wrinkled as a mummy's, the voice scrambled back at him, then blinked out of sight like a bursting bubble. For a few seconds, Joey gaped at the empty space his twin had occupied, then, finally daring to believe that the apparition was really gone, flopped back down on the grass.

At first he couldn't think, he could only rest. But gradually, as the pain and fatigue lost the worst of their edge, Joey began to wonder what had just happened.

Eventually he decided that, by using the voice's strength, he'd given it power over him, but not total control. It couldn't take over his existence, or hold him to the Labyrinth, unless he gave it permission, or it broke his will. Maybe he'd defeated it simply by continuing to resist it no matter what it offered or threatened, or how badly it hurt him.

Or maybe that explanation was dead wrong. He couldn't even pretend to understand this kind of crap, and it didn't matter anyway. What did matter was that he might not be safe even now. He needed to get out of here before the voice came back for another round, or the ground shattered and dropped him into the Void.

Spastically, teeth gritting, he dragged himself to his feet and stumbled over to the beanstalk. By the time he got there, he had to clutch it for support. Wondering grimly how he was supposed to climb all the way to the sky, he set his foot on the rubbery base of the lowest leaf.

For the first few yards, the ascent was as difficult as he'd feared. His muscles trembled and cramped. Every time he moved, he expected to fall. But as the broken ground fell away beneath him, his pain and weariness dissolved, and a sense of elation took their place. He climbed faster and faster, until he was rocketing up as quickly as the voice had hurtled down. In another minute, he plunged into the white cloud. Suddenly he felt a floor under his sneakers, and the stalk melted away inside his grasp. The creamy vapor disappeared.

-THIRTY-FIVE-

San Francisco.

When the cloud dissolved, Joey found himself standing in front of a heavy punching bag. Elsewhere in the large, square room, all but unidentifiable in the darkness, were speed bags, free weights, and Nautilus machines. A web of glinting Nihil cracks ran through two adjacent walls and half the ceiling. The air smelled of sweaty laundry and liniment.

He shook his head in amazement. He knew this place. He'd learned to box here, trained with this equipment until he died. He was back in Franklin's Gym.

Or was he? He'd already learned the hard way that the Tempest, or at any rate, some of the horrors lurking in its depths, could re-create scenes from a spirit's past. He strode to the nearest wall, and, a little hesitantly, tried to push his hand inside it.

His fingertips sank into the plaster without resistance. He stuck his head through and out into Vallejo Street. It must be late. Like the gym, the thoroughfare was all but deserted, but, hand in hand, a shaven-headed boy in a studded leather jacket and a pale, angular girl with spiky magenta hair and black lipstick were strolling by.

Neither one noticed him. Overhead, above a crumbling,

soot-stained brick building so ruinous that its decrepitude had almost certainly been embellished by the Shroud, the stars burned cold and clear.

Joey had assumed that if he made it out of the Labyrinth, he'd reappear in the place where he'd gotten hurt. But all the evidence indicated that, though he didn't understand the reason for it — so what else was new? — he'd popped out in a place he loved instead. In the Shadowlands of San Francisco.

Which, he realized with a jolt of terror, meant he was in desperate trouble. Since he'd been ordered to check in with George every day—

But no. Now that he'd been reminded of his shackles, he saw that, though he still had his clothing, the restraints were gone. He guessed he'd left them behind when his last real body — and wasn't *that* a creepy notion? — had been smashed to pieces on the rocks. Come to think of it, he didn't have the baton, either, but he no longer cared about that. What mattered was that, at long last, he was free.

What made it even better was that his mind seemed calm and quiet. His thinking had a clarity that had been missing for so long he'd forgotten what it was like. He felt *light*, the way he used to when he trained with weights strapped to his wrists and ankles, then took them off.

The difference was the absence of the voice. He doubted it was gone forever. He hadn't won that huge a victory. Probably no one ever did. But for the time being, it had crawled away to lick its wounds.

He felt a swell of elation. Against all odds, everything he'd hoped for had come true. He'd made it home with the know-how to help his daughter. He'd visit her in her dreams—

His speeding thoughts lurched to a halt. Right, in her dreams. Which he could do because Elaine had taught him how. Elaine, whom he'd last seen in terrible danger in the Tempest.

CARAVAN OF SHADOWS

He was pretty sure he loved her, though he hadn't gotten around to telling her so. How could he do anything but try to race to her aid? But conversely, now that he was finally in a position to make contact with Sarah, how could he even consider leaving?

He realized then that even silencing your Shadow didn't guarantee that you wouldn't have a divided mind. And that the freedom he'd yearned for could be as heavy a burden as slavery. With George, the little rat-bastard, calling the shots for both of them, it hadn't really mattered that Joey cared about Emily and Sarah on one hand, and Elaine and his friends in the caravan on the other. Now, however, he was going to have to choose between them.

Scowling, he slumped down on a bench and tried to think.

-THIRTY-SIX-

When Joey slipped into Sarah's dream, she was riding a school bus. She still had the body of an adult, but he could tell from her ponytail and the books in her lap that she was supposed to be a kid like the other passengers. Her eyes were downcast, and none of the chattering children were talking to her.

As desperately as Joey wanted to appear to her, now that the moment had come, he experienced a sudden attack of stage fright. What if meeting her old man's ghost terrified her? What if she didn't even care that he'd come back? What if he said something stupid, something that screwed her up worse than she was already? He told himself that it wouldn't do any harm simply to watch the dream unfold for a few more seconds. Maybe it would help him understand her.

Brakes squeaking, the bus rolled to a stop. Sarah got off, and he followed her. Together, they trudged up the sidewalk. When they came in sight of the place where their seedy apartment building had always stood, she froze. For a moment, Joey was equally startled, even though he knew this was a dream. Because the structure was gone. A condemned office building with graffiti-covered walls and boarded windows had stolen its place.

Sarah peered wildly about. Joey looked where she was looking. While their backs had been turned, the entire street had changed. Now nothing looked familiar. The sky was gray, and a cold, moaning wind had begun to blow.

Sarah looked at her empty hands and let out a tiny whimper. Joey realized that somehow she'd lost her books.

Her panicky expression spurred him into action. Concentrating, he materialized in the dream. He popped in behind her so he wouldn't scare her unnecessarily.

His throat felt clogged. He swallowed. "Sarah? Sweetheart?"

She spun around and gaped at him. "Daddy!" She threw herself into his arms.

Dazed, he thought, she seems so big. This is what it feels like to hug her now that she's grown up.

"Daddy!" Sarah repeated. "I was lost."

"I know." Exerting his power, he tried to mold the landscape. The dream stuff resisted for an instant, then flowed into the proper shapes. The wind died, and the sun came out. Reluctantly he let her go, so she could look around. "But it's okay now. See, we're back on our block. And there are your books on the grass."

She said, "Good. I thought—" Suddenly, her smile fading, she peered at him. He was glad that she didn't look frightened, just thoughtful. "Wait. This isn't right. I'm not a kid anymore. I haven't lived here in a long time. And you... died. This is a dream."

"Yeah," Joey said, "but not an ordinary one. Can you feel a difference?"

She nodded. He noticed that her hair had rearranged itself, losing the ponytail in the process. "Kind of. Things are more in focus. It's almost like being awake."

"That's because I'm not just something your imagination cooked up. I really am your daddy's spirit. I came back to talk to you, the only way I can. I've been trying to reach you ever since I died. Actually, I did, once, last Halloween.

I helped you when those punks tried to rape you. But then I got jerked back to the other side."

She stared at him. "That was you?" He nodded. She hugged him again. "Oh, daddy, I love you! I missed you so much!"

"I know. I missed you, too." He paused. What was happening between them was so sweet that he didn't want to risk spoiling it. But he knew he had to. "Do you know why I worked so hard to come back?"

She hesitated. "Because you love me?" Suddenly there was a phony, guarded note in her voice.

"Sure," he said, "but there's more to it. I'm worried about you."

She stepped away from him. A stain of bright red lipstick oozed across her mouth. "Now you sound like mom."

"Is that bad? She's pretty smart."

"Yeah? Well, she doesn't have the right to run my life. Neither do you, no matter who or what you are."

"Don't play that game. You know I'm really your father." He sensed that she did believe, that she'd accepted his presence as unquestioningly as people usually accepted the strange things that happened in dreams. "I don't want to push you around, just talk. It's not every day you get a visit from a dead relative, so why don't you give me a break? It's not like I'm going to blab your secrets to anyone else, and nothing you could say could make me love you any less."

She grimaced. "Where's all this coming from? What do you know about my life anyway?"

"I thought you understood that. I've watched quite a bit of it. I've seen you nearly die twice, once when you were attacked and once from an OD."

She glared at him. "All right. Maybe, just maybe, I do have some problems. So what? How is talking going to fix them? Do you have some magical words of wisdom to make everything all right?"

Joey sighed. "No. I want to help, but I don't know if I can. But I at least need to find out if what happened to you is my fault. I'm afraid of the answer, but I've got to know."

Sarah blinked. "Your fault?"

"Yeah. When a kid messes up, it's usually because the parents messed her up, isn't it?"

Sarah slumped. He could see the anger draining out of her body, and a kind of weariness replacing it. "Oh, daddy, of course it's not your fault."

"Then whose is it?"

"Nobody's. Just forget about it, all right?"

"I can't, if you won't help me understand." He felt an ache in his chest. "Has your life been so awful that you can't even bear to tell about it?"

She hesitated. "No. I guess I'm *ashamed* to talk about it, even in a dream, even to you. Especially to you. But all right." She sat down on the curb, and Joey sat next to her. Except for the faint hiss of her breathing and the muffled thump of her heart, this illusory version of San Francisco was altogether silent.

Looking straight ahead, she murmured, "I was a really happy little girl. Even though it bothered me when you came home all beat up after a fight, and drank and took pills to kill the pain. Even though I understood, as much as a kid could, that you and Mom were worried about money. And that she didn't think you were ever going to be a big-time boxer, but you wouldn't listen to her."

Inwardly, Joey cringed. "She didn't come right out and say it until that last afternoon, but other than that, you had it all figured out."

"Then you got shot. I was so heartbroken that I thought crazy things. I *hated* going to see you. It made me mad that no matter what I said or did, you'd just *lie* there. I wondered if you'd gotten your brains blown out on purpose, so you wouldn't have to be mom's husband or my father anymore.

Maybe we were so horrible that we'd *driven* you to it."

Joey shook his head. "Oh my god. How could you ever think that?"

She scowled. "I'd seen you hit mom, remember? And I'd heard her warn you that you could get hurt being a bodyguard. You went off and did it anyway, like that was what you wanted. Hell, I was a kid. I didn't know what made sense and what was stupid. Only that I felt miserable and angry and guilty, and couldn't deal with any of it."

"And your mother couldn't help you?"

Sarah shrugged. "I didn't see her much. With you gone, the money problems got worse. She had to work two jobs. Still, I guess she did her best, but she had her own bad feelings to contend with. And sometimes I pushed her away, because I blamed her for what had happened as much as you or myself." She smiled wryly. "I must have thought there was plenty of blame to go around. Look, I feel like this is coming out in a big tangle. Is any of it making any sense?"

"Yeah," said Joey heavily. "And what it adds up to is, your problems *are* my fault."

"No! That's not what I'm saying. You wanted to know about me, and I'm just trying to tell you. After a while, the pain of losing you eased up, even if it never went away completely. But by that time, I was a teenager, and somehow, I was turning into a different person. I stopped wanting to be a good student, or a good citizen, or any of that garbage. I had a chip on my shoulder. I liked breaking rules, getting away with stuff, and partying. But at the same time, I didn't like myself anymore. I hated the sadness in mom's eyes when she caught me screwing up. I hated it when people called me a drunk and a tramp. I hated knowing they were right.

"I still do. But I don't blame you for it. It was nobody's fault you got shot, nobody but the guy who pulled the trigger. I know that now. Besides, if you'd been around to raise me, maybe I would have turned out different... maybe not. I don't think anyone's life turns out badly because she lived through one big tragedy, except on the Movie of the Week. A thousand *little* things pushed and nibbled at me. A lot of it would have happened whether you were there or not. And when you get right down to it, I made my own mistakes, with my eyes wide open. Nobody held a gun to my head and forced me."

Joey's eyes smarted. He took her hand. "In other words, you forgive me."

She scowled. "In other words, you didn't do anything terrible to be forgiven *for*. But take it that way if you need to."

He sat quietly for a few moments, mulling over what she'd told him. Eventually he said, "Look, you admitted you don't like being the way you are. You also said you're responsible for what you do. Doesn't that mean you can change?"

"Whoa. I talked about my stupid life to let you off the hook. I wasn't asking for a lecture."

"I know. But when I see you hurting, I have to try to make it better. Don't you believe you can turn things around?"

She grimaced. "No, not anymore. It's like swimming out to sea. If you go too far, you can't make it back to shore. I wake up in the morning wanting a drink. I've got my whole day, my whole life, built around getting the next drink, and the next pill. If you haven't been there, you wouldn't understand."

"But I have. After I died, I got hooked on" — he realized he didn't have time to tell her the whole story of the past year, about the rush he'd felt mauling his opponents in the ring, or the lure of his dreams — "well, a couple of things."

She raised her eyebrows. "Dead people have drugs?"

"More or less. I don't really know how I'm going to get along without them, but I'm about to find out. The point is, people *can* shake addictions. You can get help from a clinic or someplace like that."

"Meetings and the twelve steps? That stuff wouldn't work for me. Deep down, I know I'm messed up, but nobody else better say it, or I go ballistic."

"You got past that with me."

"Only because you're my daddy, and I'm asleep. I think it lowers your resistance."

"If you work at it, you can open up to other people, too. Heck, it's just talking."

"Even if I could," said Sarah, "it's too late. I've messed up too many times, in too many different ways. I've been so mean to mom. Yelled at her. Lied to her. Stolen from her. I was kicked out of school. I've got a rap sheet—"

Joey knelt in front of her, gripped her forearms, and looked her in the eyes. "You know damn well your mother still loves you. And you're still young. You have time to get an education or do anything you want. You can't just give up on life. If you were looking at it from the outside, you'd see what a valuable thing it really is."

After a moment, she said, very softly, "I do want to change. But I'm scared. What if I can't stand being straight? What if I try to be good and blow it?"

"Then try again. As long as you don't give up, you'll get it right eventually. Look, when you wake up, you may not remember all of this. You may not believe I was real. But promise me you'll grab the phone and go meet with somebody right away."

"I promise to try. But if I forget, or screw up some other way, you can tell me again, can't you? I want you to come back."

"And I'd like to. But I don't know if I'll ever be able to."

She cocked her head. "Why not? Won't God let you?"

He sighed. "No. If there is a God, I haven't run into Him yet. I have some friends far away, in terrible danger. I have to go to them." Though Sarah didn't look at all reproachful, a pang of guilt shot through him. "It's not that I care more about them than you and your mom. I couldn't love anybody more than you guys. It's going to tear me apart to go away.

"But I've spent the last year trying to hold on to what I had when I was breathing, and it doesn't work. You can *love* what you left behind, but you can't *own* it anymore. I'm part of the world of the dead now, and I have to build a new life there."

"Yes," she said, "I understand."

"See, your mom doesn't need me anymore. And I've just done pretty much everything I can for you. I can't fix your problems, much as I'd like to. It's like you said yourself. Only you can live your life. You have to take responsibility—"

Sarah grinned and pressed her fingertips against his lips, silencing him. "Chill. I get the point. I'm going to miss you, just like I always have, but it's all right. At least we got to see each other one more time."

He stood up, then lifted her to her feet. "Don't forget the call. Make it the instant you wake up."

"I'll try. I really will."

"I love you."

"I love you, too."

They hugged. He kissed her cheek, and tasted a salty tear. Then he shifted his awareness back into his real body.

He looked down at his sleeping daughter. She was smiling and crying at the same time. Her halo shone pale blue and vermilion, calm and happy, but with a silver thread of melancholy stitching the edge.

He wondered if she really would make the call. If she would keep the appointment. He could stick around and see.

No, he couldn't. He didn't have time. Besides, he had a hunch that if he didn't leave now, he never would. He turned and strode through the bedroom doorway.

-THIRTY-SEVEN-

As Joey was about to skulk under the green-tiled, dragon-capped arch, he heard feet pounding in step. Peeking warily through the opening, he saw a column of Legionnaires marching toward him down the steep slope of Grant Avenue. The soldiers were armed with clubs and knives, and wearing green domino masks.

Joey doubted that any of the San Francisco Hierarchs, even Vincent's, were actively hunting him at this late date. But that didn't mean they wouldn't recognize him if they came face to face with him. Crouching low, he melted through the wall of the souvenir shop on his left.

Inside, he hid in a shadowy corner well away from the windows. A chimp-sized teak statue of a laughing Buddha stood by his feet, and a rack of shoddy martial-arts weapons, nunchaku, sai, tonfa, and the like, hung beside him. Missing the comforting heft of his baton, he wished the weapons were on his side of the Shroud.

The soldiers strode by and turned down Bush Street. Joey slipped out onto Grant and deeper into Chinatown, past window displays of worry balls, coolie hats, fake pigtails, and intricately carved elephant tusks. The sky above the pagoda-style roofs was still black, though off to the east, it showed a tinge of gray. Somewhere, muffled by walls and distance, a stereo played the grating new rock music he'd never learned to appreciate. The cool breeze carried the scent of the sea.

Two blocks up the hill, he came to Old Saint Mary's. The grimy, gargoyle-encrusted Gothic cathedral, its stained-glass windows a parade of martyrs suffering gruesome deaths, looked jarringly out of place in the midst of the surrounding mock-Asian architecture. Grateful to escape one of the district's main drags, he headed down a twisting alley. A gray cat seemed to stare at him for a moment, then resumed licking its forepaw.

The back streets were as maze-like as he remembered. For a few minutes, he was afraid he'd lost his way. Then, rounding a corner, he saw a tiny square containing a kite shop, and beyond it, the passage that led to the Buddhist temple. He quickened his pace.

The garbage cans in back of the restaurant stank as foully as on his last visit, but tonight no one was slumped in the shadows behind them. Joey glided through the temple door and on up the narrow stairs.

In the hall of worship, candles glowed and sticks of incense smoldered, filling the air with the scent of myrrh. Nobody, Quick or Restless, was around.

Joey frowned. All right, genius, he thought sourly, now what? Park your butt and wait for a Renegade to show up? For all he knew, they'd abandoned this hideout. But on the other hand, he didn't know where else to look. Pondering what seemed like a crappy set of options, he prowled aimlessly toward the far end of the room.

Then, suddenly, the hairs on the back of his neck stood on end. Though he hadn't heard a sound, somehow he knew that he was no longer alone. Full of mingled hope and anxiety, he turned.

Two tough-looking Asian wraiths were pointing weapons at him. Their halos burned murky red with hostility. The taller of the two had a bow and arrow. The other, a chunky, shirtless guy with a pornographic girl-and pignosed-demon tattoo on his chest, had a pump shotgun. The firearm reminded Joey fleetingly of Holliday.

Evidently there were still sentries watching the temple after all. Joey smiled. "Hi. I hope you guys are in the tong. The mask is lost."

"The scythe is drowned," replied the gunman solemnly. Then he sneered. "But guess what. That password's months out of date. And this place is holy, off limits to all white devils. Make a move if you want to. You've got until the count of three, and then I'm going to shoot. One, two—"

"Hold it!" Joey said. "I know one of your top men. I was here in March, when the Legionnaires burst in on him and a couple other Renegade honchos. I don't know if he got away, but if he did, it was thanks to me. He's the one I'm looking for."

The tattooed man frowned. "Mr. Hong told me something about that. You're a mercenary."

"Wrong. I was George Montaigne's slave, but I'm not anymore."

The tattooed man's eyes flicked toward his companion. "He's got the facts right. What do you think?"

"If Mr. Hong doesn't want to see him," the archer replied, "we can kill him in the cellars just as easily as here." The comment reminded Joey that there was supposed to be an extensive tunnel system under Chinatown. In past decades, smugglers, white slavers, and opium sellers had used it.

"All right, white trash," said the gunman. "Turn around and put your hands behind you."

Joey obeyed. Footsteps whispered toward him. Cold, hard rings snapped shut around his wrists. Remembering George's manacles, he had to struggle not to flinch. A bag slipped over his head.

One of his captors spun him around, then shoved him. "Move," said the man with the shotgun.

The pair marched him outside and through more winding alleys. He suspected they doubled back repeatedly to confuse his sense of direction. Finally they took him back indoors and down a spiral staircase. As they descended, his skin began to crawl. The place below was giving off the nerve-wracking vibes of a site with a bloody history.

Judging by how long it took to get to the last step, it was also deep underground. The air was cold, and smelled of damp earth and rock. Off to his left, water dripped. The plink-plink-plink sound echoed. Instinct told him he'd alit in a low, cramped passage.

One of his captors pushed him forward, then, a minute later, jerked him to a stop. A pair of footsteps hurried away, then returned.

The Asians goaded him on. Abruptly he felt the walls widen around him, as if he'd stepped into a room. Voices murmured.

His captors grabbed his arms, halting him, then pulled downward. He guessed they meant to force him to his knees. "That won't be necessary," said a bass voice. "Just remove the hood."

The sack slid off Joey's head. Blinking, he looked around. He and his escorts were standing in front of a throne. In it, studying him, sat the heavyset Asian he'd last seen fighting Hierarchs in the temple. The tong leader had traded his suit and tie for an embroidered blue silk robe and a mandarin's cap, but he still had his curved sword lying in his lap. Other ghosts, a seeming mixture of thugs and bureaucrats, stood along the rough stone walls. One, a wizened old man with a bald dome of a head and wispy white whiskers, sat brushing ink on parchment at a table in the corner. Yellow and white globes shed a soft glow, which, though electrical in origin, was evidently meant to look like candlelight.

"Hello," Joey said. "Thanks for seeing me. My name is Joey Castelo. And I understand that you're Mr. Hong."

The Renegade leader inclined his head. Joey sneaked a peek at his aura. It was an iridescent haze, unreadable, the way George's often was. "Yes. Good evening, Mr. Castelo. Or good morning, now, I believe. My associate has advised me that you feel you saved me, and therefore I'm in your debt."

Joey suspected it would be a mistake to come on too strong with this guy. As he recalled, the Renegade was pretty damn haughty. "Not exactly. For all I know, you would have gotten away without me. But at least I made it a little easier."

"Perhaps," said Hong, "but only after you discovered you were in danger, also. Only after your master lured me into the trap to begin with. We lost good people that night. I could argue that on balance, you owe *me*, and that it's a debt requiring payment in pain."

Joey was glad that wraiths couldn't sweat. He hoped his nervousness didn't show in his halo. "If you did, you'd be as unjust as the governors. George set you up, I didn't. I was just his Thrall. I had no idea what he was planning. Look, I'm here to ask a favor. Since I'm an outlaw myself, I didn't know who else to turn to."

Hong fingered the scarlet tassel tied to the pommel of his sword. "And what might that favor be?"

"For it to make sense, I should probably tell you what I've been up to." As quickly as possible, he told about his joining Elaine's troupe, her problem, and the caravan's flight from her enemies. He watched for some sign that he was arousing Hong's interest, maybe even his sympathy, but the swordsman's round face remained impassive.

When he finished, the Renegade said, "Very well, now you've told me. Yet I fail to see how any of it concerns me."

"I've heard there are wraiths who know how to buzz around the Tempest quickly. A big shot like you must have one on his payroll. I want you to have him take me back into the storm."

"To help your friends. It's entirely possible that they've already perished."

Joey said, "I won't believe that until I get proof."

"Even if some did survive, escaping, or, as seems more likely, being taken prisoner, how long has it been since you fell over the cliff?"

"As near as I can make out, four days. Somehow, I lost some time before I reappeared in San Francisco. And then I lost some more" — he realized he didn't need to tell Hong about Sarah — "ah, getting to you."

"Then I doubt your friends are on the mountain anymore. How do you expect to find them?"

"I don't want to go to the mountain. I want to go to Elaine's Heaven. If she hasn't shown up there, her fellow Heretics should be willing to search for her. Maybe they'll even understand why people were after her in the first place, and will know where to look."

Hong turned his head. "Chaoxing."

The elderly calligrapher rose stiffly and hobbled over to stand before the throne. "How may I serve you?" he asked in a quavering voice.

"Do you know the particular Heaven this barbarian is referring to?"

"The Church of the Holy Covenant," murmured Chaoxing. He sounded like he was sifting through his memory. He peered at Joey. "What terminals did you pass along the way?"

"What are terminals?" Joey asked.

"Places where the Byways widen out, and you can rest."

"Oh, those. A field covered in snow that felt warm, but still melted if you held it. A valley with flowers that trilled. A hill with blue pyramids. A hot spring. And the mountain where we got attacked. It had a giant chessboard made of red and black moss, and the pieces to go with it."

Chaoxing looked up at Hong. "I believe I do know. He and his companions were nearly there."

Joey winced. If only the Spectre in the swamp hadn't attacked them. They might not have stopped to rest. They could have made it. It was enough to make a person crazy.

"Then you could take him," said Hong. "The question is, should I permit it?"

Joey said, "Do you *really* think I was in on the plot to catch you?"

"No," said Hong. He nodded to the man with the shotgun. Glowering, he removed Joey's handcuffs. "And perhaps I am, in some sense, indebted to you, though it's a precept of the Blue Lotus Society that no disciple can owe anything to a non-Chinese. But be that as it may, the Tempest is dangerous. Chaoxing is a valuable resource" — the calligrapher bowed — "and his existence, like my own, belongs to the Jade Emperor. I can't jeopardize him merely to satisfy a personal obligation. Can you give me another reason?"

Joey rubbed his wrists. The cuffs had made them ache. "I told you how I think George led Elaine's enemies to us, and how he chucked me off the cliff. If I get a chance, I mean to pay him back. You guys want him killed too, don't you?"

Hong nodded. "Yes. But I'm not sure that even his punishment justifies the risk."

"Oh, come on! I thought you were a fighter, but you talk like an accountant!"

Some of the onlookers muttered. Since they were doing it in Chinese, Joey couldn't understand them, but they sounded mad. Hong raised his hand, his loose sleeve sliding down his meaty forearm, and they shut up. "I am a warrior," the Renegade said coldly. "One who's studied Sun Tzu enough to understand the necessity of subduing his passions, even the thirst for revenge."

"Is Sun Tzu the guy who said your enemy's enemy is your friend? The one thing I do understand about Elaine's troubles is that it's the Laughing Lady's people who are out to get her. Whatever they want, you should be against."

After a moment, Hong nodded. "Very well. That's a valid point. Chaoxing will assist you." He looked at the bent old man. "What will you need?"

"The usual," said Chaoxing. "A length of rope. Weapons. A hatchet for me." He looked inquiringly at Joey.

"Some kind of club," Joey said. "It's what I'm used to."

"And a club for Mr. Castelo. I'd also be grateful if someone would clean my brushes."

Joey inferred from this last request that they were going *now*. Eager as he was to begin his search, a twinge of fear stabbed through him. On his last passage through the Tempest, he'd nearly died three times.

Chaoxing waved his hand at an archway. "This way, please."

The room beyond the opening was a web of cracks and crevices, all ultimately connecting to the hissing, shimmering pit in the middle of the floor. It was the biggest Nihil Joey had ever seen. A half dozen wraiths armed with pistols and naginata were stationed around it, probably to keep Spectres from climbing out.

Joey peered apprehensively into the depths. "Don't stare at it," Chaoxing said. "It's been known to bewitch people. You said you want to journey quickly, and this gate will let us do precisely that. Unfortunately, that's because it doesn't open on a Byway. It will drop us in the heart of the storm, where the greatest danger lies. Can you face that?"

Joey thought of the horrors he'd glimpsed in the churning mist. He held in a shiver. "If you can, I can."

Chaoxing lifted a feathery white eyebrow. "Really. I've been practicing the Harbinger's art for five hundred years, and I still find it challenging."

"I'm sorry if that sounded disrespectful. I didn't mean it to be."

The old man smiled. "That's all right. I'm glad you have spirit. You'll need it. Here's our equipment."

Joey turned. A small woman in green pajamas was scurrying toward them, taking tiny steps. A flesh sculptor had shrunk her feet to a fraction of their normal size. She gave Chaoxing a hand axe and a length of blue rope and Joey what he took to be a mace, a stick with a ridged darksteel head.

"Thank you," said Chaoxing. The woman bowed and minced away. The calligrapher knotted one end of the rope around his wrist and passed Joey the other. "We're going to clasp hands. But if something breaks our grips, this is our safety line."

Joey knotted it around his forearm. "I understand."

"Try very hard to keep your head. Remember who you are and what you're doing. And no matter what happens, leave the driving to me."

"Okay."

The old man grasped Joey's hand. "I like to run and jump. It's easier if you don't give yourself time to think about what you're doing."

"That works for me."

They sprang forward, Chaoxing now moving as agilely as Joey. Just as they leaped, the old man yelled, "Geronimo!"

-THIRTY-EIGHT-

The Tempest.

One moment, Joey and Chaoxing were falling feet first. Then the world went black, and they were tumbling. Joey gripped the calligrapher's bony hand. Sheets of orange lightning flared, revealing black thunderheads all around them, and broken ground far below. He and his guide were skydiving without parachutes.

Just as he realized they were falling, things changed. A surface rammed itself against his feet. Off balance, he would have sprawled on his face if Chaoxing, who'd somehow braced himself, hadn't held him up.

Joey peered about, trying to understand what had just happened. He and Chaoxing were standing in a barren field littered with bones and rocks. A freezing, screaming wind, far more powerful than the gusts that leaked into the Byways, drove filthy tatters of mist before it. Joey leaned into it to keep from staggering.

As near as he could make out, Chaoxing had — what was the sci-fi word for it? — *teleported* them to earth. He would have asked to make sure, but he doubted that the Asian would hear him over the howl of the storm.

Chaoxing raised their joined hands and gave them a

shake. Joey got the message: hang on. He nodded, and the landscape shifted.

Now they were on a hillside. Below them, barely visible in the gloom and billowing fog, sat a huge mound of currency. The wind was tearing it apart and blowing the bills away. Several pale, naked figures snatched at them frantically. After a couple seconds, Joey noticed that the heap wasn't shrinking. Somehow it was creating new money to replace the old.

Suddenly he sensed a presence at his back. Lifting the mace, he lurched around, glimpsing jagged twelve-inch fangs and burning yellow eyes. The landscape blinked.

He and Chaoxing stood in a dilapidated beach shelter. For the moment at least, they'd left the fog behind. A child's bloated body lay face down in the sand at the edge of the surf. The waves crashed over it, clawed at it, straining to drag it out to sea. The lightning in the clouds burned blue and red.

Frowning, Chaoxing peered this way and that. The wind began to gust in rhythmic pulses. The regular beats bothered Joey, though he didn't know why. He was glad when the old man blinked them out.

During the jumps that followed, Joey and Chaoxing sometimes lingered in a place for as long as a minute. Presumably Chaoxing was resting, or figuring out where to go next. More often, the scenes flashed by: a blackness divided by rivers of molten lava; a cannibal banquet in a gaslit hall; a prison with human-sized praying mantises for guards.

Though nearly every vista was uncanny, at first Joey kept reasonably calm. But gradually he started to sense something going wrong inside his mind. His thoughts felt fractured, off kilter, as if with every jump, he were leaving a piece of his sanity behind.

He kept reminding himself that Chaoxing had warned

him the journey could play tricks with his perception. However he felt, he was probably fine. That reflection helped until he and his companion popped back into the pavilion on the beach.

Scowling, Chaoxing pivoted, evidently studying the lay of the land. Joey felt an urge to grab him and spin him around. Instead, he merely squeezed the old man's hand. The calligrapher turned to face him.

"What's wrong?" Joey yelled, trying to insert his words between the rhythmic shrieks of wind.

He only caught part of Chaoxing's reply: "...a maze... wrong turn... again." Evidently to facilitate thought, the old man squinched his eyes shut.

Veils of sand blew down the beach. Lightning blazed, and the child's corpse twitched. Maybe the waves were shifting it, but it looked to Joey like it was striving to move itself.

The roar of the wind kept on subtly changing until suddenly, he realized it had become a giant's booming laughter. At that instant, far out to sea, a huge mass like an island rose from the water.

Joey instinctively recoiled from it. Then the scene shifted.

For a few moments, he was deeply relieved just to get off the beach. Then the streams of lava flashed past, and after them, the prison.

Evidently Chaoxing didn't know what he was doing. Lost, he was jumping down some of the same blind alleys he'd already tried.

Joey felt his thoughts unraveling. He had to get off this merry-go-round before he went crazy, or turned back into a vegetable. He tried to pull his hand out of Chaoxing's, but the old man clung to him. Furious, Joey swung the mace over his head.

Then, for some reason, a picture popped into his head. He saw himself as he must have looked in the ring this past year, snarling like a mad dog, savaging someone he'd already beaten unconscious. He realized he was losing control again, and this time he didn't even have the voice to blame.

Sickened, he lowered his weapon. He was grateful that Chaoxing was so intent on his work that he hadn't even noticed the threat.

The two of them reappeared in the shelter. The disembodied laughter throbbed on and on, like a scratched record.

The mass in the ocean was too distant to see clearly. The heat lightning only glinted off a bewildering jumble of contours. Still, Joey thought that portions of the thing were moving. The small corpse in the seething foam lurched to its hands and knees, struggled to rise, slumped back down, then started to crawl toward the shelter.

Chaoxing squared his shoulders, like he was about to attempt something particularly difficult. The world blinked. When Joey perceived what was happening, a fresh blast of panic rocked him.

This time, he and Chaoxing weren't flashing through a series of unrelated scenes. They were flickering across the surface of the waves like a skipping stone, leaping farther every time, and hurtling straight toward the hulking thing in the water.

At the speed they were traveling, they should have reached it almost instantly. They didn't. It was a lot farther away than Joey had thought. And a lot bigger. Soon it loomed so huge that it all but eclipsed the sky. Lightning pulsed, and its features swam out of the murk. It was a single creature, a beast so immense that dinosaurs could have lived on it like fleas. Each of its countless globular eyes swiveled toward the travelers. Tentacles the size of skyscrapers swayed in their direction, and maws like colossal caverns gaped to gulp them down.

Joey realized he could still hit Chaoxing, and stop

rocketing forward. He'd drop in the raging ocean, but that seemed vastly preferable to meeting what lay ahead.

Sobbing, he threw the mace away and buried his fist in his pocket.

A final leap carried them inside one of the monster's mouths. Gargantuan teeth, gray streaks in the darkness, plummeted toward them.

Joey screamed. Then, once again, he and Chaoxing were falling through open sky. Evidently his guide had guessed correctly. The only way out of the cul-de-sac had been through the most terrifying thing inside it.

The towering black storm clouds kept blinking from one configuration to another. Apparently Chaoxing had decided that the next leg of their route ran through midair. Even though the calligrapher had gotten him safely to the ground before, Joey was a little surprised that the endless fall didn't bother him. Maybe the encounter with the island creature had overloaded his fear circuits. Or maybe the haziness still gnawing at his thoughts was to blame. Either way, for the moment, he wasn't complaining.

Pain stabbed up his forearm.

He snapped his head around. A bird with puke-yellow feathers had sunk its talons into him. No bigger than a robin, it bobbed down and bit him.

He lashed his arm like a whip, shaking the little monster loose. Wings beating, claws outstretched, it flew at him, and he saw it had Emily's face. It was still chewing a mouthful of his flesh.

As he swung back his arm to bash it, a flock of the creatures hammered down on him like hail. Each had the features, twisted with hate, of someone he cared about. Elaine. Artie. His mother. Fat old Bob Franklin. Sarah as she was today, and the child/daughter of his dreams.

Thrashing, he punched and tore at them until the survivors flapped away. His brain was full of static. He looked around and saw an old Asian man. The geezer seemed to be yelling, but he couldn't make out the words.

Then he noticed the cord connecting the old man's outstretched arm to his, and his thoughts snapped back into focus. He and Chaoxing had let go of each other's hands to fend off the birds, and because they were no longer in physical contact, the Asian couldn't pop them around. A field of thorny vines, slithering over each other like a nest of snakes, hurtled up at them. Joey's fear of falling, so pleasantly absent moments before, surged back.

Twisting, flailing, he grabbed for Chaoxing's hand. He couldn't reach it. A dozen vines reared like cobras. In another moment, he and the old man would crash down in their midst.

Chaoxing lurched toward him. *Flew* toward him. The Asian snatched his hand, and the world flickered.

Joey popped onto level, grassy ground. The landing threw him off balance. This time, Chaoxing fell down with him.

Joey raised his head and looked around. He and his companion were on the spacious front lawn of a country mansion. Judging by the vintage roadsters and uniformed chauffeurs waiting by the entrance, the owner was hosting a party. Anguished faces, their eyes weeping dark sap, bulged from the twisted bark of the nearby trees.

Just as Joey noticed the faces, Chaoxing carried him on through three more jumps. The last one put them on a Byway, a tunnel through the fog. Up ahead, the passage widened.

Chaoxing pressed him downward. "Sit. Breathe slowly. It will calm you."

Joey did as he'd been told. After a while, his fear faded, and the sensation that his mind was splintering disappeared.

Chaoxing untied their wrists, then used the rope to wipe the pus-like gore of the birds off his hatchet. "Better?" he asked.

"Yeah," said Joey, climbing to his feet. "Are we there?"

"We are," the calligrapher said. He waved the axe toward the spot where the Byway widened. "Your destination lies through there."

Joey shook his head. "I hoped you could take me fast, but I never dreamed it would be this fast. You're amazing. Terrifying and out of your mind, but amazing."

Chaoxing inclined his head. "Though today I serve the Emperor, once I was a guildsman, and the guilds guarded many powerful secrets. Charon was rash to abolish us. If he'd had us beside him in his time of troubles, he might still reign today."

"Well, I'm glad I had you with me in mine. Thank you."

Chaoxing bowed.

"Please thank Mr. Hong for me, too," Joey continued. "Tell him that now, I owe him."

"That will please him."

"Do you want to come on with me? You could rest up before you head back. I'm sure Elaine's Saints and Covenanters would make you welcome."

"Thank you, no. My duties await me, and, since I intend to return to Chinatown via the Byways, I have a journey of many days ahead. Good-bye, Joey Castelo, and take care. I sense that your troubles are far from over."

Joey grimaced. "Why am I not surprised? You be careful, too."

The old man smiled, turned, and hobbled down the path. His bites and cuts stinging, Joey watched him for a moment, then turned and ran in the opposite direction.

- THIRTY-NINE -

Heaven.

The Byway led Joey to a hilltop where the air abruptly turned from cold to balmy. Pinkish heat lightning flickered, vaguely revealing the landscape of Heaven spread out below. He could make out forests and meadows. Lakes and winding streams. Clumps of houses, and, not far away, the spires of a building resembling both a castle and a cathedral. In the darkness, it was hard to guess exactly how large the country of the Holy Covenant was, but he got the impression that it was roughly circular in shape.

He couldn't help feeling a little let down. Some wraiths insisted that the Far Shores lay *beyond* the Tempest, and had suns, moons, and stars. But, domed as it was by churning thunderheads, this territory was obviously just another eternally overcast eye in the endless storm. The fact diminished it somehow, made its claim to be any kind of paradise seem laughable.

But his disappointment only lasted a second. After all, he hadn't come because he believed the place was really *the* Heaven, but to rejoin Elaine and his friends, or to organize a rescue mission. Joey scrambled on down the path.

The path took him into a network of canyons and gullies.

The broken land resembled a maze of moats and earthworks protecting the pleasant-looking country beyond. He was glad that someone had marked the trail with a series of white stone crosses eight feet tall.

As he rounded the next bend, a clear soprano voice cried, "Halt!"

He jerked to a stop and looked up. From a narrow gap in the canyon wall stepped an angel, or, more likely, a ghost sculpted into the shape of one. Her face was as perfect as Chris's, but as austere and forbidding as his was warm and friendly. She had long golden hair, white-feathered wings, and a snowy robe with gilt trim. Her halo, orange and light green with edgy mistrust, and the leveled crossbow in her delicate hands undermined the illusion of divinity.

Joey reasoned that her presence shouldn't have surprised him. If he remembered the Bible correctly, even the original Heaven had angelic soldiers.

The angel sidled along the ledge, making room for her male counterpart to emerge from the crack. This sentry held a sword, its blade rippling with blue flame, in his left hand, and a crossbow with a pistol grip in his right.

"Are you a believer?" the woman said.

"Yes," Joey said. "Well, a friend, anyway. I need to see the Saints."

The angels exchanged glances. Their auras took on the flickering, multi-colored look that meant they didn't want anyone reading their emotions. Then, spreading her wings, the woman jumped to the canyon floor. Joey got the impression she couldn't fly, but her pinions could give marginal service as a half-assed parachute.

When she had retrained her weapon, the male angel leaped. Up close, his sword radiated the chill of Underworld fire. "We'll take you to someone who can help you," the woman said. She and her partner edged behind Joey. "Walk on, please."

"You guys are treating me like a prisoner," Joey said. "As long as you get me in to see the Saints, I don't mind, but is something wrong?"

"Generally speaking, new members of the flock arrive with one of our missionaries to vouch for them," the woman answered smoothly. "When strangers come alone, we have to take precautions until we're sure they mean no harm. It's nothing personal, believe me."

Joey had a hunch that while she might not have lied, she hadn't told the whole truth, either. "Whatever. Look, my name is Joey Castelo. If my friend Elaine Forrester — Margaret Elaine Rochelle to you guys — got here, maybe she mentioned me. She's a Saint herself."

As soon as the words were out of his mouth, he sensed the angels tensing. For some reason, it had been exactly the wrong thing to say.

He wondered if Chaoxing had delivered him to the right Heaven. It seemed unlikely that the shrewd old man would make a mistake, but on the other hand, it would be just his luck. "Are you guys in the Church of the Holy Covenant?" he asked.

"Oh, yes," said the woman, her voice brittle with hostility. "Keep moving."

"Will you just tell me if you know Margaret Rochelle—"

A freezing point jabbed him in the shoulder. He leaped forward, slapping at his back till he was sure he wasn't on fire. "Shut up and walk," the male angel said.

Okay, Joey thought, it's official. I'm in trouble. He wondered if he should make a break for freedom. But maybe this was a misunderstanding, one he could clear up if he kept his head. It had better be, because if Elaine's own people wouldn't help him, he couldn't imagine who would. Besides, he'd need the voice's power to get away from two captors who had the drop of him.

The rocky canyon trail suddenly opened into rolling

fields. Evidently, unconstrained by the natural laws that molded the world of the Quick, the terrain in a Far Shore could vary nearly as unpredictably as the geography of the Tempest itself. Off to the right, barely visible in the gloom, lines of men surged back and forth. A voice barked commands, and wood clacked on wood. Apparently soldiers or martial artists were drilling with staves or clubs. Ahead, on a hilltop, loomed the imposing structure Joey had glimpsed before. Ivory crosses capped the turrets, and winged archers paced the battlements. Banners bearing the monogram *ED* and what he took to be a shepherd's crook flapped in the breeze.

"Keep moving," said the female angel. "We're going to the citadel."

When Joey and his escorts reached the fortress, they marched him under a portcullis and across a cobbled courtyard. They ushered him through a pair of massive brass-studded doors and the hall beyond. A few wraiths with hunched, nervous looks watched the small procession from the shadows.

Two flunkies in purple choir robes pulled open a final set of tall, arched doors. The panels were carved with scenes from the life of Christ. Joey started across the threshold, then froze.

The lofty chamber before him looked like it had once been some kind of council chamber. Three horseshoe-shaped tiers stair-stepped from the floor to the eggshell-colored walls. But someone had smashed all the ornate, high-backed chairs except the one directly opposite the entrance. In it slouched a tall, rawboned man with piercing brown eyes, bristling white eyebrows, a Santa Claus beard, and a mane of silvery hair. Dressed in a rust-red robe and leather sandals, he looked like Joey's image of Moses or John the Baptist, but black veins wormed through his halo. In his left hand, he cradled a crystal globe like Elaine's. The key shed gold and green light, though that too was laced with strands of darkness. Beside him, a trophy case of similar orbs feebly reflected the glow.

On the tiers beneath him lounged George, Holliday, a cloaked man in a red and white enameled fox mask, and, to Joey's amazement, the tuxedo-clad Spectre who'd tried to recruit him immediately after his death.

And above and behind them all, her wrists and ankles spiked to a splintery wooden X-shaped rack, hung Elaine. Judging by the way her head lolled, she was unconscious. Joey gaped at her for a moment, then lunged forward.

Suddenly Holliday was on his feet, and the revolver that had been tucked in his vest was in his hand. "Stand still," he said.

The sight of the gun jolted Joey back to his senses. Lurching to a halt, skidding on the marble floor, he looked at the man with the key. "Are you one of the Saints? You've been tricked. That girl—"

"Silence!" bellowed the man in the chair. His voice, or perhaps the will behind it, rocked Joey backward like a hard punch to the jaw. "I'm Eric Danziger. The *only* Saint. All others are false prophets." He peered past Joey. "Where did you find this man, my daughter?"

"He showed up at the border," the female angel said. "He asked to see the Saints, and then he said he was a friend of the Great Whore."

"We know him, Your Holiness," said Holliday. "He was one of Miss Forrester's companions. He died a second death falling off a cliff, but apparently it didn't take."

"Listen to me," Joey begged. "That guy in the tux is a Spectre. Whatever he's told you—"

"I bade you be still!" Danziger said. "How dare you presume to instruct the Lord's right hand. I know what Travanti is. I know all my servants, and the roles they're fated to play in God's design." He paused, as if trying to squelch his anger. When he spoke again, his tone was gentle. "My son, when you made common cause with Margaret Rochelle, you threw in your lot with the Antichrist. Now you've invaded the kingdom of Heaven itself with vile intent. Your sins cry out for damnation. Nevertheless, Christ and I, in our infinite mercy, will forgive you if you repent."

Joey dropped to his knees. "I'm sorry. I do repent. Please, teach me how to be good and serve the church."

"Liar!" Danziger screamed. "Pharisee! Do you think I can't see into the core of your wicked heart? Take him to the barracoon."

George cleared his throat.

Danziger looked at him. "Yes, my son?"

"Your Holiness, this man is my property. I've owned him for a year now. Dr. Holliday and Mr. Travanti agreed to return him to me if he could be recovered."

Holliday pushed his blue glasses up to the bridge of his nose. "If you want him back, why'd you toss him off the cliff?"

"I was overexcited," said George primly. "He'd given offense, and needed to be chastised." He sneered at Joey. "One imagines he still does."

Travanti and Holliday exchanged glances. "It was part of the deal," the bounty hunter conceded.

"Well, I wasn't a party to the deal," Danziger said petulantly. "My angels caught him inside Heaven's bounds. He's mine now."

"Well, technically, no," the man in the fox mask said. "Not according to the laws of Stygia."

"This isn't Stygia," Danziger said, sounding not nearly as arrogant as he had before.

"If Your Holiness will return the Thrall to me," said George, "I'll strive, through the application of rigorous discipline, to grind the wickedness out of him."

Danziger grimaced. "All right. In recognition of your

service to God, and in hopes of saving the slave's benighted soul, I give him to you."

"Thank you, Your Holiness," said George. He reached inside his grimy raincoat and brought out Joey's manacles. Evidently someone had climbed down the mountainside and recovered them.

Up until now, Joey had been struggling to block out the sight of Elaine's crucifixion. To ignore the maddening irony that the haven she'd sought so desperately was under her enemies' control. If he lost his composure now, if he provoked Holliday or the angels into killing him, he'd lose whatever forlorn chance he had to help her.

But when Joey saw the shackles, he snapped. He leaped up and whirled, hoping to snatch one of the angels' weapons.

"No!" Danziger shouted. His aura and the glow of his key pulsed, dyeing the walls crimson. Joey felt immense power throb around him. It was like being struck by lightning, but without pain. Stone tentacles shot out of the floor and whipped around his ankles.

Thrown off balance, he fell. With a double crack, his immobilized ankles snapped.

He must have blacked out, because suddenly George was crouching over him. The little man had already locked a cuff on his left wrist and was about to do the same to his right.

Joey tried to jerk his arm back, but the pain in his ankles made him spastic and slow. The bracelet clicked shut. The marble tentacles released his legs and slid back into the floor.

"That's that," said George, standing up. "Will your Holiness permit me to withdraw?" Danziger nodded. "Come with me, Peter, and we'll discuss your attitude further in our quarters." Perhaps he didn't realize that Joey could no longer walk, or maybe he expected him to crawl.

"Go to hell," Joey snarled. The familiar coldness and nausea flowed into his body. He was already so miserable that for once, it didn't matter. But then, nothing did. Bound and crippled by the manacles, he felt he had no hope of saving Elaine.

"You have to learn to obey," said George. He reached into his pocket, brought out Joey's baton, pulled it to its full length, and started to beat him. Joey felt the first three blows. The fourth one lashed him across the temple and buried the world in darkness.

-FORTY-

Joey awoke in a dark room on a cold wooden floor. Outside an ox-eye window, sickly green lightning flickered within the writhing clouds.

At first he couldn't remember where he was. But when he rolled onto his side, his chain clinked, and his memory flooded back.

"How do you feel?" asked George softly.

Joey's head jerked up. George was sitting on the edge of a canopy bed. He'd shed his raincoat to reveal his yellow suit. As Joey recalled, the garish outfit had gotten dirty and wrinkled in the Byways. Evidently someone had cleaned and pressed it since.

Joey felt a surge of rage. He almost scrambled up and lunged at George, even though he knew the shackles would hurt him as soon as he started to make his move. "You son of a bitch," he said.

George pouted. "There's no need to be unpleasant. If you'd simply pretended your spirit was broken and followed instructions, you would have spared the sensitive Mr. Montaigne the ugly necessity of thrashing you. I daresay he found the experience as distasteful as you did."

Sneering, Joey clambered to his feet, realizing as he did that, though he still ached, his ghostly body had largely healed its cuts and broken bones. "Oh, yeah? How did it stack up to tossing me off a cliff?"

George's beady eyes widened. "Good lord, I know what I said downstairs, but surely *you* weren't taken in. You must understand *why* I pushed you."

Joey's anger yielded ever so slightly to uncertainty. "It sure as hell seemed like you wanted to kill me. Especially about the time my head smashed open on the rocks."

George sighed. "I should have expected this. But when one is accustomed to seeing like an eagle, it's difficult to remember that the average man is nearly as blind as a mole."

"Just tell me what you're talking about."

"A Spectre's claws and fangs are as lethal as darksteel. If they kill you, there's no chance of cheating Oblivion. Perceiving you to be mortally wounded, the quick-thinking Mr. Montaigne contrived you an alternative demise, one which afforded the hope of resurrection."

"If you expect me to thank you," said Joey, "you're going to have a long wait. Because I know you sold us out and led Holliday and his buddies to the caravan. I thought so before, and now that I see you here" — he waved his hand at the sparsely furnished, vaguely medieval-looking bedroom — "I'm sure of it."

George shook his head. "You don't grasp the subtleties of that maneuver, either. Do you recall that after we fled from our nemesis in the swamp, Elaine was too tired to navigate?"

"Yeah."

"And surely you remember how, when I was trying to come to terms with my feelings concerning Beverly's suicide, I went prowling around the oasis by myself."

"Uh-huh. Get to the point."

"Before I encountered you, I explored in the opposite direction. And discovered the caravan had ventured down a blind alley. Later, when Holliday took me prisoner, I knew the rest of you had nowhere to run."

"Maybe we could have outfought him, if you hadn't helped him sneak up on us. You pointed the lookout position out to them, didn't you?"

"It wouldn't have mattered if Artie had warned you. I told the enemy otherwise, but I lied. You were outnumbered. You know what Holliday's guns can do. And what condition the caravan was in. The nightmares left most of you too weary and too frazzled to use your special talents."

"You didn't know that for sure."

"Didn't I? You must have surveyed the battlefield, if only briefly. Did you spy Chris in his ogre form? Did you notice Elaine casting any helpful illusions, or putting any of your foes to sleep? Did you hear Kimberly wailing her battle-cry?"

Joey scowled. "No," he admitted.

"No. *You people didn't have a chance*. I tried to arrange matters so everyone would be taken prisoner instead of killed, and you personally would be delivered into my custody. I hoped that, conspiring together, we could eventually liberate the others.

"Unfortunately, things didn't go precisely as planned. I meant to locate you instantly. Use the shackles to paralyze you, thus ensuring that no one would do you harm. But you entered the fray before I spotted you. One of the Spectres ignored its orders and ripped you to shreds. And afterwards, there was never a way to free our comrades unaided. All I could do was keep pretending to be a rogue and bide my time."

Joey realized he believed him. With the boxer at his mercy, George didn't need to lie. Yet he felt an obscure reluctance to let the little schemer off the hook. "Do you really expect to convince me you changed sides to help the rest of us? I think you did it to save your own skin."

George drew himself up straight, as if for an indignant retort, then grimaced and spread his hands. "Naturally I wanted to survive. Does anyone ever do anything for just one reason, or completely lose sight of his own best interests?

But I swear, I was trying to look after the rest of you as well."

Joey sighed. "Okay. Fair enough. Did everybody else come through the fight?"

George hesitated. "No. We lost one of the jugglers."

Joey's grimaced. "Damn."

"Perhaps my ploy wasn't so clever after all," George said somberly. "Perhaps I should have sacrificed myself. It's conceivable that in a fair fight—"

Joey squeezed the little man's shoulder, surprising himself in the process. He hadn't felt this kindly disposed toward George in a long time. "Don't second-guess yourself. If everybody else made it, I suppose you did the right thing. Anyway, what's done is done."

George smiled wanly. "Thank you."

"Obviously, you understand what's going on around here. Fill me in, and then we'll figure out what to do about it."

"Very well," said George. "It all begins and ends with Danziger. Years ago, he was an ordinary Holy Covenant Saint, if that isn't an oxymoron. Just one member of a council of prelates established to govern this place till Christ Himself turns up at the end of time."

Joey nodded. "I'd figured out that much."

"Unfortunately, for some reason, he went mad, and became a Spectre. And when he did—"

"He decided he wanted to run the show all by himself," Joey interjected.

George frowned. "Who's telling this story? But you're right. Naturally, he needed powerful help to stage a coup. I don't know why he didn't seek it in the Tempest. Perhaps at that point, he didn't think of himself as a Spectre. Deranged as he is, he may not even now. At any rate, he appealed to the Laughing Lady, and she loaned him one of her Legions."

"Why?" Joey asked. "What was in it for her?"

"Danziger pledged her an annual tithe of souls to feed

her forges. A secret supply she needn't share with the other Deathlords."

Joey scowled. "Nice."

"Isn't it?" George said sardonically. "Danziger and the Hierarchs attacked the rest of the council by surprise and overwhelmed them. He declared them false Apostles, and himself the only true Saint and monarch. I gather that most of the populace accepted the fait accompli. After all, they'd settled here because they believed in their church's authority, and Danziger, ebon-stained aura or no, was now the only holy man left. Besides, they lacked the means to defy him. The few who tried were among the first to trudge away to Stygia in chains. Over time, the occupying Legionnaires withdrew, as he replaced them with a loyal, indigenous force of angels."

Joey nodded. "I can guess the next part, too. Danziger didn't want any new Saints showing up to challenge him. The Laughing Lady promised to make sure they wouldn't. Her agents are supposed to pick them off as soon as they enter the Shadowlands."

The sky outside the circular window blazed white with a particularly brilliant flare of lightning. Thunder, which was usually inaudible inside a Byway, terminal, or Far Shore, boomed.

As the echoes faded, George said, "Yes. Actually, Elaine died within days of the coup, before the Lady's safeguards were fully in place. That's why she was able to escape. There are no Holy Covenant missionaries of the old school left to guide spirits here anymore. They've all been reindoctrinated or eliminated."

"God knows I'm not complaining, but I'm surprised Danziger didn't kill Elaine as soon as he got his hands on her."

George shrugged. "Perhaps he feels that her torture provides an object lesson to those who might seek to overthrow his regime. Considering the harsh and capricious nature of his rule, the land must still harbor closet malcontents. Or perhaps, after years of absolute control, he simply feels secure enough to indulge his natural sadism."

Joey frowned. "Okay, I think I've got the basics. But there's still one thing that doesn't add up. Danziger's obligated to ship people to the Laughing Lady. Elaine said her religion isn't huge. We can assume that only a fraction of the members turn into wraiths, and only some of those ever make it to Heaven. Isn't His Holiness giving away more souls than he's taking in? Isn't he going to wind up boss of an empty country?"

"He's not so insane that he hasn't thought of that. Did you notice soldiers training on your way in?"

"Yeah. Oh. I get it. New recruits, right? He wants to take over some other Far Shores."

George nodded grimly. "Travanti says that he and his tribe will help if promised a share of the spoils. Fitzroy — the fellow in the fox mask, the Madwoman's emissary — is offering troops in exchange for a split of the conquered territory. Holliday is contemplating joining the venture as a mercenary officer, and I've been retained as a military advisor."

Joey raised an eyebrow. "You?"

The little man bristled. "Our George can discourse on Caesar and Clausewitz with considerable erudition."

"Yeah, but how are you on Sun Tzu?"

George cocked his head. "*You've* read *The Art of War?*"

"Not so's you'd notice it." Joey's momentary amusement gave way to renewed anxiety. "This war thing really bothers you, doesn't it?"

"Yes." George stood up and started pacing. "Generally speaking, one Far Shore doesn't make war on another. Nor does Stygia. The Hierarchs persecute Heretics in the Shadowlands and Byways, but they usually stop well short of invading other nations in the Tempest. And *no* state, even the most depraved or barbaric, has ever sealed a military alliance with Spectres. That's climbing into bed with the Void itself."

George's mouth twisted. "Perhaps I'm overreacting. After all, this so-called Heaven and any neighboring territories only constitute one tiny backwater of the Underworld. Still, here one can see the old order, the old understandings, the old balance of power crumbling. I can imagine this conflict *spreading*. Chaos and destruction engulfing everyone everywhere. Oblivion rising to drown the wreckage. Prophets have been foretelling Doomsday ever since Charon disappeared. Perhaps we're witnessing the start."

Joey tried to imagine the whole universe, the halves belonging to Restless and Quick alike, dissolving into nothingness. He couldn't. The idea was too huge, weird, and terrible for him, and, judging by George's slack-jawed, freaked-out expression, that was just as well. Hoping to snap the little man out of his funk, he said, "When I was alive, people called that the domino theory. If something bad happens one place, it'll spread everywhere, like flood water. If Communists took over Vietnam, they'd eventually grab all of Asia and finally the U.S., too. Except it didn't happen that way, did it?"

George gave a grudging little smile. "I suppose not."

"Then don't go nuts over a bunch of mumbo jumbo. You're not the type. Concentrate on how to help our friends."

"All right." George scratched his receding chin. "It's going to be difficult even with your assistance. My powers have no meaning away from the Shroud. Have you learned to weave illusions yet?"

"Sorry. Elaine said that won't happen for a long time. Maybe never."

"Drat. Well, at least you're still abnormally strong and quick."

Joey hesitated. His instincts told him not to undermine George's confidence, yet he felt that he owed a comrade in a dangerous exploit the truth. "Uh, not really. That Superman stuff came from my Shadow. I had to give it up to keep from dying for keeps."

George gaped at him. "Oh, no."

"Don't panic," said Joey. "I'm still a professional fighter. I'm still tough." He realized he was saying it for his own benefit as much as his companion's.

"I know," muttered George. He turned to the window and stared out at the clouds. "Still, we'll have to choose our moment with exquisite care. Play a waiting game. Perhaps in a few days, when Holliday and the others trust me even more—"

"A few days!" Joey exploded.

George spun around. "Keep your voice down! We can't afford to let anyone overhear us!"

Joey knew George was right. Trying to dampen his anger, he took a deep breath. "Elaine's *suffering*. What's more, in a few days, Danziger could decide to kill her. Or those darksteel nails could do it whether he means them to or not. Kim and the others could get shipped to Stygia."

"Surely," said George, "slaves with their talents—"

"Danziger needs souls for the tribute, right? If he's worried about unrest, wouldn't he rather send outsiders, any outsiders, than his own people? Look, the odds were a million to one that I'd ever show up to help you, but here I am. You've already had more luck than you had any right to expect. It's time to make your play."

"You don't understand what we're facing," George replied. "Holliday and the Spectres are bad enough. But Danziger considers himself the hand of God, his followers believe it, and somehow, in this place, that makes it true. Sometimes he works miracles. Makes things happen just by willing them. You know how he made the arms shoot out of the floor."

Joey didn't like the sound of that at all. He did his best to hide his uneasiness behind a sneer. "Big deal. All us spooks have our cheesy little tricks. Danziger isn't all-knowing, or he'd see through your lies. And he's not all-powerful, or he could have knocked off the rest of the council without any help from the Hierarchs."

"Perhaps he isn't omnipotent, but I fear he's far more formidable than we are. Reluctant as I am to say it, we may find that the most we can accomplish is simply to save ourselves. Slip away. Our friends wouldn't want us to perish—"

"Damn it, no!"

George gazed pointedly at the manacles. "Mr. Montaigne can compel you if he deems it necessary."

"It always comes down to that, doesn't it? Well, not this time. If you want to run out on the others, you'll have to leave me behind, too. Danziger can ship my crippled, puking carcass to the fires. You know, every once in a while, you act like a stand-up guy. I start to think I was wrong about you. Then you turn back into a rat."

Quivering, George glared. Joey stared right back at him, and after a few moments, it was the man in the yellow suit who looked away. "I keep thinking about Beverly," he muttered. "And something Travanti said. He claimed my Shadow is very strong."

"Now there's a shock."

"I don't *want* to be a rat or a weasel or any of the other epithets people hurl at me." George sounded like he was pleading. "I want to be loyal and true. But fate, or at least elementary prudence, never permits it."

Joey sighed. "I don't know what to tell you, except that there's never going to be an easy time to do what's hard, or a safe time to take a risk. You just have to go for it."

George grimaced. "You know, you're right. And by god, if the canny Mr. Montaigne can't outwit the likes of Eric Danziger and his assistant maniacs, who can? Let's do it. But we should at least wait until our principal adversaries are absent from the fortress. Fortunately, his Holiness likes to review his new troops, and march in solemn procession through the various hamlets, with his lieutenants and any distinguished guests in tow. I imagine it makes him feel papal. If I could find an excuse to remain behind—"

"Tell him you want to torture me some more."

George nodded. "That's good. He'll sympathize with that. And after he's gone…"

-FORTY-ONE-

Head bowed, shackles clinking, Joey trudged along two paces behind George like a properly cowed and obedient slave. He wasn't sure that his acting was really necessary. The shadowy stone corridors were all but deserted. Maybe, over time, Danziger had given most of the fortress servants to the Laughing Lady. Or maybe he'd drafted them into his newly enlarged army. In any case, parts of the building seemed virtually abandoned. The candles and oil lamps were unlit. The air smelled musty, and dust lay thick on the furniture. No doubt the corners would have been full of cobwebs had Heaven possessed any spiders to spin them.

His grimy trench coat flapping, George led the way down a wide, curving staircase and into the central hall. As they'd expected, an angel, tall, golden-haired, alabaster-skinned, and handsome enough to pose for Nazi propaganda posters, was standing watch in front of the entrance to the throne room. But luckily, for the moment at least, there was no one else in sight.

George sauntered up to the sentry. "Hello," he said. "I'd like to go inside."

"No can do, Mr. Pryor," said the angel with a New Jersey accent. "His Holiness doesn't want anybody messing around in there while he's away."

"But you know me," said George, edging sideways. The angel reflexively pivoted, keeping the little man in front of him. "I'm in His Holiness's army, too. I want to give my Thrall here another look at the Whore's humiliation. It will help him learn obedience. Perhaps even steer him toward our faith."

"That would be great," said the guard. "But it'll have to wait."

By now, George had the angel facing directly away from Joey. The winged man had a mole on the back of his neck, perhaps the only flaw in his unearthly beauty. George twitched a fingertip, and the chain between Joey's cuffs disappeared. He eased the baton out of his pocket, extended it, and slammed it down on the sentry's head.

The blow landed with a sharp crack. The angel crumpled. Lunging, George just barely managed to catch him. He and Joey didn't want the stunned man thumping, or his scabbard clanking, on the floor.

"Drag him inside," said Joey. He pulled open the tall door, lavishly carved with scenes of the Passion and Resurrection, in front of him, then gave a start of surprise.

Helpless as Elaine seemed, Danziger must have been at least a little worried that she could escape on her own or concerned that someone would try to rescue her, because he'd posted a second angel in the chamber. This one, a willowy woman wearing a glittering platinum chain and diamond-studded medallion, had been sitting on the middle tier beneath the crucifixion rack, tuning a small golden harp. Now she leaped to her feet and grabbed the hilt of her sword. Her halo blazed red.

Joey was sure he and George couldn't con her, not when she'd already spotted her unconscious comrade in the little man's arms. Their only chance was to keep her from yelling for help. He sprinted at her.

As he'd hoped, threatened by his charge, she was more interested in defending herself than shouting. She whipped out her sword and gripped it in both hands. The blade burst into hissing violet flame. She bounded off the risers and landed in a martial-arts stance, knees flexed, dainty white feet at right angles.

Her weapon gave her the longer reach. Hoping to get inside it, Joey tried to knock the blade aside.

The flaming sword swept up before the baton could hit it, then streaked down. He snatched his arm back to keep from losing a hand.

Radiating chill — he wondered fleetingly if some magic in the sword made the user impervious to its fire — the sibilant blade struck at his head. He parried, once again with no time to spare. Metal clanged. The shock of the impact jolted his arm and rocked him back a step.

He felt like he was moving in slow motion. He'd gotten so used to depending on the fury of the voice that he'd all but forgotten how to fight without it. He had a hunch that he'd better remember fast.

Snarling, the angel thrust at his chest. He stepped into the attack, slipping just to the side of it, and swept his club in a backhand blow.

But the sword-fighter was moving, too. Spinning away. Instead of catching her squarely in the head, the baton merely grazed one of her wings, tearing loose two gleaming feathers. At the same instant, she kicked backward. Her heel caught Joey on the knee. He reeled and fell on top of one of the toppled, broken chairs, smashing it to splinters.

Graceful as a ballerina, wings half spread, the angel whirled and rushed him. The burning sword hurtled down. He threw himself to one side, narrowly avoiding the attack, rolled, and scrambled to his feet. Luckily, though his knee throbbed, it also held him up.

Sapphire eyes shining, the angel moved forward. He retreated behind another ruined chair, then kicked it into her shins.

She stumbled back. He sprang at her, swung, and the baton crunched against her temple. For a split-second, he thought the blow had won the fight for him. Then, somehow, she slammed the butt of her sword hilt into his ribs, knocking him sideways. Her wings flapped once, cracking like a whip, restoring her equilibrium before he recovered his. Her weapon whirled over her head—

A second blade, this one rippling with crimson fire, popped from between her breasts. She made a choking sound and fell. Her robe began to smolder.

Straining, bracing one foot against her back, George dragged his sword out of her body. A moment later, the corpse dissolved, leaving only her weapon, jewelry, and burning garment behind. "Drat!" said the small man in a rapid, feverish voice. "I should have waited. I took the other guard's sword. This one shouldn't have allowed herself to forget there were two of us."

"Yeah," said Joey. "Thanks for bailing me out. I was in trouble."

"You're welcome," said George, sounding calmer. He pocketed the dead woman's medallion. "But I'm sure you could have bested her in time."

Joey shook his head. "My rhythm's off. I'm slower, but I'm not sure how much. I can't tell what will work, and—" He grimaced. "Never mind. I'll be all right next time. Let's get Elaine."

He'd been struggling not to think about what had been done to her. He'd been afraid it would make him crazy. But now, as he looked up at her motionless body, a kind of anguish overwhelmed him. For an instant he was sure she was already dead. Then he remembered that if that were so, she would have dissolved like the female angel.

Standing on Danziger's throne, he took hold of the torture rack. Fortunately, it wasn't bolted to the wall, just hanging from a hook like a picture frame. Gritting his teeth, using every bit of his strength, he lifted it down. The chair groaned ominously. George grabbed the bottom of the rack, and together they set it gently on the floor.

Elaine never stirred. Joey desperately wanted to wake her up, but realized that it might be kinder to let her sleep through the next part of the operation.

George reached inside his coat and brought out the claw hammers he'd pilfered from a storeroom. Kneeling beside the splintery wooden X, he and Joey set to work pulling out the heavy darksteel nails.

The task turned out to be every bit as unpleasant as Joey had expected. The spikes were in deep. He had to gouge Elaine's flesh to get the hammer claw under the nailhead. When he pried, her wrist bones cracked. And as the spike lurched out, squealing, a fraction of an inch at a time, it jerked back and forth, tearing its socket larger. The absence of blood didn't make the wound look any less gruesome.

He wrenched out three nails while George awkwardly managed one. Then he stroked Elaine's cheek. "Sweetheart? It's Joey. Can you hear me?"

She didn't respond.

"Shake her," said George. "Or pinch her. Someone could burst in on us at any moment."

"No. Not yet. She's been hurt too much already. Give her another couple seconds, and then I'll see if she's dreaming. If she is, I can make contact that way. Elaine, *please*, you've got to wake up."

The illusionist shifted her shoulders. Her long-lashed eyes fluttered open. "Joey?" she whispered groggily.

His throat felt clogged. "Yeah."

She blinked as if her eyes were tearing up. "I had a terrible dream. You were dead."

"Well, I'm not." He smiled wryly. "I mean, no more than usual."

"We have to make ourselves scarce very quickly," said

George. "I can appreciate that you're in pain, but—"

Elaine's head snapped toward him. Wide-eyed horror drove the drowsiness out of her face. She scrambled backward, halfway off the X.

"It's all right," said Joey.

Her maimed hands clumsy, she clutched at him. "No! He sold us out! He *smiled* while they nailed me down! He'll hurt us!"

"No," Joey insisted. "I know it seemed like he was a traitor, but trust me, he's not. Relax, and for god's sake, keep your voice down."

She gazed into his face. He could tell from the way her mouth tightened that she was trying to calm herself. "Okay. If *you* say he's all right, I'll believe it. Do you know where our friends are?"

"Yeah. We're going after them next."

George opened the display case beside the throne. "Can you tell which key is yours? Does it matter?"

Her face twisted. "It doesn't matter at all. I don't want any of them."

"But you might need one," he replied, "to plot our course away from here. Or... well, who knows?" He stuck two crystal globes in his trench coat pockets.

Joey gently squeezed Elaine's shoulders, then strode to the unconscious angel and stripped him of his sword belt and robe. When he saw the guard's crotch, he winced. Evidently, Joey thought, Danziger wanted his soldiers to resemble angels in every respect. The guard was as sexless as a Ken doll.

Joey buckled on the belt, then carried the robe to Elaine. "Lots of the people around here wear these. Put this on over your clothes, keep your head down, and with luck, nobody will recognize you. Then we'll sneak out the back door."

She tried to stand up. As soon as she put weight on her wrists and ankles, she gasped and flopped back down. "Oh, god," she whimpered, "that hurts."

"Don't worry about it," said Joey. "I'll hold you up. Or carry you if I need to."

She shook her head. "I don't want to slow you down. I saw there are guards on the wall. If one of them did recognize me, if you had to run—"

"Please," said George, "don't distress yourself needlessly. Your artful rescuers have matters well in hand. All we need is a diversion to draw the sentries' attention." He waved the flaming sword, drawing a scarlet arc in the air. "One or two fires should do nicely."

-FORTY-ONE-

Head bowed, shackles clinking, Joey trudged along two paces behind George like a properly cowed and obedient slave. He wasn't sure that his acting was really necessary. The shadowy stone corridors were all but deserted. Maybe, over time, Danziger had given most of the fortress servants to the Laughing Lady. Or maybe he'd drafted them into his newly enlarged army. In any case, parts of the building seemed virtually abandoned. The candles and oil lamps were unlit. The air smelled musty, and dust lay thick on the furniture. No doubt the corners would have been full of cobwebs had Heaven possessed any spiders to spin them.

His grimy trench coat flapping, George led the way down a wide, curving staircase and into the central hall. As they'd expected, an angel, tall, golden-haired, alabaster-skinned, and handsome enough to pose for Nazi propaganda posters, was standing watch in front of the entrance to the throne room. But luckily, for the moment at least, there was no one else in sight.

George sauntered up to the sentry. "Hello," he said. "I'd like to go inside."

"No can do, Mr. Pryor," said the angel with a New Jersey accent. "His Holiness doesn't want anybody messing around in there while he's away."

"But you know me," said George, edging sideways. The angel reflexively pivoted, keeping the little man in front of him. "I'm in His Holiness's army, too. I want to give my Thrall here another look at the Whore's humiliation. It will help him learn obedience. Perhaps even steer him toward our faith."

"That would be great," said the guard. "But it'll have to wait."

By now, George had the angel facing directly away from Joey. The winged man had a mole on the back of his neck, perhaps the only flaw in his unearthly beauty. George twitched a fingertip, and the chain between Joey's cuffs disappeared. He eased the baton out of his pocket, extended it, and slammed it down on the sentry's head.

The blow landed with a sharp crack. The angel crumpled. Lunging, George just barely managed to catch him. He and Joey didn't want the stunned man thumping, or his scabbard clanking, on the floor.

"Drag him inside," said Joey. He pulled open the tall door, lavishly carved with scenes of the Passion and Resurrection, in front of him, then gave a start of surprise.

Helpless as Elaine seemed, Danziger must have been at least a little worried that she could escape on her own or concerned that someone would try to rescue her, because he'd posted a second angel in the chamber. This one, a willowy woman wearing a glittering platinum chain and diamond-studded medallion, had been sitting on the middle tier beneath the crucifixion rack, tuning a small golden harp. Now she leaped to her feet and grabbed the hilt of her sword. Her halo blazed red.

Joey was sure he and George couldn't con her, not when she'd already spotted her unconscious comrade in the little man's arms. Their only chance was to keep her from yelling for help. He sprinted at her.

As he'd hoped, threatened by his charge, she was more

interested in defending herself than shouting. She whipped out her sword and gripped it in both hands. The blade burst into hissing violet flame. She bounded off the risers and landed in a martial-arts stance, knees flexed, dainty white feet at right angles.

Her weapon gave her the longer reach. Hoping to get inside it, Joey tried to knock the blade aside.

The flaming sword swept up before the baton could hit it, then streaked down. He snatched his arm back to keep from losing a hand.

Radiating chill — he wondered fleetingly if some magic in the sword made the user impervious to its fire — the sibilant blade struck at his head. He parried, once again with no time to spare. Metal clanged. The shock of the impact jolted his arm and rocked him back a step.

He felt like he was moving in slow motion. He'd gotten so used to depending on the fury of the voice that he'd all but forgotten how to fight without it. He had a hunch that he'd better remember fast.

Snarling, the angel thrust at his chest. He stepped into the attack, slipping just to the side of it, and swept his club in a backhand blow.

But the sword-fighter was moving, too. Spinning away. Instead of catching her squarely in the head, the baton merely grazed one of her wings, tearing loose two gleaming feathers. At the same instant, she kicked backward. Her heel caught Joey on the knee. He reeled and fell on top of one of the toppled, broken chairs, smashing it to splinters.

Graceful as a ballerina, wings half spread, the angel whirled and rushed him. The burning sword hurtled down. He threw himself to one side, narrowly avoiding the attack, rolled, and scrambled to his feet. Luckily, though his knee throbbed, it also held him up.

Sapphire eyes shining, the angel moved forward. He retreated behind another ruined chair, then kicked it into her shins.

She stumbled back. He sprang at her, swung, and the baton crunched against her temple. For a split-second, he thought the blow had won the fight for him. Then, somehow, she slammed the butt of her sword hilt into his ribs, knocking him sideways. Her wings flapped once, cracking like a whip, restoring her equilibrium before he recovered his. Her weapon whirled over her head—

A second blade, this one rippling with crimson fire, popped from between her breasts. She made a choking sound and fell. Her robe began to smolder.

Straining, bracing one foot against her back, George dragged his sword out of her body. A moment later, the corpse dissolved, leaving only her weapon, jewelry, and burning garment behind. "Drat!" said the small man in a rapid, feverish voice. "I should have waited. I took the other guard's sword. This one shouldn't have allowed herself to forget there were two of us."

"Yeah," said Joey. "Thanks for bailing me out. I was in trouble."

"You're welcome," said George, sounding calmer. He pocketed the dead woman's medallion. "But I'm sure you could have bested her in time."

Joey shook his head. "My rhythm's off. I'm slower, but I'm not sure how much. I can't tell what will work, and—" He grimaced. "Never mind. I'll be all right next time. Let's get Elaine."

He'd been struggling not to think about what had been done to her. He'd been afraid it would make him crazy. But now, as he looked up at her motionless body, a kind of anguish overwhelmed him. For an instant he was sure she was already dead. Then he remembered that if that were so, she would have dissolved like the female angel.

Standing on Danziger's throne, he took hold of the torture rack. Fortunately, it wasn't bolted to the wall, just hanging from a hook like a picture frame. Gritting his teeth, using every bit of his strength, he lifted it down. The chair groaned ominously. George grabbed the bottom of the rack, and together they set it gently on the floor.

Elaine never stirred. Joey desperately wanted to wake her up, but realized that it might be kinder to let her sleep through the next part of the operation.

George reached inside his coat and brought out the claw hammers he'd pilfered from a storeroom. Kneeling beside the splintery wooden X, he and Joey set to work pulling out the heavy darksteel nails.

The task turned out to be every bit as unpleasant as Joey had expected. The spikes were in deep. He had to gouge Elaine's flesh to get the hammer claw under the nailhead. When he pried, her wrist bones cracked. And as the spike lurched out, squealing, a fraction of an inch at a time, it jerked back and forth, tearing its socket larger. The absence of blood didn't make the wound look any less gruesome.

He wrenched out three nails while George awkwardly managed one. Then he stroked Elaine's cheek. "Sweetheart? It's Joey. Can you hear me?"

She didn't respond.

"Shake her," said George. "Or pinch her. Someone could burst in on us at any moment."

"No. Not yet. She's been hurt too much already. Give her another couple seconds, and then I'll see if she's dreaming. If she is, I can make contact that way. Elaine, *please*, you've got to wake up."

The illusionist shifted her shoulders. Her long-lashed eyes fluttered open. "Joey?" she whispered groggily.

His throat felt clogged. "Yeah."

She blinked as if her eyes were tearing up. "I had a terrible dream. You were dead."

"Well, I'm not." He smiled wryly. "I mean, no more than usual."

"We have to make ourselves scarce very quickly," said George. "I can appreciate that you're in pain, but—"

Elaine's head snapped toward him. Wide-eyed horror drove the drowsiness out of her face. She scrambled backward, halfway off the X.

"It's all right," said Joey.

Her maimed hands clumsy, she clutched at him. "No! He sold us out! He *smiled* while they nailed me down! He'll hurt us!"

"No," Joey insisted. "I know it seemed like he was a traitor, but trust me, he's not. Relax, and for god's sake, keep your voice down."

She gazed into his face. He could tell from the way her mouth tightened that she was trying to calm herself. "Okay. If *you* say he's all right, I'll believe it. Do you know where our friends are?"

"Yeah. We're going after them next."

George opened the display case beside the throne. "Can you tell which key is yours? Does it matter?"

Her face twisted. "It doesn't matter at all. I don't want any of them."

"But you might need one," he replied, "to plot our course away from here. Or... well, who knows?" He stuck two crystal globes in his trench coat pockets.

Joey gently squeezed Elaine's shoulders, then strode to the unconscious angel and stripped him of his sword belt and robe. When he saw the guard's crotch, he winced. Evidently, Joey thought, Danziger wanted his soldiers to resemble angels in every respect. The guard was as sexless as a Ken doll.

Joey buckled on the belt, then carried the robe to Elaine. "Lots of the people around here wear these. Put this on over your clothes, keep your head down, and with luck, nobody will recognize you. Then we'll sneak out the back door."

She tried to stand up. As soon as she put weight on her wrists and ankles, she gasped and flopped back down. "Oh, god," she whimpered, "that hurts."

"Don't worry about it," said Joey. "I'll hold you up. Or carry you if I need to."

She shook her head. "I don't want to slow you down. I saw there are guards on the wall. If one of them did recognize me, if you had to run—"

"Please," said George, "don't distress yourself needlessly. Your artful rescuers have matters well in hand. All we need is a diversion to draw the sentries' attention." He waved the flaming sword, drawing a scarlet arc in the air. "One or two fires should do nicely."

-FORTY-TWO-

Standing between Travanti and Fitzroy, Holliday listened to the two dozen villagers, assembled on the common between their oddly rounded little houses, recite intricate contrapuntal catechisms and sing hymns of praise. The worshippers reminded him of ragged, hard-scrabble sharecroppers. He felt as if they'd been babbling for hours. At the front of the delegation from the castle, Danziger cast a cold eye on the performance.

Travanti tugged on his shirt cuff, making sure it protruded properly from the sleeve of his tuxedo jacket. He whispered, "Enthusiastic, aren't they?"

Holliday snorted. "They're scared that if they get the words wrong, or don't seem adoring enough, Danziger will punish them. Maybe even ship them to the Lady's forges."

Travanti's green eyes shone like a cat's. "I know. That's what makes it funny."

Holliday felt a pang of disgust. He relished the way people instinctively cringed from him. It showed respect. And of course he humbled the insolent as required. But that was different than forcing wretches who were already deferential to do tricks like animals in a circus. He couldn't see the point. In fact, the pastime struck him as unmanly.

"I believe I'll take a stroll," he said. "I'll see you back at the fort."

Travanti lifted an eyebrow. Holliday was impressed anew by just how deceptively realistic the Spectre's mask actually was. "I suspect His Holiness won't appreciate your leaving."

Holliday grinned. "Do you think he'll try to stop me? It would make for a livelier minstrel show than this one." He turned and ambled away.

No one interfered. In a minute, he'd left Danziger and his absurd seraphic honor guard far behind. As was often the case, getting away by himself relaxed him. His cape flapping in the mild breeze, he hiked on across the rolling hills, past white, star-shaped wildflowers gleaming in the perpetual gloom, and an occasional gnarled, mossy oak. Off to the right, amber lightning pulsed. At the moment it was steady as a heartbeat.

He wondered what to do about Danziger's offer. In some respects, it was tempting. He'd spent his adolescence listening to survivors of the Twenty-Seventh Georgia Volunteer Infantry, the local regiment, yarn about their adventures at Seven Pines, Mechanicsville, Cold Harbor, and Malvern Hill. He'd always wondered what it was like to be a soldier. To fight in immense battles as opposed to paltry skirmishes like the one at the OK Corral. And if, as seemed likely, Danziger emerged from his crusade victorious, his captains stood to garner huge rewards. He might even appoint a particularly valued officer governor of some of the conquered lands.

But on the other hand, Holliday was already sick of the Heretic's posturing, hair-trigger temper, and general lunacy. It was scarcely any wonder that the Saint and the Deathlord of Madness got along. Of course, as far as he was concerned, *most* of his employers were at least slightly unbalanced. Perhaps you had to be a little touched to rise in the Hierarchy. But it was one thing to roam the Shadowlands bounty-hunting on behalf of men like Clement Purvis. He rarely had to see the sons of bitches. It would be something else entirely to spend months at Danziger's side, especially if it meant rubbing elbows with a pack of Spectres as well.

Waves of light bleached the churning clouds ahead. Cooler now, the wind whispered. His boots swished through the grass.

Actually, he suspected he might feel uneasy about the invitation even if Travanti were Nathan Bedford Forrest and Danziger, General Lee. He'd made it clear that if he joined the cause, it would be as a free mercenary, not a slavish convert. Yet even so, it would mean giving up a measure of independence for the duration.

And, his liaisons with the Earps and Roger Weiss notwithstanding, Holliday was fundamentally a lone wolf. Perhaps he'd be a fool to deny his nature, no matter what inducements were in the offing.

Pale light continued to stain the patch of sky directly in front of him. Abruptly, removing his tinted spectacles, he stopped to squint at it. He wasn't sure, but the glow seemed different from the heat lightning flickering elsewhere.

The wind gusted. Now it felt even colder, and he realized it bore the sound, thin with distance, of excited voices shouting. Slipping his glasses back on, he sprinted for the top of the next rise.

Reaching it, he spied Danziger's cathedral-palace. Parts of the edifice were on fire. Flames danced in some of the windows, gilding gargoyles, bringing stained-glass scenes to brilliant life. Angels and flunkies rushed pails of water from the well and cistern to the fires. This close, he could hear them crackle.

Holliday smiled. He thought he knew how the fires had started. For some reason, Martin Pryor had begged off the excursion to the village to turn his coat again. In all likelihood, the shifty little bastard, with or without the aid of his allegedly fractious slave, had freed Miss Forrester from the rack, indulged in a bit of arson to divert everyone's attention, and sneaked her away.

Even though Holliday hadn't anticipated the treachery, he didn't blame himself for the debacle. He'd delivered Miss Forrester to Danziger as promised. It was the Saint's job to manage her after that, and even with a traitor on the payroll, it shouldn't have been all that difficult. Hell, most people had so little notion of honor that they betrayed each other constantly. Sensible men made allowances for it. If Danziger hadn't had such a penchant for cruelty, he could have killed his prisoner immediately, and prevented the problem from ever arising. And now, to all appearances, his soldiers didn't even realize Miss Forrester had disappeared.

What it all added up to was that the master of Heaven and his cherubs were as bumbling as Shelley and his thugs. Holliday decided to heed his misgivings. Turn down the holy madman's commission and make his way back to the Shadowlands. It would be nice to see the moon and stars again.

But first he'd hunt Miss Forrester one last time. To satisfy himself that he truly had avoided the ignominious failure predicted by the cards, and to wring a second bounty out of Danziger. Reasonably certain he knew where his quarry was heading, he loped in that direction.

-FORTY-THREE-

Hunched over, looking even more ratlike than usual, George crept through a stand of pine trees. At least they looked like pines, though they had an odd, sharp smell that reminded Joey of a hot engine. He was bringing up the rear with Elaine cradled in his arms. He'd insisted on carrying her to give her ankles a chance to heal.

The angel sword he'd stolen hung at his side. The scabbard kept bumping his thigh. He wished he'd left the weapon behind. Who did he think he was, Zorro? Besides, he kept expecting the thing to trip him.

George raised his hand, signaling a halt. "If memory serves, it's just ahead," he whispered.

The ragged holes in Elaine's extremities had shrunk, but they hadn't closed entirely. "Can you walk?" Joey asked her. It would be hard to carry her and sneak through the trees too.

She nodded. "Sure."

As gently as possible, he set her on her feet. Her face contorted, and he grabbed her.

"I'm all right," she said, her voice brittle with pain. "It just hurt for a second."

George said, "You could wait here."

"No," she replied. "We shouldn't split up. By now,

someone may be chasing us. Let's just move, all right?"

They slunk forward through the pines. Joey hovered behind Elaine, poised to catch her if she staggered, but she never did. Somehow, stiff and trembling, she managed to move along as quietly as her companions.

When they reached the edge of the woods, Joey saw what Danziger had called the barracoon. Situated near another warren of ravines which bordered on the Tempest, the slave prison was a large, square pit. A pair of bored-looking angels lounged in chairs overlooking opposite ends, reminding Joey of lifeguards. Wooden ladders lay half hidden in the grass.

He turned to Elaine. "Can you put these guys to sleep? Or make an illusion to distract them?"

She grimaced with effort. Her muscles clenched. After a few moments, she said, "No, not yet. I'm sorry."

"It's okay," said Joey. "I can use the workout." He reached for his sword, then unbuckled and laid it on the pine needle-littered ground instead. "To hell with this thing. I'll do better with my club."

George smiled grimly. The expression looked fake, as if he were imitating the daredevil hero of some movie. "I'll take the man on the right."

"No, you won't," Joey replied. "You don't know how to fight."

George looked hurt. "I acquitted myself admirably before."

"You stabbed somebody in the back. If you get another chance to do that, fine, but otherwise, stay out of sight."

He extended the baton and gathered his strength like a runner at the starting line. He needed to close with one angel and finish him off before the other got into the action. If he wound up battling both at once, they'd beat him for sure.

His mouth felt dry. He wondered if he'd fight any better this time. Joey sprinted into the open.

His sneakers pounded the earth. Still, for a moment, the

angel he was charging didn't move. Stupidly, he dared to hope that he could knock the guy out before he even realized he was in trouble. Then the other sentry yelled, "Watch out!"

The nearer angel, virtually a twin to the one Joey had KO'd outside the throne room, looked up, goggled, and lurched out of his chair, upsetting it in the process. His sword rasped from its sheath in a blaze of silver fire.

Joey swung his baton at the burning weapon. Metal rang, the cold flame chilled his hand, and the sword flew out of line. He faked a blow at the guard's head, then kicked him in the knee. Bone cracked. The angel staggered backward.

About to lunge after him, Joey glimpsed movement from the corner of his eye. His sword now drawn and weeping scarlet flame, white wings flapping, the second angel soared into the air.

It hadn't occurred to Joey that the one of the sentries might actually know how to fly. He'd counted on the angel having to circle the pit, not being able to hurtle straight across. Recognizing he had only seconds left to nail his first opponent, he abandoned caution and sprang.

Despite his injured knee, the angel executed a deep fencer's lunge. His point stabbed Joey in the chest. But at the same instant, the boxer twisted. Instead of penetrating deeply, the sword skated along his chest and forearm, then tore free. And now he was inside his adversary's guard.

He battered the angel with all his might, using the baton and his left fist, too. The soldier collapsed.

Joey whirled, searching frantically for the second angel. Even so, he would have missed him if a particularly bright flare of green lightning hadn't cast a winged shadow on the grass.

He dove to the ground. A flaming sword lashed through the space his head had filled an instant before. The angel circled, no doubt for another pass.

Joey realized that if the airborne warrior had the sense to stay high, it would be almost impossible to club him. Scrambling up, he snatched the first angel's sword from a patch of coldly smoldering grass.

The flying sentry dove. Joey hurled the sword. Considering that he'd never even thrown a knife before, he did better than he had any right to expect. The blade, a white wheel of fire, *almost* hit the angel, tumbling past just inches from his body.

The guard's weapon streaked at Joey's neck. He ducked, and the angel wheeled and soared higher.

Joey frantically looked for the blade he'd thrown, but didn't see it. Pivoting to face his opponent, he wondered if he could jump high enough to grab him and drag him to earth. It didn't seem likely.

The angel screamed. Flinging away his sword, which fell like a meteor, the red flames dying before it hit the ground, he slapped frantically at a mass of white fire licking up his leg.

Joey realized his wild throw had done some damage after all. The sword had caught in the skirt of the angel's robe and set it ablaze.

Shrieking, the guard crashed to earth, then melted into nothingness.

Elaine and George rushed out of the evergreens. The little man said, "Nicely done!"

Rubbing his shallow, stinging cuts, Joey uttered, "Thanks. Let's get everybody out of the hole."

When Joey peered down into the barracoon, the elation of victory faded, even though George had warned him what to expect. There were about a dozen prisoners altogether, the other survivors of the caravan and a few presumably lapsed members of Danziger's flock. Each lay on a sort of narrow table, gagged and bound with dull gray wire. Since ghosts couldn't die of hunger, thirst, or exposure, such treatment couldn't kill them, but it had to be excruciatingly painful.

Joey hastily lowered a ladder. Worried that Elaine would have trouble clambering up and down, he said, "Stay up here and keep a lookout." She nodded. He hugged her, then climbed into the pit. George followed him.

Using their stolen hammers, they tore at the wire restraints. George started with Kim, and Joey with Artie.

When he got the gag off, the comedian turned his head. "Hey, Martin," he croaked, "I know some people have trouble making up their minds — my third wife lumbers Godzilla-like to mind — but this is flat-out silly."

"I know how it looked," said George, "but I give you my solemn word, I didn't betray you." He removed the gag from Kim's mouth. "Are you all right, little nightingale?"

Kim swallowed. "Is Elaine here?" she asked. To Joey's surprise, her magical voice was only a little hoarse.

"Indeed she is," said George.

"Then I'm okay," the little girl said bravely. She blinked as if her eyes were full of tears.

Artie said, "You can finish getting me off this bargain-basement ottoman in a second. For now, help Chris. He's over there." He nodded at the far end of the pit.

Wondering what the problem was, Joey said, "Okay." He strode down the aisle defined by a double line of tables.

Chris lay motionless in a deep pool of shadow. Even with the keen sight of the Restless, Joey had to get close to make out what had been done to him. When he did, he winced.

Chris hadn't been tied to his table. He'd been spiked there like Elaine, but more thoroughly. Gray nailheads studded every part of his body. Two more forged of darksteel jutted from his eye sockets.

Joey pulled those out first, then went to work on the rest. For a while, Chris seemed unconscious, but as the boxer dragged a thin spike like a hatpin out of his stomach, he gasped and bucked.

Joey grabbed him and struggled to hold him down. "Don't thrash around! You'll tear yourself up even worse!"

"Pete?" the actor groaned.

"Yeah. Welcome to the jailbreak."

"Saw you fall," Chris said. He sounded half delirious. "Glad you made it back. They nailed me down so good, I couldn't change form. Only way to hold a guy like me…"

"Don't talk," said Joey. "Save your strength."

By the time he drew the rest of the nails, George, Kim, Artie, and another survivor of the caravan, the latter three hobbling like mortals a hundred years old, had gathered around him. Gazing longingly at the ladder, George said, "Surely, time is of the essence." Then he scowled. "Oh, to hell with it!" He started prying at the wire binding one of the other captives.

Artie helped as best he could, cutting his hands in the process. "You know, Martin, old goiter, if you tell anyone I said this, you'll hear from my lawyers, but maybe you aren't a total waste of ectoplasm after all."

"My name is George," the man in the trench coat said. "George Montaigne. And my comrade-in-arms is Joey Castelo." A strand of wire snapped, whipped into the air, and nearly jabbed him in the eye. He flinched. "And you may rest assured that the patrician Mr. Montaigne is unaccustomed to this kind of brute manual labor."

"I can see that," said Artie. "Maybe you could have gotten a gig at Goodwill."

In a few more minutes, everyone was free. With a lot of help, even blind, maimed Chris made it up the ladder. Elaine stooped and gathered Kim in her arms.

"Well," said George sourly. "If it's emancipation day." He waved his hand, and Joey's bracelets dropped off. By the time they clanked on the ground, the chain had reappeared between them. George picked the shackles up, began to stow them inside his coat, then tossed them into the pit instead.

Joey's eyes stung, and his throat felt swollen. He said,

"Thank you."

George shrugged and averted his face. He seemed more embarrassed than he ever had over any selfish or underhanded act.

A hand tapped Joey on the shoulder. He turned. A plump, maternal-looking woman with curly brown hair, her flesh striped with ligature marks, peered up at him. "Thank you for freeing us," she said. "But what happens now?"

"My friends and I are going to find the nearest Byway and get out of this place. I don't know exactly where we'll wind up. We'll look for someplace safe. You guys can tag along, or you can stay and try to hide from Danziger and the junior bird-men. It's up to you."

"Oh, no," Elaine whispered.

Joey whirled. "What's wrong?"

She pointed toward the rolling hills farther inland.

At first, in the gloom, Joey didn't see anything. He was just about to say as much when he spotted the gleam of a blue and purple halo. Though the figure it outlined was still far away, he could just make out the shape of its slouch hat, and the short cape flapping around its shoulders.

"Holliday," said George. He sounded sick.

Joey said, "Listen up, gang! Somebody's after us, so we're going into the canyons. I know most of you feel like crap, but you have to travel fast anyway. Those who are able will help the ones who need it. Somebody grab those swords. We may need them. Go on, *move!*"

Two minutes later, they were scrambling down a slope into the mouth of the first ravine. Pebbles slid and rolled beneath their feet.

A limping black teenager in a torn brown shirt said, "Look, maybe we shouldn't run. If there are fifteen of us and one of him—"

Artie said, "He has guns, and knows how to use them. In the open, he could pick us off at long range."

The kid grunted and quickened his pace, drawing ahead.

"What I didn't mention," Artie murmured to Joey, "is that the son of a process server is bound to catch up with our little gaggle of gimps. I suppose it's too much to hope that a punch-drunk gorilla like you has a long-term strategy."

Despite his fear, Joey forced what he hoped was a confident-looking grin. "Want to bet? For starters, we're going where it's so hard to see and hear that if you caught a break or two, you might be able to shake even a good tracker off your trail."

Artie raised an eyebrow. "In other words, you plan to run this bunch of defenseless cripples straight on into the Tempest."

"Bingo," Joey said.

-FORTY-FOUR-

The Tempest.

The canyon itself didn't change where it ran into the storm, but beyond a certain point, it was full of writhing vapor. As Joey half carried the blind, crippled Chris across the border, he realized that he'd never tried to simply step from a Far Shore or Byway into the surrounding chaos before. He was going to look pretty stupid if he bounced off the invisible wall that held back the mist.

But that didn't happen. Instead, freezing wind knifed into his body. Chris gasped and shuddered.

Joey turned to look back across the threshold. As he'd feared, some of Danziger's former subjects were balking.

"Step lively," George said brightly. "We'll only be inside for a little while, just long enough to elude pursuit, and then Elaine will guide us to a path."

"Trust me," said Artie, "there can't be anything worse in there than what's behind us."

The dumpy, brown-haired woman grimaced. "You're right about that. I don't even want to imagine what His Holiness will do to us if he catches us again." She marched forward, squinching her eyes shut just before she stepped into the fog. With obvious reluctance, the other apostates followed.

The fugitives scurried on. The wind shrieked, and blue

lightning flickered. Kim gasped and pointed. Joey jerked around in time to see a creature like a many-legged alligator with a toddler's face crawl into a cave.

After a while, Joey said, "Okay, you guys keep running. Lose yourselves. I'm going to wait here and try to stop Holliday."

Elaine said, "No! You can't!"

Joey grimaced. "It's not like I want to, but somebody needs to at least slow the bastard down. Otherwise, he'll catch us all for sure."

"But he's deadly! You won't have a chance by yourself!"

"Thanks for the vote of confidence. Look, those of you who really know how to fight, or have special powers, are too chewed up to do your stuff. So it really is better if everybody books."

"I'm not chewed up," Kimberly said.

Joey blinked. "What?"

"I'm all right." Now that she mentioned it, he realized that, though a little gimpy, she'd been trotting along more nimbly than most of the others. "And my voice is all right." She sang a note he could feel in his teeth and bones. "I'll stay with you."

His grimy coat and garish striped necktie whipping in the gale, George put his hand on her shoulder. "Sweetheart, I don't think that's a good idea."

Kim pouted. It made her look younger, yet even more determined. "Pete, I mean Joey, needs me. And everybody said I could come on the journey, and help with stuff like a" — she hesitated, seemingly groping for the right term — "an equal partner!"

Frowning, Joey considered the offer. He hated the idea of endangering her. But she was right. If her voice could work its magic, he *did* need her. And if he tried and failed to stop Holliday by himself, the bounty hunter would keep chasing the caravan, and she'd be in mortal peril anyway.

He tried to smile. "Okay, kiddo, it's you and me. Just like in Galveston."

Elaine squinched her eyes shut. Her fists and jaw clenched. Joey was sure she was trying to make an illusion, to demonstrate that she was sufficiently recovered to stay and fight too, but nothing happened.

When she finally gave up, she looked like she was struggling not to cry. "You two be careful," she said harshly.

Artie draped Chris's brawny, mangled arm across his own narrow shoulders, relieving Joey of his burden. "Yeah, watch your backs. We don't want you chumps embarrassing us, capeesh?"

"If that lame sketch about the governor and the chambermaid doesn't embarrass you," Joey replied, "I don't think we could." He reached for Elaine, but she twisted away. The rebuff hurt, but he realized she wasn't truly angry. She was afraid that if he touched her, or said anything tender, she'd break down. "Well. If we pull this off, I'll fire Holliday's gun. One shot, then two close together, then one more. If you hear that, backtrack and find us. Now, you guys get moving."

George slapped him awkwardly on the back. Then he and the others hurried on down the ravine.

Joey looked down at Kim. "Okay, partner, here's the plan. Your job is to spook Holliday like you did the exorcist. And to make sounds come from different directions to distract him."

Looking solemn, she said, "Okay. I can do it."

"I know you can. Now, what I *don't* want is for you to try to really hurt him." He knew that would require making herself a target. "That's my department." Looking around, he spied a rocky outcropping partway up the canyon wall. He pointed at it. "Climb up there and hide. No matter what happens, don't let him see you."

She nodded. "I get it." He squeezed her shoulder. She

turned and clambered up the slope.

He waited a moment, making sure she could manage the ascent, then strode a few yards down the gully. He crouched behind an egg-shaped boulder mottled with a rash of pinkish crystals, pulled his baton to its full length, picked up a round rock the size of a tennis ball, and started watching the trail.

Now concealed on her perch, Kim wailed. Long, quavering howls alternated with sudden sobs and cries. The noises seemed to come from one location, then another, then everywhere at once.

After a while, a dark figure, not a solid form like Holliday's but a smear of shadow like the Spectre that had maimed Joey, appeared on the ridge above Kim's hiding place. The boxer was terrified it would notice her and attack, but it just glanced around, then faded back into the fog.

As time crawled on, he wondered somberly if anyone had ever truly managed to catch Holliday off guard, in any circumstances whatsoever. The gunman seemed to have a sixth sense that warned him of danger.

In general, the more Joey contemplated his chances, the more dismal they appeared. In Salt Lake City, he'd had the voice to power him up. He'd had Kim and three other people helping him. And they'd still been lucky to escape with their lives. It was as if Holliday wasn't human. The way he'd pursued the caravan across America and the nightmare landscape of the Tempest, he seemed like an incarnation of death itself.

And now, just to make the situation *absolutely* hopeless, Joey's talent for fighting was screwed up. He wasn't even as tough as he'd been before his Shadow started helping—

He scowled and gave his head a shake. He didn't know if Kim's eerie song was unsettling him, or he was just naturally scared, but he had to stop thinking negative thoughts. Otherwise, he'd defeat himself before Holliday even appeared.

Damn it, he'd been fighting since he was a kid. Maybe he'd never been a champ, a Joe Louis or a Muhammed Ali, but he'd been good. And he still was. He'd proved it beside the barracoon. Good enough to give any skinny, pasty-faced geek in a stupid cowboy outfit a really bad day.

Holliday glided silently out of the murk.

He'd buttoned his caped coat and turned up the collar, to ward off the cold. He had a revolver in each hand. If Kim's screeching bothered him, no one could have told it from his cool, alert expression. He approached a side passage snaked that away from the primary canyon, then stooped to examine the hard, pebbly ground. Apparently he was reading a sign. It only took him a second.

As he straightened up, a sharp cry rang out, seemingly just behind him. He spun fast as lightning, then, seeing nothing, pivoted forward again.

As he proceeded down the ravine, phantasmal outbursts sounded all around him. Each time, the result was the same. He whirled instantly, unerringly, toward the apparent location of the noise. But he never seemed startled. Never snapped off a shot at empty air.

Joey's skin crawled with anxiety. He told himself that, the bounty hunter's composure notwithstanding, his plan could still succeed. He didn't really need Holliday rattled. He just needed him to come close and turn his back.

The gunfighter stalked nearer. One of his boots creaked. Joey caught the oily smell of his guns. Across the ravine, a shrill, disembodied voice screamed, "Boo!"

Holliday swiveled toward the noise and Joey surged to his feet.

He would have sworn he hadn't made a sound. But Holliday started to wheel back around, so swiftly and gracefully that Joey was sure he'd be dead before the stone left his hand.

Kim popped up from her hiding place and shrieked. Just

the fallout from the cry stung Joey's skin. One ear melting into a shapeless lump, suddenly positioned between two attackers, Holliday actually hesitated.

Joey threw the rock.

He might not know how to fling a sword, but he'd thrown plenty of baseballs. The stone thumped Holliday on the side of the head, knocking off his blue glasses. He staggered, and Joey rushed him.

Holliday recovered his balance, and lifted his guns. Joey plowed into him and drove him reeling backward.

The boxer knew it was all up to him now. Kim couldn't blast the gunman a second time without nailing him as well. He had to stay right on top of Holliday, pound him hard and fast, make it impossible for him to aim. He swung madly. The blows cracked and thudded.

Meanwhile, Holliday tried to batter him with the revolvers. Despite the pale man's blinding speed, Joey's superior skill at hand-to-hand combat enabled him to block most of the attacks, and those that landed did less damage than his own. It was only natural. A heavyweight hit harder than a lightweight.

The baton smashed Holliday in the mouth, shattering teeth. Lurching backward, Holliday tried to point a six-gun. Joey lunged, brushed the weapon aside, and punched his adversary in the stomach.

In the small part of his mind that could still think, not just flow with the action, he felt a swell of exultation. He knew he wasn't out of the woods yet. Until he actually knocked the gunfighter out, any wrong move or split-second hesitation could bring disaster. But if he didn't screw up, he was going to win. Whip the most dangerous opponent he'd ever faced. Without the voice's fury sizzling down his nerves.

Kim yelled, "Behind you!"

Not again! Joey thought. What could it be this time? The bounty hunter still had both guns in his hands!

He knew he had to see what was wrong, but he didn't dare turn his back on the revolvers. He grabbed Holliday and swung him around, almost as if the two of them were waltzing.

For an instant, in the dark and the billowing mist, he still couldn't see the problem. Then magenta lightning flashed, and he spied a double-barreled derringer floating in the air, aiming itself at his head.

He tried to keep Holliday's body between himself and the hovering gun. The bounty hunter resisted with all his might. The derringer whirled around them like a planet orbiting a star, seeking a clear shot.

Joey saw that in a moment, it was going to get one. He flung Holliday away, slamming him into the canyon wall, and dove.

The small gun barked twice. Sprawling on the ground, Joey tensed for the impacts of the bullets, but they didn't come. Inches from his feet, two patches of rocky soil dissolved in crackling ripples of black flame.

Kim started to sing a loud, sustained note, not the sound that corroded flesh, but another tone. Joey had no idea what she was up to, and no time to wonder. He had to get back in Holliday's face. He scrambled up, spun around, and froze.

Hatless now, his white face scraped and frayed in the shiny, bloodless manner of the Restless, his pale, piercing eyes glittering, the bounty hunter stood with his back to the gully wall. He already had Joey covered. "The cards were right about you," he said thickly.

Kim kept wailing. Joey lunged for the cover of an almost cube-shaped, blue-veined boulder. He sensed he wouldn't make it, but he had to try.

Holliday's guns swiveled, tracking him. Then thunder, or something like it, roared.

Holliday's gray-blond head snapped up. Toward a wave of loose rock sweeping down the side of the ravine.

The bounty hunter tried to leap to safety, but even he wasn't quite fast enough. Thudding and crunching, pounding and shaking the ground, the avalanche engulfed him. Only one white hand, still clutching a gun, protruded from the newly created heap of stone. The fingers tightened spasmodically, firing a shot, then evaporated into nothingness.

Feeling dazed, Joey crept forward. When the floating dust stung his eyes, and he picked up the fallen six-shooter, he started to believe that he really had survived.

Kim slid down the canyon wall on her bottom. She looked half joyful and half horrified at what she'd done. He picked her up and hugged her.

"You should have told me you can sing down stone walls," he said.

"I didn't know it," she croaked, sounding as if she'd contracted laryngitis. Evidently she'd strained her voice. "But all of a sudden, I remembered that in science class, my teacher said sound can break things, and make avalanches. So I gave it a try."

"Uh-huh," he said, trying to look stern. "But weren't you supposed to keep your head down?"

"I didn't think Holliday would shoot at me until after he got rid of the big, strong grown-up," she answered, still sounding froggy. "Besides, when I promised, I had my fingers crossed. Sort of. Inside my head."

Joey grinned. "Well, I guess we can let it go this time. You did great, honey. Thank you." He squeezed her, set her down, and pointed the revolver at the sky. "Let's call the others, and brag."

-FORTY-FIVE-

Heaven.

Some of Danziger's new recruits, or as Robert Fitzroy privately thought of them, the Laughing Lady's cannon fodder, stood, bows in hand, at the shooting line. Many looked sheepish, one or two as if they were struggling not to cry. His crystal orb flashing crimson rays and his voluminous robe swirling about his lanky legs, their master strode back and forth, berating them.

Bored, Fitzroy watched the tongue-lashing from under a nearby elm. Travanti lounged beside him, reeking of cologne. Ordinarily, the man in the fox mask might have shunned a Spectre's company. But given that he was an emissary, come here to cement a grand alliance, such rudeness would be less than politic.

Besides, he had to admit, Travanti offered a refreshing change of pace from both Danziger and many of his own fellow minions of the Seat of Succor, in that he wasn't mad. Depraved, yes, but not demented.

Long ago, when Fitzroy was still breathing, he'd been mad himself. His lunacy had manifested itself in grandiose euphorias, suicidal melancholies, and violent rages. He'd had the ludicrous suspicion that he was Michelangelo reincarnate, and an insatiable craving for absinthe that steadily rotted what little sense he possessed. As a result, he'd spent thirty-one years making himself and his family miserable. Finally, fleeing in terror, convinced that other artists, envious of his genius, were stalking him, he'd blundered into the path of a speeding coach.

And, just as pious souls had always predicted, death had ended his affliction. Evidently his insanity had arisen from a defect in his brain, as opposed to any sort of weakness in spirit. Grateful for his deliverance, he'd striven with considerable success to become the most dispassionate, rational ghost the Underworld had ever seen. It was one of existence's little ironies that, due to the nature of his passing, he'd found himself conscripted into the Madwoman's service anyway.

He idly fingered the pommel of his rapier. He also carried a .38, discretely holstered in such a way that his short red cloak concealed it. "I'll bet you an obolus the lads shoot worse next time."

"Because they'll be too nervous?" Travanti's green eyes gleamed. "Nonsense. Fear is the ultimate incentive. Your own mistress understands that nearly as well as my people do. Did you ever hear the story—" An angel raced over the top of a nearby hill, his aura blazing orange with dread. "Hm. Speaking of fear, what's this?"

The winged soldier charged on down the slope and prostrated himself at Danziger's feet. Fitzroy surmised he was babbling a message. He hurried forward to find out what it was. His eyes narrowed with curiosity, Travanti followed.

When they were halfway there, Danziger threw back his head, howled like an animal, and raised his crystal in both hands. The orb flamed scarlet and black, as the golden-haired angel, still groveling on the grass, exploded as if he'd swallowed a live grenade.

The novice archers recoiled. Fitzroy realized that suddenly, he was none too eager to go any closer himself.

But he knew his duty, and he didn't believe Danziger was crazy enough to harm him and risk losing the Lady's favor. He marched on, and so, for whatever reason, did his Spectral companion.

When they got close enough, the Stygian bowed. "What's wrong, Your Holiness?"

Trembling, his face, beard, and robe spattered with steaming scraps of angel, Danziger glared. "The Great Whore has escaped! This, this idiot let Martin Pryor's Thrall hit him over the head!"

"Was Pryor in on it too?" Fitzroy asked.

"Yes!" Danziger screamed. "What did I just tell you?"

"I promise, everything will be fine," Travanti said soothingly. "Judging from past experience, the woman's harmless. All she's ever done is run from us. That's all she'll do now. But we'll recapture her, just to set your mind at ease."

"Yes," Danziger said. "We have to get her." He turned, glowering at his soldiers, gorgeous angels and unaltered new recruits alike. "Do you hear me? I want search parties! Look everywhere! Start with the barracoon. Her friends are there."

With commendable alacrity, the officers began forming the men into squads. Perhaps fear *was* the ultimate incentive.

Danziger turned to Travanti. "Give me your hand."

For once, the doomshade seemed nonplussed. "Excuse me?"

Danziger grimaced with impatience. "You're one of God's angels of wrath. A prince of Hell. By attuning myself with you, I can project my power into your domain."

Fitzroy reflected that if Danziger wanted to commune with a Spectre, or something very like one, he had only to look into his own heart. It was, of course, an observation best kept to himself.

Travanti extended his manicured hand and Danziger

clutched it to his chest, raising the key over his head.

Their auras and the crystal globe began to pulse in unison, like three hearts beating in time. The color of the radiance grew darker and darker, until it seemed less like light than a throbbing blot of shadow. Yet, paradoxically, it stabbed and dazzled the eye. Spectators averted their gazes.

Fitzroy shared their discomfort. But he also wanted to see what would happen next, both to satisfy his innate curiosity and to honor his obligation to gather intelligence. Squinting, he studied the scene as best he could.

The blackness strobed. Gradually the lightning in the churning thunderheads began to flash in sync with the pulsing. Then, suddenly, streaks of darkness arced away from the central mass of shadow in all directions. They shot so high and flew so far that Fitzroy couldn't tell where they came down. Beyond the bounds of Heaven, he presumed.

An instant later, the shadow structure vanished. Both Travanti and Danziger looked unsteady on their feet.

But the lord of Heaven wasn't ready to rest. "Now," he said brusquely, "can you and your followers search the ring of Tempest bordering my land?"

As if trying to match Danziger's vigor, Travanti stood up straighter and adjusted his lapels. "It'll take some time. We're talking about a big piece of real estate, bigger than anyone who thinks in only three dimensions can imagine. And I'm a stranger hereabouts. I don't know if I can get the local Spectres to help me. But yes, we can do it."

Knowing his mask would conceal his expression, Fitzroy allowed himself an undiplomatic scowl. He hadn't grasped the point of Danziger's magic, and he didn't understand the tack the discussion was taking now. "With respect, Your Holiness," the diplomat said, "I think it highly unlikely that the fugitives will venture into the Tempest. Why the devil should they? No one except a Spectre can survive there for long. If you really mean to catch them, you'd better send your fastest troops and best trackers down the Byways."

Danziger smirked like a prankster who'd just set up a particularly vicious practical joke. "Trust me, my son, that won't be necessary."

-FORTY-SIX-

The Tempest.

Elaine shivered, rubbed her forearms, and tried to keep her teeth from chattering. She was colder than she'd ever been before. In the Shadowlands, freezing temperatures could make wraiths miserable, but not actually harm them. She was beginning to wonder if the same was true of the chill that pervaded the Tempest.

The caravan was hiking along a ridge. They'd clambered from the canyon floor to higher ground in the hope that it would help them spot a Byway. The tradeoff was that up here, they were more visible to others, and, with no stone walls to block the howling wind, fully exposed to the elements.

Hands jammed in his pockets, shoulders hunched, a sword swinging at his side, Artie trudged along ahead of her. He looked odd without his straw hat, which had been lost when Holliday and the Spectres captured him. Suddenly he lurched to a stop. "Oh, joy," he said.

Elaine moved to his side and looked over the edge of the cliff. A number of withered, hairless, naked figures were skittering up the rocky slopes below, leaving a trail of pus-colored slime on the stone.

She was afraid, but not as much as she supposed she

ought to be. The cold and her leaden fatigue seemed to take the edge off, she thought. And she certainly wasn't surprised at this new danger. It was the third time since reuniting with Joey and Kim that the caravan had been attacked.

Artie's sword hissed out of it sheath and burst into silvery flame. Just what we need, she thought fleetingly, something to make it even colder. She stared at one of the monsters, willing it to sleep and forcing it to fall in a cascade of pebbles. It vanished into the shadowy depths below.

Along the narrow trace that passed for a trail, most of her companions dropped rocks over the side. Knocked from their perches, some of the Spectres plummeted. Others climbed on. Kim wailed. Her cry echoed through the craggy, fog enshrouded landscape.

A cold, greasy hand clamped shut around Elaine's ankle and yanked her off her feet. This can't be happening! she thought. She couldn't have missed seeing one of the creatures climb right up underneath her. But obviously it had, and now it dragged her toward the edge. She scrabbled at the ground, trying to anchor herself, but found nothing to grab.

Then Joey was beside her. Dropping to one knee, he swung his baton, breaking the Spectre's forearm in two.

But instead of falling, the creature somehow surged onto the ridge to grapple with its attacker. Another monster scrambled up and threw itself on Elaine.

The creature's eyeless, earless head was a long, flexible cone with a triple ring of needle-like fangs lining the sphincteral mouth at the end. The mouth darted at her eye. She grabbed the Spectre's head, and it twisted back and forth, trying to break her grip. Its coating of rancid jelly squished through her fingers.

Artie appeared behind the monster and slammed his blazing sword into its back. It jerked, went limp, and dissolved in a ripple of shadow. Behind the comedian, another Spectre climbed into view.

Joey, who'd already gotten rid of his previous opponent, pivoted and took a swing at it. Recoiling from the blow, it floundered off the edge.

Elaine scrambled to her feet and looked up and down the ridge. The Spectres were gone, destroyed or driven back. To her relief, all of her companions had survived, though several had cuts and raw, round bite marks.

Chris, who'd recovered the power to change his form only minutes before, massaged three parallel scratches in his gleaming pewter hide. "This is getting old," he said.

George nodded grimly. He had one of the circular wounds in the exact center of his forehead, making him look like a cross between a sleazy grifter and an Asian deity. "Even the stalwart Montaigne is forced to concur," he said, taking a crystal orb out of his raincoat pocket. He also had Holliday's revolver and derringer. Unfortunately, the guns were empty, and their ammunition buried inside what had proved to be an immovable mass of rock.

The little man smiled at Elaine. "Perhaps it's time for another attempt at navigation."

She wanted to refuse. But she owed it to them to try, even though she knew it would be futile. She took the globe. It shone sky-blue and umber upon her touch.

When the refugees from Heaven had learned she was a Saint, when they'd first seen a key burning in her hand, they'd cried out in wonder. A couple had fallen to their knees. Even now, some still watched her with a kind of forlorn hope, but the majority looked like they weren't expecting anything much.

Pretty smart on their part, she thought grimly.

Elaine projected her awareness into the crystal. In a moment, she made contact with the rudimentary mind that dwelled at the heart of the light.

Instantly it filled her with the knowledge of Heaven's location. This close to the Far Shore, there was none of the cloudy uncertainty that had frustrated her before. She could feel the place, the way a compass sensed north.

No, she thought. I don't want to go back there. I want to go away. Point me to the nearest Byway.

The orb radiated dismay. Though it didn't speak in words, she understood its reply. It was supposed to guide her *to* Heaven. She was supposed to want to go.

Do what I tell you! she commanded.

She *thought* she felt its resistance crumble. Then what had become a wearily familiar sequence of jagged shapes and garish colors flashed before her inner eye. Conceivably they had some sort of meaning, but if so, she had no idea what it was.

She raised her head. The raw need in her companions' faces wrung her heart. She despised herself for letting them down. She scowled to keep from crying.

"Nothing," she said curtly. "Same as before. Either it doesn't want to tell me where a road is, or it can't."

Joey squeezed her shoulder. "It's all right. We'll find one sooner or later."

Artie stroked his chin. "I wonder."

"Sure we will!" said Chris. "You can't give up!"

Artie rolled his eyes. "Spare me the pep talk, Gorgeous George. I'm not throwing in the towel, I'm thinking. You ought to try it some time, assuming you can pry yourself away from the mirror."

"Have you figured something out?" Joey asked.

"For starters, we seem to be deeply, sincerely, painfully, can't-find-our-butts-with-a-map-and-a-flashlight *lost.*"

"Wow," said one of the Covenanters, a freckled, frizzy-haired guy in a tattered plaid shirt, "thanks for the tip."

"Please," said Artie, "no sarcasm. Leave it to the professionals. As the alderman said to the stripper, I'm coming to a point. The question is, *why* are we lost? Every time our fearless leader goes into her trance, the Sacred Paperweight *does* point to Heaven. Which has enabled us to schlep along parallel to the border. According to George, who *slowly* gathered info while the rest of us were tied up in a hole — not that I'm bitter, you double-dealing skunk — there are several Byways running out of the burg, more or less at regular intervals. Why haven't we stumbled across one?"

Elaine said, "Do you think the key is lying?"

"I doubt it," said George, cinching his trench coat belt tighter. "You said it doesn't seem all that bright, not clever enough to turn tricky on us, and it *wants* you to go to Heaven."

"I agree," said Joey. He peered over the cliff. Elaine did the same. As far as she could see, nothing else was climbing up at them. "Could Danziger hypnotize us at long range? Fix it so we can't see the Byways?"

Artie shrugged. "For all we know, perhaps. Or maybe he erased them — not the whole network, of course, just the bit of it linked to his borders — or shifted them to a different level of reality. Philosophers claim the landscape of the Tempest is both hyperdimensional and fluid, and our new friends" — he shot the former citizens of Heaven a leer — "say His Flatulence can do damn near anything when he's sufficiently ticked off."

"If you're right," said Chris, "we will never find a path."

"Which means we'll have to slip back into Heaven," said George.

Elaine's wrists and ankles had finally healed, but now she could have sworn she felt a jab of pain shoot through them. "No!" she cried. "That's suicide!"

"Maybe not," said Joey. "Maybe we could pick up a Byway from there. If not, we'll hide out until the roads reappear. I'm sure they won't stay gone forever."

Elaine glared at him. "Danziger can work miracles. He's got an army. Do you think he won't find us on his home ground?"

"If worst comes to worst," Artie said, "if some search party does find us, maybe we can make them sorry they did.

This little band can be pretty tough, and you, my succulent papaya, are a card-carrying Saint yourself. Maybe, on Heavenly turf, you can match Danziger trick for trick."

"That's insane!" Her eyes aching, she wheeled and blundered a few paces down the ridge.

She expected a number of people to scurry after her, but she only heard one set of footsteps. She recognized the creak of Joey's sneakers. She imagined him holding up his hand, signaling everyone else to hang back.

He put his muscular arms around her. She yearned to relax against him, but held herself rigid instead. "I don't blame you for being scared," he said.

"How kind of you."

The sarcasm didn't seem to faze him. "In the last year, I've been through some nasty stuff. I don't guess any of it was as bad as being crucified. But we can't wander around in the Tempest forever. It's only a matter of time before we run into something we absolutely can't handle, like the island monster I told you about."

"Maybe it will at least destroy us quickly. Danziger will make us suffer."

"Not if we beat him." She tore herself out of his embrace. Spun around and opened her mouth to protest. "Come on, Artie's got a point. If you don't have even a little Saintly mojo, how come you can light up a key?"

"I don't know. Who cares? It's not like it's doing us any good. What's important is, I can't do anything else. Nothing but the same stupid tricks I've always done."

"You won't know until you try."

"I don't even know *how* to try."

"You're good at changing people's dreams. Maybe now you can do the same thing to the waking world. Just focus, let the juice flow, and twist things around the way you want them."

"Just like that," she said bitterly. "Wouldn't that be convenient. But I don't think Danziger's miracle-working is a discipline like dream-shaping. I don't think it can be taught, or figured out. It's like the exorcists' power. It comes from his faith. Probably the faith of the people around him, too.

"And I already told you, my faith is gone. If I had even a grain left, I lost it when I met His Holiness himself. See, when Danziger was breathing, he wasn't *just* a Saint. He was one of the first and greatest. A brilliant evangelist and organizer. The whole religion might have died out if not for him. All the time I was growing up, my parents and teachers held him up to me as the perfect example of what I was supposed to become. If *he* could turn into a monster, and overthrow whatever Saints were still sane, that's the ultimate proof that the Church of the Holy Covenant is a crock. And I wasted my whole life on it. I thought I was God's little darling, and I was a joke."

Joey grimaced. "I don't know what to say to that, considering I never believed in your church in the first place. I guess I've seen too much human weakness and meanness to believe that any person's really holy. But I believe in you."

"So do I," said a husky female voice. Startled, Elaine peered around Joey. The plump, motherly-looking woman had crept up behind him. "Or at least, I want to. I'm sorry for butting in on your conversation. But I just had to say, my friends and I didn't know another Saint would ever come. His Holiness said he was the last one. The only real one. If you *could* stop him, everyone would be so grateful. Our home never seemed quite like the Heaven in the Bible, but it was nice. Now people feel like they're in Hell."

Elaine felt a pang of shame. "I'm the one who should be sorry, because I haven't even asked your name."

"Caroline Teasdale, Your Holiness."

"Please, don't call me that. I swear to you, I'd save everybody if I could. I don't know how. But maybe those of us in this little group can help each other." She looked up at Joey. "Okay, we'll go back to the Far Shore. I know we don't have any other choice. But not for a confrontation. To find a road out of here."

If only it could happen just that way, Elaine thought desperately. But her every instinct told her otherwise. She reached deep inside herself, searching for a trace of the quasi-divine power everyone seemed convinced she could summon at will. She came up empty.

- FORTY-SEVEN -

Heaven.

A shadow shifted in the trees ahead. Joey ducked behind an ancient oak spotted with yellow moss, then peeked around it.

For a moment, nothing moved, and he wondered if the gloom and his edginess were playing tricks on him. Then he glimpsed the double arch of snowy wings stained mauve by the glimmering lightning above.

The caravan had sneaked back into Danziger's kingdom about forty-eight hours ago. Currently Joey's companions were resting in a pair of abandoned huts in a clearing not far away from his present location. Most of them needed it. Skulking around in enemy territory wore down a person's nerves even if he had a nearly tireless body.

But Joey didn't feel too tired. Or maybe he needed a break from Elaine more than he needed to sit down. Though she was trying her best to hide it, he could tell she'd convinced herself they were all as good as dead. He hated to see her that way, and he had no idea how to snap her out of it.

He'd gone off by himself to hunt again for the entrance to a Byway, only to run into an angel.

He guessed it could be worse. The winged soldier, an

archer just a tad fleshier than Danziger's average angel, could have spotted *him*. The question now was, should Joey try to take the guy out, or let him wander on his way unmolested? He was still thinking it over when he spotted two more angels, walking along parallel to the first.

Evidently an entire squad of warriors, spread out in a line, was searching the woods. One of them was bound to spot the clearing. Anxious to get there first and warn his friends, Joey wheeled and hurried through the brush.

The ground was treacherously uneven. Occasionally he lurched against a branch and made it rustle. Still, he thought he was moving pretty quietly until a white arrow thunked into the tree beside him. Silently cursing the keen senses of his fellow spooks, he began to run.

Behind him, someone shouted. Footsteps pounded after him. Realizing that if he fled back to the shacks now, he'd lead the enemy to Elaine, Joey veered sharply to the right.

His new course sent him splashing through a shallow stream, then racing uphill. An arrow whizzed past him and buried itself in the ground. He wondered if he could lose his pursuers once he made it over the rise. Then he heard movement on the other side of the hill. The golden heads of another row of angels bobbed into view.

Flicking his baton to its full length, he charged the soldier directly in front of him. If he could break through the line, maybe he could still escape. It seemed unlikely, but it was the only hope left.

The warrior, a slim woman whose blond curls showed a trace of auburn, drew her ivory bow. Joey leaped to the side, and the arrow streaked past him. He rushed her.

She raised the bow like a quarter staff, but too slowly. He lashed the baton against her temple. As she collapsed, he leaped over her, then had to twist in midair to avoid spitting himself on a long, thin, flameless darksteel blade. Landing, he slipped on a patch of fallen leaves, and dropped painfully to one knee.

His new opponent was the man George had identified as Fitzroy, the Laughing Lady's ambassador. In contrast to the white splendor of the angels, his russet mask and clothing blended into the dark. It was no wonder Joey hadn't seen him.

The Stygian had a rapier in one leather-gloved hand and an automatic pistol in the other. The blade drew little circles in the air. He said, "Drop your weap—"

Joey threw the baton at him, then scrambled up and charged him.

The club rang against the metal fox mask. Fitzroy staggered. His gun banged, but the bullet whined over Joey's head. Lunging past the point of the sword, he punched Fitzroy twice, once in the stomach and once in the solar plexus. The man in red fell backward, sitting down hard on the ground.

Joey ran down the hill. I'm getting away! he thought. Maybe I've disrupted the search enough to keep the angels from finding the clearing. Maybe—

Without warning, he fell to the ground.

He guessed he'd tripped. He tried to spring back up, but his right leg folded up in a burst of pain. He looked down at it to see an ivory arrow sticking through his thigh.

Hands trembling, he hastily broke off the triangular darksteel point, then pulled the shaft out. The sensation of the wood sliding through his flesh was excruciating.

Once again, he attempted to stand. This time, he made it. But his head swam, and he found he could only hobble. Blazing swords at the ready, four angels bounded down the hill and surrounded him. He couldn't have handled that many even if he hadn't been wounded. He raised his hands.

Fitzroy strode toward him. The Stygian had already sheathed his rapier, and now he stowed the gun away under his cape, freeing his hands to examine the baton. He telescoped it shut, extended it again, and rapped it against his palm. "Nice little weapon," he said, tucking it under his arm like a swagger stick. "Put your hands behind your back."

Joey obeyed. "Don't hurt me," he said, trying to sound frightened. It wasn't all that hard.

"I don't particularly want to," said Fitzroy. "Of course, I can't speak for His Holiness."

Cold, hard rings snapped shut around Joey's wrists. Chained again. He felt sick to his stomach.

As somebody frisked him, he said, "Elaine is the one you really want. If I guide you to her, will you let me go?"

The man in the fox mask chuckled. "Am I supposed to believe that the supporter who's repeatedly risked destruction for her sake has suddenly decided to sell her out? I think you want to take me on a wild-goose chase."

That was exactly what Joey wanted. "No. Honest to god. Up to now, I have been loyal, but I've got my limits. I've seen how Danziger treats his prisoners."

"Well, be that as it may, I'm afraid you've got nothing to trade. I already know your friend's approximate location. I may not be in Holliday's league, but I'm a fair diviner and manhunter myself. That's why, in his continued absence — I take it you people killed him? — I volunteered to take charge of this part of the search." He looked at the angels who'd gathered around him. "Let's move out. See that this chap stays quiet, and keeps up with us. And put away the swords. We don't want the other fugitives to see us coming."

The angels spread back out into formation, except for two who stayed at Joey's elbows, dragging him along when he limped too slowly to suit them. Which was frequently. His wound throbbed with every uneven step.

Green and ochre lightning flickered across the sky. The shadow of a colossal fish glided through the thunderheads. Joey couldn't tell if it was an actual creature or just another, darker mass of vapor.

After about a quarter of an hour, Fitzroy halted and pulled an oval, silver medallion out of his shirt. He took off his mask, revealing a lean, rather pleasant-looking face, and pressed the trinket to his forehead.

"This is it," he said to Joey's escorts. "Team Three has found them." He put the mask back on and waved his arm. Angels up and down the line passed the silent signal along.

As they neared the clearing, Joey realized just how desperate the caravan's situation actually was. He kept glimpsing more and more angels creeping through the trees, converging on the clearing.

Artie had maintained that their little band was tough enough to defeat an enemy patrol, and Joey had agreed. But, evidently confident of finding Elaine by supernatural means, Fitzroy hadn't divided his force into smaller search parties. His soldiers were all right here. Hundreds of them.

Elaine had warned that something like this would happen. Why the hell hadn't Joey listened to her?

Actually, he knew why. Staying in the Tempest would have been just as disastrous. They hadn't had a good choice to make. Joey clenched his shackled fists.

The huts appeared among the trees. Wearing his hulking, spiky-knuckled monster body, Chris lounged outside, standing watch. Suddenly his head craned forward, peering. Then he ducked into the dilapidated shack on the right. Joey was grimly sure the actor had spotted the enemy too late for it to do any good. It had probably been too late from the moment Danziger's troops encircled the woods.

Fitzroy shouted, "Hello the houses!" The fox mask gave his call a hollow, echoing sound.

No one answered.

"In the name of His Holiness Eric Danziger, anointed Saint of Heaven and the Holy Covenant," Fitzroy continued, "you're all under arrest. Come out with your hands up. You're surrounded and overwhelmingly outnumbered. We can burn you out with flaming arrows, at no risk to ourselves."

Still no reply. Joey could picture Elaine, George, and the others, jabbering back and forth, trying to figure a way out.

"All right," yelled Fitzroy, "roast if you want to. Light

them up, ladies and gentlemen." Though out the darkness, streaks of light appeared as angels drew their swords to kindle shafts with oily rags wrapped around the heads.

Then the scent of roses wafted through the air. Arpeggios of harp music lilted from all directions. Golden rays fell from the sky, illuminating the clearing like a spotlight. Overhead, inside the amber haze, winged giants peered down. Though only vaguely visible, their beauty put Danziger's dwarfed angels to shame.

Then, as if ignited by the beams from above, a brilliant light blazed inside the shack that Chris had entered. Every chink in the walls shone like a strand of white-hot metal.

Joey's guards gaped at the spectacle. Fitzroy said, "What the hell is this?"

Elaine stepped out of the hut. The near-blinding light came with her. It emanated from the key she was holding over her head. Spots on her wrists and ankles, the places where the spikes had pierced her, shone like miniature suns.

"I'm Margaret Rochelle," said Elaine. Her voice was clear and steady. "A *true* Saint, not a Judas, or a demon of the Void. Lay down your weapons."

"Conceivably you do have some power comparable to Danziger's," said Fitzroy coolly. "But I doubt you can hold back all these arrows at once."

"Of course I can't," Elaine replied. "But God can." She turned, peering into the faces of the angels. "I know that many of you serve Danziger unwillingly. You understand that he's evil. You've prayed for deliverance. Well, I'm it. And all your violence and idolatry, all the sins you've committed in the tyrant's name, can be forgiven. But only if you renounce him."

"This is ridiculous," the man in the fox mask said. "My friends here know they're God's champions. You can't sway them from their duty with a pretty light."

"It's the pure light of a Saintly key," Elaine replied, "untainted by the poison of Oblivion." The white glow threw gorgeous rainbows beams. "These sons and daughters of the Covenant recognize it even if you don't. What's more, they hear the hypocrisy in your voice when you talk about their faith. They know *your* only God is the Hierarchy."

"Antichrist!" screamed an angel across the clearing. She drew her burning arrow back to her ear.

The harp music suddenly ended in a sharp, dissonant crash. The winged archer collapsed, and her shaft flew wild. Her fellow soldiers flinched.

"I still believe," said Fitzroy calmly, "that whatever tricks you've mastered, you can't protect yourself against all of us at once. I'm going to give you till the count of three to set the crystal down. Otherwise, we'll shoot you. One..."

"Wait," said Elaine. "God loves even His wayward children. He'll strike you all down if you force His hand, but He doesn't want to. Perhaps we can reach an accommodation."

Fitzroy said, "What do you have in mind?"

"You want to take us to Danziger. We want to go, to overthrow him. We'll allow you to escort us, but we won't submit to bonds or shackles."

The Stygian hesitated and Joey felt that he could virtually read his mind. The masked man doubted that Elaine really had the power to give him significant trouble, but he wasn't sure.

"If I were you," said Joey, "I'd take her up on it. She can work all kinds of miracles. I've seen it. How do you think we made it through all the trouble we've had up to now? Besides, look at your soldiers. They're scared. They're used to obeying anybody who can light up a crystal ball and talk religion, and they've got no reason to love you. They know damn well that usually, Hierarchs persecute people like them. What makes it even dicier is that Danziger had their sex organs removed, did you know that? Don't you think that deep down, even the real fanatics would like to have them back?

"In other words, in a situation like this, you can't trust them. Push them, order them to shoot down a Saint, and they could turn on you.

"Why risk it? You want to hand us over to His Holiness, and we're going to let you. You'll have us surrounded by all these guards. What difference does it make whether we're shackled?"

"I have no reason to trust your advice, either," Fitzroy said dryly, "but I can't find a flaw in your logic." He pivoted toward the clearing. "You'll have to surrender your weapons. Your flesh-sculptor friend will have to stay in human form."

"The key is sacred," Elaine said. "I won't give it up. But you can have everything else."

"It's a deal," said the ambassador. "Bring out your people. They can leave their swords in the cabins." He glanced at Joey's guards. "Unchain him, then take him to his friends."

A soldier unlocked the manacles, then shoved Joey forward, though not as roughly as before. Ahead, hand in hand, George and Kim crept into the open. Angels strode out of trees to take the captives in hand. The smell of roses, the false sunlight, the hazy forms of the winged titans, and Elaine's luminous stigmata disappeared, while the glow of the key dimmed to its normal intensity. It was as if God, satisfied with the bargain Elaine and Fitzroy had struck, was turning His attention elsewhere.

Joey wished *he* could feel satisfied, or at least encouraged, but it wasn't possible. As a shaper of dreams, he could sense when someone else was using the art, even if she was performing a feat he had yet to master. So he knew that Elaine hadn't really tapped into the same mysterious power source as Danziger. The supposed manifestations of her Sainthood had been illusory, a magnificent improvisation that put anything she'd created on stage to shame. The archer had passed out because she'd put her to sleep, or maybe Kim had zapped her with her voice. The deafening discord of the harps could have served as a cover for the little girl's shriek.

Thanks to the illusionist's efforts, the captives would march unfettered. In all probability, the angels would treat them with respect. But Joey was certain that when they reached their destination, Danziger would expose her bluff and destroy them all.

-FORTY-EIGHT-

Joey hobbled toward Elaine. He wanted to take her in his arms, but her expression stopped him in his tracks. She looked as cold and aloof as she ever had in the days when the troupe was touring the Shadowlands.

For a moment, he thought she blamed him for her capture. That she hated him. Then something hidden deep in her eyes, or maybe just his instincts, told him otherwise.

She still loved him, but she was terrified. She wanted to touch him as much as he did her. But she was afraid that if she didn't keep up the front of a Saint on crusade, stern and self-possessed, their captors might still chain them.

She was probably being smart, but it hurt to know he would never get another chance to hold her, or tell her how he felt about her. He gazed back at her, trying to broadcast warmth and reassurance, then turned away. His chest felt tight, and his throat swollen.

The angels frisked everyone but her, then started the prisoners marching through the forest. The illusionist walked at the head of the captives. The light of her key, a rippling silver and orange now, played across saw-toothed leaves and wrinkled bark.

Caroline Teasdale crept up beside Joey. "Elaine looks like Joan of Arc," she murmured. She glanced furtively at the angels, as if afraid they might punish her for the comparison. "Like I imagine Joan of Arc, anyway."

Joey remembered that Joan of Arc had been burned at the stake. "Yeah," he said heavily.

"Can she really save us?" the plump woman asked. "Beat Danziger and his army too?"

Joey hesitated. "You saw what she did back in the clearing. Have faith." He dropped back to trudge beside George.

Joey could tell from the trapped look in the little man's darting eyes that he understood the nature of Elaine's charade. Probably everyone from the troupe did. Gamely striving to hide his fear, George said, "Well, here we are, bound for the headman's block again. I suppose it would be churlish to complain. It's only to be expected that fate, having imbued young George with a hero's mettle, sends him heroic challenges as well."

"Yeah, right." Joey lowered his voice to a whisper. One of the keen-eared guards might overhear him anyway, but it was a chance he had to take. "Be ready to move."

"Do you have a plan?" George whispered back.

"I wish. I just know that they won't leave us unchained forever. We have to grab any chance that comes along."

George nodded somberly. "I'll pass it on."

The woods gave way to rolling meadows dotted with clusters of cottages. Occasionally an angel slipped away from the column, then returned with other wingless people. And sometimes villagers joined the procession by themselves.

Joey fantasized that the newcomers were members of a resistance movement, freedom fighters gathering to rescue the caravan. In his heart, he knew better. Much as the living members of her church might have revered Elaine, the people of Heaven didn't know her. Maybe her illusions could awe them, he thought. Maybe many of them yearned to see Danziger overthrown. But he was sure that they still wouldn't rebel on her behalf, not against so terrible a master.

They just wanted to witness whatever was going to happen.

The farther Joey limped, the weaker and more painful his leg became. His ghostly body could shrug off many injuries in a matter of minutes, but a darksteel wound was different. After a while, Chris took his arm and helped him along.

At last Danziger's cathedral-fortress loomed out of the dark. The colored flames of angel swords burned along the battlements, and a crowd had congregated outside the walls. Joey wondered if someone had run ahead to announce the procession's arrival.

Suddenly red light, laced with a spider web of black, flowered on the parapet above the portcullis. Joey suspected that Danziger had simply stepped dramatically from the shadows at his back, but it looked as if he'd popped out of nowhere. The onlookers flinched.

As far as Joey was concerned, the Heretic lord didn't need theatrics to be scary. The malice in his eyes was enough. Dry-mouthed, the boxer thought, I should have stayed with Emily and Sarah.

Then he realized that in effect, he'd wished Elaine were facing this psycho without him. A wave of self-disgust washed some of his dread away. He and his friends had escaped Giovanni magic, Doc Holliday's cold, murderous competence, and the horrors of the Tempest. Surely they could find a way out of this jam, too. He began to look around him.

The procession stopped a few yards short of the gate. The angels ushered the prisoners to the front of the formation. Fitzroy said, "Here she is, Your Holiness, as promised, compliments of the Seat of Succor. The other fugitives as well."

Joey tensed. He suddenly perceived that the caravan *might* have a chance, if only a slim one. Except that too many files of angels were blocking his way.

Danziger frowned down at Fitzroy. "Why aren't they in chains? Why does the Great Whore still have her key?"

"I could march them faster unshackled," the man in the fox mask answered smoothly. "And I thought that since the crystal is sacred, it might be better for you to take it away from her yourself."

"Perhaps you're right," Danziger said, his long hair, beard, and robe stirring in the wind. "Step forward, my daughter."

Her key shining peacock blue and emerald, her face serene, Elaine stepped out of the column. Joey and her other friends tried to do likewise.

Danziger waved his empty hand. His orb pulsed crimson. An invisible force, irresistible as a tsunami, swept Joey and the others back among the soldiers. It drove the front ranks staggering back a pace or two also, even tumbling a couple angels off their feet.

Only Elaine was unaffected. Now she stood alone, on the patch of ground between the wall and the crowd. "Here I am," she said.

"And about time, too," Danziger answered, leering. "Now we can pick up where we left off. I hope you weren't too upset with me for veiling the Byways from your sight. The curse would have worn off in time, if you had time left."

"I didn't even know about it," Elaine lied. "I didn't try to run. I've been in seclusion, praying and meditating. Preparing for this meeting. As a Saint of the Holy Covenant, I ask you to repent."

Danziger smirked. "Do you now?"

"Yes," she said, staring up at him. "It isn't too late for you, Eric. You could be a good man again. You were once. What happened to you?"

The question seemed to surprise him. "Why, nothing radical, really. I was always a leader. In life, I saved thousands of souls. Established hospitals and missions. Defended the church against its enemies. When God sent me onward, I assumed it was for eternal rest, but I was mistaken. In a vision, He told me my work had barely begun. The world of the dead is as sinful as that of the Quick. It's my task to cleanse it, and so preserve it from Oblivion."

"I think I understand," said Elaine, a hint of amazement in her tone. "You were *bored*. You still had people kowtowing to you, but it wasn't the same. They deferred to the other Saints just as much, and there was really nothing much for you to command them to do. You wanted some big project to make you feel important again, even if it involved murder, torture, and war."

Danziger shook his head. "Poor lost child. God gave you eyes and yet you do not see."

"I can see the darkness in your aura. The mark of damnation."

"No, daughter. Forget the notions you learned from your Skinlands Bible. During my time here, God has granted me a new and greater revelation, a gospel for the dead. He showed me that He encompasses good *and* evil. He's mercy and love, but wrath and vengeance, too. My" — he faltered — "I mean, *His* ways are unfathomable, untrammeled by petty human notions of right and wrong. And for the blasphemy of thinking otherwise, He condemns you to the Pit."

"No," said Elaine. "You don't speak for God. I do." Drawing on her powers of illusion, she re-created her radiant stigmata. Her key and halo flared with a blue and yellow light. She turned it into a roaring fire, a blaze that shed the heat of Skinlands flame.

People cried out and jerked backward. His leg aching and quivering, Joey spun around.

Danziger's wave of power and the angels' own nervous shifting back and forth had broken up the tight ranks of their formation. It had even nudged Joey closer to his objective, or vice versa. Many of the troops stared at Elaine and Danziger.

CARAVAN OF SHADOWS

Yet it was still no good, because at least a few of the others were doing their jobs. Even when Elaine had burst into flame, they'd kept an eye on the other prisoners.

If only I weren't hurt, Joey thought disgustedly, maybe I could get past them.

A response whispered through his mind. *I could help you. But I won't, ever again. Die with me, brother. Let's dance in the Void.* He couldn't tell if it were really the voice, or just his imagination.

It suddenly occurred to him that his friends weren't injured. Maybe one of them could reach the prize, if he knew it was there for the taking. Joey looked around, only to discover that the same random motion that had opened gaps between the angels had separated him from his companions. If he shoved his way to them to whisper instructions, the guards would realize something was up.

Elaine was right, he thought in despair. Our luck's run out. This time, we are going to die.

Then he turned back toward the cathedral-castle and realized they might have a chance after all.

According to Caroline Teasdale, Danziger really could work miracles, make things happen just by wishing them. But he wasn't psychic or all-knowing, and judging by his expression, the glare and heat of Elaine's fire had startled him. Was it possible she could bluff him the way she had his troops?

"Surrender!" she shouted. "Lay down your key. God's flame doesn't hurt the righteous, but it will burn you." The pillar of phantasmal fire shot higher than the rampart, then bent over Danziger, reminding Joey of a rearing snake.

For one more moment, the Spectre looked shaken. The crimson glow of his crystal dimmed. Then, suddenly, he giggled. "I should take one of those memory courses. Doc told me you were an illusionist. A cheap carnival trickster." The scarlet light flared, and forked blood-red thunderbolts split the sky.

In the next instant, Elaine's key exploded. Bits of crystal peppered her face like buckshot. Her fake fire blinked out. An unseen force slammed her to the ground like a fly swatter mashing a bug, jerked her ten feet into the air, and wrung her body like a wash rag. Bone snapped and crunched.

Horrified, Joey knew that the odds against reaching his goal no longer mattered. In the face of Elaine's agony, he simply had to act. As he pivoted and lunged, his leg buckled, nearly dumping him on the grass. By sheer will power, he forced it to support him, then staggered on.

He squirmed between a pair of angels. Shoved a third one out of the way. Then two more rushed him with blazing swords upraised, one from either side. It was obvious that whichever one he turned to face, the other would cut him down from behind.

A brilliant flash and a deafening boom exploded across the landscape, as shocking as the unexpected detonation of a bomb. Considering the punishment Elaine had taken, she should have been unconscious, or delirious with pain. But Joey could only assume she'd glimpsed his predicament, and managed one last illusion to help him.

Startled, both angels faltered. The one facing the blast threw his arm across his eyes. Joey sprang in close to the other and hit him, a fast one-two to the jaw and gut. His sword tumbling from his fingers, the winged man fell down. Joey turned and scrambled on.

Another angel ran at him. The boxer knew Elaine couldn't afford any more delays. Danziger's Oblivion-tainted magic might destroy her any second. Still, Joey had no choice but to defend himself. Anguished, furious, he raised his fists.

Then Chris appeared behind the angel's snow-white pinions. Blurring from human to monster so fast that the transformation left gashes in his pewtery hide, he raked the angel with his talons. Elsewhere, Kim howled. Either Elaine's torment or the diversion afforded by her last trick had spurred the rest of the caravan into action.

Joey hobbled on, only to discover that his quarry had disappeared into the milling, babbling crowd. He frantically looked around. After a couple seconds that felt like a lifetime, he spotted the man he wanted.

Fitzroy was edging out of the press. Elaine's final illusion and the disturbance he could see erupting in the center of the column had made him wary. He had his automatic in hand.

Joey's leg had gone numb. He stamped his foot, but it didn't help. Snarling, he charged the Stygian.

For a moment, it looked as if, in the sudden confusion, Fitzroy didn't see him coming. But then the masked man turned, assumed a wide-legged stance, and pointed the gun at Joey.

Joey dove in a flying tackle. The pistol barked, but the shot missed him. He slammed into Fitzroy's knees, hurling him to the ground.

He madly battered the thrashing Stygian, pounding dents in the fox mask. Fitzroy made a choking sound and stopped moving.

Joey snatched the gun out of the ambassador's red-gloved hand and tried to spring to his feet. His wound turned the motion to a spastic clamber. He lurched around toward the gatehouse.

Either Danziger hadn't noticed the commotion among the spectators, or he wasn't concerned, because he was still busy with Elaine, slowly, slowly crushing her ravaged body like someone crumpling paper into a ball. Holding the gun in both hands, Joey drew a bead on him and fired. The automatic bucked.

Joey had never shot a bow. It would have been useless to grab one, even if the crowd had left him room to use it. He *had* fired a pistol before, but he was no sharpshooter. He missed. Fired again. The second bullet chipped the block of stone in front of his target's leg.

From the corner of his eye, he glimpsed angels charging him. Elaine fell to the ground with a leaden thud, and Danziger whirled to glare at him. Joey sensed a power building around him, like lightning preparing to strike, or a bear trap about to snap shut. Trying to ignore every distraction, he aimed, and squeezed the trigger.

The pistol banged. Danziger's head jerked backward, but he stayed on his feet. Even as Joey fired a fourth round, he wondered if the mad Saint's powers made him bulletproof.

Then Danziger tottered in a circle. The key dropped from his hand and shattered on the rampart. Waves of darkness swept through his body, and then he faded away.

Suddenly the eternal night was absolutely silent.

Joey had a hunch he knew what the Covenanters were thinking. Maybe they'd hated Danziger, but they'd worshipped him too, as the living emblem of their faith. And Elaine hadn't exactly whipped him in a fair fight, with a genuine display of Saintly power. Considering that someone else had fired the fatal shot, while she lay crumpled in a heap, it was debatable whether she'd beaten him at all. The flock didn't know whether to proclaim her the new boss, or rip her and her companions limb from limb.

George scrambled out of the mass of soldiers and dropped to his knees beside her. "Please, Your Holiness, get up."

At first, Elaine didn't move. Then her torn, eyeless face turned slowly in his direction.

"Please, rise," said George, taking hold of one of her arms. "The invaluable Mr. Montaigne is here to assist. Your faithful followers need to see that you're all right."

She nodded.

He helped her to her feet, then put his arm around her. She raised her shaking hand, and blue and gold light streamed through her fingers. The crowd gasped.

Because she was holding up a key. Once again, Joey could guess what the Heretics were thinking. She was hurt too badly to cast another illusion. Therefore, God Himself must have given her the orb, to replace the one that Danziger had broken.

Joey knew better. Back in the throne room, George had stolen two crystals. Through some sleight of hand, he must have concealed the extra one when the angels searched him. A moment ago, he'd slipped it to Elaine, the folds of his voluminous coat hiding the transfer from the crowd.

Elaine drew a ragged breath. "It's over," she croaked. "No more fighting. No more punishment. No war. Everybody put up your weapons. Everybody go home."

Metal rasped metal as the assembled angels, looking sheepish, sheathed their swords.

-FORTY-NINE-

Elaine twitched and shuddered, looking as if she were dying a second, final death. Joey, sitting in a chair beside her ornately carved canopy bed, had to keep reminding himself that just the opposite was true. She was actually healing, her pale, bloodless cuts closing, her twisted body gradually straightening itself out. The process made him think of one of Sarah's childhood toys, a grinning rubber doll which, no matter how she bent and squashed it, always shifted back into its original shape.

He started to take Elaine's hand, then, afraid he'd hurt her, hesitated. Though still eyeless, she reached out and twined her fingers in his.

"You're going to be okay," he said.

"I know that," she said with a trace of her old snappishness. "In case you've forgotten, I've been dead years longer than you. I do understand how it works."

He smiled. "You know, you're a lot more irritable than Emily, and she wasn't even a Saint."

"Any woman who could live with you is, by definition, a saint."

Someone rapped on the arched, paneled door. "Yeah?" Joey said.

George stuck his head into the richly furnished chamber. "Mr. Fitzroy has awakened."

"This can wait until you feel better," Joey said to Elaine. "We can lock him up. I'm sure Danziger built himself a dungeon."

"No. You guys know I trust you to handle it. Do whatever you think is right. I just want this whole thing to be over."

"Okay," said Joey, standing up. Self-conscious with George leering in the doorway, he lowered his voice. "I love you."

"I love you, too," she said, smiling. His leg still stiff, he gimped across the parquet floor.

As he and George headed down the murky, musty-smelling corridor, the little man asked, "Has she discussed our rewards?"

Joey raised an eyebrow. "Rewards?"

"Yes. That's the reason we're here, remember? To secure wealth and position for the eminently deserving Mr. Montaigne."

"Give her a break. As bad as Danziger messed her up, she might be sick for hours yet. Anyway, I'm not sure this place even has money, or dukes and barons, or any of whatever it is you've got in mind."

"Then it's in desperate need of social engineering," George replied, "and fortunate to have a political philosopher of Mr. Montaigne's caliber to guide its progress."

Joey shook his head. "Like I keep saying, you'll never change."

George grinned. "And why, pray tell, would one tamper with perfection?"

They descended the curved staircase. The winged guard in the hall below looked at them like he was wondering whether to salute. Most of the castle staff had the same uncertain air. At this point, they weren't sure what their duties were, or in what spirit they were to be carried out.

George entered the throne room. Joey started to follow,

then, on impulse, turned to the angel. "You know my friend Chris? The big, blond, good-looking guy?"

The guard nodded.

"Well, the new Saint isn't anti-sex, and Chris is a topnotch flesh-sculptor. You might want to talk to him when he comes out. Avoid the rush." He gripped the angel's shoulder, then opened one of the tall doors. In the carving at eye level, the three wise men were laying their gifts before the manger. They looked a little dazed, as if it hadn't quite sunk in that their long journey was over. He knew just how they felt.

Unmasked, his scabbard empty, Fitzroy sat on one of the risers, with Chris, Artie, and Kim gathered around him. The Stygian rose and gave Joey a smile. "Hello, Mr. Castelo. I keep shooting perfectly good darksteel at you, and nothing happens. When I get a chance, I'll log some time on a pistol range. But first we need to discuss more important matters."

Joey felt vaguely uneasy. He didn't like the diplomat's air of confidence. "You mean, what we're going to do with you."

Fitzroy said, "No, or at least, only in passing. I mean relations between our two sovereigns. From my mistress's perspective, Danziger's no great loss. He had unusual powers, but they worked nearly as erratically as his judgment. I'm not convinced they would have functioned at all at any distance from this particular Far Shore. Your friend Elaine has her own talents, not as unique, but nothing to sneeze at. She now controls this kingdom and its army. I don't see why the Seat of Succor shouldn't make the same pact with you people that it did with him. Stand with us, and one day you'll rule a realm as great as Charon's."

The offer was so unexpected that for a moment, Joey and his friends could only gape. Then Kim said, "No! We don't want to fight wars!"

"I can understand that a pretty little girl wouldn't," Fitzroy replied. "but your elders may feel differently."

"I wouldn't talk down to her," Artie said. "She doesn't like it, and she's got a talent, too, a voice that could fillet you like a mackerel. What's more, she's right. We don't want to conquer anybody."

Fitzroy frowned. "Are you sure you speak for Her Holiness?"

"Count on it," said Chris.

"Well, you really owe it to yourselves to reconsider," said the man in red. "The Laughing Lady has a great deal invested in this venture. Her Legions are ready to march. If Miss Rochelle refuses to honor the commitments made by her predecessor, then I suspect they'll march on you. For better or worse, your little country is strategically located, a springboard to many other lands beyond. And my mistress has never been one to let those who try to thwart her go unpunished."

Joey felt sick. The danger and horror weren't over after all. They were just beginning.

George snorted. Clearly puzzled by the little man's show of amusement, Fitzroy turned toward him.

"Really," said George, "with whom do you think you're dealing? Manifestly, someone less resourceful than the perspicacious Montaigne. He's already dispatched couriers to friends scattered throughout the Shadowlands. If those good people fail to hear from him at prescribed intervals — as you may rest assured they will, should your troops assail Heaven or any of its neighbors — they'll see to it that certain missives reach the Madwoman's fellow Deathlords."

The Stygian grimaced. "I assume that the letters detail what might be viewed as my mistress's... indiscretions."

"And what a list it is," said Artie, grinning. "Let's recap for any viewers just tuning in: hoarding souls, plotting to carve out her own private empire in the Far Shores, cozying up to Heretics, and even, god help us, Spectres. All, obviously, in an effort to amass enough power to grab Charon's throne.

"Not that I'm criticizing. I think it's great. Someone's finally found a way to bring the other Deathlords together. They'll team up to squash her like a bug."

"How can she know," Fitzroy asked, "that you won't expose her anyway?"

"Why should we?" Joey replied. "We're Renegades. What do we care which Deathlord winds up on top? They're all the same to us."

"Perhaps so. Still, it's only fair to warn you that as a rule, the Lady doesn't capitulate to attempts at intimidation."

"Oh, come on!" Joey said. "She's lost her allies, her beachhead, and the secrecy the whole plan depended on. It's over. How did she get where she is, if she isn't smart enough to cut her losses?"

The ambassador sighed. "All right. You make a good case. I dare say she probably will decide to direct her efforts elsewhere. After all, she has other minions, and other schemes as well." He smiled wryly. "At any rate, from my personal perspective, there's one positive thing about your ploy. A threat is worthless unless someone delivers it. Ergo, you'd do well to let me go."

"We probably would have anyway," said Joey. He noticed the Hierarch's dented mask on the floor, picked it up, and tossed it to him. "We aren't going to punish any of the angels for stuff they did, so we might as well let you off the hook, too." He smiled at Kimberly. "Would you please make sure this guy gets across the border without somebody lynching him?"

"Sure!" she said. Her eagerness reminded him of his own little girl's excitement when entrusted with some exhilarating bit of responsibility. Fitzroy put on his mask, bowed, and followed the singer out of the room.

Mindful of the sharp ears of their fellow wraiths, Joey and his companions sat quietly until they heard the door to the courtyard latch. Then Chris asked, "Did you really send messengers?"

"Of course not, bonehead," Artie said. "When did he have a chance? I guess we should, though. Danziger must have had some Harbingers on the payroll."

"That was fast thinking," said Joey. "I figured we were screwed."

"It was nothing," said George in an utterly unconvincing attempt at modesty. "An elementary blackmailer's precaution." He coughed. "Not, of course, that a virtuous fellow like Mr. Montaigne has ever engaged in such practices himself."

-FIFTY-

Joey's eyes blinked open as he woke from a dreamless sleep. After turning his back on the fantasy world in which the voice had hoped to trap him, he'd wondered if he'd ever sleep again. But obviously he was still clinging to some mortal habits. He'd drifted into a doze after making love.

Wanting to caress Elaine, he groped for her, finding her side of the feather mattress empty. Rolling over, he saw her standing at the stained glass-rimmed lucarne window, gazing out at the rust-red lightning. Her halo shimmered pale blue and green with a trace of silver at the edge. Apparently she was lost in thought, and perhaps a little sad.

Joey watched her for a moment, savoring the lovely lines of her back. Then he threw off the tangled covers, winced at the chill of the dank air on his skin, got up, and put his arms around her waist.

"Surveying your kingdom?" he asked. "Or should that be queendom?"

"Just thinking about our friends who didn't make it. I wish I really were a holy woman. Maybe then I could bring them back, like Lazarus."

"Remember that you didn't force them to come. You didn't even ask them. They wanted to. And they helped us do something good. We didn't just save your neck — though that would have been enough for them — we freed this place from Danziger. We stopped a war."

Elaine nodded. A stray wisp of her black hair tickled Joey's nose.

"So, please," he continued, "I miss them too, but don't beat yourself up."

"I won't," she said. "Maybe because we did accomplish something, I don't feel as down on myself as I used to. I may not be God's special pet, but that doesn't mean I'm worthless."

"It's good you feel that way. I don't imagine your subjects want a mopey boss. God knows, it used to get on *our* nerves."

The strobing lightning turned from rust to teal. A shape like the bladed leaves of a Venus flytrap appeared in the churning thunderheads.

"My subjects," murmured Elaine. "I guess they are, or at least they seem to want to be." She shook her head. "First the church, then the troupe, now this. It's like it's my destiny to be responsible for people."

"Could be," he said. Up in the raging sky, the jaws of the flytrap started to close. "You're pretty good at it."

"But if I do stay on as any kind of leader, things will have to be different. The people will have to accept me as an ordinary, fallible human being. I can be an advisor, a senator, or even a president if that's what they really want, but not the Great and Powerful Oz."

"I think they'll go for it, especially if you kind of ease them into it. I know they came here because they were true believers, but still, after everything Danziger put them through, some of them must have started to suspect that Saints aren't perfect. And if knowing you doesn't convince them, nothing will."

She jabbed her elbow into his stomach.

"Ouch!" he said. "To tell you the truth, I was hoping you'd stay on as head honcho. Because it fits into a plan I've been thinking about. I've got a lot of time, maybe *all* of time, ahead of me. I should try to do something worthwhile with it. Otherwise I might go stir-crazy, like Danziger. And you have to admit, the Underworld has plenty of room for improvement."

She turned and put her arms around him. "What do you have in mind?"

Now that the time had come to explain, he hesitated. What if she thought the idea was as crazy as Danziger's ambitions, or just flat-out stupid? "I wasn't the greatest student. If I could have gotten away with it, I would have cut every day to train at Franklin's Gym. But I guess I learned a little, because I remember something from American History. Did you ever hear of the Underground Railroad?"

She nodded. "The network that helped runaway slaves get to freedom."

"Right. What would you need to run an operation like that? Tough, smart agents who hate slavery as much as you do. Experienced travelers with a good excuse for wandering around the Shadowlands, like, they're touring entertainers. People like us and our friends.

"And you'd want a safe place outside Hierarchy territory to bring the Thralls to. I was thinking, here. Sure, the road's dangerous, but now that we know the way, I think we could handle it." He faltered. "What do you think?"

Her dark eyes shone. She gave him a long, soft kiss. "I like it a lot," she said.

-EPILOGUE-

Travanti felt a change in the atmosphere as soon as he marched his retainers back into one of the gorges at the rim of Heaven, something beyond the thinning of the fog and the abatement of the freezing wind. A kind of psychic taint, present at the time of his departure, had disappeared. He halted uncertainly.

Strands of her platinum-blond hair stirring in the breeze, Saundra, his current lover, came to stand beside him. Her stinking, rotten skull-face was incapable of expression, but he could read her concern from the orange tinge that washed through her black-veined aura. "Is something wrong?" she asked.

"I think so, but I'd like to do a divination to find out for sure." Knowing that, as ever, his mask would reflect his expression, he smiled at her. "Would you help me?"

She flinched. "Me?"

He nodded. "Please."

"But *why*? What have I done wrong?"

"Nothing," he assured her. "I just feel like using you. Anyway, you have to learn to make friends with pain."

She took a step backward. Leering Spectres suddenly clustered around her. No doubt recognizing that if she resisted, they'd be only too happy to force her, she stopped retreating. Trembling, she stripped, then laid her voluptuous body on the stony canyon floor.

Travanti held out his hand. Someone put a gray iron knife in it. He knelt at Saundra's side and set to work. She struggled to hold still. Her comrades stared avidly, savoring every cut.

Quick augurs could interpret the pattern of fate from a sacrificial victim's organs. Similarly, Travanti gleaned some information from Saundra's pale and bloodless internal structure. But he learned more from the flashes of agony that blazed through her aura, and the precise manner in which she twitched and writhed.

In fact, it was the most informative reading he'd obtained in years. Some aspect of recent events had sent exceptionally strong vibrations singing through destiny's web. At the end, images paraded before his inner eye. An avalanche burying Holliday. A crystal flaming in a mangled hand. A dark-haired man and woman kissing behind an oval window.

"Damn," he said.

"What's wrong?" asked Pablo. Except for his single opalescent eye and barbed brown mandibles, his shadowy form was all but invisible, even from three feet away.

Travanti stood up and brushed off his pants. "Miss Forrester and her friends didn't just elude us. They came back here and destroyed Danziger. Sickening, isn't it? The idiot had an army, and all that power. Yet he still couldn't handle what should have been, at worst, a petty annoyance." The scar Joey had given him twinged. He rubbed it through his mask.

"Are we going to keep hunting the Saint lady?" Pablo asked.

Travanti sighed. Pablo was a useful tool, ferocious yet obedient, but not particularly bright. "Not now. It's too late to help Doc or Danziger, or salvage the great alliance. Castelo and his friends control the army now, and are surely on the lookout for us. What's more, the tide of fortune is running in their favor. But don't worry, we won't forget them. Someday, when their guard is down and their luck has turned, we'll come back and get even with them for ruining our plans." He held out the knife, and someone took it. Saundra was still squirming and whimpering on the ground. He gave her a little kick. "Rise and shine, my darling. It's time to go."

Grunting, clutching the lips of her largest wound together, she clambered spastically to her feet. Then Travanti led his band into howling darkness.

-ABOUT THE AUTHOR-

Richard Lee Byers holds an MA in Psychology. After working for more than 10 years in an emergency inpatient psychiatric facility, he left the mental health field to become a writer.

He has written over ten novels, three of which are Young Adult titles, including *Dead Time*, *Dark Fortune*, *The Vampire's Apprentice*, and *Netherworld*.

His short fiction has appeared in numerous magazines and anthologies, including four White Wolf Publishing World of Darkness Anthologies *Dark Destiny I*, *Elric: Tales of the White Wolf*, *Death and Damnation*, and most recently, *Truth Until Paradox*.

A resident of the Tampa Bay area, the setting for much of his fiction, he has taught Writing Horror and Dark Fantasy at the University of Tampa, and currently teaches Fiction Writing at Hillsborough Community College.

CARAVAN OF SHADOWS

Excerpted from
Midnight Blue: The Sonja Blue Collection
Paint it Black
Available from White Wolf Publishing /Borealis
in April, 1995

Thou who, abruptly as a knife,
Didst come into my heart; thou who,
A demon horde into my life
Didst enter, wildly dancing, through
The doorways of my sense unlatched
To make my spirit my domain.
                    - Baudelaire, "The Vampire"

Chapter 3 Page 398-401

I have to give the dead boy credit; he has the trick of appearing human nailed down tight. He's learned just what gestures and vocal inflections hide the fact that his surface glitz isn't there to disguise basic shallowness, but an utter lack of humanity.

I've seen enough of the kind he imitates: pallid, self-important intellectuals who pride themselves on their sophistication and knowledge of what's "hip," sharpening their wit at the expense of others. Like the vampiric mimic in their midst, they produce nothing while thriving on the vitality of others. The only difference is that the vampire is more honest about it.

I work my way to the bar, careful to keep myself shielded

from the dead boy's view, both physically and psychically. It wouldn't do for my quarry to catch scent of me just yet. I hear the vampire's nasal intonations as it holds forth on the merits of various artists.

"Frankly, I consider his use of photo-montage to be inexcusably banal — I've seen better at Olan Mills!"

From whom did the vampire steal that particular drollery, I wonder. A dead boy of his wattage doesn't come up with bon mots and witty remarks spontaneously. When you have to spend a lot of conscious energy remembering to breathe and blink, there is no such thing as top-of-your-head snappy patter. It is all protective coloration, right down to the last double entendre and Monty Python impersonation.

It will be another decade or two before the vampire dressed in black silk and leather with the stainless-steel ankh dangling from one ear and the crystal embedded in his left nostril can divert his energies to something besides the full-time task of ensuring his continuance. And I doubt this dead boy has much of a chance of realizing that future.

I wave down the bartender and order a beer. As I await its arrival, I catch a glimpse of myself in the mirror backing the baill lack major psionic muscle. Sure, they might have enough mesmeric ability to gull the humans in their vicinity, but little else. Compared to my own psychic abilities, the art-fag vampire might as well be packing a pea-shooter. Still, it isn't smart to get cocky. Lord Morgan dismissed me in such a high-handed manner, and now he's missing half his face.

That's what you get for being smug.

I shift my vision from the human to the Pretender spectrum, studying the vampire's true appearance. I wonder if the black-garbed art aficionados clustered about their Mandarin, their heads bobbing like puppets, would still consider his pronouncements worthy if they knew his skin is the color and texture of rotten sailcloth. Or that his lips are black and shriveled, revealing oversized fangs set in a perpetual death's-head grimace. No doubt they'd drop their little plastic cups of cheap blush and back away in horror, their surface glaze of urbanite sophistication and studied ennui replaced by honest, old-fashioned monkey-brain terror.

Humans need masks in order to live their day-to-day lives, even among their own kind. Little do they know that their dependence on artifice and pretense provides the perfect hiding place for predators. Predators like the vampire pretending to be an art-fag. Predators such as me.

I tighten my grip on the switchblade in the pocket of my leather jacket. Midnight! Time to drop your masks!

"Uh, excuse me?"

I jerk around a little too fast, startling the young man at my elbow. I was so focused on my prey I was unaware of his approach. Sloppy. Really sloppy.

"Yeah, what is it?"

The young man blinks, slightly taken aback by the brusqueness in my voice. "I, uh, was wondering if I might, uh, buy you a drink?"

I automatically scan him for signs of Pretender taint, but he comes up clean. One hundred percent USDA human. He is taller than me by a couple of inches; his blond hair is pulled back into a ponytail. There are three rings in his right ear and one in his left nostril. Despite the metalwork festooning his nose, he is quite handsome.

I am at a loss for words. I'm not used to being approached by normal people. I tend to generate a low-level psychic energy field that most humans find unnerving, if not antagonistic. In layman's terms: I tend to either scare people or piss them off.

"I — I—"

I shoot my prey a glance out of the corner of my eye. Shit! The bastard is starting to make his move, hustling one of the more entranced hangers-on.

"I realize this is going to sound like a really dumb come-on," he says, shooting me an embarrassed smile. "But I saw you from across the room — and I just had to meet you. Please let me buy you a drink."

"I, uh, I—"

The vampire is escorting its prey outside, smiling widely as it continues to discourse on Post-Modern art.

"There's something I have to take care of — I'll be right back! I promise! Don't go away!" I blurt, and dash off in pursuit of my target for the night.

•

I scan the parking lot, checking for signs of the vampire's passage. I pray I'm not too late. Once a vamp isolates and seduces a human from the herd, he tends to move quickly. I know that from my own experience at the hands of Sir Morgan, the undead bastard responsible for my own transformation.

The vampire and its prey are sitting in the back seat of a silver BMW with heavily tinted windows; their blurred silhouettes move like shadows reflected in an aquarium. There is no time to waste. I'll have to risk being spotted.

The imitation art-fag looks genuinely surprised when my fist punches through the back window, sending tinted safety glass flying into the car. He hisses a challenge, exposing his fangs, as he whips about to face me. His victim sits beside him, motionless as a mannequin, eyes unfocused and fly open. The human's erect penis juts forward, vibrating like a tuning fork.

I grab the vampire by the collar of his black silk shirt and pull him, kicking and screaming, through the busted back windshield. The human doesn't even blink.

"Quit yer bitchin'!" I snr. To the casual observer I appear to be no more than twenty-five. Tricked out in a battered leather jacket, a stained Circle Jerks T-shirt, patched jeans, mirrored sunglasses, and with dark hair twisted into a tortured cockatoo's crest, I look like just another member of Generation X checking out the scene. No one would ever guess I'm actually forty years old.

I suck the cold suds down, participating in my own form of protective coloration. I can drink a case or three of the stuff without effect. Beer doesn't do it for me anymore. Neither does hard liquor. Or cocaine. Or heroin. Or crack. I've tried them all, in dosages that would put the U.S. Olympic Team in the morgue; but no luck. Only one drug plunks my magic twanger nowadays. Only one thing can get me off.

And that drug is blood.

Yeah, the dead boy is good enough to have fooled another vampire. But didn't.

I study my prey speculatively. I doubt I'll have any trouble taking the sucker down. I rarely do, these days. Least not the lesser undead that stap as I hurl the snarling vampire onto the parking lot gravel. "Let's get this over with, dead boy! I've got a hot date!"

The vampire launches himself at me, talons hooked and fangs extended. I move to meet the attack, flicking open my switchblade with a snap of my wrist. The silver blade sinks into the vampire's chest, causing him to shriek in pain. The vampire collapses around my fist, spasming as his system reacts to the silver's toxin.

I kneel and swiftly remove the vampire's head from his shoulders. The body is already starting to putrefy by the time I locate the BMW's keys. I unlock the trunk and toss the vampire's rapidly decomposing remains inside, making sure the keys are left in his pants pocket.

I look around, but, remarkably, there are no witnesses to be seen in the darkened lot. I move around to the passenger side and open the door, tugging the still-entranced human out of the car.

He stands propped against the bumper like a drunkard, his eyes swimming and his face slack. His penis dangles from his pants like a deflated party balloon. I take his chin between thumb and forefinger and turn his head so that his eyes meet mine.

"This never happened. You do not remember leaving the bar with anyone. Is that clear?"

"N-nothing h-happened."

"Excellent! Now go back in the bar and have a good time. Oh, and stick that thing back in your pants! You don't want to get busted for indecent exposure, do you?"

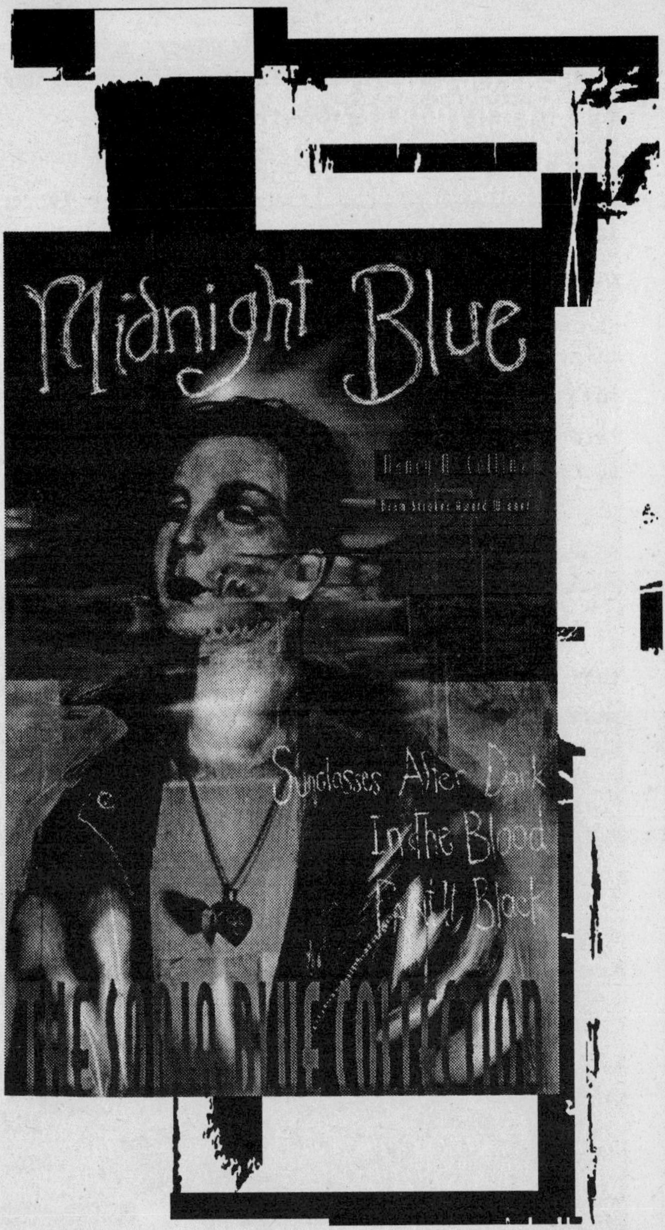
Midnight Blue
Sunglasses After Dark
In The Blood